"If you've be... adventure, *The Landlord's Black-Eyed Daughter* is not to be missed! Mary Ellen Dennis crafts a swift and bawdy tale that skillfully blends the classic poem 'The Highwayman' with elements of historical romance and the Gothic novel—and manages a happy ending as well. Enjoy!"

—Mary Jo Putney, *New York Times*
bestselling author of *The Bargain*

"Dennis's wonderful retelling of Alfred Noyes's 'The Highwayman' is, quite simply, remarkable."

—*Booklist* (starred review)

"Dennis's novel reimagines the tale of the star-crossed lovers and incorporates a bit of the paranormal to heighten the suspense and the passion. The fast pace and clean, clear writing style suit the adventure/romance."

—*RT Book Reviews*, 4 stars

"Themes of reincarnation and redemption elevate Dennis's homage to Alfred Noyes's poem 'The Highwayman'… An entertaining eighteenth-century romp."

—*Publishers Weekly*

"A dash of humor, a splash of the paranormal, and a dollop of danger—and let the adventures begin… A fast pace, fluid writing, and an exceptionally well-crafted plot make this an enjoyable read."

—*Library Journal*

Praise for *The Landlord's Black-Eyed Daughter*

"Riveting… Rich in historical detail, *The Landlord's Black-Eyed Daughter* sweeps you along on waves of atmosphere and passion… I couldn't put it down."

—*Linda Banche Romance Author*

"Gorgeous… Ms. Dennis writes this story as if she's actually lived it."

—*Dark Diva Reviews*

THE GREATEST LOVE ON EARTH

MARY ELLEN DENNIS

sourcebooks
casablanca

Copyright © 2011, 1997 by Mary Ellen Dennis
Cover and internal design © 2011 by Sourcebooks, Inc.
Cover illustration by Phil Heffernan

Sourcebooks and the colophon are registered trademarks of
Sourcebooks, Inc.

All rights reserved. No part of this book may be reproduced in
any form or by any electronic or mechanical means including
information storage and retrieval systems—except in the case
of brief quotations embodied in critical articles or reviews—
without permission in writing from its publisher, Sourcebooks,
Inc.

The characters and events portrayed in this book are fictitious
or are used fictitiously. Any similarity to real persons, living or
dead, is purely coincidental and not intended by the author.

Published by Sourcebooks Casablanca, an imprint of Sourcebooks, Inc.
P.O. Box 4410, Naperville, Illinois 60567-4410
(630) 961-3900
FAX: (630) 961-2168
www.sourcebooks.com

Originally published in 1997 by Pinnacle Books, an imprint of
Kensington Publishing Corp., New York

Printed and bound in Canada
TR 10 9 8 7 6 5 4 3 2 1

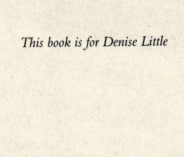

This book is for Denise Little

"It's a girl," said the Bearded Lady. "But her's not breathing." Carefully, the Bearded Lady extended the lifeless infant toward Angelique Kelley.

"You did your best," said Sean Kelley, patting the Bearded Lady's shoulder. "There was no midwife handy, and our wee one came early."

Nine-year-old Brian O'Connor had been crouched outside the circus wagon. Now he burst through the doorway and raced across the wagon's narrow interior. Grasping the baby, he held her by the ankles and slapped her slippery bottom.

"Brian!" Sean roared. "Are you brainsick?"

"Brian, *s'il vous plait*," Angelique cried.

"Hush," Brian said. "Listen!"

The baby girl mewed piteously. Then she sneezed, screwed up her tiny mouth, and wailed. Brian placed her upon her mum's bosom, and the babe's yowls subsided.

"*Merci*," Angelique whispered.

"There was something in a book 'bout spanking a dead baby alive. You always say reading's a waste of time, but I'm glad I read that book."

"A miracle," said the Bearded Lady.

As if she understood, the baby gurgled.

Tears streamed down Sean's face. "Me daughter," he bragged, "sounds like a calliope."

"What's a calliope?" Embarrassed by Sean's tears, Brian counted his toes.

"A musical instrument. I shall buy one for our circus. That'll increase business tenfold. Wait till you hear the calliope's whistle, lad. 'Tis a siren one cannot fail to notice. Seductive, tempting, irresistible."

"Seductive, tempting, irresistible," Brian parroted.

Outside the wagon, a short distance away, another circus performer squatted like a toad—a turbulent toad. The Gypsy's concoction had cost dear. Angelique had swallowed every bite of the spiced pudding and gone into early labor, yet she was still this side of the grave.

The French wench was a cat with nine lives, damn it, and she had eight lives to go!

One

WISH I COULD FLY WITHOUT A NET.

Hands pressed against her heart, Calliope Kelley watched a lone sparrow hawk glide across the sky.

"Happy birthday, Calico Cat," Brian said.

He had sneaked up behind and tugged her long braids as if they were whips to tame his lions and tigers. *Ouch!*

Her braids felt like a hangman's noose as Brian wrapped them around her neck and stepped in front of her. He wore fawn-colored trousers tucked into high black boots, and a loose white shirt. Peeking from the shirt's pocket was a dime novel. Brian always carried books. He had taught Calliope how to read and, when she wasn't performing or helping with chores, she eagerly scanned pages.

"Let go of my hair, Brian O'Connor," she stated with defiance, but couldn't control a tear or three.

"Sorry, puss." He released her braids. "Guess I pulled your weeds too hard."

"My hair ain't weeds," she said, her tears forgotten.

"Papa says weeds are not valued where they grow. Mum says flowers are cherished."

"True." Brian bowed, then handed her a clown's bouquet of paper flowers. He did it so quickly she couldn't decide if he had drawn it from his sleeve or the pocket of his breeches. She hated being fooled.

She hated her name too. Calliope Angelique Kelley. It was pronounced cal-*eye*-oh-pee, but some people said cal-eee-ope, which was wrong, wrong, wrong! Brian had nicknamed her Calico Cat because, he said, her brown hair had glints of reddish gold and her gray-green eyes slanted like a tiger's. Other circus performers called her girl. "Stay away from the tent ropes, girl." "Don't be playing near the elephants, girl." Golly Jehossafrat!

This afternoon she had blown out the candles on her birthday cake and wished her name was Mary. Mary was a fine name. Nobody in the whole world was called Calliope. Everyone else had a person's name.

Calliope stood outside the performers' entrance to the big tent. She had just finished her Jockey's Act, not that she did much. Wearing soft leather boots, tights, leotard, and skirt, she straddled Marianne Defossey's shoulders. Marianne stood on top of Big John's shoulders while their horse galloped 'round the ring. Last week Calliope had practiced a pirouette on her toes, followed by an upward leap and spiral, but when Papa watched, she had missed and tumbled from her horse to the dirt. What a hullabaloo! She had merely hurt her pride and behind, but Papa said, "Wait a bit, me darlin' daughter. Practice makes perfection. 'Tis no need to be taking foolhardy chances."

It wasn't fair. When Mum rehearsed, she sometimes stumbled and fell. Mum had even tried to somersault forward, an almost impossible feat for a ropewalker. By Calliope's reckoning, Mum had been close to death seven times. She had fallen twice while climbing to the top of the tent. Luckily, the distance had not been great, and she had ended up with what Papa called "piddling boo-boos." Once Mum had eaten canned beans and suffered from a ghastly bellyache. Then there was the time she had been pushed from the wagon by mistake while crossing a stream. Papa said he had to turn her inside out and bail her breadbasket. Last Christmas she had been scratched by a lion with a toothache, and last month she had been shot at during a circus parade. Thank goodness she had been swinging from the small parade trapeze and the gunshot missed. Mum said the bullet parted her hair down the middle like Papa's, and Papa said she must wear a big hat for her next march-past. Papa was so funny.

Calliope peeked through the tent's opening. Papa stood by the center pole. White cuffs hung from the sleeves of his gray linen jacket. He wore a batwing collar and a black cravat, and his necktie's knot sported a diamond pin as big as an acorn. Papa looked downright purty with his round, rosy face, green eyes, and wavy black hair. Mum and Papa had met in Paris, France.

Mum considered herself an equilibrist, but other performers called it ropewalking. Mum used a net for rehearsals, never during her act. High above the audience, she danced with the grace of a ballerina. Then, blindfolded, she would perform backward somersaults.

Calliope thought her mum, Angelique, was the most daring performer in Papa's circus. If only Mum wouldn't insist on perfecting that forward somersault. If only Brian O'Connor wasn't besotted by Mum's beauty.

Brian loved Angelique, and why not? Everyone adored Sean Kelley's "French Angel." Everyone said how Calliope was such a skinny little thing, all arms and legs, with a sassy mouth to boot—nothing like her mother.

But now she was eleven. Older. Tomorrow she'd be eleven and a day. Soon she'd play center ring, just like Mum. Then Brian would love *her*.

Calliope watched Marianne perform a fork jump, leaping from the ground to her horse, alighting astride its dappled back. There was scattered applause.

Maybe it was the recent outbreak of cholera, thought Calliope, but the audience seemed restless, mean tempered. Papa had sensed their unease and begun his show with Brian's wild cats. That held their interest, but they hadn't laughed much at the clowns. And they seemed downright bored by the Jockey Act.

Papa signaled to the band member who played a steam piano on wheels, and Calliope heard the music's tinny whine taper off.

"My friends," Sean began.

"We ain't your friends," shouted a beefy, red-faced man. "And if'n you cain't do your show better, we want our two bits back."

"My friends," Sean repeated, his clear voice reaching every seat. "You have just heard a modern marvel of musical mechanism, a gen-u-ine calliope. The tones of this incredible instrument are so powerful they can be heard five miles away, and yet they are as sweetly soft as a lover's lute."

The beefy man guffawed. "Lover's lute, my ass! The wife's piana can be heard ten miles away, more's the pity."

A wave of laughter followed the heckler's words.

"Rotten side-whiskered son of a hyena," Brian muttered.

Calliope wished she could cuss like a man. "Why is that gilly so mean?" she asked.

"Who can tell about gillys? They all sound growly. I wish Sean had taken the circus straight to New York."

Calliope slanted a glance toward Brian. His mother, a circus equestrian, had died before Calliope was born. Sean and Angelique had taken the orphaned boy into their care and raised him. He was, in effect, her big brother. Calliope knew she couldn't marry her brother, and she was glad Brian was not truly related by blood ties. Because she planned to marry him when she grew up. Then, lickety-split, they would have a baby named Mary.

What if her first child was a boy? Well then, she would christen him for the state where he was born. Dakota. Montana. York. Unless, of course, he was born in Missouri. You couldn't call a lad Miss Ouri.

"Look at your papa, Calico Cat." Brian pointed toward the ring.

Sean, unperturbed, waved a slender gold-headed cane. "And now, my friends, if you will kindly give me your attention, the Sean Kelley Circus proudly presents its star attraction. Our French Angel, at great danger to her lovely person, will tiptoe across the rope. Lay-deez and gen-tul-men, she will dance through the air straight up to heaven." He winked toward the red-faced, side-whiskered man. "And don't be tellin' me how your wife dances across the sky like an angel, though I sure-fire pity her for the divil she wed."

This time the laughter was good-natured.

Calliope watched the beefy man's wife jab him in the ribs. His mouth opened then closed. Whatever remark he meant to shout became an unintelligible gurgle.

Angelique had entered the ring.

Calliope gasped. Mum had sewn a new costume. Beads sparkled at her bosom and between her legs. The tights and leotard were flesh-colored, and from a distance she appeared naked. Good thing they were performing in Missouri, because she'd never get away with it in Boston. Calliope sneaked a peek at Brian. His dark blue eyes looked moonstruck, and his lips wore a doltish grin.

Her heart plummeted to the bottom of her boots. No matter how hard she tried, no matter how fast she grew, she would never look like Mum.

Angelique entered the ring swiftly, her honey-colored hair streaming behind her. Reaching the center pole, she posed *en pointe*. Then she began a slow accent up a swinging ladder, held steady by Papa. The band played a waltz.

Calliope's gaze followed until Mum safely reached the platform.

Excitement charged the audience, but there was still an almost imperceptible murmur of discontent.

Calliope sighed. What would make the gillys happy? Couldn't they see there was no net beneath? Did they want Mum to walk through the air without a rope?

"Lay-deez and gen-tul-men," Papa announced after Mum had danced to the middle of the rope, "our French Angel will execute a back somersault blind-folded. We need complete silence. Will the fainthearted among you please shut your eyes?"

A drum rolled, and the audience hushed. Good. Mum had their attention.

The calliope player hit a key by mistake.

A discordant whistle echoed throughout the tent.

Startled, Angelique dropped her blindfold. The piece of black material floated toward the ground. Angelique's spell was broken.

"Does she want it brung up again?" roared the red-faced man. "I'll climb that there ladder fer a kiss at the top."

"What's the Angel doing now?" cried a woman, rising to her feet.

Noting the waning interest of her audience, Angelique had performed a series of double somersaults.

"That ain't nothin'," Redface said with a sneer. "My young'un can jump from the roof of our barn backwards an' spin his way down like some damfool twister. French Angel, my ass! She's a cheat!"

The crowd rumbled loudly. Calliope thought they sounded like lions and tigers with bellyaches. She watched Angelique tense her body and spread her arms. "Mum's going to try a forward somersault, Papa. Stop her, oh please, stop her."

Calliope's plea was unnecessary, for Sean had

already seen his wife's anger and sensed her injured pride. Dropping his cane, he cupped his hands around his mouth.

"Cease, me precious darlin'!" he yelled. "There's no net beneath. Do not be attemptin' a foolish stunt for these hooligans. New York—we planned to show the forward in New York."

If Angelique heard her husband, she gave no sign.

Calliope watched, praying. In a back somersault, shoulders flexed naturally, and swinging arms gave additional momentum. "Somersaulting forward reverses natural reflexes," Papa had once said. "The body generates a gravitational pull." Calliope wasn't sure what gravitational pull meant, but she thought it might mean Mum's arms were no help because they got in the way.

Angelique leaped high. At the same time, she lowered her head.

"Your arms!" Calliope screamed.

"Do not be forgettin' to wrap your arms about your chest," Papa warned, "or they'll catch between your legs."

Brian pressed Calliope's face against his ruffled shirtfront. Despite the book in his pocket, she could hear the thud of his heart.

"Angelique, no, please, God, no." Brian's voice was an anguished moan.

Wrenching free from his grasp, Calliope ran through the tent's open flap, her gaze riveted upwards, her whole world reduced to a pair of slipper-clad feet. And yet she thought she saw a sag in the rope. *Impossible!* The rope was always guyed-out, stretched tight by Big John or Bobby Duncan or Jack the Giant.

Angelique's golden hair whipped around her throat as she teetered sideways. Her fingers scratched at the air, reaching toward heaven. Then one dainty foot stepped on a cloud that wasn't there, and she plummeted toward earth.

Two

EVERY FLY, FLEA, AND MOSQUITO HAD JOINED THEIR parade, yet stinkbugs and hellish heat didn't seem to plague the crowd. Pasting a smile on her face, seventeen-year-old Calliope Kelley listlessly waved her American flag toward several people standing by a metal pole. A clock, flanked by cast-iron cherubs, perched on top of the pole. Noon.

Sunlight hit ground-floor windows, casting a reflection of backwards letters across the pink brick sidewalk. Perspiration trickled down Calliope's brow. She reached for Napoleon's ruffled collar, planning to cleanse the moisture away.

Napoleon oink-oinked indignantly.

Heat made everything blurry. Sidewalk children wavered like the stripes in Calliope's fluttering flag.

God had already begun baking the city when the circus arrived at dawn. They had anchored their showboat on the Mississippi alongside *Lady Franklin*, the ferryboat to Prairie du Chien. Despite the sultry heat, Calliope had helped unload the equipment. Then she had harnessed the bandwagon's twelve dappled grays. It was hard work, but she did it without grumbling. She hardly ever complained, at least not out loud. Six years ago she had complained about a saggy tightrope. But no one would listen to an eleven-year-old circus brat with a vivid imagination. Not even Brian.

In the years following Angelique's death, Calliope had taken over many of her father's duties. Jocko had helped, thank goodness. Although she found she had a good head for figures, balancing the books and keeping the circus from financial ruin, it was Jocko who supervised the roustabouts. Jocko had created their banner line, the paintings of sideshow attractions displayed on separate sections of canvas. His paintings were so pretty, Calliope thought they could decorate a lady's boudoir, not that she'd ever been inside a lady's boudoir. Jocko wouldn't talk about the life he had led before he'd joined her circus, but she didn't care. Let him disguise his face with clown paint during a show or hide behind a wagon when an official of the law paid a call; she'd never give him away.

Jocko hired the new acts. "No performer will bargain with a girl," he had insisted, "and when Sean is guyed-out, he can't tell good from bad."

Guyed-out. Tight as a tent. Poor Papa. He drank more every day, every week, every month. He had a great tolerance for whiskey and would remain sensible through the opening spectacle and performances, announcing each act with competence. After the show he'd drink himself insensible. There was no cure for Sean's malady. Not even a leprechaun with a pot of gold could ease the sorrow from Papa's broken heart.

Panama Duncan had tried, along with several other women, but to no avail. *The Irish can only love once,* Calliope thought. Lucky she was half French and if necessary could love as often as she wished.

"Sit still, daughter! You squirm with more zeal than the blasted piggy," Sean admonished. His shirt collar was askew, his vest buttoned wrongly, and his stovepipe hat tilted over one bloodshot eye. And yet his gloved hands expertly flicked the reins that controlled two white horses. "Wriggle again, and you shall become supper for the hungry beasties."

"Yes, Papa." Smiling at her father's threat, she glanced back at the wagons. Three animal dens contained lions and tigers. The Sean Kelley Circus wound through the streets of McGregor, Iowa. Calliope squirmed because she was hot. Because Napoleon—balanced precariously beside her on the buggy seat—smelled like rancid bacon. And because she hated sitting still.

Following the cats were eight medieval knights in shining armor mounted on black steeds, and five velvet-clad Ladies of the Court atop chestnut mares. Close on their heels trotted Calliope's famous horse, the blind, beautiful Dublin. Next, a lumbering elephant with an ornate silk blanket decorating his rubbery sides, a golden howdah on his back.

Clowns marched with their dogs and ducks, while a few rode in tiny carts drawn by ponies or goats. Calliope glimpsed Jocko, almost hidden behind his cluster of balloons. She waved her flag and called,

"Sakes alive, Jocko, it's hot!" But the bandwagon's musicians drowned out her words with earsplitting sounds that could burst the starched pinafores of every Mary who jumped up and down along the pink sidewalk's edge.

"He flies through the air with the greatest of eeease," Sean sang in his rich yet strident baritone. "This daring young man on the flying trapeeeze."

"Papa, you're bluffering loud enough to beat the band!"

"Bluffering?" Red and blue plumes waffled as the buggy horses pranced and shook their braided manes. Grinning at his daughter, Sean sang one octave higher. "His figure is handsome, all girls he can pleeease, and my love he purloined her away."

"No man would dare steal me away, Papa, most especially the hateful gilly-galloos." The word galloo was a corruption of the Dutch word *gelubt* which, according to circus performers, meant eunuch. Awkwardly, Calliope leaned sideways and kissed Sean's chin. "I shall never marry and leave you, Papa."

"I should hope not," he said, his voice gruff. "'Tis barely out of nappies ye be."

"Papa, I'm seventee… almost twenty!"

Today was her birthday, though they'd not cele-brate the event, since it brought back memories of Angelique. Could Papa be remembering? He had lapsed into silence, thank goodness, but now Napoleon commenced oinking again. Damn and blast!

Calliope scratched the golden-colored pig behind his ears and tidied his silken clown ruff. Napoleon Bonaparte was small and lean. A leading circus attraction, he performed a number of stunts. He rolled a vinegar barrel by trotting hind-legged against it and rode the hooped sides as it rotated. He answered questions with guttural grunts and spelled P-I-G and C-O-R-N by nudging letter cards with his snout. He even worked a teeterboard and wove a figure eight between Jocko's legs as Jocko sang the ballad "Root, Hog, or Die."

Today Napoleon wore a diaper with a hole cut to let his curly tail stick through.

Thank goodness for the piggy-knickers, Calliope thought, wrinkling her nose. She couldn't wait to hand the malodorous porker over to Jocko.

❧

Surrounded by buckets of water, Calliope stood inside the menagerie tent. She clutched a soapy broom. Hot and tired, she watched her caged animals drowse or pace apathetically.

Outside, a storm was brewing. She heard distant thunder and wished it would rain. After the show. Or during the show but after the gillys had paid. Before, during, after, she didn't care. Anything to do away with this sticky heat.

Maybe there *was* hope for rain, she thought, at the sound of a second thunderclap.

The tent's entrance opening was suddenly filled with the form of a tall man who stood outlined against the flare of lightning. Calliope stifled a scream. This man looked like the very devil himself. No. Not the devil. More like a savage black panther.

A panther with dark blue eyes.

"Brian?" She blinked several times, wondering if he really stood there, wondering if the man in high leather boots, tight cavalry pants, and bare chest was really Brian O'Connor. Perhaps the pending storm played tricks on her mind and memory. "Brian, is it truly you and not some ghost?" To her surprise, the caged animals began to spin, and the menagerie tent turned as gray as an elephant's hide.

Alarmed, Brian watched Calliope's face lose every stitch of color. She pitched forward but caught herself in time, leaning on the broom as if it were a crutch.

"You're wetter than Pachydermal," he teased, tossing a valise and his dusty shirt toward the hay-strewn corner. "And wouldn't Sean be vexed if he saw his wee daughter washing a prodigious elephant? What would he say about your cobwebby chemise tucked into a pair of me old tatter'd breeches?"

"Nothing. Papa wouldn't care one whit."

Calliope replied so loftily, Brian knew her defiant statement was a fib. She dropped the broom and swiped at her untidy hair with a muddy hand, leaving a daub across her forehead.

She said, "Panama wears less when she does an arabesque on Pachydermal's trunk. I'm always holding my breath, waiting for her boobies to fall out during the opening spec."

"Panama still performs?"

"Not really, Brian. All she does is ride and posture."

"When I left, she was a trapeze artist."

Calliope snorted. "I would never call her an artist. She could swing, but she lacked grace. Now she's become top-heavy, like a ship with billowed sails."

"Why does Sean keep her?"

"We can't lose Duncan. Panama married him. Bobby Duncan, the Kid Show strong man. Remember?"

Brian nodded as he pictured Bobby Duncan. Well structured with cast-iron muscles, every bit of common sense Duncan's head lacked was stored inside his powerful arms and shoulders.

Had Panama's marriage changed her? Or did she still spread her legs for everyone from Kid Show to clown? Talented Panama! She might lack grace under the Big Top, but she performed well beneath the wagons.

Hunkering down, Brian plunged a dipper into a bucket of clear water and sipped, cooling his parched throat.

"Are you planning to kiss me hello, Mr. O'Connor?" Calliope tossed her waist-length hair. "It is the best of greetings, for I have no braids to tug."

"I miss your braids, Calico Cat. You look different."

"I look older. I *am* older."

"Truly, puss?" Rising, Brian leaned against a tent pole. "I see a dirty-faced urchin."

"Dash it all! You sound like Papa."

"How is Sean?"

"Fine." She raised her chin. "He's wondrous fine."

"What's wrong, lass?"

"Nothing."

"What's wrong, Calliope?"

"Why should you care? You abandoned me."

"It wasn't you I abandoned. It was the circus."

"It's the same thing." She hesitated then said, "If you must know, Papa drinks."

"Sean is Irish."

"You're Irish. Do you drink lots, Brian? Do you get guyed-out every night?"

"I've had myself a few nips too many." Today, for example. He had fortified himself well, fearful Calliope would condemn him with her large cat eyes. Because he *had* abandoned her. He had left after Angelique's burial. He had just turned twenty-one, and the woman he loved... worshipped... He had lost his angel, so he escaped. The youth fled. Sean's child could not.

Child? Calliope spoke true when she said she'd grown older. Older and beautiful, with a fey Irish quality. Nothing fey about the quality of her breasts straining the lacy confines of her chemise. His old boyish trousers looked absurd. Except when she turned, showing a saucy rump. Except where they hitched up between her thighs.

"Liquor makes you forget," he said. "Sean drinks to forget Angelique."

"No, Brian. Papa drinks to remember." She kicked the wash bucket with one bare foot. "Where did you go when you left the circus?"

"Out West."

"What did you do?"

"I fought with bloody sabers and bloody guns."

"But the war between North and South is over."

"I fought a different war, puss, a daft war. I fought Indians."

"Are you back forever?" she blurted.

"There's no such thing as forever."

"The circus is forever."

"Nothing is forever. Haven't you learned that yet?"

"The circus is forever," she insisted. "Have you returned home?"

"Home? No. Yes. I suppose I have." He glanced at the lions. "I see Leo and Duchess recognize my scent, even after all this time."

"You raised them from cubs, Brian. You raised me from a cub too. We had no secrets. Sometimes we played clowns. Together we rode Pachydermal's howdah during parades, and you always threatened to push me from my high perch. We were such good friends. Can we be friends again?"

"Does Sean have a place for me? Is there a position? I won't play roustabout or vendor."

She nodded toward the cages. "We need a cat tamer. The man we have now begs to retire. You can be his assistant tomorrow night. The lions recollect your scent, but our tigers are new. Bengals cannot be trusted when they perform with lions."

"Do the lions and tigers share the ring?" he asked, quirking an eyebrow.

"Yes. It's what makes our show unique. Do you want the position? Cat tamer?"

Cat eyes. Calico Cat. Child of Angelique. No, not a child anymore. "Yes," he said. "I'll find Sean straightaway."

"Don't bother. *I* run the circus."

He bristled. "I'll not take orders from a lass."

"Then leave again and be damned!"

She doesn't mean it. He gazed at her wee hands curved into fists. He admired her mouth, now set in a pretty pout. The tent's nebulous illumination could not diminish the reddish-gold glints in her brown hair. Her eyes kept changing from gray to green to gray again.

Her lovely chin tilted higher than a proper colleen's chin should tilt. Stubborn. Prideful. Just like Angelique.

"Sheathe your claws, puss; I'll stay." He glanced through the open tent flap. Lightning silhouetted the backyard. An Opener leaned against the Red Wagon. Soon he'd talk the crowd into buying tickets. One vendor, a Bugman, stopped to converse, holding his basket of chameleons.

Calliope was a chameleon, Brian thought as he thrust his hand inside his trouser pocket. Lord, she could change her moods as easily as her eyes flip-flopped between gray and green, as easily as a chameleon changed color.

His fingers found an object amid his coins and pocketknife, and he withdrew a crumpled piece of paper. "Happy birthday, Calico Cat."

"Golly Jehossafrat! How could you remember?"

"How could I forget? Didn't I help the stork deliver you?"

"The Bearded Lady delivered me."

"But I spanked you awake."

"If you ever try that again, I'll spank you back." Accepting his gift, she smoothed the paper until she found a gold chain and a tiny horse charm. "Oh, my goodness. It's lovely, Brian. Thank you. I shall keep it forever, even though you say nothing is forever. Will you attach its clasp, please?"

"Of course." He linked the chain, removed his fumbling fingers from her nape, then said, "I've got another gift for you, puss. Turn around."

She made an about-face in time to catch a gush of cold water. "Stop it, Brian!"

"Wash down the elephant," he chanted, sloshing more water.

"I'm not an elephant. Aren't you the confused, boy-o?"

"It's time for Calico Cat's Saturday bath."

"Saturday was yesterday." She held up her hands. "No more shenanigans. I'm cold."

"Are you not shamed for the fibbing, lass? 'Tis hotter than the devil's front parlor."

Swiftly, before Brian could react, Calliope propelled herself forward and batted the bucket away. But her whirring motion sent them both tumbling to the straw.

"Be careful of Pachydermal's feet," she said. "He could crush us to bits in an instant."

Brian held onto her shoulders and rolled them over, away from the elephant, until he was on the bottom and she was on top. "I'm not cold anymore," she whispered, burrowing against the warmth of his sun-bronzed skin.

"Sleepyhead. You're Bo Peep with a cage full of cats but nary one sheep."

"If I'm sleepy," she groused, raising her head, "it is not because your chest is pillow-soft. Anyway, sheep have no…" She smiled. "No horse sense. The nursery rhyme tells Bo Peep to leave them alone and they'll come home, but I don't believe that for one moment. Her sheep will doubtless be eaten alive by wolves."

"*I* came home."

"Yes, lad, but *you're* the wolf."

Distracted by the flushed face so close to his, Brian couldn't think of a witty backchat. Her lips were creased into a smile of invitation. *I look older. I am older.* What had she meant by that? He had taught her how to ride bareback. Had another man taught her how to ride with passion? He turned her over, straddled her hips, kissed her, and grinned. If another lad had tutored Calliope, he had neglected to instruct her on how to pucker properly. Her lips were closed, even though he had felt them push against his with undeniable eagerness. She looked like a woman but kissed like a child.

Slowly, deliberately, he traced her mouth with the tip of his tongue, until he felt the soft, moist, inner edges of her lips yield. She gasped and wriggled both hands between her waist and his, trying to push them apart. Good. Tussling made the contest more exciting, more fulfilling. He pressed closer, letting her feel his hardness. He sensed she wasn't ready for the ultimate thrust, but she stopped struggling. In truth, she lay so motionless he wondered if she had fainted.

"Are you all right, puss?"

"Fine. I'm wondrous fine." Freeing her hands, she twined her arms around his neck.

He could see the adorable blush that stained her cheeks. His tongue discovered her earlobe and traced the contours of her inner ear.

"Wolf," she hummed.

Her breasts were so close to his mouth, he couldn't resist. Through the chemise, he sucked her breast until he felt her nipple expand and her body begin to writhe. Lowering one bodice strap, he took a moment to cherish the sight of her firm young breast. It was fuller than he had expected, milk white except for her rosy nipple.

He wanted to maneuver his body so his knees cradled her face and she could take him into her mouth. He hoped the other lad, her instructor, had taught her how to do that. At the same time, he felt a brief, unwelcome stab of resentment. *He* should have been her teacher.

She placed her small palm on top of his hand and pressed, until he was compelled to mold his fingers around her breast. Gently, he flicked her nipple with his first finger.

Her writhing halted abruptly as, almost languidly, she spread her legs.

Thunder sounded. Louder. Closer.

His deft fingers reached between them for the buttons on her trousers. With a purr she raised her knees, plowed the ground with her heels, wriggled her rump, and molded herself against his hand.

Stifling a groan, he rubbed his thumb and little finger back and forth, gently digging into the juncture between her thighs and mound. He ached to taste the sweet nectar situated between his thumb and finger, but they were still clothed. Time to remedy that situation.

"Brian, oh, Brian," she cried, "I've missed you so much." Then she whispered, "You must teach me what to do."

The flaps of the tent swayed from a sudden gust of wind. A lion roared.

You must teach me what to do. Despite the lion's thunder, Brian heard her plea. Every word branded his soul as he realized she had never lain with a man before. Her smile of invitation had been a smile of trust. Her close-lipped kisses were the result of her inexperience.

Selfish bastard! Why did he assume she wasn't a virgin? Had his years away from the circus turned him into the worst kind of gilly?

Regaining his feet, he scooped her up and set her on her feet. She stepped away and yanked up her chemise strap. Then she hid her face with her hands.

Was she laughing at him? No. She was weeping.

He pulled her against him, planning to halt her tears with a friendly embrace. A mistake! Beneath his tight pants, he felt arousal once again. This young colleen had bewitched him. He wanted to drop her trousers, his trousers, and achieve immediate satisfaction.

Instead, he dropped her and doused himself with cold water from a third rinse bucket. "Why do you weep like a banshee, Calliope?"

"A banshee wails of death," she gasped, crossing herself.

Perhaps he *had* become a gilly. He'd forgotten circus folk were so superstitious. "Why do you cry, puss?"

"Because I did something wrong."

"You did nothing wrong. It was my fault. We haven't seen each other in years, and yet I took your love for granted. Stop crying, please. You did nothing wrong."

"But I must have. You stopped. You wouldn't teach me." She gazed upwards, where rain spattered the canvas like a drumroll. "When I fall from my horse, I must mount him again. That's how I learn."

He burst out laughing.

She stamped her small foot. "Why do you chortle like a hyena?"

"Because I have never heard anything so naïve." *Or so provocative.*

"Could you not finish what was foolishly begun?"

"You misread my intentions, Calliope."

"Liar!"

"If we had truly finished your lesson in love, I would have been sacked by Sean. And this before I've presented myself to him or tamed one cat."

"Milksop! Papa wouldn't sack you. *I* run the circus."

"And *I* would rather pet Bengal tigers than a grubby urchin in tattered breeches."

Enough! He'd apologized sincerely, and she'd called him a coward. No one called Brian O'Connor a milksop, not even Miss I-run-the-circus!

"Thank you," she said, lifting her chin.

"Are you daft, lass? Why would you be thanking me?"

"Because I believed you a man, Brian O'Connor. But now I see you are merely a spalpeen in manly form."

He winced. This time her verbal fisticuffs had been delivered below the belt. Glancing through the open tent flaps, he saw the backyard was mired in mud. The rain's drumroll had become a whole orchestra, and yet the Bugman still stood there, conversing with his friend the Opener.

Beautiful chameleon-cat! Brian shifted his gaze to Calliope. Her skin was a golden hue except where the cobwebby chemise exposed the mounds of her creamy breasts. Her gray-green eyes blazed, and her mouth was bright pink, somewhat swollen from the press of his lips. Chameleons didn't have stingers, but cats had claws. He would have to avoid those sharp clinging needles. During the last seven years he had experienced so much hate, he didn't have room for love. Not pure love. Not Calliope's love.

Three

MUSICIANS SAT ON FOLDING WOODEN CHAIRS. THEY had just finished playing for Jocko and Napoleon's performance.

"What are you reading, Calliope?"

"Huh?"

Jocko chuckled. "It must be a good book, sweetheart, for you've blocked out all else."

She raised her face from the folds of her red cape. "In truth, it's a mighty fine book. Brand spanking new. See?"

"*Barriers Burned Away*," he said, squinting through his heavy clown's greasepaint, "by Edward Payson Roe."

"It's made up but tells all about the Chicago fire."

"Lucky we bypassed Chicago last October during that holocaust, eh Calliope?"

"They say a cow kicked over the lantern in Mrs. O'Leary's barn. It's happy I am that we have no cows in our circus."

Jocko toed the dirt with his oversized shoe. "We

have a kicker, though, and you'll be using her for your performance tonight."

"What do you mean? What's the matter with Dublin?"

"He's a bit lame in his left hock. That man you hired yesterday, Brian O'Connor, smoothed on liniment. But you'll have to ride Susan."

Calliope had named the new mare herself. Susan B. Anthony was a beautiful chestnut, well schooled when she behaved. But sometimes she tended to play the rebel, kicking out with her hind legs. Since Calliope's final stunt relied on perfect timing, a break in stride could be dangerous, even fatal.

"Susan has been a good little lady during rehearsals," Calliope told Jocko, "and tonight's gilly-galloos seem friendly. They won't startle the mare when Papa asks for silence."

"If the audience is friendly, why do you call them gilly-galloos with that tone of insult in your sweet voice?"

"Because they killed Mum. You weren't there to see, Jocko. They wanted her to fall. They willed her to fall."

"I thought you said Angelique was felled by a saggy rope."

"She was! But the gillys bruised her pride, first."

Jocko toed the dirt again. "Who would want your mother dead, Calliope?"

"I don't know. I've racked my brains for six years and can suppose only that someone desired Mum's favors and was rebuffed. She was so beautiful, so…"

"Yes? Go on."

"So in love with Papa. Would you kill for love,

Jocko?" When he nodded, she said, "Truly? You're not clowning around?"

He smiled at her choice of phrase. Then he scowled. "Yes, Calliope, I would kill for love."

Stunned by the intensity of his tone, she swallowed another question and gestured toward the people surging up and down the tent's aisles. "Look at their rumps sway, Jocko, like smug-assed monkeys. They are galloos, and when I have enough money, I'll spit in their faces." She slammed the book against her leg. "Just see if I don't."

"Then I guess the gillys are safe from your spittle, for no matter how large the crowd or how fine the show, we always seem to come out even." Removing a derby and white stocking cap, Jocko ran gloved fingers through the flattened strands of his ash-blond hair. "Duncan wants more pay."

"Horse dung! Panama wants a boodle of coins to buy fancy duds. The answer is no."

Calliope was tempted to tell the clown her secret, but not even Papa knew. Only Big John, who had sworn to keep his silence when he took her savings and invested it with the leading brokerage firm of Jay Cooke and Company. Soon she would have enough money to make Sean Kelley's circus the finest in the world. Soon she would have enough to spit.

"Were you buried in your book," Jocko said, "or did you see the tiger claw O'Connor's trousers?"

"I was in the toilet," she blurted with a blush.

Papa shouldn't have let Brian play cat tamer so soon, she thought. Papa was delighted to see Brian. They drank together for hours. One could hear their

Irish ballads from every wagon, every muddy inch of the backyard. She was almost certain Brian had sought out Panama after Papa passed from singing to snoring. Damn and blast! The horny boy-o courted a lump on his noggin from Duncan's hammy fist.

After mulling it over in her mind, Calliope had justified her actions inside the menagerie tent. A result of the sultry heat. The storm. The excitement of Brian's return. Her wet chemise had been responsible for the ache in her breasts. And the moisture between her thighs? Well, that was easy to explain. Didn't she always feel like running for the toilet and taking a pee when raindrops drummed against the tent's tight canvas?

"Did the tiger hurt Brian?" she asked Jocko.

"A scratch. There was more damage to his trousers than his flesh. Will you join me in Clown Alley after the show, sweetheart? I'm not supposed to tell, but the crew has baked up a surprise birthday cake larger than center ring, and I must escort you to the Cook Top."

"My birthday was yesterday." Calliope saw Jocko smile beneath the painted frown dipping toward his chin.

"Yesterday we were busy with the rainstorm," he said. "Aside from nature's elements, we had to contend with human nature. While you juggled receipts inside the silver wagon, O'Connor, Jack the Giant, and Panama disappeared. Duncan was in a rage."

Jack the Giant? Perhaps Brian had not sought out Panama. Calliope wondered why she felt such profound relief. Brian didn't mean anything to her. The heat. The storm. Before she could summon any more justifications, she heard Papa's voice announce her act.

It began with the parade knights, now dressed as Cossacks, who stood on top of their galloping horses and raced around the ring. From their midst, as if by magic, emerged Calliope. Clothed in tights, leotard, and short ruffled skirt, she sat sideways on Susan B. Anthony, her legs crossed one over the other, the fingers of her right hand clasping the mare's mane. Then, rising to her toes, she performed a series of dazzling stunts.

With perfect precision, Big John's gray Arabian appeared next to Susan B. Anthony. On the stallion's hindquarters, behind Big John, stood Marianne. Next to the Arabian galloped a riderless black.

"One, two, three," Calliope counted, knowing her fellow equestrians did the same.

She leaped high in the air and somersaulted, alighting on the gray stallion's haunches. Marianne somersaulted at the same time, landing atop Susan B. Anthony, while Big John cartwheeled onto the black horse. The audience cheered as all three performers reversed their routine.

With a grin, Calliope nudged Susan from the ring, riding her away from the bright lanterns, through the performers' entrance. Susan had been a perfect lady and would receive a special treat in her feed bag.

The Cossacks joined Big John and Marianne as Calliope collected props for her final stunts.

The musicians executed a drumroll.

"Lay-deez and gen-tul-men," Sean shouted. "Pre-senting a performance the likes of which you have never seen before. Our star equestrian, Dream Dancer, will dazzle you with her daring, be-muse you with her beauty…"

Beauty? That was new, thought Calliope. Had Papa finally conceded that she was out of diapers?

"We need complete silence," Sean continued, "for one muffled oath, one misplaced sigh, one lover's kiss…"

Lover's kiss! Hah! Brian's second kiss had been very wet. He couldn't even kiss like a gentleman.

The band played "El Caballero."

Calliope slapped Susan lightly on the haunch, and the chestnut, mane and tail flowing, pranced into the ring. Calliope followed on foot, bowed to the audience, and removed her cape. She now wore a white evening gown with a small bustle and Chinese-style slits up both sides. Her arms were covered by elbow-length kid gloves, and in her left hand she carried an ostrich-feather fan. Seizing Susan's mane, she flipped onto the mare's back.

Jocko entered the ring, stuck the ostrich-feather fan in his hat brim, handed Calliope a gun, and retreated, all the time expressing exaggerated gestures of fearful concern.

She fired at a target, releasing a flock of pigeons. They flew straight toward her, alighting on her outstretched arms. At Calliope's command, Susan halted and knelt in the center of the ring. A spotted pony trotted around the ring, harnessed to a cart with a cage labeled HOTEL DES PIGEONS. The birds flew into the cage, and the pony withdrew.

Calliope dismounted to thunderous applause.

Papa's voice: "Lay-deez and gen-tul-men, Dream

Dancer, the loveliest daughter of the Sean Kelley Circus, will now attempt a daring and difficult feat. Atop a galloping horse she will leap through a circle of fire. Again, I must ask, no, *beg* for silence."

The slits in Calliope's long gown allowed her to land astraddle and rise to her feet. Quickly, she adjusted her balance to Susan's stride.

Jocko and Brian entered the ring and secured a hoop onto an iron block.

What was Brian doing here? It was supposed to be another clown. Brian still wore his animal-tamer's costume, including the clawed trousers. Forget Brian! Her stunt depended on split-second timing.

The audience hushed.

The music's tempo increased.

Susan quickened her pace from a controlled canter to a gallop.

Calliope watched the mare intently. Still, from the corner of her eye, she saw Brian strike a wooden match on his boot heel and light the hoop.

"Now!" she screamed, and Susan leaped gracefully through the air. They cleared the fire.

Someone tossed a flowered nosegay into the ring. Susan shied and kicked out with her hind hooves. Calliope felt herself falling. Her legs became tangled in her long skirt, and she realized she'd have to land on her back or her head.

She didn't. Brian caught her neatly in his arms, presented her to the crowd, and kissed her. The audience whistled and applauded.

Limp with relief, Calliope snuggled against Brian's chest as he carried her through the performers' entrance. He ignored the laughing crew and continued walking until he was outside the tent. Then and only then did he put her down.

She stared up into his eyes, trying to fathom his expression. Finally she said, "Why were you in the ring?"

"Jocko told me about Susan. I mistrust a kicker."

"Thank you."

"And why would you be thanking me?"

Tears spiked her lashes. His voice sounded like yesterday's voice. Teasing but not teasing. Brian but not Brian.

"Catching you was a reflex," he said. "Out West I caught many ladies."

Anger dried her tears. "I suppose you kissed them too."

"Of course. Most kissed me back."

Avoiding Brian's smug face, she turned away from him. "It was not necessary to pluck me from the air, Brian O'Connor. I would have landed fine."

"You're on the dot, me precious darlin'. They do say that cats are predisposed to alight on their wee paws."

His bedeviling brogue was so close to her ear. She felt him pull her against the length of his body. His fingers caressed her horse charm. She swayed backwards, leaning, and could feel his tense thigh muscles through his shredded trousers. His fingertips traced her bodice, as if he contemplated the fit of her gown. Apparently satisfied, he reached beneath her corset and began to circle her nipple with his first finger. Her nipple grew taut.

Brian kissed the perfumed masses of Calliope's hair, then jerked his head back. Damn! Yesterday he had determined that there would be no impassioned foolery between them. And yet he felt resentment gnaw at his brain like a mouse nibbling at a piece of trap cheese. *She* was the reason his trousers were clawed. Groggy-eyed from lack of sleep, he had performed with bravado rather than common sense, and one astute tiger had caught him off guard. Why shouldn't *she* burn with the same passions that had kept him awake last night?

Testing her resolve, and his, he rubbed his thumb very lightly across her nipple, back and forth.

Calliope chewed her bottom lip but couldn't quite stifle her moan. "El Caballero" reverberated inside her head then became swallowed up by the vast expanse of starry sky. Brian's other hand, the one that didn't caress her breasts, slid through the slit in her skirt, and her whole world turned topsy-turvy. She saw the stars change into sparks of fire, but the fire was above her head while the star's pointy spikes had somehow snagged her slippers. Her graceful balance, always a mainstay in every performance, had flown just like her flutter-winged pigeons. She began to pitch forward.

"Whoa, puss," Brian said, his voice a tease. "Must I catch you twice in one night?"

His words halted her motion as she remembered. "Did you see who tossed the nosegay, Brian?"

"No. Perhaps it was a gilly."

"That's impossible. The ring is a goodly distance from the crowd, and the flowers had no propelling force like… like a cannonball."

"Don't fret, honey. You probably have a secret admirer. A roustabout. Or a knight. Or a clown."

"That doesn't make any sense, Brian. Everyone knows how skittish Susan is."

"Maybe 'everyone' didn't think it through. In any case, your secret admirer's crafty plan failed. You're mine, puss. I caught you. I earned you."

As Brian's deft fingers stroked again, the nosegay incident receded, tucked away inside her mind along with Angelique's saggy rope. "I was truly a liability tonight," she said, "but I have always been accountable for my debts, and I shall pay. If you want me, I'm yours."

Brian winced at Calliope's genuine simplicity, guilelessness beyond his comprehension. His passion still burned, but he knew he must douse his fiery instincts, and hers, for good. He must whip his pretty circus puss with sharp, stinging words. He had never struck his cats. The loud snap of the whiplash sufficed, even though they oft glared at him with murderous intent. Yet now, before he lost complete control—

"Brian," she cried, "my legs feel like beeswax. I… I'm falling."

"When you fall, you must mount again," he said. "That's how you learn."

She stiffened her body. "Are you making fun of me? You sound so strange. Maybe we should go inside the silver wagon. Jocko will direct the rest of the show, and we can still make the grand finale."

"We'd never make the finale, Calliope. In any case, I don't want to tumble you amidst Sean's greenbacks, coins, and receipts, for I might be accused of stealing Sean's money rather than his daughter's virtue."

She cringed. All of a sudden, from a distance, she

heard laughter. Only one person laughed like that, like the shrill whistle of a mare in heat. Panama.

"Hurry," said Brian, "before we are discovered. What would people say if they found the cat tamer taming the circus owner's prize kitten? Mount me, puss."

"No!" Calliope stepped forward. With dismay, she felt her gown's bodice rip. "Why do you sound so nasty?"

"Yesterday you wanted to learn. You called me a coward and a liar. You said I was a spalpeen in manly form."

She whirled about, holding the torn edges of her bodice together. "Does a hasty fondle make you a true man?"

Her eyes were stormy, staring at him with murderous intent. "The deed," he said, "was performed to make you a true woman."

"How charitable you are, my lad. But I would rather pet Bengal tigers than a conceited boy-o wearing tattered breeches. Oh, God, I am such a ninny. You seek to gain favor so I might print your name above mine on the playbills. Did you toss the nosegay, Brian, trusting that after you caught me I would swoon with lustful gratification?"

"Lustful gratification?" He laughed. "How bookish we have become, puss."

"I am the star performer, and don't you ever forget it. Toady bastard!" she screamed, her anger building. "You're no better than the damn gilly-galloos."

"Don't cuss, Calliope."

She raised her chin and for the first time, Brian realized how much she resembled her father.

"I shall do whatever I damn well please," she said.

Four

A NEW RAILROAD CIRCUS,
FOR WHICH SEAN KELLEY HAS BUILT
NINE CARS OF HIS OWN!

Expressly for the Transportation of the
Performers, and so Ingeniously Constructed As
To Be Taken With Their Contents
FROM THE TRACK TO THE TENT!

Congress of Equestrians Starring
DREAM DANCER

Wild Animals Under the Fearless Direction of
BRIAN O'CONNOR

A LIVE ELEPHANT
CLOWNS—CLOWNS—CLOWNS
Starring JOCKO and his Performing Pig
NAPOLEON BONAPARTE

ADMIRING JOCKO'S ILLUSTRATED HANDBILL, CALLIOPE remembered how he had been reluctant to add that last line.

"Gillys love your wee piggy," she had insisted, "and the spalpeens will pester until the whole family, kit and caboodle, buy tickets."

"It just means we'll have to guard the sidewalls more closely," Jocko had grumbled.

But Calliope always had her tent sidewalls carefully patrolled because children would sneak inside the loose canvas flaps. She didn't want to forfeit even one coin, especially since she must now replace the huge amount she had spent to build and furbish her railroad cars.

The railroad was a necessity.

Last year their baggage stock had dragged show wagons through what seemed like hundreds of muddy roads as they traveled to Indiana and Illinois. "Jonah's bad luck," circus performers called the stuck wagons. It had been cold and miserable, but that was the easy part.

Leaving Iowa City for Richmond, they had sloshed around in ooze as thick as pea soup, found bridges washed out, and finally turned back. Nor could they make any of the next three towns. In desperation, they discovered a railroad and rode it to Muscatine, Iowa— which wasn't on their schedule. But they hastily passed out handbills and gave a show. Then they moved on to Fort Madison, partly by train, partly by steamboat. At least a dozen performers had quit.

Yes, the railroad was a necessity, and Calliope was proud of the designs she had drawn up with Jocko.

The cars were built to her specifications. Each had an extended covered platform with a door leading inside so any person could move easily and safely from car to car. Jocko had painted pictures of wild animals on the outside slats. Following the engine was an open gondola for band members. When Papa's circus came to town, the hulligans always knew they had arrived, no matter how early in the morning or late at night.

This year Calliope planned to entertain in Omaha, North Platte, Cheyenne, and Denver. They would have to leave the rail and go overland some 110 miles to play Denver, but she felt it would be worth the effort. Along the way they'd play Central City, Golden, and Boulder.

God had finally smiled upon her, for she had chucked Jay Cooke and Company just in time.

Following a disastrous summer of more mud and rain, she had reluctantly withdrawn her profits from Cooke. Then the nation plunged into a depression. The depression, said every newspaper and politician, was triggered by the failure of Cooke's brokerage firm.

A depression didn't seem to hurt the circus. People were eager to part with a few hard-earned coins to enjoy spectacular events, especially Papa's elephant. Other circus owners had offered huge sums for Pachydermal, but Papa always refused. One farmer had been so awestruck by the elephant that he purchased tickets for his family with enough cured pork to last a whole month. Calliope had savored every bite, suppressing her guilt. Because each morsel reminded her of Jocko's pig. "I'm eating Napoleon," she had said, then wondered why Brian and Jocko laughed so hard. It wasn't all that funny.

Now she dabbed at her mouth with a white linen napkin, even though her plate of scrambled eggs and buttered toast remained virtually untouched. She sat in the pie car. The bench that bounced her skirted bottom and the table that held her late afternoon repast were attached to the diner's floor with wooden struts. A window was only a few inches from her elbow. Other rain-spattered, soot-streaked windows stared at her like the haunted eyes of sea monsters or gargoyles— nightmare-eyes. But she was definitely awake and, at least for the moment, alone with her thoughts.

Omaha. Cheyenne. Denver.

Colorado. The first five letters spelled color. Despite her exhaustion and fanciful images, she smiled. Colorado was a wild, free land whose mountain peaks were so close to the sun they burst into flaming shades of reds and purples at dawn and dusk. Or so she'd heard.

"The damn train's moving too fast," Brian said, entering the pie car. "My cats will be ill-tempered."

"We have to reach Kansas by daybreak. In any case, we go no faster than usual."

"Are you blind? Look out the window. We move so swiftly, the shapes blur and fade."

"The driver... *engineer* is following my orders. I suppose you'd rather be mired in muck, Brian. Have you not noticed the foggy rain?"

"All the more reason to slow our speed, Calliope."

She resisted her impulse to glance out the window. "Did the train's sway interrupt slumber or pleasure?"

"What the hell are you babbling about?"

"Where would Panama be resting her overblown body? Did you not lead her to the wild-animal car? Perhaps Panama's musky scent was the reason for your cats' growly agitation. There's enough room between the cages, and I should imagine bumpy speed would be an inspiration. A precipitous aphrodisiac."

To her dismay, he burst out laughing.

"Precipitous? Aphrodisiac? Can you not abandon your wordy book pages for plain circus talk? That gibberish sounds like a gilly-galloo's."

"It does not! I sound like a lady."

"Is it bumpy speed that inspires you, my lady? Would you like a tour through the wild-animal car?"

"I have more important matters on my mind. For goodness sake, Brian, sit down."

"Thank you, Miss Kelley, but I do not need your permission to sit or stand, or lie prone for that matter."

"I don't give a damn if you join me or tumble to the pie car's floor. You can go straight to the devil!"

"Now you sound like a circus roustabout." Sliding onto the bench next to Calliope, Brian stretched his long legs under the table. "Panama is with Duncan, seeking protection. Your performers are frightened."

"Truly? But do they not remember the fagged-out horses, leg-weary after sloshing through Jonah's bad luck? Last year the company was always tired and hot tempered. Even the clowns lost their wit."

"Your performers don't dispute the necessity of train travel, Calliope. They merely request that you slow down."

"I can't slow down. We have to reach Washington, Kansas, tomorrow, arrive when our dated posters say we will. I have debts to pay. How happy would the company be if I lose my circus to creditors?"

Somebody would be happy, she thought. Because *somebody* had put a spell on her circus. Horse dung! *Somebody* couldn't control the weather.

Brian circled her shoulders and drew her close. "Poor lass," he said softly. "Don't cry."

"I'm teary from the engine's smoke, that's all." Blinking furiously, she pulled away. "Where's Papa? In the stock car watching over the horses?"

"Sean is inside the sleeper, where he snores with whiskey-induced bliss."

"Papa is tired from loading the train."

"*Papa* didn't load the train, Calliope. You did."

She chewed her bottom lip, unwilling to discuss Sean's flaws with Brian. Papa was her problem. So were the horses, and she couldn't allow their fragile legs to be strained or broken. She hated giving in to Brian's demands, but she really had no choice.

"All right. I'll tell the driver... engineer to slow down. I won't have the menagerie in a fret and my performers seeking protection."

"That's a dear lass." Brian rose to his feet. "I'll calm my cats and your horses."

"Is Dublin all right?"

"Yes. Although blind, Dublin understands. It's Susan B. Anthony who worries me. She kicks at the car with her hind hooves and passes along her fear. We could have a horse mutiny on our hands."

"Mutinies are conducted aboard ship." When he didn't respond, she stood. "I'll take care of Susan."

"Stay here and finish your meal."

"I'm done."

"But you've barely chewed your toast."

"It's cold."

So are you, Brian thought. He contemplated her shivering form and pale face with concern. He and Jocko had tried to lift burdens from her small shoulders, but it was like trying to halt last season's mud slides. Sean drank morning, noon, and night, damn his soul, and despite Calliope's objections, they'd soon have to hire another ringmaster.

Poor wee lass. Her beautiful eyes were smudged with fatigue. Her hair, neatly plaited in one thick braid, appeared too heavy for her head. Yet he had to admit Calliope operated their company with competence far beyond her years. A shame it was that the bright lettering on their railroad car read THE SEAN KELLEY CIRCUS. Calliope deserved recognition. With her book learning and aptitude for sums, "Dream Dancer" could challenge the most astute businessman. But female circus performers were considered dunderheads with loose morals, far lower on the social scale than actresses.

Brian's mother, an equestrian, had believed the lies of a rancher named Aaron Fox, had believed she was wed with words spoken by Fox's friend, who wore a borrowed frock coat and clerical collar. When Maureen O'Connor discovered Aaron's duplicity, it was too late, for she had already conceived his son. Maureen fled and joined Sean's circus, riding her horses with daredevil carelessness. Luckily for Brian, she had not miscarried. Maureen confessed all on her deathbed, coughing her life away. Consumption. Brian, age seven, had listened to her whispered words.

And how would Calliope react when he left the circus? Abandoned her again? He did not plan to play cat tamer forever—nothing was forever. Calliope wanted to be a lady, but he wanted to portray a gentleman even more. She had learned from newspapers and books. So had he. Brian knew where his father's ranch was situated: Colorado Springs. Aaron Fox would pay dear, if only to avoid embarrassment. Eventually, the circus would reach Denver. According to Brian's map, Colorado Springs was less than seventy-five miles away.

"I'll soothe the cats," he said, bringing his attention back to Calliope. "Then I'll tell your damfool engineer to slow down."

"Thank you. Meanwhile, I'll soothe Susan."

"Please, lass, let me…" He swallowed the rest of his words, for Calliope was already brushing crumbs from her gray skirt and dark green spencer. A portion of her skirt and petticoats caught on the splintery bench, and Brian could see her red flannel calf-length drawers.

"You'd better go," she grumbled, yanking her garments free, "before I change my mind."

He gave her a mock salute then opened one of the pie car's windows and vaulted through.

The stock car followed the pie car, so Calliope need only cross from one platform to the other. She noted with satisfaction that the striped awning above was secure. Fortunately, raindrops, not snow or hail, peppered her train. Gripping the platform's railing, she leaned out, craning her neck to obtain a better view. She watched Brian spread his arms and jump from stock to cat car. He preferred to travel on top of the train so his animals wouldn't become further agitated by the scent of horses. Daft boy-o! The cats were caged. So what if they smelled horseflesh? Men enjoyed courting danger. If Brian's feet slipped—

They didn't. He disappeared inside the cat car, and Calliope shook the moisture from her long braid, wondering why she had even bothered to watch.

After passing through the small entrance door at the front of the stock car, she took a moment to let her eyes adjust to the dim light. Then she glanced around. Dublin stood majestically reposed. Recognizing her scent, the blind horse greeted his mistress with a whinny.

Susan, however, was indeed unsettled, kicking out in an almost mesmerizing rhythm of continuity. She hated the restrictions of a railroad car, and Calliope seriously considered hobbling Susan's hind legs. The chestnut communicated her fear and rage to stock horses, performing steeds, and bandwagon drays. They, in turn, tossed their heads and rolled their eyes.

Although the car was lengthy, the odor of dung overpowered the scent of neatly piled leather harnesses and thick straw bedding. Calliope wrinkled her nose, as if by that action she could stop breathing. The train swayed and shook like an overweight belly dancer.

"Hellfire," she swore, rubbing Dublin's velvety nose. "I'll tell the driver to slow down. Dated posters be damned! If we arrive late, I'll shorten the parade." Incredibly, as if she had communicated her thoughts to the driver… engineer… the train reduced its speed. "Now we're moving at a snail's pace, Dublin," she fumed, "slower than molasses in January."

Thoroughly annoyed, Calliope maneuvered around her stallion's haunches and gazed through a small window.

The sky was dove gray between sheets of pelting rain. She raised the window high enough to poke her head outside and discovered that they approached a wooden bridge stretching across a muddy, swollen river. Vertical slanted supports and horizontal cross-pieces held up the bridge, but they looked worm-eaten, pitted, ancient. No wonder the engineer had slowed on his own.

Susan kicked hard at the car's slats. As Calliope walked toward her skittish mare, she heard a god-awful noise outside the window. It sounded like a wet towel being snapped. No. More like a tent's center pole cracking.

The stock car jolted to a halt, tilting at an awkward angle. Calliope lurched across the car and pitched forward, into the side-slats. She felt a stabbing pain behind her eyes and pressed her hand against her forehead. When she drew her hand away and stared at her palm, she saw blood.

For a moment she just stood there, totally confused.

Papa wouldn't let her perform in tomorrow's show. He'd say she was too fuzzy-minded. He'd say she was dotty, crocked, off her feed and—*what show*? If the train didn't start moving, there would be no Kansas engagement. God, her head hurt.

The horses made such a commotion. Why did the car slant? Had they missed the bridge? Derailed? Suppose the engine was on fire! She had read newspaper articles about trains exploding like sticks of dynamite.

Add this disaster to Angelique's saggy rope and the nosegay, she thought, staggering toward Dublin and the window. Then she stopped short. She had already looked through the window. The train approached a river and bridge. Her head ached.

If the horses would only hush, maybe she could figure out what was happening. Brian had said that her performers were in the front cars. Papa dozed inside the sleeper. So, as far as she knew, only she and Brian occupied the back cars. Had his growly cats escaped from their cages when the train jerked to a sudden halt?

Forget Brian! She couldn't remain motionless while the minutes ticked away.

"Think about your horses," she said, hoping the sound of her voice would dispel her swither. "Think about getting out of this sloping coffin."

Striving to remain calm and reasonable, she unfastened the cross-ties around her animals' necks and then tugged at the side door's sliding panels.

"Calliope!"

"Brian?" She tugged harder, wondering if he hung outside the train.

"Move away from the door!"

"Where are you?" Glancing over her shoulder, she thought she could distinguish light near the back entrance. "Brian, for the love of God, where are you?"

"Inside the stock car. Calliope, step away from the opening. Too late! Press yourself against the slats!"

Following his command, she barely avoided a trample by the stampeding horses surging through the gaping side door.

"No! Stop! Dublin! Susan! Blackie! Stop! Brian, I released their ropes."

"Stay very still, Calliope."

His voice sounded closer.

"But a few horses have already jumped, and—"

"Don't move! I think I've got… yes… the side door's shut enough to keep the others inside."

She heard the sound of a snapping whip. The remaining horses reared, pranced, snorted. Brian shouted with pain. Calliope carefully sidled toward him. She had no fear of her horses, finally subdued by Brian's whip, but she couldn't see. Dust from trampled straw filled the car's interior, thicker than the outside fog, and she felt her eyes accumulate powdery debris.

"Brian, I can't find you."

"Near the window."

"Are you hurt? What a daft question. Of course you're hurt. I heard you yell. What happened?"

"Right… arm's… broke or sprained," he panted. "Hoof caught my elbow."

"Oh, no. Where's the medicine box? I have to set the bone."

"Calm down, lass. Are you all right?"

"Yes. But you're hurt."

"Forget about me. Take care of the horses. They'll topple the car if not secured."

Eyes tearing, Calliope caught a halter and led a bandwagon dray toward his cross-tie.

"No," said Brian. "Tether him at the rear of the car."

"Why?"

"For balance. Don't ask questions. Damn useless arm!" His voice was filled with frustrated anger.

Even working quickly, it took her several precious minutes to tether five horses. Her head felt better, merely a throb, but her eyes still stung, and she rubbed them continuously.

"Balance," she muttered, her nimble fingers securing the last knot despite a lack of illumination. "I would trade all my horses for Pachydermal."

"If you had an elephant in here, you'd be dead."

"What do you mean?"

Before Brian could reply, the car pitched forward. Calliope lost her footing. Instinctively, she reached out and flung her arms around the neck of a sturdy dray. The car teetered then settled. Releasing her pent-up breath, she stroked the frightened animal's sweaty withers and haunches.

"Brian, are you all right? Where are you now?"

"Directly behind you. Grab my left arm, and I'll pull you the rest of the way."

"Rest of what way?"

"We have to get out onto the platform."

"How? Your right arm's useless, the car is dark, and we're climbing at a slant."

"Pretend you're rope-walking. Angelique taught you. One foot in front of the other. Remember?"

"Why can't we go through the side door?"

"We're on a bridge, over water."

"What happened?" she finally asked, moving hesitantly, holding Brian's outstretched hand for direction.

"The trestle beneath our wheels snapped. Pie car's gone."

She halted, consumed with panic at the image of her stock car following the pie car's descent. Her escape from death had been a miracle. If the train had been going a wee bit faster—

"Keep moving, Calliope!"

"Sorry, I'm sorry," she gasped, thinking how her whole world had reduced itself to the inside of one smelly railroad car.

After an eternity, they reached the door. Brian pulled her forward in front of him. Then he pushed her rump through the opening. At any other time she would have sputtered with indignation at his bold touch on her backside, but she felt so happy to be outside standing on the small rickety platform.

Or was she happy? The bridge appeared fragile as an eggshell, and she could hear creaking timbers. Below her feet, undulating water surged against the wooden supports. For the first time she had a clear idea of what had occurred, and she realized the stock car's front wheels balanced precariously on the edge of broken railroad ties. At least fifty feet of open space loomed between the bridge and the water. She had learned to swim at an early age, but the swollen river looked like a watery grave, beckoning her to seek solace beneath its boiling caps of brownish spray.

"Your head's bleeding," Brian said, joining her on the platform. "No wonder you sounded so muddled."

"I bumped my head against the wall. It's nothing."

"Are you sure?"

"Yes."

"Then let's go."

"Where?"

"Back. Along the bridge."

"No. We have to go forward."

"We can't. There's a gap."

"I don't care. Papa needs me. I have to find Papa."

"Others will take care of Sean. There's no time to argue. The bridge might collapse at any moment."

"Papa needs me," she insisted, maneuvering her leg over the platform's railing.

"Wait! Get back here, you daft colleen! That's better." Leaning way out past the railing, he studied the damage. "The trestle's still attached on this side. Okay, puss, you've walked the rope. Now you must pretend the trestle is a circus ladder. Strong winds will make the wood feel as if it's swaying, and there's no ringmaster to hold it steady. Rain will make the crosspieces slick, so you must move tortoiselike. Do you understand?"

"Yes."

"Get rid of your skirt and petticoats."

Her fingers fumbled at buttons. Then, almost daintily, she lifted her trembling legs one at a time until her garments lay in a heap. Mesmerized, she watched the wind send her skirt and petticoats spiraling through the sky.

Brian captured her chin with his left hand, drawing her gaze away. "Calliope, look into my eyes. We'll make it safely across the trestle, I promise."

"We? You have to go back along the tracks."

"Not a chance." He released her face. "I'll stay close to you, just in case you slip and fall."

"Then what, Brian? Will you catch me with your good arm and hang onto the trestle with your teeth? Go back along the tracks, and that's an order."

"I won't take orders from a lass!"

"Damn your manly pride! In another moment you'll faint from pain, and I'll have to carry you across the trestle."

Brian gazed at her slender form, appearing even frailer without the weight of her skirt and petticoats. Her flannel drawers would have dropped to her ankles had they not been attached to her bodice. The nasty gash on her forehead looked like a second eyebrow. Yet he knew that she would make good her threat, even if it killed them both!

"All right," he said, "I'll wait here. When you reach the others, have Duncan rig a harness. He can haul me to safety. Does that appease your *womanly* pride, Calliope?"

"Yes. That sounds like a good idea. Yes."

"I'll follow until you reach the trestle. Thank God you're wearing slippers rather than boots. It will give you a better grip, and you can pretend you're a monkey."

"Monkeys don't wear slippers."

"For once in your life, will you not bandy words?"

With his left arm, Brian swung her up and over the platform's railing. Straight away the pelting rain soaked her green spencer and red drawers. Adjusting her balance to compensate for the gusty winds, she walked the length of the narrow gap between the railroad ties and open space, wondering how she would free her horses and menagerie. Thank goodness her valuable elephant had ridden up front.

Directly ahead was a gaping abyss where the track had been. A rail twisted away into the darkness. Ties splayed out from the other rail like the spokes of a rimless wheel. Once again she was almost over-whelmed by her miraculous escape from death. She cast a quick glance below and saw that the pie car had smashed against an embankment. One end of its crushed remains lay immersed in water.

"Don't look down!" Brian shouted.

"Huh? Oh. Yes. Dizzy."

His good arm circled her waist as he righted her against the car's slats. "Do you have the throw-ups, lass? It's okay if you do. Spew with the wind, not into it. Why don't you say something? Are you all right? Calliope, answer me!"

"Fine. I'm wondrous fine," she said, and heard him chuckle. How dare he laugh when any moment they could both plummet through infinity? "Why do you chortle like a hyena?"

"Because you always say you're fine when you're not. Look up or straight ahead, but don't look down."

Her dizziness receded. Choosing to look straight ahead, she noticed several performers standing on the other side of the gap. They surrounded the engine and assembled ropes.

She took a deep, calming breath, lowered herself to the second crosspiece, and began to inch sideways along the trestle. The first crosspiece was directly above her head. Splinters pierced her palms as she fought to steady her grip on the slippery wood.

The wind loosened her braid, whipping hair into her eyes, and she felt as blind as Dublin. Dublin! She must find her beloved horse. And where was Papa? Why wasn't he with the others, shouting encouragement? The sleeper appeared undamaged, but it had halted before reaching the end of the bridge. Had somebody helped Papa emerge safely from the car?

With her mind focused on that single thought, she finally reached Bobby Duncan's outstretched hands. He had positioned himself on his belly, his enormous torso suspended out over the embankment. Bobby grasped her wrists. Calliope's breath caught in her throat as his grip loosened. She honestly thought he might drop her, but he swiftly pulled her up and over.

She shook with relief as she staggered to her feet. Through the thin soles of her slippers, she felt cinders and pebbles. Her sore feet reminded her that she was alive, safe, and she stifled an urge to shout with joy.

Duncan stood in front of her. For a moment she rested her cheek against his chest. Then she jerked away. "Bobby, help Brian. We must rig a harness."

"What for?"

"To save Bri—"

"Miss Kelley, he's here."

She whirled about in time to watch Jack the Giant and three crew members lift Brian from the beam and haul him up the muddy embankment. His mouth grimaced with pain, but his expression showed a certain satisfaction, and she recalled her earlier conclusion that men enjoyed courting danger.

"Damn your soul," she raged. "I told you to wait."

"And I told you I won't take orders from a wee lass. Are you all right?"

"Fine. I'm wondrous fine."

"Good. 'Tis pleased I am you're not angry."

Ignoring his injury, Brian joined the guying-out

crew. Hellfire! If he could disregard his injured arm, she could forget her sore feet and the gash in her forehead. She could be as brave, or as foolish, as a man. "Are there any performers trapped inside the car?" she asked Duncan.

"No, Miss Kelley. Me and Jocko walked through 'em all. Everybody got out."

Thank God, Papa's safe.

"Where's Jocko, Bobby?"

Duncan pointed toward the water below.

Calliope rubbed rain from her eyes with her fingertips. She could hear the screams of drowning horses. Bent on rescue, a few performers had already plunged into the swirling river. But they weren't able to get very far. The current fought them, despite the ropes knotted about their waists. Slipping and sliding down the embankment, she headed toward them. After attaching a rope around her waist, she waded into the water and immediately saw Big John leading Dublin. Her throat was so full of tears she couldn't gasp out more than a brief "thank you." Then she clutched Dublin's halter and guided her stallion over the slippery rocks until they reached land.

Brian covered her with a blanket. She shrugged it off. "Are you daft? I must find my other horses and keep their heads above water."

"The company needs you."

"You need to be fixing your arm."

"Later."

"Susan?"

"Jocko brought her to shore." Brian hesitated then said, "Her legs are shattered."

"No, Brian, no." Calliope heard the sound of a gunshot. "Was that Jocko? Susan?"

"You would not have the mare in pain, would you, lass?"

She closed her eyes and pictured the beautiful chestnut leaping through hoops of fire, and she hoped with all her heart that heaven comprised pastures of clover and God would be a gentle ringmaster.

With a sigh, she opened her eyes, stiffened her shoulders, and squinted up toward the train. "What's the damage, Brian?"

"We were lucky, Calliope."

"Lucky?"

"Yes. The pie car's smashed to kindling, but it's empty. A wee bit earlier, and we would have been trapped inside."

"The saggy rope and nosegay," she murmured.

"What did you say?"

"Nothing. Go on."

"Performers were knocked about, and a few sustained injuries, some serious."

"Where's Papa? Is he hurt?"

"I've not seen Sean."

"We must find him."

"Don't fret. Sean's somewhere. Slow your pace, puss, or else you'll just slither around in the mud."

"Here comes Jocko. Have you seen Papa, Jocko?"

Beneath soot and grime, the clown's eyes looked stricken. "Sean searched for more whiskey, Calliope, perhaps a bite to eat. He—"

"The pie car!" Racing around the embankment, she splashed through shallow water.

"Hide your eyes, Calliope!" Brian yelled.

But he was too late. Much too late. Despite the rain and fog, she saw her father clearly.

Sean Kelley lay in a mass of bloodstained wreckage, with a splintered piece of scantling driven through his head.

Five

"YOU'RE MAKING A MOUNTAIN OUT A MOLEHILL, BRIAN O'Connor."

"I forbid it!"

"A tempest in a teacup."

"Did you hear me, Calliope? I forbid it!"

The toss of her head caused hairpins to fly. Her neat bun unraveled, and thick strands tumbled to her waist. "You also forbade me to play here in Concordia, and as you can plainly see, news of our train wreck had brought every bloodthirsty gilly-galloo straight to our tents."

"Your father is dead, Calliope."

"My father died seven years ago when Mum fell from the rope."

"You've not even wept."

"Why should I mourn? Sean is with his Angelique."

"Do you wish to join them? I won't allow it."

"And I shall do as I damn well please. The cats are not yours. They belong to the circus. If you interfere…"

"Finish your threat. Would you truly sack me?"

"Sack yourself, Brian. I don't care."

She walked a few paces away. Then she glanced

around the Cook Top's corner, toward the backyard. A dozen or more people lined up for her Kid Show—Jocko's bright banner line proclaimed: CONGRESS OF FREAKS. Since the Outside Talker had been badly bruised during the wreck, Jack the Giant stood on a bally box. "Come one, come all!" he shouted. "Watch Duncan, the strongest man in the world, heftin' up the fattest lady. I ain't promisin' nothin', but mebbe, just mebbe, you'll see a princess with three titties."

Calliope gasped. They didn't have a princess with three breasts. They didn't even have a princess. But then Jack wasn't "promisin' nothin'."

Making an about-face, she lifted her chin. "Don't you understand, Brian? I must present a wild-cat act. This is no pumpkin fair. Anyway, I won't give *him* the satisfaction."

"Him? What the bloody hell are you talking about?"

"I don't know who… who he is… but whoever he is, he wants to destroy my circus."

"Listen to yourself, Calliope. You sound like an owl."

"I don't care if you call me an owl or a monkey—"

"Monkey?"

"—but *somebody* killed Mum. *Somebody* loosened the rope, and you'll never convince me otherwise."

"I suppose *somebody* sabotaged the bridge."

"No. I think the killer invited Papa to the pie car, planning to throw him from the train. Just like Mum was thrown from her wagon seat many years ago when we crossed that chancy stream."

"Damn it, puss, you're still brainsick. Angelique's fall from the wagon and rope were accidents, and Sean wanted more whiskey, or perhaps some food."

"Papa never ate unless I practically hand-fed him, Brian, and I keep no whiskey inside the pie car."

"Maybe Sean was searching for you."

"I think he was searching for Angelique."

"What?"

"Papa was muzzy-minded. You said so yourself. 'Sean sleeps with whiskey-induced bliss,' you said. I think a very large, very evil leprechaun put a bug in Papa's ear."

"That makes no sense, puss. Suppose he did wait for Sean? In that case, your leprechaun would have been trapped inside the pie car when it plunged."

"Not if he saw us there. He had no way of knowing we'd leave for the stock and cat cars, so rather than wait for Papa, he went away. He was probably damning his luck and—"

"Why would the evil leprechaun want your parents dead?"

"They were your parents too!"

"Why, Calliope?"

"I don't know. At first, I thought Mum might have rebuffed an admirer. But Papa..." She swallowed a lump in her throat as big as an acorn. "Perhaps the leprechaun is a saboteur for another circus."

"Forgive me, honey, but our piddling show is of little consequence compared to Phineas Barnum and the other traveling circ—"

"That's not true! Disregarding my equipment, I have unique Kid Show performers. And Dublin. And Napoleon. And Pachydermal. Before I was even born, Mr. Barnum gave Papa Pachydermal. Mr. Barnum bought him from the Royal Zoological Gardens of

London, and there are circus owners who would kill for 'The World's Largest Elephant.'"

"Have you had many offers?"

"Yes. Papa…" She swallowed again. "Papa always turned them down. Well, I'm Sean Kelley's daughter, Brian, and they don't scare me one whit. They shan't get my elephant, no matter how often they threaten or bargain or—"

"They won't have to threaten or bargain, Calliope, not if you persist with this mad scheme."

"I shall persist. God smiled when the rain stopped, allowing our guying-out crew to rig nets and rescue the menagerie animals. Pachydermal was already safely across. But our wreck cost us five horses, including Big John's and Marianne's trained mounts. The trapeze artist has a sprained wrist. Our ropewalker is suddenly afraid of heights. He says he keeps imagining swirls of water below. Half the clowns are injured. Panama's ill. And your right arm is in a sling."

"My left is not."

"Are you daft? The cats can smell weakness. What good are you to me mauled or dead?"

"What good are you to *me* mauled or dead?"

She heaved a deep sigh. She wanted nothing more than to give up the fight and let Brian take over her responsibilities. He stood there, tall and strong, his body rippling with sinewy muscles, as solid as the center pole that kept her Big Top from folding. His shirt was unbuttoned, revealing the resilient hair on his chest. His eyes were a turbulent blue, almost black, and his lips were set in a scowl. Twice she had felt those same lips caress with kisses that left her knock-kneed.

I was only eleven when Mum fell to her death, but I saw the way Sean and Angelique suited each other. If Mum was distressed, Papa would lead her to their wagon. Later, she'd be all secret smiles. Brian could make me feel that way.

Calliope pictured Panama Duncan. Furtive smirks rather than secret smiles. Everybody knew about Brian and Panama—except dull-witted Bobby.

"If I should die inside the cat cage," she muttered, "it would cure Panama's illness helter-skelter."

"What does Panama have to do with this? She means nothing to me."

"And I do?"

"Yes!" Brian turned away to control his temper and collect his thoughts. What *did* Calliope mean to him? He hadn't embraced her since the night after his return, yet he had no doubt she'd respond. She was—he searched for a word. Ardent? Warm-blooded? No. Hot-headed. Impetuous, he concluded, his anger building anew.

Logical arguments had failed. Could he possibly woo her into submission? Caress her into obedience? Stroke her into capitulation as he would a bristling cat? It had always worked with other women.

But Calliope wasn't like any other woman Brian had ever known. She was sensual and naïve, all at the same time. She was like a young swan gliding across the water. You'd admire a swan, but you'd never muss its feathers and ruin the effect.

The Cook Top was deserted and they were completely hidden from the backyard—no! He might be a bastard by birth, but he wasn't a bastard by nature and he couldn't take advantage of her recent emotional turmoil.

"Horse dung!" she shouted. "You care! Hah! You'd say anything to keep me from the cage!"

All his clear reasoning disappeared. *Yes, anything*, he thought, stepping forward.

Calliope saw Brian's wicked expression and stumbled backwards. He moved closer, reaching out with his good hand to stroke her loosened hair.

"Leave me alone, Brian O'Connor. That won't work either."

Any other words she might have flung at him were swallowed up by his kiss. His lips were rough, demanding, possessive. When she would have moved her head away, she felt his hand catch the back of her neck, keeping her pinioned. She struggled weakly but he continued, his mouth a hot branding iron, designating ownership.

"Suppose you swoon inside the cage," he said, his lips finding the hollow at the base of her throat.

She fought to regain her breath. "I won't swoon."

His hand released her neck, and his good arm circled her waist, drawing her closer. When had her blouse and chemise slipped from her shoulders? His lips found her breast, and his tongue circled her nipple.

"I don't want to see your lovely bosom slashed to ribbons," he said as his arm abandoned her waist and his fingers caressed her buttocks.

"Please, Brian, I..." She couldn't go on, because he was lowering her to the ground, removing her skirt and petticoats with one-handed expertise, straddling her hips, pressing his thumb against her flannel-clad belly button. She forced her eyes to gaze skyward until she focused on the top of the tent. Small banners fluttered, finally merging into a whirling merry-go-round of cloth and canvas and clouds.

"Not one paw must mar your belly," he said.

This was no lesson in love! Brian was playing her like a real calliope. She began to struggle in earnest, aware that only her drawers and his trousers kept them from commingling.

"Fraidy cat," he taunted. Rising to his knees, he bent forward and kissed her eyes shut. "Beautiful legs," he murmured, caressing the inside of her thighs. "I feel them quiver. Will they shake so in the ring? Will they become the target for a tiger's fangs? Answer me, Calliope." His probing touch traveled toward the vee of her drawers.

Her answer was an astonished gasp as his fingers deftly rubbed the red flannel. She craved nothing more than to arch her back and crush her swollen nipples against his chest. Her hips began to rise, responding to his rhythmic rub.

"Now!" she screamed.

"Patience, puss. I must make you wet first."

Wet? What on earth was he talking about?

"I'll be wet," she cried, opening her eyes. "I'll be anything you want me to be."

"Then play the equestrian, not the cat tamer."

"Brian, please. Please, please, please—"

"Hush." His hand found her belly button again then wriggled beneath her drawers, his first finger moving unerringly toward the core of her sensations, and she knew she'd soon succumb—beyond hope, beyond recovery, beyond consciousness.

Every instinct urged her to thrust her legs toward

the tent banners, yet somehow she managed to resist. If she gave in to her body's demands, she would accede to his demands. If Brian possessed her, he would possess her circus.

She willed herself to go limp. Awkwardly, he began to unbutton his trousers with one hand.

That was all she needed. With every ounce of strength she could muster, she cracked her palm against the side of his face. Then, ignoring his look of stunned surprise, she slapped him again.

He rose to his feet and loomed above her, holding his face. "You cannot whop a Bengal, Calliope."

"I'll have a whip in the ring. I had none handy when you attacked."

"You did well without a whip. I apologize, Miss Kelley. I would never force myself on an unwilling lass. I thought you wanted me as much as I want you."

"I did… I do," she replied with complete honestly. "But I want you to love me, not use me for your own advantage."

"What advantage?"

"'Be the equestrian, not the cat tamer,'" she mimicked. "If you had not gabbled those very words—"

"Then you still intend to play cat tamer?"

"Yes."

As she staggered upright, he said, "I shall leave tonight."

"Why? Because I resisted a tumble in the dirt?"

"No. I've told you many times I won't take orders from a lass."

"And I won't take orders from *you*, Brian O'Connor!"

"The animals may belong to the circus, your

circus, but the act belongs to me. I promised to play ringmaster, and I shall keep my word. But if you pirate my act, I'll leave directly after tonight's show. It's *your* choice, lass."

Six

JOCKO'S ASH-BLOND HAIR WAS HIDDEN BY A WHITE stocking cap. From a distance he looked bald. His putty nose looked like a red doorknob. His face was covered by charcoal. His mouth turned down at the corners, and white creases circled his eyes. He wore baggy trousers, a tunic expanded by hoops, and a derby hat that had seen better days. Jocko's specialty was pathos.

"You look wonderful, Calliope," he said.

Brian scowled. "You look like a gazoony."

Ignoring Brian, she tucked her shirt more securely into her breeches, and her rolled-up pant legs into her boots. She had bound her breasts. Her too-long shirt cuffs were hidden by her riding gloves, and her hair had been stuffed into one of Sean's caps. Her best idea was to invade Clown Alley and fashion a handlebar mustache beneath her nose. Maybe it wasn't her best idea. She kept stifling the urge to sneeze.

She couldn't appear as herself, because it would startle the women in her audience. She knew they'd be shocked at the sight of a female tamer. They might even faint.

"Will Junior direct the cats through the chute?" she asked Brian.

"No. My cage-boy still nurses three bruised ribs. I forbade him to enter the tent, and *he* at least listens. Jocko and I will direct the cats."

"Now just a minute!"

"Would one ringmaster and one clown hinder your performance, Calliope?"

"Of course not, Brian, but—"

"There will be more than one clown," Jocko interjected. "All our Joeys, Augustes, and Charlies will be stationed outside the ring."

"Why?"

"If the cats give you any trouble, we'll divert the gillys while you make your escape."

"I don't anticipate trouble, Jocko. I've known these cats since they were cubs. I've fed and watered them." She wrinkled her nose and adjusted her mustache again. "I've even cleaned their cages."

"It's different inside the ring," Brian said.

"I've watched you hundreds of times and memorized your every move. I'm not scared."

"You should be scared."

"Well, I'm not!"

"Tigers are the most cunning. Lions give warning, since they have a slow way of turning before they strike. The black panther is a killer."

"We don't have a panther. You mention the word 'killer' only to frighten me."

"I thought nothing scared you." Brian's batwing collar bobbled, betraying emotion. "Will you not agree to either lions or tigers? It's far less dangerous."

"No. The posters announced both together. I'll be giving the gillys what they paid for."

There was a burst of applause, which meant Big John and Marianne were finished. Calliope had asked them for a Stall Act, lengthened by superfluous business, padding her shortened circus program. They had to contend with new mounts, too. Apparently they had been successful.

"Good luck," said Jocko.

"Aren't you going to wish me luck, Brian?"

"You don't need luck. You need savvy. Jocko, make sure the cage is secure and the clowns are in position. Where's Napoleon?"

"Asleep in his baby buggy."

"Good. Keep your pig away from center ring. I don't want the cats to catch his scent."

Calliope waited impatiently, coiling and uncoiling her whip. She had asked to be introduced as Brian O'Connor because the posters carried his name, but Brian said no. Even if she insisted on pirating his act, he wouldn't allow her to steal his name. So she was Kelly Green—Kelly Green, the fearless cat trainer.

Once, a long time ago, she had wished to be called Mary. Papa called her Dream Dancer. *Papa.* Calliope swallowed a sob.

Her thoughts were straying because she was scared. No, not scared. Nervous. Cats could sense agitation. So she had better lose these damfool whim-whams before entering the cage.

Brian's introduction was brief and brusque. "Ladies and gentlemen and children of all ages," he said loudly, gesturing with his cane. "Our lions and tigers appear together. It is very dangerous, so we need complete silence. If anybody has to cough, do it now."

There were several hacking gags, followed by laughter. Finally, the crowd hushed.

"Pre-senting Kelly Greeneyes, the fearless cat tamer."

Greeneyes? He was making fun of her. Furious, Calliope glared at Brian. Then she strutted into the ring-sized cage and slammed the door behind her.

The chute's wooden entrance panel opened. The first tawny lion appeared, followed by another. Leo and Duchess.

Six tigers entered the cage. Although Calliope had played with them all, even petted their smooth coats, she felt her stomach tighten. The knuckles of the fingers that held her whipstock and hickory club stretched white. She snapped her whip and the beasts settled. So far, so good.

Not so good. One of the tigers was slinking toward her, his ears flattened, his tail swishing softly. Plato. Sweet, lovable Plato, whose lips were now curled in a nasty snarl.

"Calliope! Brian, get her out of there!"

"Shut up, Jocko! She must not lose eye contact."

"Eye contact," echoed Calliope, staring at the huge cat.

Brian spoke true when he called me a gazoony. I acted like a stubborn woman. No, child. Why did I insist on doing this daft thing? I could have dismissed the cat act and paraded the train-wreck performers around the arena. That's who the gilly-galloos came to see.

She snapped her whip.

Plato's ears twitched forward. His muzzle seemed

to expand in a tiger smile as he mounted his pedestal. Calliope could almost hear him purr.

Triumphantly, she tossed her head. The cap flew free and her hair tumbled down. At the same time, she sneezed, losing her mustache.

"It's a girl!" screamed a gilly.

"Catch m' wife. She's fainted."

Calliope slanted a glance toward the seats. Movement surged like a tidal wave as some women pitched forward in faints while others stood, trying to get a better view. Swooning women outnumbered the avidly curious ones. Clowns climbed the guardrail, carrying vinegar and salts. *Damn and blast!*

"Don't look away!" Brian shouted.

"Huh?" With a quick jerk of her head, she returned her gaze to the cats.

Plato chased his tail, exciting the lions.

Calliope could sense the old lion-tiger jungle hatred flare. Sure enough, Leo sprang from his high pedestal, landing within inches of Plato. They both locked together, struggling fiercely for tooth-and-claw advantage.

While Brian rattled the cage with his iron bar—a signal for the cats to retreat through their chute—Jocko ran to open the door and found it stuck.

Calliope brandished her club at the flailing cats then gave Leo a generous clout on the top of his head. The lion let go the tiger's neck, and Plato scampered through the chute. Eyes smoldering, Leo turned, glared, and growled.

Now was no time to play fearless Kelly Green or even courageous Kelly Greeneyes. Dropping whip, club, and gloves, Calliope ran toward the exit where Brian was throwing his whole body, including his hurt arm, against the stuck door. She could practically feel Leo's hot breath on her neck, his fangs severing her throat.

The door finally opened, and Jocko tossed something inside the cage.

Leo skidded to a halt and swiped at the object with his paw.

As Jocko pulled Calliope through the opening, her eyes widened with horror. *Napoleon.* Jocko had baited the lion with Napoleon.

Listening to the screams of the audience, she began to laugh hysterically. Then avoiding Brian and Jocko, she covered her mouth with both hands and lurched as fast as she could from the tent. She finally halted by a patch of weeds. She bent over and clutched her stomach, fighting to control the nausea that threatened to overwhelm her.

"I've got you, lass."

"You were right, Brian. I couldn't tame the cats."

"No, Calliope, *you* were right all along. The cats became agitated by Napoleon's scent. Somebody pushed his buggy close to the cage. Somebody *wanted* the cats to attack."

"Who, damn it, who? And please do not tell me I sound like an owl."

"I don't know, honey. Jocko's damn clowns were all over the place. Your leprechaun could have posed as a clown."

"What's happening inside the tent?"

"The clowns are calming the children while Big John and Marianne—"

"I can't breathe, Brian. Binding. Too. Tight."

He tore at her shirt and the binding that held her breasts. Then as she again slumped forward, he caught her waist with his left arm.

She took a few deep breaths, but it didn't help. Despite Brian's support, she felt herself falling.

"Are you planning to faint, Calliope? Don't faint. The tent is already chock-full of swooning women. Can you sit? Good lass. Now place your head between your knees."

She did, but briefly. Lifting her face skyward, she screamed, "He's dead!"

"Napoleon's but a wee piggy. It's far better—"

"Papa's dead!"

"All right, I understand."

"I loved Papa so much, but he didn't love me, only Mum. If he had cared for me, he'd still be alive, because I warned him about the leprechaun, and I scolded him for drinking, but he wouldn't listen because he didn't love me enough. He loved me but not enough."

"*I* love you, Calliope."

She burst into tears.

Brian realized she was weeping for Sean, finally mourning her father, and he felt an urge to join her, to cry with profound relief. He had watched the lion chase her across the ring and his heart had stopped beating. In that instant, he knew how much he loved his stubborn, prideful colleen.

Helping her rise, he pressed her face against his chest. "I shall always love you," he crooned, "just like Sean loved his Angelique. Cry your sorrow free, puss. Cry for Sean and your drowned horses and Napoleon."

"It hurts to cry."

"I know. But when you can smile again, I'm going to ask you to marry me. You had better say yes, Calliope, or I swear before God I shall toss you back inside the cat cage and open the chute."

"Yes," she said, her voice muffled by his shirt.

"I can't hear you."

She lifted her face. "Yes, damn you, yes!"

Brian's lips claimed hers, and Calliope didn't care if he possessed her body, her circus, her soul. Her breasts were already bared. All she need do was pull her boots and trousers free and mount him, as he had once suggested. She wanted him so badly, more than her circus, more than her pride.

"Now!" she cried.

"No, my love, not until we are wed."

"Fraidy cat," she said, her voice half tease, half taunt.

"*You* are the cat. *I* am the tamer. And I shall protect you from your wicked leprechaun, I promise."

Calliope had a sudden thought. Irish folklore never told of lady leprechauns, but could her death-dealing gnome be a woman?

Seven

"AH, HEEBIE, HEBBY, HOBBY, HOLE, GOLONG," CHANTED the Rope Caller, boss of the guying-out crew. His men worked their way systematically around the tent, taking up slack in the canvas.

For the third day in a row, windy weather threatened the circus and the result could be a blowdown.

Wind storms are unpredictable monsters, Calliope thought. Her rope caller was usually adept at reading warnings in the sky, always ready to drive an extra stake line, guy down the Big Top, or move in a barricade of wagons to break the wind's force. She would rely on his advice, even though yesterday he had suggested she cancel the show and the storm had not arrived.

Her gaze was drawn to the horizon, where a barn suddenly burst into flames. If the capricious winds shifted, burning bits of debris might blow in their direction. She would have to issue orders not to open for business until the barn fire was extinguished. Pachydermal must be hitched to a wagon, ready to collect poles. The crew must be prepared to tear the tents down quickly if catastrophe struck.

Catastrophe! First the train wreck and Papa's death, then the near fatal attack by Leo. Performers grumbled that the Sean Kelley Circus was cursed. Accidents happened in threes, they said, several packing up and leaving.

She knew the real reason they fled. It was because a woman ran the show, which was so unfair. She had never been late with their pay. She had settled their doctor bills and would soon build a new pie car. She had never stinted on food or costumes, and despite Brian's insistence that she shut the circus down, she kept it going.

Last night she and Brian had squabbled, their words more gusty than the wind. He had concluded that her death-dealing leprechaun didn't exist. Napoleon's baby buggy, he said, had been unintentionally bumped or wheeled toward the cat cage. The nosegay had been tossed into the ring by an admirer. Sean had visited the pie car for food and drink. Therefore, Calliope had no reason to keep the circus open. She should sell it, the sooner the better. After she sold it, Brian wanted her to meet somebody, but he wouldn't tell her who. She had finally pleaded a headache and promised to make her decision by the end of the week.

Simply stated, she didn't want to choose between Brian and her Big Top. It would be like choosing between popped corn and candied apples. Calliope loved them both.

And what about Jocko? After Brian had abandoned the circus, Jocko had been there to help. Calliope had always suspected Jocko used his clown's greasepaint to hide from the law and now she was certain. Two

days ago, when the sheriff had eyeballed the premises
and collected fees for her permit, a young deputy had
handed Calliope a somewhat blurry photograph.

"Have you seen this man, Miss Kelley?"

"What's he done? Why is he wanted?"

"Murder." The deputy removed his hat and wiped
his sweaty brow with a bandanna. "Eight years ago,
Bret Johnson set fire to an Atlanta brothel. One whore
burned, but she was shot first."

"What makes you think this Johnson person is with
my circus?"

"Your handbills. The man I heard about owned a
wild pig he trained to do tricks. The pig was no bigger
than a dog."

"Eight years is a long time, and Georgia's far away
from Colorado."

"The murdered whore had a powerful friend and
he's kept the case open. There's still a reward."

"I've never met a man named Bret Johnson,"
Calliope had said, her voice sincere, "and our wee pig's
only thirteen months old. Would you like to meet her?"

"Who, Miss Kelley?"

"The piggy."

"No, thank you just the same. I'd like to meet your
elephant, though. Never seen me an elephant. 'Spect
I never will again."

"Come along, then. My elephant is in the menagerie tent."

"What's that powerful smell, miss?"

"Elephant dung."

"Could I have a piece? Just to prove I seen an
elephant?"

"Of course. One silver dollar, sir, if you please. Then you may collect all the elephant dung you want."

"Thank you, Miss Kelley."

Calliope had not questioned Jocko. The deputy's picture was blurry, she justified. The name was different. It was none of her business. Jocko posed no threat to her circus, but where would he go if she closed? Other owners would turn him in for the reward.

"If this continues," said Brian, "we might as well tear down and move on."

She hadn't heard his approach and jumped at the sound of his voice. "But we've traveled a hundred miles to play Denver. We can't leave."

"Sure we can. Or sell the circus where it stands. We've had three offers."

"We? It's not your circus yet, Brian O'Connor. And how do you know about those bids?"

"They were in the silver wagon."

"They were on the desk, under a sheaf of bills." She thrust her hands in her pockets to keep from pounding his chest or scratching his face. She sewed pockets on all her skirts to hold her keys and the peppermint candies she collected to treat her favorite monkeys. Her fingers curled around the mints, which also eased her performers' frequent indigestion. "You've been snooping."

"As my wife," said Brian, "everything you own belongs to me."

"I'm not your wife yet."

"Marry me tonight and sell the circus tomorrow."

"We shall play Denver first."

"In a windstorm? With over half the acts gone and more leaving every hour?"

"Leave with them, Brian. That's always been your answer. Leave and be damned!"

"It seems to me I've heard this same song before. Do you want to have another clem?"

"We should have three fights," she said sarcastically. "Three's the magic number. Three disasters and three clems."

"When did you become a gilly, Calliope? When did you lose your superstitions?"

"When Papa died and I inherited his circus."

"You inherited Sean's debts. Give it up."

"No!" Removing her hands from her pockets, brandishing her fists toward the sky, she wailed, "The leprechaun's winning and he doesn't even have to kill another soul."

"You're shaking like a leaf, puss. Come inside the silver wagon and rest a while."

"I can't. See that barn on fire? I have to order the elephant hitched—"

"It has already been taken care of."

She wanted to tell Brian she was in charge, it was her circus, but she was too tired. Brian was wrong. She wasn't shaking like a leaf. She shook like tent canvas. In fact, the whole Big Top convulsed as if it writhed in the throes of a fever. There would be no performance tonight.

Allowing him to lead her into the silver wagon, she collapsed atop a red-cushioned sofa. Beneath the rolled-up sleeves of her blouse, her arms were dotted with gooseflesh.

Brian opened a desk drawer, removed a bottle, and poured, filling a glass. "Drink this, Calliope."

"Where did the whiskey come from?"

"I found it while *snooping*. Here, take the glass."

"You know I don't drink, Brian. Even if I did, I would never guzzle before a show."

"I don't want you to guzzle. I want you to relax. And unless the winds die down, there's no chance we'll open."

She accepted the glass from his outstretched hand. She swallowed. Fiery liquid burned its way down her throat and brought tears to her eyes. "This is awful," she gasped. "How could you and Papa tolerate the taste?"

"It's an acquired taste, Calliope, like caviar. Have you ever eaten caviar?"

"The quick lunch wagon serves it every day," she quipped, leaning against a cushion. "Where did you taste caviar?"

"At an officers' ball. Slow down, puss. You don't have to consume it all at once."

"How could you and Papa tolerate the taste?" she asked again.

"Flavor is not always the reason a person drinks. It's the effect afterwards."

"What effect? I don't feel a thing."

"Have another wee sip. I said sip, Calliope, not guzzle."

"But if I sip, I don't like it. When I drink fast, it's much better. See? All gone. May I have some more?" She accepted another portion and gulped it down. "More?"

Brian sat next to her on the sofa. "When did you last eat?"

"This morning, I think." She giggled. "I ate caviar for breakfast. More, please."

Quirking an eyebrow, he poured. "Is that enough? No? I'll give you all you want, puss, but if you should get corned and spew it up, don't be blaming me."

"Papa could drink day an' night an' never spew," she said indignantly, draining half the glass. "I'm his daughter an' part Irish. You once said Sean's Irishness… inside the menagerie tent, you said… I forget."

"I said liquor makes you forget, and you said it helps you remember."

She rose to her feet, swaying. "I was wrong, boy-o. All my problems seem blurry now."

Although her problems had become blurry, the silver wagon's interior was discernible. Bookshelves, Brian, sofa, Brian, the desk where she counted receipts, a candle mired in tallow, Brian. Why did her gaze always return to him? Because his denim trousers clung to his long legs like a cowboy's, and his blue shirtsleeves were rolled up above his elbows, revealing muscled forearms bronzed by the sun. His dark hair was as thick and shaggy as a lion's mane. His eyes were bluer than his shirt. His lips were smiling.

"Ah, little girl," he said, "you're corned."

"Not true. A lay-dee's never corned."

"I've known several corned ladies."

"Lay-deez and gen-tul-men," she chanted, placing her empty glass on the desk. She grabbed the bottle from Brian and waved it around like a cane. "Pre-senting a performance the likes of which you have never seen before. Dream Dancer will dazzle you with her daring—" She paused to hiccup. "Why aren't *you* guzzling, Brian?"

"I must remain sober."

"Why?"

"Liquor not only helps you forget. It makes you ardent."

"So what? You've been ardent before. Me too." She squinted at the nearly empty bottle then staggered toward the middle of the wagon. "Where was I? Oh, yes. Dream Dancer will dazzle you with her daring, be-muze you with her bosom."

"Bosom?" Brian sat back and crossed one leg over the other.

"Why are you simpering like an uncaged tiger?"

"A lady simpers, Calliope. A gentleman smirks."

"Why are you smirking? What did I say? Do you prefer the word breast to bosom?" She tucked in her chin and looked down. "Damn! Where are my breasts?" Dropping the bottle, she tugged her blouse free from her skirt's waistband, then her shoulders, then her arms and wrists. "That's better. Now I have breasts. Where was I? I forget. I remember. And so, my friends, we need complete silence, for one misplaced sigh, one lover's kiss... Won't you please kiss me?"

"No." Brian stifled a sigh. The candle's wispy glow revealed Calliope's breasts, pushing against her oftwashed, oft-mended chemise. "That's why I didn't sip or guzzle, for we would never stop with one kiss."

"You don't love me," she wailed, tears brimming.

Brian stood. "Now I see Sean's Irishness in you, puss."

"'Tis proud of my Irish heritage I am."

"Are you planning to entertain me with a crying jag?"

"Oh! Why are you so nasty?"

"Because I don't intend to lie with you, not until we are wed."

"'Cause I don't 'tend t' lie with you, not till we're wed,'" she mimicked, catching the end of her braid and pulling it across her face, forming a mustache. "Pray tell me why you must develop scruples this very evening."

He grinned. "If I can wait a wee while longer, you'll collapse in a heap or spew your breakfast, assuming you had breakfast. Nobody can drink a full bottle of whiskey that quickly and feel no effect, even if they had just consumed a full meal, which you have not."

"Don't gabble so fast. You're makin' the wagon spin."

"I warned you." Stepping forward, he caught her about the waist. "Do you have the throw-ups, lass?"

"Dream Dancers never spew." She felt the whiskey rise in her throat and swallowed hard. "Do you hear the music, Brian?"

"I hear the wind."

"It's the same thing." Cocking her head in a listening pose, she sang, "Now this boy that I loved, he was handsome, an' I tried all I knew him to please, but I never could please him one quarter so well, like the lass on the flying trapeze."

"It's the *man* on the flying trapeze, and I do believe I prefer your crying jag to loud drunken singing."

"You an' Papa sang the night you came home. I can beller if I want." She tried to wink but closed both eyes and couldn't open them again. "He flies through the air with the greatest of ease," she warbled tremulously. "This daring young man on the flying trap—"

She took one deep breath, then another, and slumped forward.

As Brian caught her and carried her toward the sofa, his hand brushed against her chemise. He felt her breasts, young and firm, and he grinned, thinking how she was too bemused to acknowledge the accidental caress. Poor lass. Tomorrow her head would feel like a balloon about to burst.

He was about to burst through his trousers. It had taken every ounce of willpower he possessed to keep from responding to her performance. Calliope was adorable, but he wanted her pure until their wedding night. He was no Aaron Fox, promising marriage in order to tumble a pretty equestrian. And yet he needed release. There was only one way. He took a few steps toward the door. Then he hesitated. Should he stick around, just in case Calliope awoke and needed him to hold her head? No. If he gauged the sound of her breathing correctly, his tipsy puss would sleep until tomorrow morning.

⤜⤛

Calliope raised her head from the cushion. The candle flickered in a widening pool of melted wax while the inside of her mouth tasted like tallow and burnt wick. Furthermore, her belly was growling ominously.

"Toilet," she moaned, trying to rise quickly. "Brian, are you awake? Brian, I have to pee and… and maybe… I think… yes… throw up."

There was no reply, and she couldn't linger. Outside the wagon, a quarter-moon shed a feeble glow, bright enough to help her find the privy, even though she had to battle strong winds. When she emerged, feeling better but still light-headed, the moon had vanished. She staggered back toward what she hoped was the silver wagon.

The wind whipped strands of hair into her eyes and molded her chemise against her body. When had she lost her blouse? She vaguely recalled weeping and singing, just like Sean!

And yet the whiskey had made her problems diminish. Diminish? They'd gone clear away.

She reached inside her pocket for candy, and sucked three mints until they were thin webs on the tip of her tongue.

Gauzy clouds released the moon, and Calliope saw she was headed in the wrong direction—and Brian raced toward her.

"What's the matter, puss?" he asked. "Are you all right?"

"Fine. I'm wondrous fine." Her heart pounded like a ring full of galloping horses. "Where have you been?"

"I took a walk."

"I may still be a wee bit corned, Brian, but I'm not daft. Nobody strolls through a dark storm. Where were you?" When he didn't answer, she whispered, "Panama."

She turned abruptly and was almost knocked to the ground by a gust of wind that pushed against her body like a giant fist.

Brian placed his arm about her shoulders, but she wrenched free. "You rejected me," she screamed, "and visited your whore instead!"

"I didn't reject you."

"I suppose you didn't visit Panama's wagon, either."

"I won't lie to you, Calliope. I saw her."

She felt as though he had slapped her face. The moon was a thin smile, turned sideways. "You said you loved me."

"Love and lust are two different things."

"Are they? Do you know what lust rhymes with, Brian? Trust. Why did you betray me?"

"Nothing happened, puss. I didn't... Panama was... I..."

"You're him-hamming."

"If I hem and haw, it's because you talk like a child."

Calliope's hands fisted. "I'm no child. Are you as blind as Dublin?" Untangling her fingers, she pulled down her chemise. "Do I look like a child?"

"Do not be baring your breasts for all the world to see."

"Are you brainsick? All the world sleeps while you stand here and gawk."

"I don't gawk, Calliope. I've seen naked breasts before. Every woman has breasts, just like every man has—"

"I don't care what every man has. Yes, I do. I'll find myself a man who won't leave me for his whore. Has Panama crept back to Duncan? Or does she wait for your return in whatever spot you chose to rut? Duncan must be lonely."

Brian laughed.

He didn't believe her! Calliope opened her mouth, planning to scream her rage. But Brian ran behind her and covered her mouth with his hand. His arm captured her waist. She struggled wildly, trying to bite his fingers and kick his legs.

"Calm down," he said into her ear. "Do you want to wake the performers? Do you want them to see you like this? Playing the jealous brat?"

She was beyond caring who saw her, but Brian's tight arm was drawing the breath from her body. In another moment, she'd faint. Already, the crescent moon was chasing its tail. She stopped struggling and stood motionless.

"I refuse to discuss this further until we are safe from the windstorm," Brian said. Slinging her across one shoulder, he strode toward the silver wagon.

Despite the discomfort of her head hanging down his back, she managed to spit out her terse response. "There's nothing to discuss."

Once they were inside, Brian circled Calliope's waist and slid her down the length of his body. He felt her breasts temporarily flatten the creases in his shirt like a hot iron. "I went to Panama's wagon," he said. "I even knocked on her door. But when she answered, I didn't want her. I want no woman but you. I'm not him-hamming. Do you believe me?"

She nodded, looking up at him with her heart in her eyes, and he silently cursed himself for his stupidity. Calliope was right about trust. "I made up some lame excuse about checking out the wagons to see how they weathered the storm," he explained, emphasizing every word. "Then I did walk around, until I saw you battling the gusts."

"I'll not share you with another woman, Brian."

"You'll not have to."

"I mean it."

"I know. Pull up your straps, puss."

"Straps?" Lord, her chemise was still down, the material caught in the waistband of her skirt. Her immediate instinct was to cover her breasts, but she murmured, "You pull the straps up, lad. I'm tired. I've fought too many battles this night. Your scruples. The wind. Jealous demons."

Chameleon! Her temper had cooled so quickly, but Brian realized it could return just as quickly. Choosing his next words with care, he said, "You shall never have to fight demons again, I swear."

She finally smiled.

He reached out, planning to cover her breasts with her chemise. Instead, he disentangled leaves and bits of twiggy debris from her hair. "Dirty-faced urchin," he said tenderly.

"We both need a bath. I wish I had that bucket of water, the one you splashed me with inside the menagerie tent. Why did you stop that day?"

"Because you were unused, innocent." He couldn't keep his gaze away from her nipples, swollen by the wind's breathy caress.

"Will you not cure my innocence?"

"I told you before. Not until—"

"We are wed. Yes, I know." Opening a desk drawer, she removed a fresh taper and held it over the tiny flickering flame of the other candle until its bottom melted, merging into the old puddle of tallow.

Lighting the fresh wick, Calliope saw Brian head for the door. "Where are you going?"

"To my own wagon." He made a sound that was half sigh, half groan. "I cannot stay here."

"Don't leave me. Please, Brian, I'm frightened."

"It's only a windstorm."

"Not the storm." How could she explain? "Last month a diddy told my fortune."

"That's nice," he said, his voice impatient.

"It wasn't nice at all. She swore I would be rich."

"And so you will. Good night, Calliope."

"Wait! The diddy had a crystal ball and she vowed I would be unlucky in love. She said I might never find happiness unless I searched for a long, long time." Walking across the small space, Calliope stood directly in front of Brian.

Even in the nebulous light, he could see her eyes were filled with anguish. "Not a very wise diddy, puss. I wouldn't have her in our circus, for she'd drive away the gillys with her dire predictions."

"I want my happiness tonight. I don't want to wait a long time." Tears streamed down her cheeks, and she clutched Brian's hand so tightly her nails dug into his palm.

"Hush," he said, disentangling her frantic grip. "It makes no sense to tear yourself to pieces over a thievish Gypsy woman."

"She wasn't thievish. I paid no coin." Kneeling, Calliope clasped her hands together. "Before God, I, Calliope Kelley, take thee, Brian O'Connor, to be my lawfully wedded husband."

He turned away, hesitated. Then he knelt, facing her. "Before God, I, Brian O'Connor, take thee, Calliope Kelley, to be my lawfully wedded wife. In sickness and health, *forsaking all others*, till death us do part."

The wagon shook with the force of the wind. Or was it the force of their vows? "If we shut our eyes," she said, "we can imagine our wagon being drawn through the sky by four ghost white horses, just like the ending of a fairy tale."

He kissed the long lashes that shaded her cheekbones.

"Teach me," she murmured, sinking to the wagon's floor.

"There is no need." He followed her descent until he lay alongside her. "Hold still." He removed her remaining clothing and his. Then he straddled her body.

"Are you saying I've done this before?" she asked indignantly. "Is it because I show no shame?"

"Never be ashamed of your nakedness, puss, for God himself created all that beauty."

"And you, not God, spanked my behind, bringing me to life. Why is there no need to teach me?"

"When the time comes, you'll know what to do."

"I have not read about this in books, Brian. I've watched the horses, but it seems... well, uncomfortable."

"It's comfortable for the horses."

She traced the ridged muscles of his chest. "You have a scar."

"Knife wound. I bested the son of an Indian chief."

She shuddered. "Did you kill him?"

"I tried not to. That's how I received my wound."

"Oh." She was suddenly afraid to explore his body further. "Are there others?"

"Let's not speak of the past, Calliope. I've known many other women."

"I meant other scars, Brian."

He chuckled. "One directly on the inside of my thigh. Would you like to heal it anew with your touch?"

"Yes," she said, reaching. But he caught that hand, then her other one, and anchored them both above her head with one of his. Her mouth opened under the onslaught of his tongue and, without conscious thought, she began to writhe.

"Slow down, puss. This isn't whiskey. Is my taste not pleasant?"

She wanted to say yes again but merely caught her breath, because his tongue had moved to her earlobe while his free hand stroked her breasts. His breath was warm, his hand even warmer. He released her arms, and she clasped him around his neck. Then she found her voice. "You are like my horses," she purred, "all power and elegance."

"And you are like my cats," he said, "all grit and grace."

She felt his lips on her breast, his tongue teasing her nipple. With fierce abandon, she moaned and once again began to writhe. He sucked each nipple in turn. Then his hands were between her thighs. Letting go the thick hair at his nape, she pushed her right breast through the wet tunnel his mouth had become.

Now his knees were between her thighs, spreading them apart. All of a sudden, as he had promised, she knew exactly what to do. Winding her legs about his hips, digging her heels into his buttocks, she rode him like she'd ride one of her horses.

"Center ring," she urged. He bucked gently, and she adjusted her rhythm to his motion. "Find center ring," she pleaded, tightening her legs. She heard the wind and the music and they were the same. She heard a drumroll. "Now!" she shouted, using the one-word signal that directed her mounts through their hoops of fire.

He obeyed and penetrated. The pain was sharp—like a knife thrower's blade. Brian kissed her deeply, breathing her scream inside his mouth, but she twisted away and he pulled out.

"It hurts," she complained, feeling betrayed.

"I know."

"How can you know?" She felt her bottom lip quiver like a child's. "A man has no center ring."

"I'm sorry, puss." Rising to his knees, he stroked the tangled hair away from her forehead.

Curious, she traced the jutting evidence of his desire with her fingertips. "It's so huge," she whispered. "That's why it doesn't fit."

The strain of fighting both his laughter and the demands of his body were almost more than Brian could bear. Yet he knew he must make Calliope wetter. How? The usual method he employed with a more experienced woman might frighten her.

"Spit on my fingers," he said.

"Are you daft? How will that make you smaller?"

He couldn't control a delighted burst of laughter. "Never mind," he said, bending forward, kissing her chin, then parting her lips and thrusting his tongue inside.

Calliope had already learned this lesson. Eagerly, she sucked his tongue while he rubbed his hand across her breasts, his first two fingers creating a vee that lightly scissored her nipples. Her mouth opened and she began to draw deep, gulping breaths. Nevertheless, she found it increasingly difficult to breathe. An incredible amount of moisture accumulated, unbidden, between her thighs.

"I'm sopping wet," she cried. "Is that usual?"

"Yes. Dear God, Calliope, I love you so much."

His words, rather than his touch, increased her passion tenfold. His lips claimed hers again. Then she felt him lower his body and guide her hand until he was fully in her grasp.

Now what?

Nothing. Passively, he let her clasp his erection. Dazed with desire, she began to insert his engorged tip. She tilted her head all the way back, spread her legs, and arched her hips. He unclasped her fingers while she urged his entry, shouting his name over and over. But he moved slowly, pausing, penetrating, pausing—

"Now, Brian, now!" She placed both hands against his buttocks and pressed with all her might.

Suspended between pain and pleasure, her senses focused on the searing intrusion of his body into hers. Then pleasure began to dominate and her pain diminished, giving way to a new sensation. She rode through a waterfall. Her mount was wet, and so was she. The wetness soothed the last remnants of her pain. She heard Brian groan. Had *she* hurt him?

The rush of the waterfall was very loud, and she wavered precariously on its precipice. Then, losing her balance, she soared through space. She must have landed inside a rainbow, because colors obscured her vision. Even through the rainbow's mist, she saw Brian's eyes, lazy-lidded yet bright with hunger.

"Good puss," he said. "That's what I was waiting for."

She felt him tense and moan. She wasn't exactly

sure what had happened because she was soaring again, ascending in a spiral, gliding earthward, cradled by clouds. The wind sang a lullaby until it was interrupted by two words: "Encore, Brian."

"Soon," he said. "Give me but a few wee moments to catch my breath."

She gasped when he withdrew. Then she buried her face against his chest, hoping she had performed well.

Once, a long time ago, she had watched a sparrow hawk and wondered how it felt to fly with no net beneath.

Now she knew.

Eight

By the next evening, the windstorm had become an occasional breeze and the charred barn was the only unpleasant image to mar a perfect landscape. The setting sun shaded distant mountain peaks, creating a vista filled with pink and blue and violet streamers. *Silk handkerchiefs*, thought Brian, *drawn from a Master Magician's vest pocket*.

Although low from lack of rain, a nearby river had enough water for bathing. There was even enough to spray the grounds so slippers, boots, and hooves wouldn't raise squalls of dust. Brian saw Calliope talking to Jocko.

On her left finger she now sported a gold ring. Before sunrise, while she slept, Brian had left the silver wagon to rummage through his trunk and locate Maureen O'Connor's wedding band. Aaron Fox had presented it to Maureen in order to satisfy his lust. Brian would give it to Calliope as a token of their love.

He had placed the ring on her finger. Then they had come together again, and he was delighted by her playful passion. She had lost every trace of modesty, insisting he lie motionless while she rode his hips. Holding back, he had stroked her body until he heard her singsong plea: "Now, Brian, oh please, now."

When he finally thrust, abandoning patience, giving in to a climatic compulsion, she had responded with imperative contractions of her own. Then she had rewarded him with a complacent smile. "Encore, Husband," she had whispered.

"Tonight, Wife. There's a method to make you wet I have not yet explored."

The image of Calliope's beautiful body surrendering to him with uninhibited rapture caused an immediate reaction, which he lowered his hands to hide.

"Thinkin' 'bout me and you behind the Cook Top?" Panama asked.

Her mouth was open in a lascivious grin and she fondled her huge breasts. Which, Brian knew from experience, were bulldozed forward by her corset stays.

Why had he ever thought her attractive? Her rust-colored hair was brittle and kinked like the end of his tightly braided whiplash. Her abundant flesh threatened to burst through her orange-and-yellow-striped gown. Her face was as wrinkled as an elephant's skin, and she hid face creases with enough paint to challenge the clowns.

Once she had been statuesque rather than stout. But now, especially today, she was a fetid puddle compared to Calliope's bubbling well of fresh spring water.

"What d'ya say? You and me behind the Cook Top?"

"There's no time," he replied lamely, unwilling to hurt her feelings. "The show begins soon and I must tend to my cats."

"Junior prods your lions and tigers into their chutes. I'm thinkin' there's one particular pussycat you want to tend, but she's busy with her clown."

"Get ready for the opening spec, Panama."

"Don't be so highfalutin, mister. Ain't you smart to housebreak the cat? Soon you'll own her circus."

"What the hell are you babbling about?"

"I'm talkin' 'bout a stroll to my wagon smack-dab in the middle of the night. I'm speakin' of you standin' there in such a sweat you don't care for Duncan's snores and the chance of a bashed head. I was of a mind to let you have me against the spokes, but then you was gone."

"I guyed-out all the wagon ties last night."

"Don't give me that, Brian. You decided to play a different game for higher stakes. I followed you. I couldn't see everything through that small window, but I seen enough."

"Damn your soul!"

"Stop snarling. You sound like one of your tigers. I don't give a fig if you diddle the boss."

"Shut up! If you keep mentioning Miss Kelley in that tone of disrespect, I'll wring your neck."

"Banana backbone! I'd like to see you try." She snickered. "Dearie me, could it be true love?"

"I'll not warn you again."

"I'm warning you, Brian. Meet me at the Cook Top before the show starts, or in the menagerie tent afterwards. If you don't, you'll be sorry."

"For some daft reason, Duncan believes his wife has been faithful. You wouldn't want to shatter his illusions, Panama, for if you did, I'm thinking it's your head he'd bash first. Duncan reacts, then reasons."

"I couldn't understand all you just said, Brian, shattering loose shins and such, but I do know one thing. If you don't meet me, you'll wish you'd never been born."

He watched her waddle away like an enormous duck. Once those swaying hips had been enticing, but now he possessed a swan. Suppose his swan already carried a cygnet? In the heat of their passion he hadn't considered that, or he would have withdrawn before spilling his seed. They must be legally wed. Why not introduce Calliope to his father and have Aaron Fox pay for an elaborate wedding and honeymoon? That would be a fine revenge, one that Maureen O'Connor would have relished.

Following this evening's performance, he would tell Calliope about his father and demand she sell the circus. Of course he'd let her choose which bid to accept, appease her womanly pride. Jocko could handle the negotiations. They would keep Dublin and a couple of other horses. It was seventy-five miles to Fox's Colorado Springs ranch, more or less.

Calliope had always wanted to play the lady. Hell, she already looked and sounded like a lady. But soon Brian would give his swan the trappings—feathery gowns, baubles, and trinkets galore.

Selling the circus would solve another problem. Brian wouldn't have to explain why she must dismiss Panama. He knew that, despite her immodesty with him, Calliope would never recover from the thought of Panama spying through the silver wagon's window.

Impatient for the opening spectacle to begin, impatient for the show to end, he ignored Panama's threats.

❧

From the corner of her eye, Calliope saw Panama confront Brian then saunter toward the Cook Top. Brian walked in the opposite direction, toward the menagerie tent.

Bringing her attention back to Jocko, she said, "So you see, I must sell the circus. I've had three good offers. If I introduce you as my manager and tell the new owner you've been with us ten, maybe even twelve years, you wouldn't have to explain your past. Last night Brian and I…" She paused, blushing. "Well, I'm sure you understand."

"Damn it! I understand perfectly."

She blinked with surprise. "Why do you sound so growly, Jocko? I thought you'd be happy for me."

"Why should I be happy because you love another?"

"But I've always loved Brian, even as a child." She stared at his face. "Oh. Oh, God. Jocko, I had no idea."

"Of course you didn't. I should have pressed my suit before he returned."

She felt tears sting her eyes. "I'm fond of you, truly, but it's not a forever kind of love."

"Do you honestly believe that Brian O'Connor will be a forever husband?"

"Please don't be horrid."

"If he hadn't returned, I could have made you love me."

"You can't make somebody love you."

"You're right, Calliope. I tried it once before."

"The woman in the brothel," she breathed.

"How do you know about that?" He grasped her arm.

"Let me go! You're hurting me!" When he didn't release her, she pried his fingers apart, one at a time. "A lawman showed me a photograph. He said your name was Bret Johnson. There's a reward for your capture."

"Why didn't you tell me?"

"Because I didn't believe him. He said you shot a woman and set fire to a brothel. He lied."

"You remind me of your father, Calliope. Sean wouldn't face reality, either."

"Are you saying it's true?"

"In a way. Clarissa tried to shoot me, but I managed to turn the gun in her direction. During our struggles, she knocked over a coal stove."

"Then it was self-defense."

"Clarissa pulled her gun because I threatened to carve her lovely face with my knife."

"Would you have done it? Cut her?"

"Yes."

Calliope pressed her hands against her heart. She had never seen this side of her clown before. Of all her performers, clowns were the most diverse, composed of distinct qualities. Joeys worked as athletes, usually on horseback. An Auguste dealt with comic farce. Charlies entertained through pathos. Jocko was a Charlie.

"Why did you want to carve her face, Jocko?"

"At one time I was a respectable illustrator. I covered the war, penning my pictures of battles and soldiers and selling them to newspapers."

"The posters and banner line. The handbills."

"When peace was declared, I found myself in Atlanta. I met Clarissa, an impoverished gentlewoman.

Sherman had stripped her plantation. Her mother had died of influenza. Her father, like Sean, existed in his own imaginary world, useless. Clarissa had one asset, her beauty. God knows she could have done better than an illustrator, but the South lacked young healthy men. I thought she really loved me."

"When did she become a—?"

"Whore? After she spent my money, every cent. I couldn't refuse her. She had been through so much and suffered so many losses. She was only sixteen. I left her in Atlanta and traveled to New York, searching for a steady job. When I returned, she had found a position."

"A position," Calliope echoed.

"She had a close friend who had also lost everything. This friend was employed by the madame of a very successful house and she convinced Clarissa to join the staff. I told Clarissa I understood, that we could start anew. She laughed and offered herself to me for a price. She said she preferred gold or greenbacks but would settle for a portrait to hang above her bed. I was such a stupid bastard. A love-struck fool."

"I don't believe you'd have really cut her, Jocko. After the fire, why didn't you explain to the law? You know, tell them what happened. That it was self-defense."

"One of Clarissa's callers was a judge, an uppercrust, powerful man. I didn't have a prayer, so I ran away. I don't like to be made the love-struck fool twice, Jane."

Calliope felt the color drain from her face. In her circus world, Jane was *the* most uncomplimentary description for a woman, short of obscenity.

"Don't call me Jane, and don't compare me to

Clarissa. I'm not a whore." When he didn't reply, she held out her left hand. "Brian and I said our vows before God."

"Did O'Connor and Panama vow too?"

"How dare you! It's not the same at all."

"Your cat tamer wants to own the Sean Kelley Circus, darling, and all for the price of one gold band."

"Are you saying Brian doesn't love me?"

"Who wouldn't love you, Calliope?" Jocko captured her face with the palms of his hands. "Why can't you think with your head rather than your body?"

"I think with my heart. I dream with my heart. I dance with my heart."

"That's no way to run a business."

"Love isn't a business."

"It is for O'Connor. He chafes under your control. He fumes at the idea of taking orders from a 'wee lass.' He wants to be the biggest toad in the puddle."

She stumbled backwards, shaking her head. "You're wrong. Brian doesn't want to own my circus. We've already had two clems because he wants me to sell it."

"For a profit?"

"Yes. No. He doesn't care about the money, Jocko, truly."

"O'Connor will abandon you. Didn't he leave after your mother's death, when you needed him the most?"

"Yes, but he was a spalpeen, not a grown man."

"Your grown man is just like my Clarissa. He'll spend all your money then laugh in your face."

"Go to hell, Jocko!"

"I'm merely stating facts, Calliope. I would never betray you." His eyes turned cold. "Unless, of course, you betrayed me first."

"Is that a threat? Are you trying to scare me?"

Circling her waist, he drew her close. "I could make you love me, but not if you sell the circus and disappear with *him*."

She struggled free. "I shall never love any man except Brian. Never!"

"I don't believe that. When Brian leaves you, another man will take his place. Your body demands caresses." Beneath the painted frown, Jocko's mouth stretched upwards in a tight-lipped smile. "To love in vain, Calliope, makes one a god. But to love again, still in vain, makes one a fool."

"You're no fool, Jocko, and I'm sure you'll find another woman to love."

"Who'd love a clown? People laugh at clowns but underestimate fools. Clowns are funny. Fools are dangerous."

"Please be happy for me."

"Haven't you noticed, my darling? Clowns are always happy, even when they're not."

❧

The Big Top was filled to capacity with children of all ages. *Children from one to one hundred*. Calliope saw several gillys wearing fancy evening clothes, as if they planned to attend a society ball after the show.

She could sit among them. Her white gown was prettier than many of their gowns. All she needed was jewelry. A necklace of glittering spangles, perhaps earrings strung together with popped corn. She could drape Duchess's cub around her shoulders, wear him as a fur piece. Rather than flowers or plumes, she could collect colorful ribbons and tie the new pig, Josephine, onto her bonnet.

Calliope pictured the lion cub trying to claw the wee piggy—not a good idea.

Collecting her props and peeking through the performers' entrance, she watched Big John, Marianne, and the Cossacks. Only five Cossacks, since the superstitious others had packed up and left. Her Kid Show entertainers had all stayed, bless their hearts. Cuckoo the Bird Girl, so perfectly tiny, marred only by a pointed head. Jack the Giant. Duncan. The Bearded Lady and her husband, the Bear Man, whose body was covered with thick fur. Even Gwendolyn, with hair five feet four inches long, who had joined the circus after their Boulder, Colorado, performance.

Damn her newest ringmaster! He had disappeared during the windstorm, having told Cuckoo the circus was cursed. No loss. He was very heavy, ate twice his worth, and often swallowed his words while announcing the acts. Brian was much better, even though he would have to double as cat tamer.

Where was Jocko hiding? He was supposed to hand Calliope her gun in exchange for her ostrich-feather fan and then, later, light the hoop. Was he off somewhere sulking?

And where was Panama? She had missed the opening spec—no big tragedy, but worrisome.

"Pre-senting our star equestrian. Ladies and

gentlemen, Dream Dancer will dazzle you with her daring, bemuse you with her beauty…"

Calliope was distracted from Brian's announcement by movement behind her. Whirling about, she saw a fleeting shadow turn the corner. Panama? Jocko?

Clowns are funny. Fools are dangerous. What had Jocko meant by that? A clever comment or a threat?

Perhaps the shadowed form was a young lad trying to enter through the sidewalls. No. Her glimpse had been brief, but the figure was definitely adult. And heavy. Jocko's girth was extended with hoops inside his clown's tunic. Panama's circumference was provided by nature. Or the fleeing figure could have been her absent ringmaster. He might have returned for one last meal, she thought wryly.

"And so, my friends, this will be Dream Dancer's final performance. You are privileged indeed to witness…"

Final performance? Damn and blast! Brian was determined she sell the circus, had just announced it to the world. Well, maybe not the world. Colorado. Brian believed she would honor his words, just as she had honored the posters in Kansas.

Damn his soul! He had no right to make up her mind for her, even though she had already decided to sell. During her act, when Jocko handed her the gun, she would shoot Brian rather than the target that released her pigeons.

Slapping Dublin's haunches a little harder than usual, she followed her prancing stallion into center ring. The band began sounding the opening strains of "El Caballero."

Before she could bow to the gillys and release

her cape, Calliope saw smoke curl through the main entrance. Helpless, she turned toward Brian, who was signaling the band to stop playing. He had seen the smoke too.

Then, quick as a wink, faster than she could believe possible, fire leaped up the tent's sidewalls and raced across the top of the canvas.

Brian cupped his hands around his mouth, shouting for the gillys to file out through the performers' entrance or beneath the sidewall flaps.

Instead, chaos exploded like a cannon. With one accord, the audience tried to rush out the way they had come in—toward the fire—and found their escape blocked by the runway and chutes. Unable to scale this obstacle, at least a dozen men and women piled up like haphazardly stacked firewood.

Clowns attempted to turn people in the other direction but were trampled for their efforts.

Calliope heard flames thundering across the Big Top. The sound released her brief paralysis. She tugged at the slits in her gown until her long skirt ripped apart. Now her legs were unrestricted and she could move. She whistled for Dublin. Miraculously, he responded, and she guided him toward the performers' entrance. Thank God he didn't need a blindfold.

She saw Gwendolyn grabbing children and handing them to Cuckoo, who shoved them through the loose canvas. Calliope ran to join them. She could smell her hair singe. The arena was filled with black fumes and the heat was intense.

"Over here, Calliope." Marianne held out her arms.

Fumbling at the ribbons around her throat, releasing

her cape, Calliope scooped up the first child she saw and passed him to her fellow equestrian. After ten more, she could barely lift her arms. Her lungs were bursting and she knew she'd have to exit soon. She heard a cry—one last child whose ruffled party dress was beginning to catch fire.

Grabbing her cape, Calliope crawled toward the little girl and wrapped her inside the cape, smothering flames. Crawling back, Calliope squeezed through the sidewall, took a deep breath, and coughed. The child lay limp in her arms but appeared unhurt, thank God.

A wavy line of people wound down to the river. They passed buckets of water to each other. Calliope knew she should join them, but she felt sluggish.

For all intents and purposes, the Sean Kelley Circus no longer existed. She could sell her railroad cars, sell the undamaged wagons and equipment, even sell her precious elephant, but she could never bargain away this disaster.

She wondered how many lives had been lost, and fought waves of nausea. The menagerie tent was gone. How many animals had escaped?

If her evil leprechaun had orchestrated this fire, he had been very successful.

Gwendolyn sat nearby. Her long hair was missing, burned away. She held a handkerchief to her blistered lips and her skin was lobster-red.

"I hurt, Miss Kelley," she whimpered.

"I know. I'm so sorry. Have you seen Brian, Gwen?"

"Who?"

"Brian O'Connor." As Calliope cleared her throat, clogged with smoke and tears, she remembered

Gwendolyn had recently joined the circus and didn't know Brian very well. "Our cat tamer, Gwen. Tonight he also played the ringmaster."

"Oh. The ringmaster. He's cold as a wagon tire."

"What?" Calliope's brain whirled like a merry-go-round. "What did you say?"

"The ringmaster was trampled."

Calliope experienced a profound sense of relief. "Lots of people were trampled, Gwen. He must have simply bided his time and—"

"No. He's dead."

"Are you absolutely certain?"

"Yes. I swear. It was the ringmaster. I watched him burst into flames, just like the others."

"What others?" Calliope knew she asked the question, but it seemed to come from far away. Brian couldn't be dead. Gwendolyn was mistaken. Dear God, you couldn't mistake a ringmaster. He wore different clothes. A starched shirt. A batwing collar. Cravat. Top hat. And he wielded a cane. Maybe Brian had shed his shirt, lost his hat, dropped his cane.

I watched him burst into flames.

"My hair's all gone. See?" Gwendolyn's blistered lips opened. She screamed and screamed and—

Calliope took another deep breath, clasped the child to her bosom, and fainted.

Nine

THE SMELLS WERE ALL WRONG—CHICKEN BROTH RATHER than popped corn and lemonade. A light breeze carried the scent of lilacs through an open window. The woman wore a dressing gown that reeked of lavender. Calliope closed her eyes.

When she opened them again, nothing had changed. Her body felt as if it floated on clouds, most likely because she rested on the softest mattress she had ever encountered. Her head was cradled by a downy pillow. Her hands were bandaged and lay atop a quilted bedspread. Tentatively, she moved her face to one side and saw a full-length mirror holding her reflection trapped within its glass. Her head was turbaned with gauze, hiding her hair. Her eyes were puffy, she had no eyebrows, and her face was covered with red welts and blue bruises. Had she miscalculated when Dublin leaped through his fiery hoop?

She squeezed her eyes shut, trying to remember. Something *bad* had happened. It was her birthday and she blew out eleven candles and wished her name was Mary and Mum fell from the rope. Brian went away.

Papa drank because he didn't love her enough, and she tried to get him to stop so he wouldn't be killed by the wicked leprechaun. A lion pawed Napoleon, and Brian said he loved her. Wind rocked the silver wagon while she learned how to fly. Jocko said people laughed at clowns, then he set fire to the Big Top. Brian went away again.

"Are you awake, dear? Try and open your eyes. I know they hurt, but do try."

Calliope obeyed, and stared at the woman who leaned over her bed. The pretty lady was old, but her chin didn't sag and her complexion was smooth as parchment. Her silver hair had been combed into a high braided circle, and her blue eyes looked sad.

Behind the lady stood a tall man. He wore a gray jacket, a white shirt, and a batwing collar. Beneath the collar was a black cravat with a diamond stickpin as big as an acorn. A top hat perched securely on his head, and he held a gold-tipped cane.

Calliope smiled. Gwendolyn was mistaken after all. The ringmaster hadn't died in the fire. Brian was alive.

"Brian. Thank God! I thought you were dead."

The lady looked up at the man. "She must mean her husband. Oh, dear."

Calliope winced. This man wasn't Brian. This man had a thick mustache, more gray than brown. His eyes were brown too, and webbed with lines.

"Then he's truly dead?" She chewed her bottom lip and gasped with pain. Her lips were swollen twice their usual size. "Gwendolyn said Brian was trampled before he burst into flames and burned to death. She watched and swore it really happened."

"Poor, poor darling," the lady said. "I'm so sorry."

"How…?" Calliope swallowed. "How did I get here? Who are you?"

"I'm Raymond Stanhope," said the elderly gentleman. "This is my wife, Ann. We brought you here to our home after you saved Pollyann from the fire."

"Pollyann?"

"Our granddaughter. Our dearest treasure. We found her in your arms."

"I remember. The little girl with the ruffled dress. Is she all right?"

"Yes," Raymond Stanhope said. "You're going to be fine too, my dear. We've had our physician salve your burns and he promised you wouldn't even carry one scar."

"How long have I been here?"

"Ten days."

"Did you say ten days?"

Mrs. Stanhope's head bobbed up and down. "May we notify your parents, my dear? They must be worried sick." Pulling a chair forward, she sank onto its cushioned brocade.

"My mother and father are dead, ma'am."

"I'm sorry. Perhaps another relative?"

"Nobody."

"We can send a servant to pack your trunks and deliver your clothes here."

"My clothes? But they burned in the fire. I'm almost certain they did."

As if speaking to a small child, Mrs. Stanhope said, "Your evening gown was beyond repair. Fortunately, your gloves protected your arms and hands and kept them from sustaining more damage. You must have lost your jewels, though you still have your gold chain and lovely horse charm. May I assume you and your husband had plans to attend the ball afterwards?"

The ball? What was Mrs. Stanhope talking about? Calliope squeezed her eyes shut. Behind closed lids she pictured row upon row of seats filled with gillys dressed in evening gowns and furs.

I didn't lose my jewels, you daft lady. I have my wedding band and necklace, all that remains of Brian.

Opening her eyes, she held in check the tears that congested her throat. She wouldn't cry. Brian wouldn't want her to weep like a banshee in front of gillys, especially rich gillys.

"If you give me your address," said Mrs. Stanhope, "we can send the servants for your belongings."

Address? The circus didn't exist anymore. But they wanted her to recite numbers and a street.

"I can't remember," she said.

"It's not important," Mr. Stanhope said. "When you are fully recovered, I shall purchase a brand new wardrobe." He waved his cane expansively. "Or if you prefer, my wife shall employ the finest seamstress in Denver."

"Please, sir, I'm sleepy."

"Of course you are," said Mrs. Stanhope. "Rest, my dear. In a little while, after the doctor changes your bandages, Cook shall prepare more broth. Perhaps a boiled egg or bread soaked in wine. You must recover quickly. Pollyann wants to thank you in person. Why, she even finger painted a picture just for you, a picture of her favorite cat."

Calico Cat. Brian. Dead.

Calliope wanted to die too. Could one bring about death by imposing one's will? In a strange way, by a bizarre twist of fate, Sean had achieved that goal, even though Calliope was still certain the evil leprechaun had lured Papa to the pie car.

What if Papa's grandchild lay beneath her tear-drenched heart? Brian's wee lad or lass. She couldn't die. She couldn't destroy Brian's seed.

A seed of an idea began to sprout.

"Can you tell us your name?" Mrs. Stanhope leaned forward.

Calliope knew she was book smart and circus shrewd. She was rash, impulsive, inventive. But could she be cunning? Devious?

"Do you remember your name, dear?"

Her mind raced. The gillys had killed Mum and Brian. They had made Mum too prideful, and Gwendolyn said Brian was trampled by gillys before he burned to death.

A new wardrobe be damned! She wanted a new life. Furthermore, she needed the kind of life that would allow her to discover the identity and whereabouts of her death-dealing leprechaun.

She would remember whatever she chose to remember and forget when convenient. She would plot and scheme and make these rich gillys pay.

"My name is Mary," she said. "Mary Angelique O'Connor."

Ten

NOT A BREEZE STIRRED. COTTONWOOD TREES AND chokecherry bushes looked like the painted backdrop for an allegorical play starring Virtue and Temperance. Calliope wriggled her toes, held captive by the patent leather toe caps on her boots. She yearned for bare feet. The grounds were verdant with thick blades of grass, except where Ann Stanhope had recently cleared a space for the new game, lawn tennis.

"And it was in… let's see now, Mary… late 1858, I believe. Everybody grabbed land, preparing for a gold strike that hadn't even happened yet." Raymond Stanhope chuckled. "They named the new town Denver City after the *Kansas* Territorial Governor, James Denver."

Calliope nodded and took several deep breaths, inhaling the sweet scent of the freshly cropped grass beneath Ann's tennis net. Four women swatted at two balls. They were clothed in striped cotton dresses with the hems of their skirts looped around the buttons at their waistbands. If they saw Raymond, the skirts would be released and allowed to fall over numerous petticoats.

The male guests wore white trousers, white shirts, and soft leather boots. Most had shed their long-sleeved short jackets. They stood on top of a knoll, watching a football scuffle on the field below.

Strolling with Raymond and his granddaughter, Calliope slanted a glance toward the tennis ladies. They looked like statues, their feet planted firmly on the cropped turf, motionless. Only the ball moved. If it happened to hit a racquet, spectators applauded politely.

Today's occasion was a picnic, and the weather had complied. Calliope's blue spoon bonnet provided decoration rather than protection from the elements. Not that she needed or wanted protection. After a winter of heavy blizzards, she welcomed the sunshine on her face.

With a slight twinge of guilt, she brought her attention back to Raymond, who veered toward the house in an effort to avoid embarrassing the tennis ladies.

"Denver City and Auraria vied for leadership in everything from miners' supplies to fisticuffs," he was saying. "Fortunately, there came a sensible day when they decided to settle quarrels by sharing a shipment of Taos lightning. That's another name for frontier liquor, Mary. It was called Taos lightning because it was wagon-trained from New Mexico. Filled with good cheer, the rival communities voted to call the settlement Denver."

"That's where you come in, Grandpapa," trilled six-year-old Pollyann. "Tell Mary, do."

"Mary already knows."

"Tell my dolly." Pollyann held up her favorite rag doll. The stitches on its face had unraveled so it had one eye, half a nose, and no mouth.

Raymond cleared his throat. "My firm, the first to make beer in Colorado, was called Mountain Brewery."

"Grandpapa rode on a wagon pulled by oxes."

"Oxen," Raymond corrected, his brown eyes sparkling with memories. "I ran a general store. To obtain merchandise, I made thirteen perilous journeys back and forth across hostile plains."

"Tell Mary 'bout the papoose, Grandpapa."

"Surprised by a band of Indians, I purchased my life by giving the chief's papoose a cup of sugar. Upon returning to Denver, I learned the rogue I had left in charge of my store had sold everything and disappeared. I was mad as hops." Raymond patted Pollyann's carrot-colored hair. "Hops are essential to beer making, so that's when I started my brewery."

In the ten months Calliope had resided with the Stanhopes, she had heard Raymond's story many times, but she added her laughter to his. She adored her guardian and occasionally felt guilty when she compared him to Sean. Raymond never drank, confessing that the production of spirits was his occupation, not a social indulgence. He had invested his brewery profits in real estate and he owned a large, successful bank. He doted on his family, especially his son Thom, his daughter-in-law Dorothy, and Pollyann. His other son, Maxey, attended Williams College in Massachusetts and was due to join them for the summer.

As if she had read Calliope's mind, Pollyann said, "When will Uncle Maxey come home, Grandpapa?"

Raymond halted midstride. "Soon. Possibly sooner than expected."

Glancing up at her guardian, Calliope noted his furrowed brow and the frown that clouded his sunny smile. Ann claimed Maxey had fallen in with a disreputable group of irresponsible rowdies and was a victim of their activities. Could Maxey have been expelled?

Influenced by Raymond's angry diatribes, Calliope was determined to merely tolerate Maxey during his visit—no more, no less.

"Dottie is beckoning, Mary," said Raymond, his eyes again filled with amusement. "Perhaps she has some girlish secret to share."

Thom's wife reclined on a cushioned chaise. By no stretch of the imagination could she be considered girlish, thought Calliope. Dottie was plump and placid as vanilla cake batter. In fact, she dressed in white lace and ruffles no matter what the occasion. Her exposed limbs and pale complexion reminded Calliope of milk diluted with water. Only Dottie's hair retained vitality. It was the color of a sunrise, the color of fire.

"Mary Angelique," Dottie called. "Come here at once."

She wasn't beckoning; it was a command. On tiptoe, Calliope kissed Raymond's weathered cheek. Then she scurried over to the reposed woman's side.

"Sit down, Mary Angelique. You are standing in front of the sun, and it hurts my eyes to squint."

"I'm sorry, Dottie." Calliope looked around for a chair.

"Share my chaise. I prefer to conduct our tête-à-tête privately." Dottie dabbed at her face with a perfumed handkerchief. "Is it not hot for April?"

"Yes, hot," Calliope agreed, sinking to the edge of the cushion and settling her blue-and-white-striped tennis skirts demurely over her ankles.

It wasn't the sun that caused excessive heat, she thought, but rather her rigid corset, crinolines, and bustle, all covered by ample petticoats. No wonder the tennis ladies couldn't move. Calliope pictured them swinging from a trapeze and stifled a giggle.

Dash it all! I'm no different. The weight of my own costume would surely cause me to fall from a trapeze. Her urge to giggle went away, because this time, if she fell, Brian wouldn't be there to catch her.

Dottie fluttered her handkerchief. "For lo, the winter is past, the snow is over and gone."

"The *rain* is over and gone," Calliope corrected. Dottie had a habit of misquoting scripture. Although Calliope didn't know the Old Testament verse by verse, she had memorized the beautiful Song of Solomon during her convalescence.

"Are you quite sure it's rain, Mary Angelique? I thought it was snow."

"If God had lived in Colorado, Solomon would have sung of snow."

Dottie's pale blue eyes widened. "You blaspheme, Mary Angelique. God lives everywhere."

He didn't live in my circus. God was elsewhere when we had our fire.

Aloud, she said, "Why do we conduct this tête-à-tête, Dottie? What do you wish to discuss in private?"

"You have an admirer, my dear. Charles Doone has requested permission to escort you to the ball tomorrow night."

"The ball?" Calliope slanted a glance toward the tennis ladies. "What ball?"

"The Spring Ball, of course. It's held on the first of May, at the Men's Club."

"Why didn't Charles ask me himself?"

"You cannot be serious. That's improper, even if you are a widow. My Thom played whist with Father for months, and lost on purpose before asking for my hand in marriage. How did your late husband propose?"

He ripped off the binding that flattened my breasts. He threatened to toss me back inside the cat cage if I didn't agree to marry him. "He proposed, and I accepted," Calliope said.

"He didn't ask your father?"

"After the war and Mother's death from influenza, Papa was indisposed. He never fully recovered from the loss of my brother during the siege at Gettysburg."

Dottie assumed an expression of pious solemnity while Calliope hid a smile with the back of her hand. It was so simple to weave a web of lies based on the story Jocko had related that last day, before the fire. *Jocko!* Calliope planned to find the clown and extract revenge. She was convinced Jocko had torched the tent in a jealous rage. She no longer believed Clarissa's death and the whorehouse holocaust were accidental.

And yet, thanks to Jocko, Calliope had a past that satisfied every strict social standard. She was an impoverished Southern gentlewoman whose family had lost everything during Sherman's march through

Georgia. She had even borrowed Jocko's background for Brian, inventing a journalist who had forfeited his vast inheritance during the last stock panic.

Yes. She could be clever and inventive and devious, even though, every once in a while, her conscience bothered her. Because she truly adored the elderly Stanhopes. Moreover, she had a feeling they might have accepted her circus background without censure.

"You must put the past behind you, my dear." Dottie patted Calliope's hand. "Charles Doone is a fine catch."

"You talk as though men were fish. I won't be bait, a worm on the end of a hook. In truth, that's a poor analogy, since worms do not have legs and breasts."

"Mary Angelique! You are much too outspoken, my dear. If you continue, I doubt you shall catch, I mean find a second husband."

"I'm not looking for a husband, Dottie."

"Nonsense. Do you prefer spinsterhood?"

"Widowhood."

"The New Testament says it is better to marry than to burn. That must mean hell. Do you want to burn in hell?"

Calliope shuddered. Dottie had pulled her reference from thin air, never realizing the images her words would invoke—a blazing tent and Brian trampled by gillys, left to burn alone. Stupid, insensitive woman!

"When there's marriage without love, there will be love without marriage," Calliope snapped.

"Is that from the Bible?"

"No. It's from *Poor Richard's Almanac*."

"Mr. Richard couldn't have been a decent Christian."

"Ben Franklin wrote the almanac."

"Then they were both heathens!"

As Calliope rose to her feet, she let her gaze sweep the landscape. Ignoring picnic guests, she imagined her circus crew guying-out tent ropes, pictured her Big Top with its colorful flags and banners, could almost swear she smelled popped corn, lemonade, and wienies on a stick.

Attempting to curb her introspection, she said, "Raymond asked me to check on the new mare. She was in a wee bit of a fret this morning and reminds me of Susan."

"Who is this Susan, and why do you compare her to a horse?"

Damn and blast! Calliope chewed her bottom lip. "Susan was a mare on my father's plantation," she said, hoping to cover her faux pas. "A chestnut like Brandywine."

"If you ask me, and nobody does, it was more than generous of Raymond to give you Brandywine."

"Yes, very generous. Please excuse me, Dottie."

"Wait! What should I tell Charles?"

"Tell him I still mourn my husband. I may burn for remaining unwed, but I prefer the heat of hell to the heat of a man's body when I feel no matching passion."

Now I've done it. Dorothy Stanhope will faint dead away.

Dottie, however, looked honestly perplexed. "What does passion have to do with marriage?"

"What is marriage without passion?"

"There are twenty-four hours in a day and night, Mary Angelique. Your act of passion requires ten, perhaps twelve minutes. It takes longer to bathe, prepare a meal, or even select a gown. My husband provides the salts for my bath, the food on our table, and the gowns in my wardrobe. If Thom must indulge in a brief, disgusting quest for pleasure, it is little to ask in return for his name, his generosity, and his protection. If it were proper, I would assign a servant the task of scratching Thom's itch."

And she called me outspoken! "Dottie, have you never felt…?" Calliope hesitated, searching for the right word. "Rapture? Desire?"

"Of course not. I am a lady, Mary Angelique, and Thom knows it. He wouldn't expect me to display desire. Passion is for paramours. Did your mother not explain all this?"

"My mother died when I was eleven, but I enjoyed my husband's caresses."

"No, my dear, what you enjoyed was the sanctity of wedlock." Dottie removed her straw hat and fanned her flushed face with its brim. "Promise me you'll consider Mr. Doone's invitation."

"I promise," said Calliope. Truthfully, she would have promised to lasso the moon or play tennis in her undergarments if it meant an escape from Dottie.

Walking toward the stables, Calliope removed her bonnet and swung it back and forth by its ribbons. She felt the sun warm her nape on either side of her neatly braided bun.

I did enjoy Brian's caresses, she thought defiantly.

Enjoy? How inadequate that sounded. She had sobbed with rapture, implored Brian to satisfy her desires, and soared through the air on wings of passion. She would never feel that way again. She would never marry.

I shall never have children. She didn't require a man to buy salts for her bath or gowns for her wardrobe, but she needed Dottie's "sanctity of wedlock" to fill her belly with a wee lad or lass.

And she couldn't reside with the Stanhopes forever. Why not? Raymond had already confessed he considered Mary Angelique his daughter. After her recovery, he presented her with beautiful clothing. Surprised by her ability to add sums quickly, he admitted that, had she been a man, he'd have offered her a position in his bank, and he often brought ledgers home for her to peruse—and correct.

The Stanhopes never questioned her new identity. Why would they? Jocko's posters had depicted her likeness, and yet only somebody searching for proof of her duplicity would note the resemblance and discover Brian O'Connor's name also dominated the posters. Calliope was safe as long as she didn't stray very far from the Stanhope estate.

Why would she want to stray? She glanced toward a row of elm trees adding beauty to the south side of the house. Plum trees were set in the front yard. A fence of evergreens were placed, each three feet apart, on the north. A haven? Or a pastoral prison?

Her days progressed in a blur of pleasant activities, but nights brought dreams of Brian. Together they circled a large ballroom filled with lighted candles. He wore circus tights, and she was naked. In her dream, Brian kissed her, his tongue caressing her tongue until a soft purr trembled in her throat. Slowly, he stepped from his tights, his erection swelling. He cupped her buttocks and pulled her close, rubbing his groin against hers. Joyously, she straddled his hips. Then she rode him like a merry-go-round horse. All of a sudden, she was balanced precariously on top of a rope that stretched from one side of the room to the other, high above the floor. Still naked, she heard the sound of laughter. A man on a swaying ladder held a candle underneath the rope's strands. She shouted Brian's name, but he didn't answer. Then she smelled hemp burning—

Calliope shook her head to erase images. She always awoke before falling and never saw the face of the man who held the candle. Jocko? She must find the clown. She had read newspapers, searching for a mention of Jocko. Or Bret Johnson. Nothing. She planned to ask Raymond to hire a detective. Even though she had previously claimed no family members existed, she would suddenly recall an uncle named Bret Johnson.

Strolling past a small pond created for ducklings and goslings, Calliope approached the rear of the carriage house, where Raymond had added stables for six horses and four milch cows. Then she circled poultry coops. Although she adored most critters, Calliope loathed the cackling hens who reminded her of gillys. Hens were like the harpies of old, defiling whatever they didn't destroy. Dottie was a hen. Thom was a rather ineffective rooster. Pollyann was a pretty duckling who had not yet joined the common stockyard of grown gilly-galloos. What about Maxey? Another strutting rooster? Or a daft turkey?

Calliope wondered how they would react upon learning about her circus background. Would they send her away? Ann, with her head in the clouds, might think it "romantic." Raymond might issue one of his hearty chuckles, or he might be "mad as hops." It didn't really matter. So far, she had played her role well. They would never find out.

Inside the stables, she stood motionless, letting her eyes adjust to the dim lighting. Partitions between the stalls extended back from feeding cribs and were formed of stout plank. Only Brandywine remained boxed in her large stall.

"And how are you feelin' today, herself?" Calliope crooned. "For sure it requires a wee bit of adjustment to new surroundings, but Mr. Stanhope will spare no expense to make you feel chuffed."

Hanging her bonnet on a bridle peg, pulling open the stall gate, Calliope walked toward the mare. Her long skirts caught in the straw, so she swiftly buttoned the material up about her waist.

"What fun we shall have together, lass. You must learn how to canter in a wide circle and bow to the birds. I've seen no pigeons in this Colorado wilderness, but they have song larks and loud crows, and that shall be our band. The rabbits and other furry critters can be our audience. I've heard frogs and crickets. Should we round them up and organize a wee circus parade?"

Brandywine's ears twitched forward.

"Have I told you about my stallion, Dublin? He's blind and yet can see better than most animals. People too. He's alive, but I know not where he resides."

Calliope's one-sided conversation was interrupted by a deep growl. For a brief moment she expected to see an uncaged Bengal tiger.

"Are you daft, girl?" she admonished. "This is no

menagerie tent, and that growl belongs to a dog, not a cat."

Curious, Calliope slipped through the gate and walked over to the next stall. In the straw lay Dottie's favorite bitch, Cleopatra. Cleopatra was a Bedlington terrier who—with her gray, woolly coat—looked like a sheep. Cleopatra and her mate, Caesar, had been transported from England. Dottie hoped to breed the dogs for profit, and apparently her plan had proved successful, since Cleopatra was busy licking the afterbirth from the last of five tiny puppies.

"Oh, you adorable things." Entering the stall, Calliope dropped to her knees and smiled at the newborns.

Cleopatra growled again.

"What a pretty picture, Mrs. O'Connor."

Calliope whipped her head about then relaxed. "Good morning, Mr. Doone."

"Won't you call me Charles?"

"Only if you call me by my given name."

"Of course… Miss Mary. Mrs. Stanhope is setting out the picnic luncheon and sent me to fetch you."

"Ann or Dottie?"

"Why, er, Dot… Mrs. Thom Stanhope. She said I might find you in the carriage house."

As Calliope stood, she watched Charles cover his eyes with both hands.

"Your, um, dress, Miss Mary."

What a hullabaloo over nothing! Calliope removed the buttons from their loops and let her skirts fall. She studied Charles while his eyes were hidden. Clothed for playing football, he wore a striped jersey, striped socks, and plain black knickerbockers. His hair was a light gold, already thinning at the forehead. A mustache of the same hue shaded his upper lip. He was pleasant looking, almost handsome, undeniably a fine catch.

"Are you decent, Miss Mary?"

"Quite decent," she replied, recalling Brian's reaction to her cobwebby chemise and tattered breeches. A small thrill coursed through her body at the memory. Then she felt a piercing sorrow so acute she doubled over.

"Are you all right, Miss Mary?"

"I feel faint… from the heat," she said, her agitated mouthfuls of air giving credence to her fib.

Charles stepped forward and helped her straighten up. His fingers accidentally brushed her breasts, and she felt nothing more than she'd have felt if an upstairs maid had helped her slip on a gown. She supposed the word for what she felt was indifference.

She breathed deeply several times and saw Charles's face turn ruddy.

No, not ruddy. Crimson, like a clown's false nose. A gentleman would never gawk at a lady's heaving bosom, at least not when the lady stood close enough to witness the deed.

"My bonnet hangs on a peg with the bridles," she said, tempted to smile at the absurdity of the situation. "Perhaps you might use the brim to fan my face."

"Don't move, Miss Mary. I'll retrieve your bonnet straightaway."

While he raced toward the rack of bridles, Calliope's brief desire to smile subsided as the echo of Jocko's voice filled every corner of the stall: *When*

Brian leaves you, another man will take his place. Your body demands caresses.

Another man will take his place. Charles Doone?

Charles worked in Raymond's bank. But his father owned several parcels of land, including sites filled with gold mines. His father was ill, bedridden, practically at death's door. Charles would inherit and—

Calliope felt a sudden breeze. Charles fanned her with enthusiasm, his gaze touching upon everything except her bodice.

"That's sufficient; I feel revived," she said, wresting the bonnet from his grip.

"May I escort you to the Spring Ball, Miss Mary?"

"I suppose you must," she teased. "We have barely known each other six months, yet you have already seen me in my underskirts."

"I'll never tell, Miss Mary. It shall remain a secret between the two of us, I swear."

"Thank you, Charles." Rising on tiptoe, she kissed him lightly on the cheek.

He ensnared her nape with his hand, captured her mouth with his mouth, and thrust his tongue inside. His other hand pressed her close, and she felt the hard bulge beneath his knickers.

Once again she experienced nothing, not even a keen interest in the warm hands that were now stroking her back. Once again she heard the echo of Jocko's voice: *Your body demands caresses.*

But Jocko was wrong. Her body didn't demand caresses unless the caresses were delivered by an Irish lad named Brian O'Connor. Had Brian thrust his tongue inside her mouth, she would have shivered with ecstasy. Had Brian pressed her body against his, she'd have mounted him, encircled his hips with her long legs, and ridden him through misty rainbows.

Only Brian, her lost love, could make her purr.

At the thought, her eyes filled with tears, and she couldn't prevent an anguished sob.

Charles let her go and stumbled backwards. Perspiration streamed down his brow. "Don't cry," he said. "I'm sorry, Miss Mary. I'm a dastardly cad. Please don't cry."

Calliope dropped her bonnet and swiped at her eyes with her fingertips. His kiss had been inconsequential, evoking naught except more memories of Brian, but how would a *lady* respond to a social impropriety of this magnitude?

"I should be shot," Charles continued. "Naturally, we shall become engaged immediately. I'll find Mr. Stanhope, and—"

"Mary Angelique? Are you still inside the stables? What are you doing?"

Dottie! "Mr. Doone and I were admiring Cleopatra's new litter of pups," Calliope said, amazed at how normal her voice sounded.

"Thank you for not exposing my brutish conduct," Charles whispered.

"Cleopatra had her puppies?" Dottie appeared, her pale face flushed with anticipation. "My goodness, I am excited, but you look flustered, Mary Angelique."

"I am flattered rather than flustered, Dottie. Mr. Doone has invited me to the Spring Ball."

"Excellent. Thom and I shall act as chaperons."

Charles will propose again during the ball, thought

Calliope. Was indifference too high a price to pay for Charles Doone's name, his generosity, and his protection?

She smelled boiling herbs and pictured an old Gypsy woman gazing into a crystal ball. The diddy had been startled by what she saw. Grasping Calliope's hand, poking at her palm with a cracked fingernail, the diddy had said, "You shall be rich beyond your wildest dreams."

Charles was rich, a gilly rather than a gilly-galloo, and he could give her children. Once wed, Calliope could search for Jocko, perhaps hire an assassin to execute the clown. Her body had healed, along with her face. The doctor had promised no scars, but she carried one just the same. Jocko was a festering scab, and she must prepare herself for the ultimate confrontation with "Bret Johnson." She must be hard as steel yet flexible as a braided whiplash.

Forget love.

Forget passion.

Brian must be avenged!

Eleven

CALLIOPE VOWED TO ENJOY THE DANCE. AFTER ALL, she was young, fit, and would be escorted by an attractive suitor who might very well become her lawfully wedded husband. After a night of tossing and turning and dreaming her Brian dream, she had decided to say yes—should Charles propose again.

The Stanhopes employed a dancing master for Pollyann. Several times Calliope had joined the little girl's lessons, quickly learning the reel and quadrille, and she soon discovered that the steps were far less difficult than Angelique's toe-heel glide along the rope. Or even Brian's supple improvisations inside the cat cage.

Before her transformation, Calliope had visualized herself attending a society ball with a lion's cub draped across her shoulders, a corkscrew-tailed piggy decorating her bonnet, or, at the very least, a white silk gown adorned with glittering spangles. Much to her dismay, tonight's party was a masquerade, and guests would be clothed as participants at a royal court. How could she concoct an elaborate costume in only one day?

"Make it simple, Mary Angelique," Dottie had

advised. "I have no skill with thread and needle, but an impoverished gentlewoman such as yourself—"

"Oh, do hush!" Although she had oft mended her undergarments and sewn pockets on her skirts, Calliope loathed the tiresome task of stitching hems and tucks and seams and pleats. Thus, she wasn't very good at it.

Raymond Stanhope came to her rescue by suggesting they summon the seamstress.

The seamstress was ill and sent her young daughter Lizbet, instead. With Lizbet, Calliope flipped through pages of book illustrations then selected material from the bolts of velvet, silk, ribbons, and lace all stockpiled on shelves inside the sewing room.

"Make it simple, indeed," Calliope muttered. Perusing her book, she learned that during the second half of the seventeenth century, petticoat breeches had been all the rage and were taken up with enthusiasm by Louis XIV and his court. It was an unusual masculine fashion, resembling knee-length trousers with the appearance of a skirt. Lizbet's nimble fingers cut and stitched until Calliope's garment was bedecked with colorful loops, bows, and lace ruffles. A small apron of ribbon loops covered the front closure. Lacy pantalets started beneath the kiltlike skirt then stopped midcalf, tied below her knees with red velvet bows. Her shoes were heeled pumps with identical bows.

A waist-length blue velvet jacket covered her chemise. Peeking from the jacket's sleeves were frilly lace cuffs that matched the bottom of her pantalets. Another froth of lace cascaded down her bosom.

Calliope left her hair unbound, a simple counterpoint to the froufrou elements of her costume. The final touch was a wide-brimmed hat with a white plume, while a Columbine half mask, decorated with gold, silver, crystals, and feathers, enhanced the green of her eyes.

Lizbet, who giggled through every sentence, even when talking about her mother's illness, stayed to help Calliope dress in the complicated costume. It would soon be dark, so Lizbet had been invited to bed down in the servants' quarters, which seemed to delight her no end. She chattered away like a snickery magpie until Calliope wanted nothing more than to stop up her ears.

"You'll bewitch them all, mistress," Lizbet concluded with a giggle, admiring her handiwork.

"Please don't call me mistress. I don't own you. Neither do the Stanhopes."

"Own me?"

"Never mind, lass." Calliope studied her reflection in the full-length mirror. Her ankles were trim, her legs firm. Yet even while performing, she had always covered her limbs with heavy tights. "Lizbet, do I look too daring? Will the others be shocked?"

The young seamstress giggled. "We followed the book pictures, mistress."

"That's true. In any case, it's too late to change my clothes. Or my mind."

"Should we braid your hair?"

"No. The French lords wore long, curly wigs."

"Is that what you be? A French lord?" With a twitter, Lizbet removed Calliope's hat and tightened the colorful ribbons that held her mask in place.

"*Oui, mademoiselle*." Calliope bent one knee in a courtly bow.

"But you're a *lady*, mistress."

"Yes, Lizbet, irrefutably, I'm a lady."

"Ear-what?"

Calliope heard the echo of Brian's voice: *Can you not abandon your wordy book pages for plain circus talk? That gibberish sounds like a gilly-galloo's.*

And her response: *It does not! I sound like a lady.*

"For sure I'm a lady," she explained.

❧

"A lady would not clothe herself in short breeches and allow her limbs to show, Mary Angelique. I've never been so embarrassed in my life."

"Why are you embarrassed?" Calliope asked as she and Dottie stood inside the entrance hall, waiting for Thom and Charles to bring the carriage 'round. "I wear the costume."

"You are a member of the Stanhope party." Dottie's pale cheeks were splotched with streaks of crimson. "I cannot begin to imagine what Ann and Raymond will say when we meet them inside the club."

"Charles complimented me on my royal garb. If he approves, I don't see why you should be disturbed."

"Of course he approves. So will every man at the ball. Are you naïve, Mary Angelique? Or have you purposely contrived to appear provocative?"

"Scotsmen show their legs. Perhaps I should have left my bosom uncovered and rouged my nipples. There were courtesans who did that, you know."

"I don't know. How would I know? I am gently bred."

"So am I! Before she came to this country, my mother was a member of French aristocracy."

"Is that true?" Dottie regarded Calliope with suspicion, and yet the expression on her face betrayed a grudging respect.

"Do you dare accuse me of telling lies, Dorothy Stanhope? In any case, you expose more bosom than I."

Dottie glanced down at her chest, her chins folding into several turkey wattles. She was costumed as Queen Bess and wore a white gown with a stiff ruff. A clever choice, thought Calliope. She had learned from her illustrated history book that Elizabeth had red hair, often decorated with jewels and plumes. Even Dottie's plucked eyebrows resembled the haughty British Queen's.

"It's a sin to show your limbs," Dottie said.

"Why?"

"Lead us not into temptation, but deliver us from debauchery."

"I believe it's evil."

"You do? Then why did you choose short breeches?"

"I believe the psalm says 'deliver us from evil.'" Calliope was tempted to giggle like Lizbet. "Why is it forbidden to show legs yet proper to display a bosom?"

"What a foolish question, Mary Angelique." Dottie's brow furrowed. "Because Eve was spawned from Adam's chest… I mean ribs. Eve was spawned from Adam's ribs, and ribs are in the chest. My goodness, everyone knows that."

Watching the men approach, Calliope swallowed her retort. Instead, she smiled at Charles and dipped into the semblance of a courtly bow. Despite Dottie's horror at bare legs, Calliope knew it was the mounds of her breasts rising above the froth of lace that captured Charles's avid gaze.

"Do we not escort the two prettiest ladies in Denver, Doone?" Thom said. Like Charles, he was of average height. Like Charles, he wore a silver cloth doublet slashed at the sleeves and chest, arriving at a point over loose knee breeches. Unlike Calliope, both men wore high-heeled boots that met the bottom of their breeches and hid their legs.

In another decade, Thom would be the image of his father, thought Calliope. What Thom lacked was Raymond's sense of humor. Thom's gallant remark had been delivered sincerely, even though his wife resembled the blown glass on a parlor lamp, and one of his ladies was clothed as a lord.

"The prettiest in Colorado, possibly the whole world." Charles extended his arm. "Our carriage waits outside."

Since the night was unusually mild, they rode in a surrey with a fringed top, and soon arrived at the club's impressive portico.

The lobby was refinished in black oak and smelled of paint and polish. After hanging their wraps inside a cloakroom, Dottie and Calliope joined the other guests strolling toward the reading room, where rugs and furniture had been removed for dancing. Fresh flowers were garlanded under ceiling beams of Mexican mahogany. Logs glowed inside a tiled fireplace. A twelve-piece stringed orchestra was flanked by a bay window. An enormous, layered chandelier had lighted tapers enclosed in glass. It cast a dreamlike quality over the guests, especially since all were costumed and most wore masks. Queen Elizabeth and Marie Antoinette were predominant. There were several Napoleons, and Calliope briefly recalled Jocko's wee piggy.

The musicians began playing. A line of bachelors immediately formed in front of Calliope.

"You are the belle of the ball, my dear," Ann Stanhope said during a pause in the dancing. Ann's silver braids were twined with pearls, and she wore a gold-and-diamond coronet.

"You don't think I'm too provocative?"

"You're from the South," Ann replied as if that explained any unconventional behavior.

Before Calliope could respond, a tall man claimed her for the next dance. Resplendent in black trunk hose that clung to his muscled thighs and calves, he wore a matching black velvet doublet, decorated with gold jewel-crusted embroidery. His hair was disguised by a white wig, secured at his nape with a black bow. His mustache and beard were ebony, neatly trimmed. A black silk scarf, complete with eye slits, covered his face from his forehead to his nose. The scarf was tied behind his head like a pirate's. Calliope didn't care for his eyes. They were a lovely dark blue, but cold and piercing. Due to the mask and wig, she couldn't determine his age.

As they strolled toward the dance floor, Calliope felt the impact of a ruthless vitality. *He is more kingly than a king, and more predatory than a pirate.*

The orchestra played a waltz. The stranger guided Calliope correctly, but she felt he was molding her body to his. "With whom do I have the pleasure of sharing this dance?" she asked.

"Edward the Sixth," he replied.

"*Bonjour*, Your Majesty. I am Louis the Fourteenth."

"Yes, I know."

"What else do you know about me, sire?"

"You are Mary Angelique O'Connor, a lovely widow descended from a French countess named Angelique Kelley. How refreshing to meet an authentic aristocrat at this pretentious ball."

Calliope meticulously counted her steps, afraid she might forget the intricate movements and step on her partner's toes. "One, two, three, one, two, three... Who told you I was the daughter of a countess?"

"That red-haired woman whose face is surrounded by a ridiculous ruff."

"I do not care for your tone of voice, sir," Calliope said, thinking his voice sounded familiar. Had he been one of the guests at Ann's picnic? But she would remember a tall, bearded man with piercing blue eyes. Maybe he was a servant on the Stanhope estate. Was she daft? A servant wouldn't attend a society ball. Anyway, he sounded too educated. Educated or not, his voice sent shivers down her back, and she didn't like the feeling... not one little bit. "Mrs. Stanhope's ruff is no more ridiculous than your wig," she said.

"Is Mrs. Stanhope your sister? Auntie?"

"One, two, three... Neither. I am a ward of the... one, two, three... Stanhope family."

"O'Connor does not sound like a French name."

Calliope had the feeling he was mocking her. "My late husband was half Irish," she said with pride.

"Half Irish?"

"His mum... one, two, three... was descended from Irish royalty."

"Indeed? I had no idea the Celts possessed an

aggregate of hereditary nobility. How did the noble Mr. O'Connor die?"

"What a rude... one, two, three... question. That's none of your... one, two, three... business. I prefer that we not... one, two, three... discuss my husband's demise. May we just... one, two, three... enjoy this waltz?"

"How can you enjoy a waltz, or any other dance, when you are counting aloud?" He pressed her so close she had no choice but to silently follow his whirling steps. "I apologize if my words have stirred up unpleasant memories," he said into her ear. "Unless I miss my guess, you are very young. Were you married a long time?"

"Not long enough," she retorted, annoyed at his refusal to change the subject.

"Were there any progeny as a result of your brief union? A son? Perhaps a daughter?"

"I have no children."

As they continued twirling around the room, Calliope felt breathless. *We're dancing too fast*, she thought, knowing that they spun no faster than the others. *He's holding me too close*, she thought, knowing that, once she had stopped counting, he held her quite properly at arm's length. *My corset is too tight*, she concluded, immediately dismayed by the realization that she wore no corset.

He didn't wear gloves, and the hand grasping hers was warm, but his blue eyes were cold. She wondered what features hid beneath his mask. An old, wrinkled brow? A crooked, warty nose? Dueling scars? She would find out at midnight, when the guests who wore masks were obliged to remove them.

Why did she have this foolhardy urge to lay her head on his chest and melt against his body? She had consumed only one glass of champagne, and yet giddiness overwhelmed her. Candles flickered, and her legs felt like melting beeswax.

As if he sensed her weak dependency, he suddenly drew her close again. She made no attempt to pull away as he guided her behind a sofa and propped her back against an ornate bookcase. She felt trapped inside a dream. Behind his mask, the stranger's blue eyes glittered, reflecting rays from the chandelier. He ignored her mask and traced the contours of her face like a blind man. She stood motionless, chin high, letting him explore, tempted to bite his fingers. No. Suck his fingers.

He toyed with the froth of lace at her neckline, his bold fingers dipping lower and lower, down into her bodice. His other hand found the ribbon loops that covered the closure on her breeches. Suddenly, he slid his hand beneath her apron. Through the layers of material, she could feel his thumb move sideways, searching, caressing.

This was total madness! She tried to tell him to stop, but a whimper forced its way up her throat. The bookcase, his hands, and his body kept her from sinking to the floor. His audacious actions were hidden from view. If anybody deigned to glance her way, they would merely acknowledge a tall gentleman doubtless discussing the book titles displayed on the shelves behind her back.

Waves of heat suffused her whole body as his thumb stroked up and down.

Ann was wrong. Mary Angelique wasn't the belle of the ball. She was the bell's clapper. Unintentionally, her petticoat breeches had become an invitation, providing easy access for a thumb that had increased its pace and was now moving in small circles.

Calliope chewed her bottom lip, thinking how she must not struggle or scream. Everyone would glance her way. She would disgrace the Stanhopes, and Dottie would say "I told you so." Tears brimmed, and Calliope realized she was about to sob with frustration.

No, not frustration. Mortification. She was about to sob with the indignity of—

"Don't cry," he said, stepping backwards. "I thought your eyes were green like a cat's, but tears turn them gray."

Why did he discuss the color of her eyes? It was her body that had betrayed her. She could still feel his thumb. With an effort, she suppressed a series of quivers. Dear God, all she wanted to do was spread her legs and—

"Did you love your husband with all your heart, Mrs. O'Connor?"

His voice was hushed, tender, yet she caught his thin thread of sarcasm. Stiffening her shoulders, raising her chin even higher, she said, "I loved him more than life itself."

"Then why do you sully his memory by allowing me, a total stranger—?"

"Stop! Not another word!"

"But I must know why you allowed my bold caresses."

"I was giddy with champagne. The waltz… All that spinning made the blood rush to my head. You took advantage of my dizzy state. You knew I couldn't struggle and draw attention. You, sir, are no gentleman."

He laughed. "And you, my darling Louis, are no lady."

"I am too a lady," she said childishly, longing to stamp her foot. "I live in a fine house with servants at my beck and call. Unlike you, sir, my fiancé treats me with respect."

"You're engaged to be married?"

"Yes."

"When?"

"That is none of your concern."

For a moment, he stood silent, thoughtful. Then he said, "I apologize for my unseemly behavior, Mrs. O'Connor. In all honesty, I must admit the brevity of your costume obscured my sense of decency. I am only human, and when you responded so ardently—"

"It was the champagne!"

"Of course. Are you still giddy?"

"I am recovered, sir. Fully recovered!"

"Then let us toast your engagement." He captured two glasses from the tray of a passing waiter. "I wish you many years of happiness, Mrs. O'Connor. I'm sure you deserve it."

"Thank you." With relief, Calliope drained the bubbly liquid from her glass. She blushed when she realized how unladylike her gesture must appear, but he merely extended his full glass, which she defiantly drained just as quickly.

He didn't toast my engagement, she thought, as he led her back to Ann. What engagement? Charles hadn't proposed yet.

Watching "Edward the Sixth" disappear into the crowd, she felt a sudden sense of loss, though she couldn't understand why. After all, kingly or not, he was the worst kind of gilly-galloo. Only a gilly would assume a circus performer would respond so ardently to his damned thumb.

But he didn't know anything about her circus background. He believed her a member of French aristocracy. Or did he?

"You're ignoring Charles Doone, Mary Angelique," Dottie said, her wide skirts swaying as she approached Calliope. "Do you wish to abort any chance of an honest proposal?"

"How do you know he intends to propose?"

"He told Thom as much. After dinner you must contrive to get Charles alone so he may press his suit. I shall relax my role as chaperon until the deed is done."

The deed, indeed! Some chaperon! A total stranger nearly ravished your precious lamb while you, my vigilant shepherd, were unaware of any devious behavior.

"Did you see the man with whom I danced the waltz?" she asked. "Do you know his name?"

"Aaron Fox," Dottie replied. "He's a wealthy rancher from Colorado Springs and reputed to be a bit of a rogue."

"A bit of a rogue? He's a contemptible son of a Bedlington terrier."

"What did you say? You spoke so softly, I could not hear you."

"I said that Aaron Fox is no gentleman."

Promptly at ten o'clock, waiters moved about, beating gongs and announcing that dinner would be served upstairs. Calliope ignored the caviar, blue points and terrapin, boiled quail and ice cream. Instead, she sipped from goblet after goblet of red wine. Perhaps the wine would dim her memory of that cocksure, officious fox.

On her left sat Charles. On her right sat Percy or Harry or Frederick—she couldn't remember—who dropped his linen napkin then reached beneath the table and ran his fingers across Calliope's ankles. The second time he tried it, she ground her sharp heel into his hand and had the satisfaction of watching him try to hide his pain.

She saw the masked Aaron Fox gaze at a beautiful blonde woman costumed as Marie Antoinette. *Bare legs be damned!* Marie Antoinette had breasts that spilled from the confines of her bodice, and she constantly rubbed them against Fox's velvet doublet.

The room felt hot. Aaron Fox must be hot in his doublet, because she, Calliope Mary Angelique Louis, sweltered in her tight jacket.

Wine flowed. Calliope caught Dottie's disapproving glare but rebelliously downed the contents from another goblet before turning her face toward Charles. "Is it not hot?" she said. "Please fan my bodice with your hat."

"I fear our wine is much too strong for a woman of your gentle breeding, Miss Mary. Why don't we excuse ourselves from the dinner table, and I shall show you the clubhouse. They open the rooms to ladies this one night."

"Yes, we must leave. I cannot fathom what he sees in Marie Antoinette, for she's very obvious and sluttish to boot."

"Which Marie Antoinette?"

"So did Brian once lust after Panama," Calliope whispered.

"What did you say… dear?"

She shook her head. "You are correct, Charles. The wine is strong, and I am not used to spirits. My papa was a teetotaler," she added, almost choking on her words. In one short evening, Mum had become a countess and Sean a teetotaler.

Charles Doone tried to hide his discomfiture. "Look, dear, others are leaving. Let's join them," he said eagerly. He helped Mary rise then placed his arm about her waist to steady her. Dear God, he thought, if she swooned from the wine, or even worse, vomited, he would never hear the end of it. She looked pale, and perspiration dotted her lovely brow. He wanted to wipe that gleaming wetness away with his handkerchief, but it might prove too intimate a gesture. Mary was such a delicate creature, far more delicate than the woman Charles was supposed to marry, a robust lady whose fortune far outweighed his own. Ill as he was, Father had caused quite a row. Mary Angelique O'Connor was an orphan, a widow, and penniless. Yet her beauty had cast a spell on Charles. After she accepted his proposal, he would give her the family ring, a cabochon beryl whose greenish sheen nearly matched the color of her eyes. This time she might *allow* him to kiss her, perhaps even kiss him back. At the thought, his groin throbbed. They had better marry soon or else he'd have to purchase baggy trousers.

Later, all Calliope could recall about the sacred

male precinct was a jumbled image of liquor lockers, a larger-than-life statue whose nakedness was disguised by flower clusters, and a billiard room filled with framed etchings of fox hunters. Fox! He wasn't a member of her group.

They returned to the ballroom. A clock struck twelve. Amid shrieks of laughter, the guests unmasked. Calliope looked around for Aaron Fox. He was missing. Damn and blast! She had wanted to memorize his scarred, wrinkled face and dismiss him from her thoughts.

Dropping her mask, she saw it trampled beneath the jeweled heels of a very stout George the First.

"Would you care to walk around the grounds?" Charles asked.

"Yes, please. Perhaps fresh air might erase foxy images."

"What did you say, dear? Are you feeling all right?"

"Fine. I'm wondrous fine. Hurry, Charles." Clasping his hand in hers, Calliope swiftly wove through the guests.

Once outside, she breathed deeply. A bright moon shone through the branches of an ancient oak, outlining a fountain where cherubim spit water toward a shallow pool.

"It's a bit gusty," Charles said, ardently squeezing her hand until Brian's gold band dented her middle finger. "Should I retrieve your cloak?"

"No, thank you. This wee breeze feels wonderful after the smelly press of all those people. I feel refreshed." *And hungry!* She hadn't touched the caviar or quail, and she'd never tasted either. Damn and blast!

Releasing her hand, Charles sank to one knee. "Mary dear, I cannot wait any longer. I want you to be my—"

"Charles Doone! I'll be damned! What the hell are you doing on your knees? Praying?"

A tall man stepped out from the shadows. He wore high boots, fawn-colored trousers, a white ruffled shirt, and a maroon cutaway coat with short rounded tails. His broad chest narrowed into a lean waist. The skintight trousers dramatized muscular legs. Moonlight shone on his thick dark hair and eyes so black they appeared to have no pupils. His nose was long and narrow, his teeth very white. He was altogether the most beautiful man Calliope had ever seen. Beautiful? Was she daft? This man was striking, devilish. If Aaron Fox was more kingly than a king, this man was more regal than a prince.

He puffed on a slim cheroot then said, "Aren't you going to introduce me to your pretty lad, Charlie?"

"She's no lad," Charles said, rising to his feet. "She's a lady."

"Yes, I can see that."

"Maxey Stanhope, I have the pleasure of introducing Mary Angelique O'Connor." Charles coughed and waved away a cloud of cheroot smoke. "Mrs. O'Connor, Mr. Stanhope."

Calliope felt as if all the color had drained from her face. So this was Maxey, the man she had vowed to merely tolerate. This handsome, princely devil was Raymond's prodigal son.

Twelve

"How do you do, Mr. Stanhope," Calliope said, hoping she didn't sound as flabbergasted as she felt.

"I do very well, thank you."

The air hummed with tension. She watched the two men as if she were a great distance away rather than close enough to see the sweat beading their brows.

"Has Charlie shown you the cherub's pool?" Cheroot smoke clouded Maxey dark eyes. "Toss a coin in the water, and your dreams will come true." He withdrew a penny from his pocket and pitched it toward the shimmering spray. "Make a wish, Mrs. O'Connor."

"It's your coin, sir, therefore your wish."

He stared at her wedding band. "My wish is you have an old husband with perpetual indigestion who would tend to ignore his young wife's indiscretions."

"Stanhope!" Charles draped one arm across Calliope's shoulders. "That's his attempt at wit, Mary. He means no harm."

"Yes, I do." With a grin, Maxey crushed the cheroot beneath his boot heel. "Does your husband conveniently linger inside, Mrs. O'Connor?"

"I am a widow, sir." Calliope raised her chin and gave him what she hoped was her best glare of disdain.

His grin faded. "Sorry. As you have just discovered, Doone has far better manners than I."

"If you had any manners at all, Stanhope, you would leave us alone." Extricating his arm, Charles smoothed his crumpled doublet. "I was about to ask Mary a very important question."

Maxey turned toward Calliope. "And what would your answer be, Mrs. O'Connor?"

"I have no idea what Mr. Doone plans to ask me."

"Does Mr. Doone usually indulge in casual conversation on bended knee?"

She was saved from making a reply by a gust of wind that sent her plumed hat spinning down the path.

Charles chased it.

Grasping her hand, Maxey sprinted in the opposite direction.

"Wait! Are you daft? Let me loose!"

He dropped her hand. "I would never take a beautiful woman for a stroll against her will."

"A stroll? We were running so fast I nearly fell head over heels."

"I've already fallen head over heels in love, Mary."

"Don't be ridiculous." Despite her admonition, she smiled.

"Mary." He recited her name dispassionately, as if it were a foreign word. "That doesn't sound right."

Calliope didn't allow her smile to falter, even though her heart skipped a beat. Had Maxey seen Jocko's circus posters? How could he? The few that remained in Denver were surely dulled beyond recognition by inclement weather. Her circus had played Boston after Mum's fall, but she had not scheduled Massachusetts again. There was too much competition from P.T. Barnum's Greatest Show on Earth.

"Mary is plain," said Maxey. "Mary is shy. Miss Mary would never attend a ball clothed in short breeches. So I shall call you Angelique, or better yet, Angel."

"And I shall call you Mr. Stanhope. Besides, you speak nonsense. An angel wouldn't wear breeches, either." Calliope felt her shoulders relax. Maxey didn't know her real identity.

"My horse is nearby," he said, "tied to an elm, still hitched to his sulky."

"Sulky?"

"I foolishly indulged in a small race for a rather large wager."

"Did you win or lose?"

"Unfortunately, my trotter stumbled."

"Is he all right?"

"You show concern for my horse but not me?"

"You seem fit, Mr. Stanhope."

"Thank you, Angel."

"Don't call me Angel!"

"Do you know much about horses, Mrs. O'Connor?"

"I have worked with them my whole life."

"In what capacity?"

I trained them to gallop around a ring and leap through hoops of fire.

"My father raised stock on our Georgia plantation," she replied. "But we lost everything during the war."

"Didn't the government make reparations to Southern land owners?"

"My mother, father, and brother are deceased. Our plantation was sold for a pittance to pay the taxes. Why did you ask if I knew about horses?"

"I was wondering if you would tend to mine." Turning left, Maxey walked toward a grove of elm trees. "I might have lamed him while racing."

Calliope understood full well his ploy to draw her away from the clubhouse, but she followed, thinking how at the age of seven she had appeared in a circus jolly starring all the clowns. The playlet was about a pied piper who lured rats and children from a village. Only fourteen, Brian had played the Piper. Clowns portrayed rats and villagers. Calliope, along with the other circus children, had followed Brian's music. After the performance ended, she'd attached herself to Brian's heels like a small shadow, still hearing his music in her head.

Was Maxey Stanhope another Pied Piper? Or a rat?

"Charles must be searching for me," she said, hoping the sound of her voice would dispel her sudden whim-whams.

"Later you can tell him you felt ill, perhaps a headache. Doone is a gentleman and would never question a lady's infirmity."

"By the tone of your voice, I assume you are not a gentleman."

"I'm a black sheep, Angel. Black sheep have a certain reputation, so if you want to return to the ball, I won't chide or scold. I'll even lead you inside. It would not hurt this black sheep's reputation to be seen with a beautiful lad."

Calliope's mind raced. Dottie, chaperon and

shepherd, waited inside the clubhouse. What would Dottie say when she saw her precious lamb without Charles? Escorted by Maxey, her infamous brother-in-law!

Raising her chin, Calliope continued walking until they reached the horse—a roan with a cream-colored mane and tail. Maxey's two-wheeled sulky was meant for one person, but after unfastening the reins and seating himself, he lifted her up and settled her on his lap. "I'm glad you wear breeches," he said, "for a full gown and petticoats would never adapt."

She leaned back against his chest. His arms encircled her shoulders while his hands flipped the reins. Her head fit neatly under his chin. His thigh muscles tensed, adjusting to her weight as the sulky's wheels hit trail ruts. Such a strange sensation, she thought. Could two people make love while riding a sulky? She would have to ask Brian.

But Brian was dead, and that familiar realization extinguished any ardent response she might have felt. "Where are we going?" she murmured into the wind.

"What did you say?"

She shook her head. It didn't matter. This whole evening was an illusion—the ball, Aaron Fox, the sudden appearance of Maxey Stanhope.

I can never marry Charles! Headache? Charles could be manipulated, but he wasn't stupid.

She twisted Brian's wedding band with her thumb and first finger. For over ten months she had performed the role of a lady. Once, a long time ago, she'd blown out her birthday candles and wished her name was Mary. Years later, she had vowed to accumulate a fortune and thumb her nose at gillys. "I'll spit in their faces," she'd told Jocko.

But fountain cherubs spit. Ladies did not.

A lady had to wear the correct undergarments, keep her legs covered but expose her bosom, pretend to be weak. A lady had to weave a web of lies in order to maintain her pose. A lady must not show rapture or desire.

Calliope wasn't sure how she felt about Maxey Stanhope, but he seemed amusing, and she was tired of playing the lady.

After a short ride, Maxey tugged at the reins, lifted Calliope from his lap, set her feet on the ground, and joined her.

"Where are we, Mr. Stanhope?" she asked. "I have the feeling I've been here before."

"Won't you call me Maxey?"

Ignoring him, she walked forward. The capricious moonlight shone down on a clearing. Even after months of rain and snow, remnants of the Sean Kelley Circus remained—blackened wagons, a piece of faded banner-line canvas, an old broom she had once used to wash her elephant.

Her charred silver wagon stood sentinel over a landscape that lay under some dread enchantment. Lions and tigers peered at Calliope through eyes blinded with the reflection of flames. Accusing eyes. Horrible eyes.

"It was the leprechaun," she cried. "It wasn't my fault!"

"What wasn't your fault, Mary?"

"Can't you hear them?"

"Who?"

"They were trapped inside chutes and cages. The people had a chance to crawl free but not the animals. Can't you hear their screams?"

The river flowed, winding past Calliope's horrific image of chaos and destruction. She could picture smoke-blackened performers toting buckets of water. But they were too late to save her circus, too late to save Brian.

Even though her body had become a solid block of ice, Calliope felt perspiration dot her brow. Stomach churning, she ran behind a copse of prickly bushes and dropped to her knees. She pictured center ring; a spotted pony harnessed to a cart with the words HOTEL DES PIGEONS. The birds were supposed to land on her outstretched arms. Instead, their wings fluttered inside her throat. She issued forth a desperate moan, clearing a path between the pigeon wings, clearing a path for the red wine that gushed through her open mouth.

"Mary? I'm here. Just go with it, sweetheart."

Wings fluttered again.

Maxey's hands grasped her shoulders. "Spirits have a tendency to fool you, Mary," he said. "A widow of your gentle breeding should have been warned. I'd bet my last dollar, if I had one, that Doone wanted you corned before he rendered his proposal."

"No," she said with a strangled gasp. "You don't understand."

"Sure I do." Releasing her shoulders, Maxey hunkered down. "I, myself, have used the very same ploy. Not for any honest proposal, but to relax the limbs and ease the conscience."

Ignoring his confession, Calliope staggered to her feet. "It wasn't my fault!" she screamed as she ran toward a large oak and beat her fists against the gnarled bark.

"What is it, Mary?" This time Maxey's voice sounded testy. "What's wrong?"

"Why did you bring me here?"

"It used to be one of my favorite haunts, but I can see there's been some sort of fire."

"Fire? It was a holocaust. People were trampled and burned to death." Vaguely, she realized her protective shell was cracking. In another moment she'd become hysterical, incautious, but she couldn't stop.

"The animals," she cried. "Lions, tigers, monkeys. Dear sweet monkeys. I fed them peppermints. The horses…"

Unable to continue, she covered her face with her hands and wept. She felt Maxey's fingertips gently caress the back of her neck. "I'm sorry, Mary," he said, his voice soft. "I didn't know. I was far away from Colorado. It was a circus fire, wasn't it? Mother wrote me a letter. My little niece was almost killed. I assume you attended the performance."

"Are you daft? I was—" Calliope's words stuck in her throat. She felt the moonlight catch in her tears as the trees whirled and the stars disappeared and the ground rose up to meet the sky. She shut her eyes.

❧

Calliope opened her eyes and gazed up at Maxey looming above her. The smell of his cheroot cleared away her first confusion. Her knuckles hurt, as if she'd lost a fistfight with a tree. She felt the hard earth beneath her body and struggled to a sitting position. "Where are we?"

"Farther down the river."

"Why is your roan not hitched to his sulky?"

"It seemed more prudent to transport a swooning woman on horseback." Maxey retrieved a silver flask from his coat pocket. "Hair of the dog, Mary?"

"What dog?"

"This is whiskey, not wine. A taste will clear your head and settle your stomach."

"No, thank you," she said then reconsidered and reached for the flask. Although her rebellious tummy had stopped churning, her breath tasted like burnt coffee. After several sips, she felt a warm languor infuse her body.

"Lean on me, Mary." Kneeling behind her, Maxey stroked a few errant curls away from her eyes. "Do you feel better?"

"Yes, Mr. Stanhope." In truth, she did feel better.

His lips brushed her forehead while one hand toyed with the froth of lace at her bodice.

"Please, Mr. Stanhope."

"Maxey." Tilting her chin so her head was cradled against his shoulder, he nuzzled her earlobe, and she felt his fingers travel beneath the lace, between the mounds of her breasts.

"You are so beautiful," he whispered, his hand cupping her breast, his other hand pressing against her breeches.

Just like Aaron Fox!

She pulled away and assumed a crescent shape, tightly pressing her knees to her chest. Then reaching for the flask again, she remembered Maxey's remark about spirits relaxing the limbs and easing the conscience.

As if he had read her mind, he said, "Would you care for more whiskey?"

"No, thank you. I appreciate your concern, Mr. Stanhope, but we must return to the ball."

"Now?"

"Yes. It's hard to explain, but this place holds memories I cannot dismiss."

"Poor Angel. You fed the circus monkeys, and then they were trapped by the fire, along with the horses. It must have been a harrowing experience for a girl raised on a plantation. You said you worked with horses."

His voice was so tender she wanted nothing more than to nestle her head between his shoulder and chin. She wanted to tilt the flask to her lips until she was beyond memories, beyond modesty, beyond shame.

Still on his knees, he kissed the nape of her bowed head. Then he dipped his hand between her arms until he fondled her breast again.

"Please stop. Passion is for paramours," she cried, parroting Dottie. With profound relief, she felt Maxey's hand immediately withdraw.

"Despite my reputation," he said, "I would never take a virtuous woman against her will." Helping her rise, he brushed away twiggy debris.

"I'm sorry, truly I am," she murmured, "but I want to go back."

Back in time before the fire, she thought. Before her words with Jocko. Merciful God, it wasn't her fault. Jocko had set the blaze.

Or had he?

Jocko hadn't been anywhere near the circus when Mum fell from her rope. Why would Jocko lure Papa to the pie wagon? And why would he place the woman he professed to love in the cat cage and then sacrifice his wee piggy to save her?

The answer was simple. Jocko had nothing to do with the other so-called accidents. He had, however, set the fire. And she would see him burn in hell for it.

Oh, if she could only toss a coin into the cherub's pool and wish away the fire, wish away Brian's death. But a penny couldn't change the diddy's fortune. A whole mountain of gold couldn't reverse her loveless fate.

She remembered her Big Top as it had once stood, capturing within its canvas the sounds of laughter and applause. She pictured Sean's twinkling green eyes and the clear lilt of his voice: "Lay-deez and gen-tul-men—"

Without warning, the image became distorted, and she pictured her papa with a piece of scantling driven through his head. "Lay-deez and gen-tul-men, the Sean Kelley Circus sets forth a truly wondrous sight. Can ye not see the specters of me dead animals? Look skyward and watch me own angel tiptoe across the stars. Watch the horses gallop through shards of moonlight. Direct your attention to the fire-garbed monkeys who swing from the branches of trees. Pre-senting Brian O'Connor, ghostly cat tamer of this haunted horizon."

Calliope felt sick to her stomach again.

Silently, Maxey mounted the roan and swung her

up behind him. As they rode, she consciously willed circus images to fade. She couldn't go back in time. Memories made her weak. Tears hurt.

When they reached the club's portico, Maxey helped her dismount, but he stayed atop his roan. "Are you planning to accept Doone's proposal?" he asked.

"Yes. Perhaps. I don't know."

"Marry me instead."

"Are you daft? You know nothing about me."

"I know you have courage. You rode my sulky."

"That was impulsive, not brave."

"You had the courage to wear breeches and show your legs."

Damn the petticoat breeches! She should have costumed herself as a courtly monk or nun. Maxey was making fun of her, mimicking Charles Doone's honest proposal. She didn't like the sound of Maxey's laughter, and she would not stand here like a stick, the target of his demented amusement.

"My breeches," she said, "were an impulse as well. Ordinarily, I am not so unladylike, so imprudent. Good night, Mr. Stanhope."

Maxey grinned. "We have already become more intimate than most enslaved couples," he said.

"Enslaved?"

"Did I say enslaved? I meant engaged." He laughed. At the sound, the roan reared up, but with a press of his muscular thighs, Maxey controlled his mount. "After all, I held your pretty head."

She sighed. "Mr. Stanhope, I admit my distress was rather intimate, and most gentlemen—"

"Black sheep."

"Most black sheep would have scurried away. Your assistance was vastly appreciated. And now, good night."

"Wait! Would you prefer a more traditional proposal?" Sliding from the roan's haunches, Maxey knelt. "Widow O'Connor, we have known each other a very short time, but the few precious moments I held you in my arms, conscious and unconscious, I was totally captivated—"

"Hush! Please get up. Someone might hear you."

"I am well aware of manners and conventions, believe me, but I have so enjoyed your company, my angel. If you delay your answer to Doone, I would consider it an honor to vie for your hand, not to mention the rest of your beautiful body. I wish to become your wedded bedmate and the father of your brats."

"Brats?"

"Children are such a nuisance, don't you agree?"

"No, I don't."

Calliope felt a sudden shiver of apprehension. Maxey seemed like an amusing rogue, but she sensed an unpleasantness beneath that handsome facade. What was he hiding? An evil soul? A diabolical spirit? Was he a demon rather than a devil? Despite her vow to forget the circus, she must be letting memories affect her, because she had the whim-whams again.

"Allow me to remove your breeches, sweetheart," Maxey continued, "and we can make babies right away. Your legs, sorry, your *limbs* are lovely, Mary."

"Do hush." Regardless of her foreboding fancies, her fear of discovery, and her ire at his bantering tone, she smiled. "First you must play whist with my guardian. You must lose on purpose and—"

"Who *is* your guardian?"

"Aaron Fox," she said, blurting the first name that came to mind. "Have you met him?"

"No. But I've heard of him. An elderly widower from Colorado Springs. If I recall correctly, he's childless."

An elderly widower? Funny, he didn't seem all that old. Of course, his wig might have hidden a bald pate. But his beard didn't display one gray hair. Nasty old reprobate! She shuddered at the memory of his bold caresses.

"Fox is very wealthy and not particularly altruistic," Maxey said. "How did you become his ward?"

"It's a long story." Suddenly, she was tired of this game. Tired? Exhausted. Her emotions had been jostled by too many back flips and somersaults. "I'll be honest with you, Mr. Stanhope. Aaron Fox is not my guardian. I met the man only tonight and danced one waltz with him."

"He must have made an impression, Angel. I'm jealous."

"And why would a black sheep be jealous of an old goat?"

"Mary! I've been searching all over for you." Charles's shrill voice was accusatory. "Where have you been? I couldn't find your hat," he added lamely.

"Due to the wine you allowed her to consume, Charlie, Mrs. O'Connor was violently ill," Maxey said, his voice oozing sincerity. "Then she fainted. I revived her, but I fear she's about to swoon again. Don't just stand there. Fetch some salts."

"You fetch the salts. I'll take care of Mary."

"Don't be an ass. Can't you see she's still indisposed?

Lean on me, Mrs. O'Connor. Let me help you to the steps. Hurry, Doone!"

Charles turned and raced toward the entrance doors.

"That was cruel," said Calliope.

"I did it to protect your reputation, Angel. Doone will be back in a few minutes, so please give me your answer."

"What answer?"

Maxey stared down into her eyes. "I must wed soon. It's somewhat complicated, but—"

"Hush! I thought you were teasing. You can't be serious."

"I've never been more serious in my life. You're beautiful, intelligent. Most heiresses are fat, grumpy, and show physical defects that—"

"Heiresses? What makes you think I have money?"

"I realize you lost your family fortune, sweetheart, but surely your husband left an inheritance."

"Dear Lord above!"

"I have no time to court you, Mary. If you prefer, I can propose again on bended knee."

"Don't bother. I can't marry you." When Maxey drew her close and tried to kiss her, she pulled away. "Try that once more, and I shall slap your face."

"But you'll like my kisses, Angel, and that's a promise."

"I'm not certain I like you, Mr. Stanhope. In any case, you've made a mistake. I'm not an heiress. I don't have a penny. I couldn't even wish at the cherub's pool."

"What a shame. Good-bye, lovely Mary. My family has a summer home in Colorado Springs, so I doubt

I'll see you again." He swung his long legs across the roan's haunches. "I don't usually make mistakes."

Calliope watched him nudge his horse with his heels. *You fortune-hunting gilly-galloo!* Shivering with trepidation, she felt his dark presence remain even after he'd turned the corner and vanished from sight.

She recalled her strange sensations during their sulky ride. If they had reached a different destination, would he have used his charms to seduce her? Would she have given in to his demands?

She felt her cheeks bake at the memory of Aaron Fox, and she almost groaned out loud. She wasn't a lady. She would never be a lady.

Just like Maxey wasn't a black sheep. He was a sheep in wolf's clothing.

I don't usually make mistakes.

"You've made two mistakes this very night, Maxey Stanhope," she murmured. "I have no valuable assets except for the mare your father gave me, and you shall see me again. Oh yes, boy-o, you shall see me again. Sooner than you think!"

Brian O'Connor stood outside the Men's Club, not far from the back entrance. He knew he should return to the club room where his blonde "Marie Antoinette" would spew her fury at his neglect, but he felt catawampously chewed up—utterly defeated—and Aaron Fox, by word or deed, never displayed that kind of emotion.

Damn Calliope Kelley!

"She's a conniving bitch!" he said aloud.

Abandoning him, abandoning her circus, choosing greener, more lavish pastures. She had run away without a qualm, hadn't even stayed long enough to see if the man she professed to love was injured or dead, while he had been desolate, nearly driven mad with grief at her disappearance.

After the fire, he and Jocko had searched high and low, but she had covered her tracks well. Not a trace—until tonight. He had been tempted to ignore the summons from his father's best friend's daughter, asking him to attend the ball as her escort. He had accepted reluctantly. Traveled to Denver. Entered the crowded club room. And immediately recognized Calliope. Who could forget those long legs beneath her provocative petticoat breeches? He learned she was posing as Mary Angelique O'Connor, a ward of Raymond and Ann Stanhope. A least she had kept her mother's name. What daft whimsy had made her add O'Connor?

It was reality rather than whimsy that had led to Brian's name change. After the fire and his fruitless search for Calliope, he had confronted his father and demanded Aaron Fox shell out enough money to take care of the circus performers' medical expenses. But instead of paying Brian to go away, the elderly Fox had been overjoyed to discover he'd sired a son, had even stated he'd gladly cover all medical expenses and acknowledge Brian as his son and heir on the condition Brian assume the name Aaron Fox III. A fair and not very difficult bargain, especially since Brian had quickly established a friendship with his father. Then, eventually, a fondness that was more binding than mere benevolence.

Abruptly, Brian turned and stomped toward the back door, his mind as whirly as a merry-go-round. He had seen the gold band on Calliope's left hand and wondered why she still wore it. Somebody said she had rescued the Stanhope's granddaughter from certain death during a horrific circus fire. Perhaps his lovely equestrian hadn't had time to remove the ring and, instead, had concocted a story about a dead husband. Widowhood was certainly more respectable than admitting she had recited her marriage vows in the midst of a violent windstorm, within the confines of a wobbly circus wagon.

She should have stuck around a wee while longer. The Stanhopes were undeniably wealthy, but compared to Aaron Fox, they were small toads in the puddle. Had she not fled, Calliope would have been wealthy beyond her wildest imagination.

He, Brian O'Connor, born on the wrong side of the blanket, was wealthy beyond *his* wildest imagination. For now he was content to manage his father's vast ranching empire, but he fully intended to amass his own fortune.

Calliope had seemed so heartsick during their waltz together, when they talked about her "dead husband." The steadfast sorrow in her gray-green eyes—what a fine performance! She had always been an exceptional player inside the ring, but she was an even better actress outside the ring. He had initiated a seduction, purposely goading her into an ardent response, hoping she'd recognize him. On the verge of admitting his true identity, she had taunted him with her betrothal.

He had found her only to lose her again.

Thirteen

CALLIOPE REMOVED BRANDYWINE'S SIDESADDLE. NEXT to the saddle she placed kid-leather boots, skirt, bustle, petticoat, and every crinoline save one. Then she grasped Brandywine's mane, swung easily up onto the mare's back, and with heels and hands, guided her 'round the clearing in a wide circle.

"Very good, lass. Let's try a back flip, shall we?"

Knotting the reins, she rose and shifted her stocking-clad feet until they adjusted to Brandywine's smooth canter.

Calliope leapfrogged, but it felt wrong. Her jump wasn't high enough, and her corset thwarted movement. Instead of flipping, she landed astraddle.

Dare she remove her blouse and corset? It was an hour past cockcrow. Last night's warm weather and capricious breezes had caused fog to roll in, so she was hidden from the house and stables. But the child wandered about, and Pollyann would enjoy nothing more than tattling. Pollyann would tattle on God if she saw God somersaulting atop a horse.

Dottie, Thom, Ann, even Raymond still slept. Exhausted, Calliope had slept too, but the dream had plagued her slumber—the jut of Brian's erection as he stepped from his tights; candles flickering; the sound of laughter; the smell of singed hemp.

This time something new had been added. In her dream she awoke to Brian's tender strokes across her back. "I'm here, puss," he said. Clinging to him, she felt his muscles tauten, and she wanted him with a hunger she had never known before. She nuzzled her face against his belly and then looked up. The man whose belly she nuzzled was none other than Aaron Fox. His blue eyes glittered through his face mask as he said, "Did you love your husband with all your heart, Mrs. O'Connor?"

Then she awoke, for real, to find her pillow stained with tears. Dragging herself out of bed, donning her clothes, she had felt a deep sense of her own betrayal.

Brandywine nickered, circling in an easy gait, her hooves skimming the dirt.

"Yes," said Calliope, "this is a daft game, and the foggy dew makes your hide slick. Should we be trying one more time before we quit?"

Rising to her toes, Calliope leaped high, flexing her shoulders, swinging her arms, holding her breath against the pain of her heavily starched corset.

"I did it!" She laughed. "It's like learning to read, Brandywine. One never forgets. Mum taught me ropewalking when I was a wee lass. I wonder if I could walk a rope."

Calliope glanced around the clearing. Even if she managed to stretch a rope between leaves and branches, she'd be seen. A *lady* didn't tiptoe across the sky.

Straddling Brandywine again, she reached for the reins. "Whoa. Such a pretty lass."

"Pretty, indeed."

"Who's there?" For a moment, Calliope thought the man walking toward her was Brian. He was tall and dark. Fog swirled, softening his features. After the first moment of shock had passed, she sat frozen, not knowing whether to dismount and run into his arms or shriek at the top of her lungs.

She did neither. Weaving her fingers through Brandywine's silken mane, she whispered, "Brian took wing and left me grounded. He's gone evermore."

"Good morning, Mary. Are you a lovely spirit or merely an apparition caused by my consumption of spirits?"

"Good morning, Mr. Stanhope. How long have you been watching me?"

"I followed the sound of your laughter. I thought I'd never see you again. Are you by any chance a ghost?" Maxey reached out and lifted her down, and she smelled whiskey on his shirt and breath. "You seem to be flesh and blood, Mary." He paused, eyeing her crinoline and rolled-up sleeves. "Most especially flesh."

She blushed, pushed him away, and retrieved her skirt and the rest of her undergarments. "What are you doing here?"

"I live here. This is my home."

"It is my home too."

He scowled. "You're no servant. Doone would never

escort a servant to the Spring Ball. Pollyann's governess? But a governess would never wear breeches."

"Won't you please, please forget the foolhardy breeches?"

"Who the hell are you?"

Calliope smiled impishly, enjoying his consternation. "A gentleman would curb his profanity and hide his eyes while I put my clothes back on. Oh dear, I forgot. You're a black sheep. Pray tell me, sir, have you been expelled from Williams College?"

For a moment he seemed at a complete loss. Then he said, "Damn! Last night I thought your name sounded familiar, but I didn't—Mary O'Connor! You saved my niece from the circus fire. Mother wrote about your courage." He scrutinized her body from head to toe, as if she were a butterfly, albeit a half-dressed butterfly, nailed to a corkwood tree. "How fortunate that not one scar mars your beauty."

"Why? What difference would it make?

"None," he said, and she heard the false sincerity in his voice. But she also realized her question was unreasonable. Visible or invisible, scars made a big difference.

Maxey lowered himself to a tree stump, crossed his long legs, and lit a cheroot. "Did you accept Doone's proposal, Mrs. O'Connor?"

"Why aren't you asleep, Mr. Stanhope?"

"Why aren't you?"

"I awoke early, on purpose, because I wanted to ride. Alone." With annoyance, she realized Maxey had no intention of leaving. He still wore the fawn trousers and ruffled white shirt from last night. Heavy lids hooded his black eyes, smudged by fatigue, and he needed a shave. "Has the family learned of your homecoming, Mr. Stanhope?"

"I shall announce my return during breakfast. It will be difficult for Father to sustain his wrath when his belly is full of fried chicken, corn bread, eggs, and bacon."

She recalled Raymond's barely suppressed anger over his son's behavior and Ann's insistence that Maxey's companions—not her son—had committed aberrant acts with a young lady of doubtful breeding. Staring down at Maxey's handsome, brooding face, Calliope said, "That is a poor diversion. Raymond's displeasure will not be digested along with his bacon."

"Do you honestly believe Father will send me away? Even black sheep have mothers. If Father disinherited me, it would break my mother's heart."

"How cold and calculating you sound, Mr. Stanhope."

"Maxey. What if I told you I was repentant?"

"Are you?"

"Of course."

"Why were you expelled?"

"I'm too old for school."

"How old are you?"

"When General Lee surrendered to Grant, I was seventeen."

"General Lee surrendered ten years ago!"

"After the war, Mother suggested Father send me on a Grand Tour if I promised to attend college."

"You obviously don't honor your promises, Mr. Stanhope."

"How can you say that? I attended. There was no promise to finish and graduate."

"It was implied. Why were you expelled? Old age seems a lame excuse."

"I'm afraid I attempted to organize a rugby team at Williams and neglected my classes. And my examinations. The chancellor was extremely rude. If I had licked his boots I might have been given a second chance, but I don't lick boots."

"I assume your motives—rugby, whatever that is— were in the best interest of the college, Mr. Stanhope."

"Maxey," he insisted, rising to his feet and crushing the cheroot beneath his boot heel.

"You're not too old for school. You're too young!"

"You've wounded me deeply, Angel, so I'll confess. Rugby wasn't the only reason for my dismissal. I don't want to shock you. Intimate details might cause you to swoon. On the other hand, you're a widow. I'm glad. There are certain rituals of the boudoir—"

"Hush! Not another word, or I shall saddle Brandywine and—"

"Brandywine? Is that her name? She's a beauty. Where did you get her?"

"From your father. A gift."

"She looks valuable. Father was very generous. He must admire you."

"I admire him. He works hard."

"Father established his fortune by fulfilling a need, Mary. The common man will spend his last cent on a beverage that causes him to ignore responsibilities and, in most cases, act the fool."

Fools are dangerous.

Where had she heard that before? Jocko!

People laugh at clowns but underestimate fools.

"You drink spirits," said Calliope. "Are you a clown?"

"Clown?"

"I meant fool."

"I'm always in control, Mary. I abhor drunks."

"But last night, I was corned…" She paused, consumed with embarrassment.

"That was Doone's fault. He wanted to take advantage of a young, virtuous—"

"Fiddle-faddle! I drank too much wine."

He regarded her with raised eyebrows. "Your honesty is refreshing, Mary. However, since I witnessed your distress, we can now be chums as well as lovers."

"We shall never be lovers, Mr. Stanhope." This conversation was treading on dangerous ground, and Calliope decided to change the subject. "From what I've heard, you don't care how your father amassed his fortune. When did you develop scruples?"

"Last night. I held you in my arms after you fainted, and you were so vulnerable, completely at my mercy."

"I was unconscious!"

"That's when I developed scruples. Did you accept Doone's proposal?"

"That, sir, is none of your concern."

She stroked Brandywine's sleek neck, thinking how Charles hadn't rendered another proposal. He had believed her explanation of a headache and seemed solicitous, but Maxey's appearance had doused Charles's ardor as effectively as the fog had blanketed the distant mountains. And Charles had said something very strange. "No parent would allow their daughter to be alone with Stanhope, Miss Mary," he had stated. "Maxey is dangerous."

Of course Maxey was dangerous, thought Calliope. If the lady gillys were all like Dottie, they'd be scared of passion and rapture, probably quake in their slippers.

"Doone's proposal is my concern," said Maxey, "for I plan to marry you."

"We've been through this before, Mr. Stanhope, and to be perfectly honest, I'm in no mood for a clem."

"What's a clem?"

Damn and blast! "It's an Irish expression. My late husband used the word often. It means an argument."

"I'd rather kiss than clem, Angel. Let's celebrate our pending nuptials."

"You can't marry me. I told you last night. I'm not an heiress."

"You didn't say anything about saving Pollyann's life and becoming my father's ward. Don't you understand what that means?"

"Yes! Your parents will take care of me for the rest of my life. So you see, I don't need a husband, nor do I want a black sheep."

"But I want you, Mary, and I need you. Father will *digest* his anger at the announcement of our betrothal. He'll be delighted at my selection of you for my wife and my plan to settle down and produce many sons. I know, I know—" He raised his arms as if to ward off a blow. "I said children were a nuisance. But having a child with you would be different."

"Why?"

"Because your background is impeccable. So is your lovely body."

"You are presumptuous, Mr. Stanhope."

"If we are to be wed, you must call me Maxey."

"Mr. Stanhope, the answer to your proposal is no."

"Am I so ugly?"

"That's a woman's question. Anyway, it doesn't affect my decision."

"Do you believe I would be unfaithful?"

"Yes."

"You said you liked children."

"I do."

"Don't you want to have children of your own?"

"Yes."

"Will you marry me?"

"No."

Maxey circled her waist and drew her close. "I need you," he said.

She wanted to reject the intimacy of his arms. If he tried to kiss her, she would knee him in his nether parts. But he merely pressed her face against his chest and stroked her tangled hair.

The smell of his shirt reminded her of Sean.

Marriage, however, was out of the question. For one thing, Maxey didn't love her. He needed her. She didn't trust him, not one whit. And suppose the rumors about his deviant behavior were true?

On the other hand, she wanted a family of her own. She wanted a life of her own. Charles Doone was the answer. Charles wasn't dangerous. Charles was safe.

Charles was boring.

The fog had evaporated, allowing sunshine to warm her body. Maxey continued stroking her hair, his touch gentle, tender, undemanding. "Beautiful Mary, beautiful angel," he crooned. Then he swiftly unbuttoned her blouse, his fingers caressing the rising swell of her breasts.

She struggled to escape his touch.

He grasped her tightly at arm's length, bent forward, and lowered his head. His teeth tugged at her chemise ribbons. His lips nuzzled beneath her open bodice. "You smell like flowers," he said, raising his face, drawing her closer, and planting a kiss on her unwilling lips.

She wrenched herself free, thinking *I warned you last night*, and slapped his face. "You smell like a brewery," she fumed, sorely tempted to spit.

He laughed, the rogue. "A brewery, my innocent Mary, is where one makes malt liquor. I have consumed too much corn whiskey, but that is not why I kissed you. Furthermore, I despise people who blame their conduct on John Barleycorn."

"Liar! Last night you said you gave ladies wine and whiskey to relax the limbs and ease the conscience."

"Did I?" A grin flickered. Then his expression turned somber. "You have nothing to fear from me, sweetheart. I told you during the ball I'd never take a virtuous woman against her will, and in your case, not until we are wed. This I swear before God."

She heard the echo of Brian's voice: *I don't intend to lie with you, not until we are wed*, but before she could tell Maxey they would never wed, Brandywine whinnied, a dog barked, and a child sang, "Way down upon the swan river, far, far, away. That's where my harp is turning over. That's where the old folks play."

With shaky fingers, Calliope retied her bodice ribbons and buttoned her blouse.

"All the world is sad and dreary," sang Pollyann. She walked into the clearing and stopped midstride. "Uncle Maxey, Uncle Maxey, you're home."

He lifted the child and swung her around. "It's the Swanee River, sweetheart, and hearts turn over, not harps."

"That's silly, Uncle Maxey. I saw a harp. It's big and wiggles unless you hold it still. Hearts are inside your bosom, so they can't turn over."

"Bosoms can't turn over?"

Pollyann giggled. "No, Uncle Maxey, hearts."

"Hearts do lots of things we can't see," Calliope said, regaining her composure. "Hearts can even break," she added softly.

"If your heart broke, you'd die," Pollyann announced in a solemn voice.

"You sound like your mother," said Maxey.

"Have you met Mary, Uncle Maxey? I went to the circus and there was a big fire and Mary saved me but my dress burned. Then I woke up and cried."

"Because the circus burned?"

"No, because my dress burned. It was my best dress. Dolly burned too. She was my best dolly."

Good Lord, thought Calliope, saddling Brandywine. *In a few years Pollyann will be a damned replica of her mother.*

"I bought you a new doll," Maxey said. "It's inside my baggage at the stage depot."

Pollyann jumped up and down. "Is she a big doll? Can the seamstress come over and sew clothes for her? Can we fetch my doll right now?"

"First I must bathe and eat breakfast."

"I want my new dolly." Pollyann stamped her small, booted foot. "I know what! Mary can wash you. She gives me a bath sometimes, and it's faster."

"That's a wonderful idea, sweetheart." Maxey grinned. "I'd enjoy having Mary wash my... ears."

Calliope felt her cheeks bake as she lifted Pollyann onto Brandywine's saddle.

"Mary says if your ears aren't clean weeds'll grow inside."

Maxey burst out laughing. Then grasping Brandywine's reins with one hand, he looked up at his niece. "Soon you must call her Aunt Mary." With his other hand, he drew Calliope close to him. "I shall find Mary's harp," he teased, dropping the reins and nibbling at her bodice.

Mindful of the child's presence, Calliope stood motionless, but she felt angrier than she'd felt when the loathsome Aaron Fox had tried to seduce her at her very first society ball.

Fourteen

SEATED AT THE DINING-ROOM TABLE, CALLIOPE RECALLED the first time Raymond Stanhope had walked her through the house.

"My house is large enough to minister to the necessities and luxuries of a moderate Republican," he had said, "but not extravagant enough to warp the manners of his children."

Even as she admired the heavy gold mirrors, frescoed ceilings, and chandeliers, Calliope had wondered what the home of an *immoderate* Republican would look like.

The Stanhope's dining room was spacious, airy, with a bay window and a fireplace. The walls were decorated with paintings. Raymond said one had been painted by a sailor home from the sea. It depicted men being eaten by whales. From inside their ornate frames, presidents Buchanan, Lincoln, Johnson, and Grant watched the Stanhope family devour meals.

Calliope slanted a glance at Maxey, who leaned against an oak sideboard. Atop the sideboard, silver platters held steaming portions of biscuits, scrambled eggs, sausage links, bacon, and fried chicken. More than enough to feed her entire staff of circus performers and then some.

Stifling an urge to scream at the waste, she scrutinized the family members situated at the large round table.

Thom shoveled eggs into his mouth as though the task was tastefully necessary.

Pollyann swung her legs back and forth beneath her chair, impatient for the meal to end.

Ann sipped from a cup of tea and nibbled a biscuit as she gazed adoringly toward the sideboard and her youngest son.

Maxey, now bathed and shaved, was relaxed, aware Raymond wouldn't rudely halt breakfast with an angry tirade.

Dottie was vivacious. Her pale cheeks flushed and her eyes glowed every time she looked at Maxey. She chattered on and on about Cleopatra's puppies and last night's ball, ignoring her food. If Maxey deigned to reply, she tossed her red hair coquettishly and bestowed a dimpled smile in his direction.

Passion might be for paramours, but Dottie wasn't immune to a primitive desire. The family didn't react to her fatuous expression—maybe they thought she smiled at the food—but Calliope, an outsider, knew Dottie was flirting. There was no other word for it. She billed and cooed like the caged pigeons that had once been a part of Dream Dancer's equestrian act.

Raymond placed his linen napkin over his plate. "Maxey, there are things we must discuss privately."

"Of course, Father, but first I have an important announcement."

"Announcement?" Raymond's mustache quivered. "Are you planning to explain your reprehensible behavior in front of the ladies? Do you expect them to protect you?"

"My disclosure concerns one lady, Father. You see, I have asked Mrs. O'Connor to become my wife. With your permission, I plan to build Mary a house on our acreage in Colorado Springs. Dottie prefers to live with you, but Mary wants a home of her own and children right away."

He didn't lie. He neglected only to mention that I refused his proposal.

Holding back the urge to indignantly rise, she waited for the family's reaction.

Their reaction was soundless amazement, as if Maxey's words were hornets tossed into the air. Everybody froze, not wanting to move and invite stings.

Dottie broke the silence first. "But you can't wed Mary Angelique, Maxey. She's promised to Charles Doone. He's already—"

"Staked his claim? No, sweetheart, though I agree Mary is an untarnished nugget of pure gold."

Only Calliope understood the real meaning behind his words. Maxey wanted an heiress, but, according to him, heiresses were fat and grumpy. Calliope's inheritance was the gratitude of Raymond Stanhope.

She felt like one of the sailors inside Raymond's framed oil painting, struggling to escape the jaws of a large black whale. Rubbish! She had the Irish whim-whams again. Maxey was no whale, and she was no Jonah.

"When did you meet Mary?" Thom asked. As

usual, he had plowed through the rhetoric and reached the core.

"I met her through Mother's letters and in person last night. The ground shook and lightning filled the sky."

"There was no storm last night," said Dottie, "just fog."

"Don't be so literal, sweetheart. When I met Mary, thunderbolts of love invaded my heart. This morning I asked her to become my wife. I know my actions were hasty, but I can't let Doone, or any other man stake his claim."

"How romantic." Rising from her chair, Ann walked over to the sideboard and hugged Maxey. Then she wended her way around the table and hugged Calliope.

"I am very pleased, son," said Raymond, his stern expression melting into a smile of gratification. "I assume your wild escapades are a thing of the past. After all, you've chosen a fine woman to share your life."

Dottie jumped up, her face as white as her ruffled dressing gown. "Have you all lost your wits? Maxey just admitted he acted in haste. If you ask me, and nobody does, it isn't proper. What will people say?"

"They'll say Uncle Maxey licked Aunt Mary's harp."

"Hush, Pollyann. This doesn't concern you."

"Yes, it does." Instinctively, the child was enjoying her mother's discomfort. "Uncle Maxey says she'll be my Aunt Mary, and he licked her harp."

"What are you talking about? What harp?"

"It was a funny. Uncle Maxey said harp, but he meant heart. The heart is 'neath the bosom. My goodness, everybody knows that," said Pollyann, sounding very much like her mother. "Uncle Maxey licked Aunt Mary's bosom."

"Hush! That's enough, Pollyann!" Dottie splayed her hands across the tabletop, presumably for support but most likely to steer clear of slapping her daughter's face. Or Calliope's face.

"Well, that settles it." Raymond's eyes sparkled with amusement. "If Uncle Maxey kissed Mary's harp, there must be a wedding ceremony."

"Not kissed, Grandpapa, licked."

"Don't be ridiculous, Papa Raymond," Dottie said, her bleached face splotched with streaks of crimson. "What do we really know about Mary Angelique? I've had my doubts from the very begin—"

"She saved your child from certain death," Ann gasped.

"And I'm eternally grateful. As I said, I've had my doubts from the beginning, and after last night, well, I'm sure you all understand."

"What did Aunt Mary do last night?"

"Shut up, Pollyann!"

"I'm afraid I don't understand," Raymond said. "You've called me ridiculous and hinted that our Mary committed some kind of indiscretion. Would you care to explain?"

"All right. I'm sure Mary Angelique encouraged Maxey's embrace and enticed him into rendering a proposal. She has a habit of doing that. Before the ball, Charles told Thom he kissed Mary inside the carriage house. Charles said Mary became distressed from his kiss, but if you ask me, and nobody does, her protest was feigned. In any case, Charles insisted he and Mary must be wed as soon as possible. You saw how Mary Angelique costumed herself, showing her limbs. I must be honest. I love Mary like a sister, but we all know she's penniless. So she uses her bodily assets..." Dottie hesitated, glancing toward Pollyann.

Once again there was silence.

Calliope's mind raced. She hadn't realized until this moment how much jealousy lurked beneath Dottie's placid exterior. Dottie would pay a servant to scratch Thom's itch, but not Maxey's. Oh no, not Maxey's.

Ann Stanhope stood straight and regal. "I don't want to hear another word, Dorothy. I love Mary like a daughter, and your daughter is alive today because of our Mary. She could have escaped without one burn, as you did. Instead, she put her life in danger. How dare you accuse our Mary of... of... How dare you!"

Dottie turned and ran from the room.

"You really should control your wife, Thom." Maxey still stood by the sideboard, and up until now a grin had creased the corners of his lips. "If kisses were enticements for marriage proposals, I would have a multitude of wives. Make it clear to Dottie that I embrace whomever I choose, and I've never made love to a decent woman against her will."

"Maxey, please! The child."

"Sorry, Mother."

Calliope lifted Pollyann onto her lap. "Do you understand what your Uncle Maxey just said?"

"No."

Hugging the child, Calliope stared directly into Maxey's black eyes. "He said gentlemen should treat ladies with respect. A man is stronger than a woman, so he shouldn't use that power to make her do things she doesn't want to do."

"Are you really going to be my Aunt Mary?"

"Of course she is," Raymond said. "First thing tomorrow I'll have my bank send through a draft to Colorado Springs. Ann, dear, you must help Mary select her trousseau. I'll advance Maxey the money necessary to begin construction on his new house. You lack funds, don't you, Son?"

"Yes, Father. I appreciate your help, since I want to make everything perfect for Mary." Having finally abandoned the sideboard, Maxey walked toward Raymond. As Maxey extended his arm for a handshake, he said, "The first room I shall build is the nursery."

"I'll send some servants to ready our summer cottage." A smile wreathed Anne's face. "Perhaps we can leave next week."

I never said yes. Raymond and Ann are making plans, but I never agreed to accept Maxey's proposal.

Everything was happening too fast. She didn't care about the impropriety, but she needed time. And yet she'd fallen irrevocably in love with Brian while washing an elephant. There had been a storm and bolts of lightning and—

Maxey said thunderbolts of lightning invaded his heart. He was full of the blarney, but he made her feel alive.

If she married Charles Doone, she'd live in Denver. With a home of her own in Colorado Springs, she could perfect her circus act atop Brandywine without fear of discovery. Or, even better, she could string a rope between two trees and practice her back flips and somersaults. Far from Denver and the scene of the fire, she'd be able to bury her memories of Brian—and her nightmares would go away.

Calliope glanced toward the sailors and man-eating whales. Painted water seemed to undulate, and once again she subdued her sense of unease.

Why condemn a man because he was too attractive? With marriage, Maxey would settle down. He would never have to search for an indecent woman to placate his desires, because his wife would keep him satisfied.

After they were wed, she would play circus equestrian inside their boudoir. You couldn't make somebody love you, but you could make him want you.

All of a sudden she pictured Jocko and heard the echo of his voice: *You remind me of Sean. He wouldn't face reality, either.*

With an effort, she put the clown's words out of her mind and focused, instead, on this morning's ride in the clearing. For the first time since the fire, she'd felt truly liberated. So tonight, while everyone else slept, she would escape from the house, bridle Brandywine, and visit the clearing again.

Perhaps a horned gilly-owl would be her audience.

At the image, she burst into delighted giggles.

Her laughter was contagious. Everybody laughed. Maxey laughed loudest of all.

Fifteen

RAYMOND STANHOPE'S COLORADO SPRINGS COTTAGE possessed an entrance hall that opened into three principal apartments—drawing room, library, and living room. A passage from the living room led to the kitchen and scullery. The kitchen fly-door swung both ways, covered with baize to filter out disagreeable smells. Sheltered by trees and shrubs, the kitchen wing included a pantry, a laundry, and servants' quarters.

A second story consisted of five spacious bedrooms.

Ann had christened their summer home Ravenspur because, during construction, she had seen a large bird with black plumage land on the unfinished roof.

In all probability a crow, thought Calliope, *but you couldn't call a beautiful estate Crowspur or Crowfoot.*

A verandah stretched across the front of the house. A shady balcony had been built over the porch. "Where ladies will find it agreeable to pass summer mornings," said Ann.

Calliope leaned against the balcony railing. Her pink peignoir fell in graceful folds from a high waistline. Long sleeves were elaborately decorated with lace, reminiscent of her Spring Ball costume. Below one lacy wrist, a diamond solitaire ring sparkled in the early morning sun. She had reluctantly removed Brian's gold band for this more ostentatious piece of jewelry, selected by Maxey, purchased by Raymond.

Her wedding would take place this September. *Less than three months away!* She caught herself chewing her bottom lip. Why did she feel so apprehensive? Maxey was the perfect fiancé, an exemplary gentleman. He was attentive and treated her with concerned kindness. He wouldn't allow her to view the progress on their new home, insisting that, when completed, it must be a surprise. Calliope didn't care. After all, she had slept in circus wagons and railroad cars and required neither drawing rooms nor sculleries.

I'd like a nursery, a library, and a balcony like this one, she mused, gazing into the distance toward the sun-clad mountains. She would feed her babies on the balcony, carry them to the nursery for their naps, then return to read.

Her newest book, *Twenty Thousand Leagues Under the Sea*, lay neglected, next to a cup of cold coffee. She preferred to prop her elbows on top of the wooden railing and daydream.

It was much nicer to dream during the daylight hours, since a change of scenery hadn't banished her nightmares. Perhaps, after marriage, sleeping next to Maxey, cradled by his strong arms, the demons would finally disappear.

From her vantage point, Calliope could see the stables and Pollyann's rabbit hutch to her right, the gardens to her left. Near the vegetable garden, strung between two tree limbs, was a clothesline covered with white sheets and drawers, petticoats and crino-lines. No union suits or trousers interrupted the femi-nine symmetry, because Thom and Maxey were in Denver. Raymond, Ann, and Pollyann were visiting Ann's widowed mother who lived in Kansas.

At the moment, only Dottie, a few servants, and Calliope occupied the cottage. Tonight the moon would be full and the clothesline empty. Tonight she would practice her ropewalking.

Several times she had managed to slip away at dawn and, without the corset, perfect her back flips atop Brandywine. But she had not yet played the equilibrist.

The door swung open, and Dottie walked onto the balcony. Since family members were absent and she was "on holiday," she hadn't bothered to bathe. Calliope wrinkled her nose. Dottie wore a white velvet dressing gown, recently laundered, but she smelled like overripe melons.

With a loud yawn, the plump woman sank onto a cushioned chaise. "Fetch me a cup of hot chocolate, Mary Angelique."

Fetch it yourself, you slothful piece of elephant flop! Aloud, Calliope said, "Good morning, Dottie."

"Do hurry, Mary Angelique. My throat is parched."

"But I've been reading my new book, and it's very good." Calliope hoped Dottie would take the hint and leave.

"I'd like my chocolate right away, and please remove that obstinate tone from your voice. After all, you shouldn't bite the hand that feeds you."

"I'd have to give it a wash before I bit," Calliope said under her breath. Descending the staircase, she walked across the living room, swung open the fly-door, and entered the kitchen.

Soon I'll be my own mistress!

Meanwhile, she had to fetch and carry or suffer the consequences. Dottie no longer hid her barbed comments unless other family members were present, especially Ann. The exception to family members was Maxey. Dottie didn't bother to hide her hatred from Maxey.

Shortly after arriving at Ravenspur, Calliope had stood on the balcony one night, thus becoming a reluctant witness to a conversation below.

"You can't really mean to marry her." Dottie's petulant whine betrayed her jealousy. "Mary's nothing more than a draggle-tailed harlot."

And you're a frowsy hag, thought Calliope. She couldn't see Dottie hidden within the confines of the verandah, but she watched Maxey walk a few paces away and light a cheroot.

She fully expected him to chastise Dottie for her draggle-tailed harlot remark, but he merely grinned and said, "I recall a time when you were rather wanton yourself, sweetheart."

"I wasn't wanton. I was foolishly in love with my husband's brother."

"And I was a mere boy, ten years younger than you."

"Eight, er, five years younger."

"Why quibble, Dot? It doesn't matter."

"It does! You've changed while I haven't. I still crave your… well, you know what I mean. And I know what you want."

"I want Mary."

"She's not what she seems, Maxey. Mrs. Brian O'Connor may have fooled others but not me. She claims she's from Georgia, and yet she uses words like wee and daft and—"

"Mary's late husband was Irish."

"Is don-a-cur an Irish word? Mary said she had to use the don-a-cur and then headed straight for the privy. Once, when a guest became intoxicated, Mary said he was guyed-out."

Calliope stifled a gasp behind her hand. She had never imagined she had become so complacent and careless. Or that Dottie was so perceptive.

"Perhaps you misunderstood."

"Perhaps. But I didn't misunderstand the impropriety of her ball costume. When I reprimanded our young seamstress the next morning, she said Mary *insisted* on wearing breeches. What's more, Mary said she *wanted* to appear provocative."

That's a lie, thought Calliope, saddened by the dishonesty, not to mention disloyalty, of the young seamstress. But then, considering Dottie's acid tongue, Lizbet undoubtedly had no choice.

"You're so dazzled by Mary's virtuous attitude," Dottie continued, "you refuse to accept any sign of duplicity. Abhor that which is evil and cling to that which is good."

Cleave to that which is good!

"Are you saying Mary's evil while you're good?" Maxey's voice was filled with scornful amusement. "Pull up your nightie, Dot. The sight doesn't tempt me. If you must satisfy your salacious appetite, find my brother."

"But Thom won't... Please, Maxey, all I ask is one night."

"No." After lighting a fresh cheroot, he turned and walked toward the stables.

The aroma of boiled milk brought Calliope back to the present. That disagreeable scene beneath Ravenspur's balcony reminded her of Brian and Panama. If Maxey had accepted Dottie's seductive plea, Calliope would have called off their engagement.

Only three months. She would make the best of an awkward situation and watch her P's and Q's—or, in this case, her dafts and donickers.

≈

"Ann insisted I take you shopping." Dottie shifted her parasol from one shoulder to the other, trying to block the sun. "I hope you appreciate Papa Raymond's generosity, Mary Angelique. Once you are wed, expensive gifts will cease. Maxey is not known for his munificence."

"And I'm not known for my avarice," Calliope said, swinging her own purple silk, cream-tatted parasol by its handle. She had no desire to hide from the sun. On the contrary, she welcomed the strong rays that caressed her cheeks.

Ignoring Calliope's retort, Dottie continued strolling past various shops. "You would have been wiser to accept Charles Doone, my dear."

"Maxey told me Charles is now engaged to a lady of fine breeding and great wealth."

Dottie wasn't even listening. "Charles would never knot his purse strings," she said.

"I shall have clothes enough to last a lifetime.

Brandywine is the perfect mount, and Maxey builds me a house. What more do I need?"

"Fashions change every year, Mary Angelique, while a woman's figure changes after childbirth."

"Ann is slender after two children. My mother remained unchanged after one."

"One? I thought you had a brother."

"I do. Did. The memory of Bret's death is still painful. Could we please talk about something else?"

"We need not talk at all. I was trying to be polite."

And I swore to be cautious! How could she have forgotten her imaginary brother, Bret? She had blurted out the name Bret when Raymond first questioned her about her family, because Jocko had been on her mind at the time. She had even planned to remember an uncle, Bret Johnson, for whom her brother had been named, and ask Raymond to initiate a quest. But then Maxey had appeared, and the scheme had gone clear out of her head.

Now that she lived in Colorado Springs, she must give up her search for the clown.

Forgive me, Brian.

Happiness was so brief, like sifting grains of sand through one's fingers. She didn't have time for revenge schemes. Furthermore, she suspected that, unlike Charles or even Raymond, Maxey would decipher her motive.

Halting, Calliope glanced into the window of a haberdashery. With a sigh, she admired the shirts, socks, and knickerbockers, especially the knickers. Since she'd become a gilly, she missed the freedom of her circus attire.

"Do you like this ensemble, Mary Angelique?" Dottie stared into a plate-glass window farther down the row.

Calliope walked forward and studied a dressmaker's dummy clothed in a plum-colored velvet jacket with gray fur and tassel trim. Beneath the jacket was a plaid skirt, swept back and decorated with a wide bow above an abbreviated bustle.

"I like each individual article of clothing," she said, "but the display is brilliant."

"What display, Mary Angelique? There's only one ensemble. The seamstress doesn't give us a choice."

"That's because she wants us to step inside and view her merchandise. Come on, Dottie, let's oblige her."

Above the doorway was a painted sign: Eve's Apparel.

Bells chimed as they entered. "That must be Eve," Dottie said, pointing toward a small woman who was busy sewing pink silk roses onto the brim of a blue velvet bonnet.

The woman looked up, bit the end of her thread, and smiled.

Calliope's breath caught in her throat. *Gwendolyn*.

It was Gwendolyn, former member of Sean Kelley's Congress of Freaks, a performer in Calliope's Kid Show, the very same performer who had sworn Brian was dead.

Gwendolyn's hair, once five feet four inches long, was now shoulder-length. The brown curls were secured behind her right ear but allowed to tumble unrestricted along the left side of her face, not quite hiding the scar that began at the corner of her slanted eyebrow and continued down past her chin.

She wore what must have been one of her own creations—a mauve poplin afternoon dress whose pink silk roses nodded from the bodice, waistline, and hem. She gazed politely at her visitors through a pair of wire-rimmed spectacles, but Calliope could discern no recognition in the young woman's brown eyes.

Have I changed so much? Why doesn't Gwendolyn blurt out a greeting, expose my true identity?

"Are you Miss Eve?" Calliope fervently hoped her voice didn't betray the distress she felt, an agitation that was turning her bones to jelly—quince jelly, since her complexion doubtless duplicated the yellowish fruit. "This is Mrs. Thomas Stanhope. I am Mary Angelique O'Connor."

"You are too familiar with tradespeople," Dottie admonished. "There is no need to introduce yourself by your Christian name."

I can't introduce myself as Mrs. Brian O'Connor, you daft gilly, thought Calliope, her mind in a daze. Gwen might remember the cat tamer/ringmaster's name.

Placing her rose-festooned hat on a shelf, the woman said, "Yes, I am Eve, manager of this emporium."

"Manager? You don't own it?" Calliope blurted, apropos of nothing, hoping her confused emotions would settle.

"The shop will be all mine soon," Eve said with pride. "My benefactor has already received half his investment, along with interest."

"May I ask the name of your benefactor?"

"Aaron Fox."

For some daft reason, Calliope wasn't surprised, even though Maxey had said Fox was not known for his altruism. Why on earth wasn't she surprised? Because Aaron Fox was a wealthy rancher from Colorado Springs? Because Aaron Fox had been turning up in her dreams almost every night? The first reason made no sense at all. The second did.

"Have you always been a seamstress?" Calliope couldn't resist asking, even though she knew she invited recognition with the question.

"I can't remember my past. They tell me I sustained burns during a circus fire." Eve studied Calliope. Then, apparently liking what she saw, she continued. "The doctors insist I was lucky. I lost my hair and partial sight in my left eye, but it could have been much worse. As you can see, my hair has grown back. Unfortunately, my memory has not."

Lucky? Calliope felt tears build behind her eyelids. She had landed in the lap of luxury, while Gwen had to start from scratch.

"I shall order my entire trousseau from Eve, Dottie."

"Your entire—?"

"There is no reason for you to remain while Eve takes my measurements. Why don't you shop for yourself and Pollyann? We can meet here in an hour's time."

"But there are other dressmakers, Mary Angelique. We should compare—"

"I admire Eve's originality."

"Mary Angelique, she's deformed," whispered Dottie, although her voice was audible enough to be heard by the window's display dummy.

Calliope gritted her teeth. "I see no deformity, especially in her creations. You can rant and rave till hell freezes over, Dottie, but you won't change my mind."

"Really, Mary Angelique, you never cease to amaze me. If you ask me, and nobody does, Maxey won't tolerate bad language. And he certainly won't appreciate a wife who maintains such a stubborn attitude."

"Maxey will appreciate a wife who can give him heirs."

With satisfaction, Calliope watched her words strike home. After Pollyann's birth, Dottie had been pronounced barren. She and Thom could provide no male Stanhope heirs, a circumstance that rankled her no end.

"Well!" Dottie's red-blotched cheeks puffed in and out. Unable to think of a sharp retort, she vented her fury on Eve. "We won't pay until the work is completed and approved by both Mrs. O'Connor"—she pointed rudely at Calliope—"and Mrs. Raymond Stanhope." This time Dottie's voice was very loud, since she apparently equated Eve's scarred face with deafness.

"Nonsense," Calliope said. "Raymond gave me a full purse. Eve shall receive her deposit today."

Dottie's pale blue eyes narrowed. "In that case, my presence here is not required, and you can walk home."

"I prefer walking. It keeps one's figure slender and firms one's legs."

"Limbs!"

"No, Dottie, legs. Maxey loves my legs. He said so." Calliope knew she was playing the brat, but Eve's bells chimed a giggle. Were they applauding Dottie's hasty exit?

Turning to Eve, Calliope said, "Shall we begin? Good Lord, I never asked your opinion. Perhaps you have orders that require your immediate attention."

The seamstress smiled. "Even if I did, I would lay them aside, Mrs. O'Connor. I appreciate your words in my defense."

"Please call me Mary. I apologize for Mrs. Stanhope. She's a stupid woman."

"But in essence, correct. I am deformed. Maybe that's why I choose beautiful fabrics and bright colors. Don't fret, Mary. The person who knows how to laugh at herself will always be amused."

"I think we are all deformed, Eve, only some people hide it deep down inside. If you were ten feet tall and had a pointy head, I would still pay for your talent."

"Good." She led Calliope toward a bead-curtained entranceway at the back of the shop. "Because my efforts do not come cheap. Many ladies assume that because I have scars on my face I should be grateful for any assignment. To their chagrin, they discover it's not true and outbid one another for my services."

Why didn't I sense the intelligence that lurked beneath Gwendolyn's long hair? Calliope mused as she entered a small room filled with bolts of fabric, measuring tapes, and a full-length mirror. *We could have become friends. But our time together was so brief. Damn! I can tell her who she is and where she comes from. But do I really want her to know she was once my Kid Show performer? A circus freak?*

No! Gwen had joined the circus because she was unhappy. She said her father beat her, and worse. Better the pain of not remembering than the painful memories of her past life.

"We can work with your hair," said Eve.

"My hair?"

"Sorry, I was thinking out loud. Your hair has traces of red and gold, and your eyes are a most arresting color, green and gray. I shall design your clothes to enhance your hair and eyes." Eve helped Calliope remove her gown. "You are very slender and need no corset. Why do you wear one?"

"The sun rises and sets every day, and ladies wear corsets."

"I don't. Why should I strap myself in like the cinch on a horse's saddle? Soon a lady will be *required* to wear a bridle and sharp bit, mark my words. If you allow me, I shall design your gowns so no corset is necessary. That too, is a talent appreciated by many of my ladies. They tell me they feel more feminine, not less."

Humming, Eve removed the corset then drew her tape around Calliope's waist, hips, and bosom. Apparently she could memorize each measurement, since she didn't write the numbers down. She was reaching for a bolt of emerald silk when bells chimed.

"Someone has entered the shop, Mary. Please wait right here."

After Eve had left the small room, Calliope stretched the silk across her face from one earlobe to the other. Then she gazed into the looking glass. Sakes alive! Her eyes were so green! Raymond's coins would be well spent. The silk was obviously imported from across the ocean. France, perhaps?

Mum had often talked about France... Paris... the Nouveau Cirque. It was the most famous circus in the world, and Calliope planned to visit it one day. Would Maxey let her? Of course he would. They could have a second honeymoon.

"You haven't had your first honeymoon yet, you daft colleen," she murmured. Ann and Raymond were making plans, rejecting first one city then another. Presently, New York headed the list.

Eve had left the fitting-room door ajar, and Calliope heard a man's voice. Why would a man shop at a woman's emporium when the haberdashery was nearby? Perhaps he purchased a hat for his wife. Although she couldn't hear his exact words, his voice sounded familiar.

Curious, she tiptoed down a short hallway until she stood behind the heavily beaded curtain. From this new vantage point, conversation was audible.

"It will be my wedding gift, Eve."

"You plan to give another man's wife a negligee? That's rather ill-mannered, Aaron Fox. Maybe the new husband won't appreciate—"

"Red, I think, or black. I'll leave the choice up to you. Any color but white. The lady is no virgin, and the gown must be transparent in all the right places."

"I don't understand, Aaron. Why do you want her to appear seductive for another man?"

"I have my reasons."

"Who is this lucky lady?"

"A woman from my past. I'll give you her name and address when the negligee is finished."

"I realize I owe you everything, Aaron, my sanity and my life, but—"

"You owe me nothing. You were a wise investment."

Calliope heard the sound of Eve's laughter.

"My apparel shop is nothing compared to the hotel you're building. I've heard you plan to include a restaurant with a stage larger than most opera houses."

Consumed by curiosity, Calliope wanted to see what Aaron Fox looked like without his mask and wig. But she couldn't casually stroll through the beaded curtain, not when she was clothed in what Brian had once called her "cobwebby chemise."

Twisting the gold horse at the end of her necklace chain, she pictured Fox's eyes, cold as a blue lake covered by a thin layer of winter ice. Then, despite her fear of discovery, she inched the beads apart and peeked into the shop.

Damn and blast! She could see Eve clearly—curly brown hair, rosy cheeks, mauve dress—but Fox stood facing the seamstress, not Calliope. She could discern only his back and broad shoulders covered by a light gray tweed jacket with black trim. His hair, partially hidden beneath a gray summer derby, was thick and unruly, the color of coal dust. If Fox was elderly, as Maxey had claimed, he had aged well.

"Holy Moses, Aaron, I left a lady waiting inside the fitting room. She's practically *au naturel*."

"Let me help you take her measurements."

"Get gone, you big oaf."

"Where's the advantage in financing an apparel shop if you won't let me help—?"

"Hush! Mrs. O'Connor might hear you."

"Who?"

"Mary Angelique O'Connor. She arrived earlier, accompanied by a red-haired dragon lady who was dressed in the latest fashion but smelled dreadful. The dragon lady was so tightly corseted she most likely couldn't breathe and smell herself. In any case, Mary said she wanted to purchase her entire wardrobe from me, and the dragon lady, Mrs. Thomas Stanhope, walked out in a huff."

Calliope could almost swear Fox's shoulders stiffened. Perhaps he remembered their waltz together. But why would that tense him up?

"Did Mrs. O'Connor recognize you?" he asked.

"Don't be silly, Aaron. I'm positive I've never mingled with rich, socially prominent families. My instincts are too base, too unconventional."

"Thank God. I'm sick and tired of pampered fillies."

"Mary's not pampered. Well, I suppose she is, but she doesn't act like it. Do you want to meet her?"

"No."

His reply was cold, brusque, absolute. Calliope shut her eyes against the hurt that inexplicably washed over her. Thus, she missed Aaron Fox's exit. Speeding down the hall, she reentered Eve's fitting room and found she was shaking from head to toe. Why? Because she had been eavesdropping? Or because Fox made her feel like a rabbit caught in a snare? Come to think of it, she had never met Aaron Fox, not really. She had danced with "Edward the Sixth." All of a sudden, she recalled a portion of their conversation.

"What else do you know about me, sire?"

"You are Mary O'Connor, a widow, descended from a French countess named Angelique Kelley."

Angelique *Kelley*? Calliope had never said her last name out loud, not since living with the Stanhopes. Had she? Of course not. She wouldn't say Kelley, conspicuous on her circus train, wagons, and posters. But she didn't remember saying donicker or guyed-out, either, and she must have. Dottie couldn't pull

those circus terms from thin air like she did her ridiculous biblical quotes. Calliope must have mentioned
Mum's full name, and Dottie had offhandedly repeated
it to Aaron Fox during their brief exchange.

Why had Fox asked Eve if Mrs. O'Connor recognized her? How had he met Gwendolyn? Was he
among the gillys who attended the circus during the fire?

Had he known all along that Mary Angelique was
Calliope Kelley? After all, she had appeared in the
opening spec, where Brian, as ringmaster, had introduced each performer.

Ann, Raymond, Thom, and Dottie had watched
her ride around the tent. But they had met her later,
bruised and burned beyond recognition. And after her
recovery, she looked so different from the lass who
rode Dublin, the lass who wore a spangled costume,
the lass known as Dream Dancer.

Aaron Fox had never seen her bruised and burned.
Were his Spring Ball actions—his effort to seduce
her—spawned by his knowledge of her true identity?
Supercilious bastard!

*I'd like to stare into those cold blue eyes and demand he
answer my questions.*

I hope I never see him again.

❧

Ravenspur was a muted shape in various shades of gray
and black. Every lamp had been extinguished by ten
o'clock. Calliope had waited until midnight. Then she
had donned her blue-and-white-striped tennis dress,
ignoring corset and petticoats. Now she stood beneath
the moon's spherical brightness and contemplated

the clothesline. It wasn't so awfully high, no higher than her forehead. If she fell, she'd merely bruise her pride—and perhaps her derriere.

She buttoned her dress about her waist, thinking how shocked Dottie would be at the sight of bare legs, or even worse, bare feet. Then, after climbing the tree and reaching the fork where the line's end had been tightly knotted, she tentatively placed her right foot upon the rope.

Good. The rope was taut. Walking to the middle, she halted. Just a wee sag, she thought, but enough to make back flips risky and a forward somersault impossible.

She heard the sound of footsteps, boots crushing pebbles into the dirt.

Arms outstretched, she twisted her head to the left. Then she gazed through the moonlit-tinted darkness at the man with long legs, narrow hips, broad shoulders, and coal-dust hair.

"Well, I'll be damned," he said. "Calliope Kelley. Or should I call you Mrs. Brian O'Connor?"

Calliope felt all the color drain from her face. Teetering on the rope's edge, desperately trying to maintain her balance, she blurted the first thing that came to mind.

"What are *you* doing here?"

Sixteen

"I LIVE HERE, BITCH!"

Calliope tried to control the thrum of her heart by breathing in the smell of the garden. A lingering scent of soapy water emanated from the clothesline, but the odor that dominated all others was Maxey Stanhope's sweating roan. The horse had been ridden hard and stood amidst the tomato vines, his heaving sides swelling and shrinking like a concertina, his music a wheezy snuffle through his distended nostrils.

Maxey didn't look much better.

His face glistened with perspiration. His mouth was partially open in what could only be described as a sneering grin. His brown boots, fawn trousers, white shirt, and fawn waistcoat were stained with dirt and dust.

"Get down from there, Calliope Kelley," he said. "That's a Stanhope clothesline, this is Stanhope property, and you're trespassing."

Her first reaction was a profound sense of relief. No more lies. No more deceit. Then she felt a panic she had never known before, not even during her performance inside the cat cage.

"Did you hear me, you conniving bitch? Get down!"

Calliope knew she must hide her fear. Maxey was a study in controlled fury. If she said the wrong thing, made the wrong move, he would explode like a stick of dynamite. Folding her arms across her bodice, she said, "I shall not come down until you are calm."

"I'm quite imperturbable, my sweet circus performer."

"That's a lie! I can see your agitation in the foamy moisture that stains your roan's flanks. He looks rein-whipped, poor thing, and the bit has chafed his mouth."

Maxey laughed, but the sound had a mocking quality. "You show concern for my horse but not me?" Swiftly walking forward, he reached up, grasped her around the hips, and pulled her from the rope.

Her head was above his, her waist on a level with his shoulders. She resisted the urge to kick with her bare feet. If she *perturbed* his nether parts, he might employ retaliation.

Still holding her against him, Maxey slid her body down the length of his, but there was no passion in his grip. Her reaction was pure terror. Maxey's arms were shackles; to struggle would sap her strength.

Brian, get her out of the cage.

Shut up, Jocko, she must not lose eye contact.

Raising her chin, Calliope deliberately stared up into Maxey's eyes. Oh, how she wished she held a whipstock and hickory club. "Let me go!" she stated with defiance.

His second laugh was a growl. "Do you want to consummate our betrothal here? The perfume of rotting roses would be suitable, don't you agree? Or perhaps you'd prefer a more intimate spot."

"I prefer my room, where I sleep alone. Your horse needs attention, Maxey, not me."

He gave a soundless whistle. "I've always admired your courage, my angel. Don't you want to hear about my discovery?"

"No. I want you to release me, right now, this very minute. I want to go straight to bed."

He removed his arms so quickly she staggered backwards. "You have backbone, Mary. Of course, I could snap that backbone in two and blame it on a fall from the clothesline. But then I would be in the same pickle as before, a black sheep with no fiancée. We wouldn't want that, would we?"

His voice sounded correct, almost teasing, however perspiration continued streaming down his face, and his mouth was still set in that scowl of a smile. "I shall leave Ravenspur tomorrow," she said. "Is that soon enough?"

"No."

"You prefer that I leave tonight?"

"No."

"But you can't want to marry me now." She felt despair at the loss of her latest dream, then, once again, a profound sense of relief.

"Riding here from Denver, I didn't plan that far ahead." Maxey walked over to his horse and loosened the cinch on its saddle, and Calliope could almost swear the bedraggled roan heaved a sigh of relief. "For the moment, my angel, you must continue your masquerade."

"Why?"

"I need Father's good will... and his money. I'm deeply in debt."

She had a sudden thought. "Our new house. You haven't begun construction, have you? That's why you refused to let me see its progress. You've accepted funds from Raymond and gambled the money away."

"Logical reasoning for a circus chit." Maxey reached into his saddlebag and retrieved a poster. "This was on the wall inside a Denver saloon. They don't bother taking down old announcements, just cover them over with new. All I could see was the name Brian O'Connor, but it was enough. I had never heard your husband's first name until one evening when Dottie said it. 'Mrs. Brian O'Connor has fooled others but not me,' she said. I guess it takes one whore to recognize another whore."

"I'm not a whore!"

Rolling the poster up, Maxey waved it back and forth, as if he waved a thick ringmaster's cane. "I tore this from the wall and saw your likeness. Very flattering, my angel."

"The artist was well schooled."

"So are you, Calliope Kelley. You've put us through our paces, tutored us to accept your sad plight, drilled us in the details of your tragic life."

"It wasn't like that at all, Maxey. After the fire, your parents assumed I was a society lady. Brian was dead, the circus had burned to the ground, and I had no place to go. Whom did I hurt by pretending?"

"Me. You've wounded me greatly," he said, his voice dripping with sarcasm. "I don't usually make mistakes."

"I, on the other hand, seem to make them a lot. If I had accepted Charles Doone, I wouldn't have wounded your pride."

"My pride is intact, sweetheart. It's my judgment that's impaired." He stuffed the poster back inside his saddlebag.

"I'm truly sorry, Maxey, but you've used our relationship for your own advantage. If you insist, I shall play out the game before I invent an excuse to leave Ravenspur." Despite her fear, she yawned. "I'm exhausted. May we continue this discussion tomorrow morning? Please?"

Maxey stepped toward her. "Certain things make sense now. Your convenient faint the night we met."

"It wasn't convenient. That was the first time I had visited the scene of the fire, and it brought back memories. I don't even know where Brian is buried. They couldn't identify all the bodies because some were so badly burned…" She paused, feeling the salty sting of tears.

"A word here and there, a mannerism," he continued, as if she hadn't interrupted him. "I thought your quaint expressions charming, but Dottie saw right through them."

"Dottie is jealous of your love for me."

"I never said I loved you. I was obsessed by your seductive beauty, deceived by your virtue." He brandished his fist toward the moon. "How you must have laughed behind my back."

"There was no laughter. I was proud to be your fiancée. And just like your pride, my virtue is still intact, for I have lain with no man but Brian. And that happened only after we had both pledged our vows before God. I care not what you believe, Maxey. It's the honest truth."

"Truth? You've deceived us all from the beginning."

"Look into a mirror. It is you who deceive. A perfect house for Mary Angelique, indeed! Your sins are far greater than mine."

"You accepted gifts under false pretenses. Clothing, the mare—"

"I saved Pollyann's life. Your parents were grateful. They would have rewarded Calliope Kelley the same way they rewarded Mary O'Connor."

"Perhaps. But they wouldn't have turned a circus whore into a Stanhope ward."

"I'm not a whore!" She shuddered from head to toe. How could she have once compared Maxey to Brian? Maxey's eyes were evil—like black beetles.

If he touches me, I'll scream.

He reached out.

I'll scream. I swear—

He swung her body around so she leaned against him. His other hand covered her mouth, pressing down so hard she knew his fingerprints would remain even after he released her.

If he released her.

Now was no time to flaunt false courage.

Kicking backwards, she lost her balance. Her dress was still buttoned up about her waist. She felt sharp rocks and pebbles shred the skin of her bare heels as Maxey dragged her toward the carriage house. She screamed into his hand until her throat was raw. Then, with the greatest effort of her life, she willed herself to stop struggling and save what little strength remained.

After they had passed the chicken coop and entered the stable, she shut her eyes and let her body go limp, hoping Maxey would believe she had fainted. But he simply removed his hand from her mouth. "Thieving circus bitch," he sneered. "Your tricks don't fool me, not any more. Stand up!"

Calliope kept her eyes closed and didn't move a muscle. She heard Brandywine nicker. If she could only manage to open the stall, mount her mare, and ride away. She would count to three and then make her bid for freedom.

She had counted to three during her equestrian act, during her waltz with Aaron Fox—

"Stand up, damn you!"

One. Two—

She felt Maxey prop her against the tack wall, felt him rip her bodice and chemise, felt a pain she had never imagined as his fingers found her breasts and squeezed her nipples.

The walls of the stable wobbled, swaying inward. Brandywine's agitated whinny vibrated. With an inarticulate sound, Calliope opened her eyes, sprang forward, and curled her fingers into claws, reaching for Maxey's eyes.

He caught her wrists with one hand while the thumb and forefinger of his other hand continued pinching her nipples. Overwhelmed by agony, she slumped against him.

"That's better," he said with a sneer. Slinging her across his shoulder, he climbed the loft ladder and tossed her onto the straw.

When she tried to crawl away, he hauled her upright and pressed her face against his waistcoat. "Don't cry, my angel," he said, stroking her tangled hair. "I would never take a woman against her will."

She just stood there, shivering, sobbing with pain and humiliation.

He said, "Aren't you going to thank me?"

"Thank you, Maxey. May I leave now?"

"I said I would never take a lady against her will. I said nothing about a circus whore."

"Maxey, please."

"When we are alone, you must call me Mister Stanhope." He gave a contemptuous push that sent her sprawling, and straddled her body. His hands hovered above her breasts. "If you do what I ask, I won't hurt you again."

"You gave me your word, Maxey. You swore before God you wouldn't touch me."

"I swore I wouldn't *lay* with you, Mary, and a Stanhope never breaks his vow."

"Then let me go."

He fumbled around in the straw and held up his silver flask. "I left this here earlier, sweetheart. One must always be prepared."

"What is it? Whiskey?"

"No. Brandywine."

"Brandywine?" For a moment, confused, Calliope thought he was talking about her mare.

"A beverage distilled from fermented apple juice," Maxey explained impatiently. "Open your mouth."

"If I drink lying on my back, I shall choke."

He helped her sit and tilted the flask to her lips. "Drink, Mary. I'm sorry I hurt you, but I lost my temper. It won't happen again."

She pushed the flask away. "Do you swear it?"

"Don't ever defy me. Drink the brandywine, my

angel. There, that's a good angel. Drink some more. When you've finished, Mary, I'll help you walk to your bedroom."

"I don't need your help," she said, vaguely aware her voice sounded slurred. Thirsty, she had gladly consumed a goodly portion of the wine. It had a brackish taste, but the first time she had tried whiskey it had tasted nasty too.

"Drain the flask, Mary. There's a good angel."

"Are you tryin' to poison me?"

"Of course not. If I poisoned you, I couldn't collect more funds for our new house."

"I feel... feel muzzy."

"Sorry, sweetheart, I forgot to tell you brandywine has alcohol."

"Donicker," she moaned.

"What? Oh, the privy." He chuckled. "I'll carry you to your room and fetch a chamber pot. You don't look well, Mary. Perhaps you've caught a chill."

"No. The wine. The wine, Maxey."

"I'm afraid you've finished every drop, my angel."

"No. No. The wine makes me ill."

"Really? Then why did you drink it all?"

"Because my throat was dry from screaming and you said... you promised... dizzy... oh, God. Gonna throw up."

"Don't you dare! Food will settle your queasy belly. Dottie's in the kitchen, cooking up a rabbit stew."

"Dottie? Cooking? Dottie never cooks. An' it's night... midnight... isn't it? Isn't it?" she cried, trying to erase with her fingers the flush that burned her cheeks.

He caught her wrists, but this time there was no malice in his grip. "Poor angel, it's way past midnight. I stopped at the house, first. That's how I knew you were missing. I woke Dottie and asked her to prepare a meal. It's a long ride from Denver, and—"

"Denver. Yes. You're angry 'bout something. Poster."

"I *was* angry. How can I stay angry at you when you're so ill?"

She groaned. "Gonna throw up, Maxey."

"No! You must not vomit, my lovely angel, my dearest angel, for if you do, I shall cover your mouth with my hand and push that bile back down your lying throat."

She swallowed. "Mus' leave," she said. "Leave Ravenspur."

"Of course, Mary, but not until you feel better."

"Why do you keep calling me Mary when you know my real name?"

"Because you look like a Mary. I never thought the name suited you, but I do now."

Seventeen

"Drink, Mary. Here, let me help you."

"Yes. Thirsty, Maxey. Where am I?"

"On your bed, inside your bedroom."

"Wha' time's it?"

"Suppertime. I've brought you some rabbit stew."

"I slept all day?"

"Yes." Maxey brushed an errant curl away from her forehead. "Your eyes are dilated, Mary. It's very becoming. Did you know whores use a plant called belladonna in order to dilate their pupils?"

"I'm not a whore."

"That's a matter of opinion."

"Who's opinion?"

"Mine."

"Thirsty, Maxey."

"How many times have I told you to call me *Mister* Stanhope?"

"Could I have water, Mr. Stanhope? Please? The wine's nasty."

"Eat your stew."

"Is it from the hutch?"

"Is what from the hutch?"

"Stew."

"Yes. In due course we eat our rabbits, Mary. Why else would we breed them?"

"For pretty. Bunny pretty."

"So are you, my pet, with your eyes all pupils and your cheeks so red. Shit! You're beginning to get a rash. We don't want imperfections, do we? I'll have to lower the dosage, although it's difficult to control what the rabbits eat. Finish your stew, my angel. Chew. Swallow. One more bite. That's a good girl."

"Gonna throw up. Can't help it, Max... Mr. Stanhope."

"No, my angel, for if you do, I'll feed you more rabbit stew. I'll hold your nose and force it down—"

"Maxey, what's that sound?"

"It's your heart, Mary. You hear your heart."

"Breaking?"

"No. Pounding."

❧

"Wha' time?"

"Morning. I brought you some breakfast, Mary."

"Don't want."

"You must eat and get your strength back."

"Privy."

"The chamber pot's right here."

Calliope thrashed her head from side to side, soaking the pillow with her perspiration. She could hear her heart. When she slept she didn't hear her heart.

"Would you prefer Dottie's help with the chamber pot, Mary?"

"Yes. Oh, yes."

"You look ill, Mary Angelique," Dottie said. "You must eat and get your strength back."

"Bunny poisoned. Tell somebody."

"Nonsense." Dottie chewed a piece of meat. "Would I eat your rabbit stew if it was poisoned?"

"Water, Dottie. Please?"

"I've brewed tea."

"Tea nasty." Calliope lowered her lashes, hoping Dottie and the stew and the tea and her pounding heart and Maxey would go away. Maxey was still in the room. She could feel his eyes staring, probing, eating her alive.

"Do you want to try the chamber pot again, Mary? Mary? Mary Angelique! Maxey, she's sleeping."

"Good. That's what she's supposed to do. Sleep."

"I don't like it, darling. She can't pee, and that could kill her."

"How many rabbits are left, Dot?"

"Ten, twelve, maybe more."

"I meant the ones we fed nightshade, you idiot."

"Don't call me an idiot. Three, I think."

"Kill them and bury them. No. Burn them. We don't want the dogs to dig them up."

"She's breathing funny, Maxey. When will she start feeling better?"

"Tomorrow night."

Calliope heard the murmur of their conversation, but she shut out their voices. Because Brian was here again. This time he held her close and told her she didn't have to drink the nasty tea or eat the pretty bunny. "Brian, please don't leave me. Please love me."

"She's awake," said Dottie.

"No," said Maxey. "She's hallucinating."

⌘

By noon, Calliope felt less muzzy. She knew she still had a fever. Her mouth was dry, her vision blurred, but she had used the chamber pot. Dottie had helped, after letting Calliope drink a glass of water.

"Don't tell Maxey," Dottie had whispered. "Despite what you might believe, Mary Angelique, I don't want you to die."

"Then why are you doing this?"

She ran her hands over her body. "Maxey rewards me well."

"Why is he doing this?"

"You'll find out tomorrow night."

After Dottie left the room, Calliope tried to rise. But using the chamber pot had exhausted her.

In what had become a habitual gesture, she pressed her fingertips against her flushed cheeks. Maxey had put a drug called belladonna in her wine, tea, and stew. He had fed it to the rabbits and then fed the rabbits to her. He could have poisoned her, but he didn't want her dead. He wanted her docile, passive, obedient. He had something in store for her, something that would break her spirit. But she was already as pliable as one of Pollyann's rag dolls, so he meant to humiliate her completely. Maxey was intuitive. He had realized pride was her one vanity. Thus, his plan would include her total degradation.

What was going to happen tomorrow night?

She felt so hot, and yet an icy chill ran up and down

her spine. When she was a wee lass, Papa had hired a tattooed snake charmer for their Kid Show. Calliope had been both frightened and fascinated by the snakes. Their black reptilian eyes were mesmerizing. She had watched a huge python for hours, wondering why his soul lay hidden behind his eyes, wondering why he stared and stared, undulating back and forth, flicking his long, forked tongue.

Brian had said the python wanted to charm the charmer.

"Does the python want to eat the charmer, Brian?"

"No, puss. The python wants to hug him."

Once upon a long time ago, Calliope had watched a snake and wondered how it felt to be trapped inside a cage with those wicked black eyes and that long, forked tongue.

Now she knew.

Eighteen

EVEN THOUGH HER LEGS FELT LIKE PUDDING, CALLIOPE managed to stagger down the hallway. Clutching the banister for support, she listened to the voices that wafted up the staircase. Dottie's voice sounded arrogant. It also sounded loud, as if her visitor was hard of hearing.

"Must I repeat myself, Eve? You cannot see Mrs. O'Connor. She's ill."

"Perhaps the sight of her new gown will spruce her up."

"She's sleeping. Her fiancé, Mr. Maxey Stanhope, says sleep is the best medicine."

"Very well, Mrs. Stanhope. Tell Mary I've sketched the pattern for her engagement party's gown, even though the event was rather last minute. I assume you've received your invitation."

"Mr. Fox's servant brought it straight to me," Dottie said, her voice loud and patronizing.

Aaron Fox? Calliope gripped the banister tightly. *No, Aesop's fox.* Of course it was Aaron Fox. Had she lost what little remained of her mind?

"Tell Mary her gown will be dark gray silk," Eve said, "draped up and over the bustle to show its floral lining in apple green, light gray and red. The underskirt will be a pale orange-yellow silk, fringed and pleated. I might sew a few pink roses at the neckline to enhance her complexion. The barbecue is Saturday. If I don't hear from Mary, the gown will be delivered on Friday."

A barbecue to celebrate my engagement. Saturday. Raymond and Ann will be home by then.

Maxey would have to kill her or cure her, and if he cured her, he would have to secure her silence. *Silence!* Dear God, why wasn't she screaming her head off?

"Eve, please help me." Even to her own ears, her shout sounded like a mousy squeak.

Maxey evidently concurred. Without haste, whistling through his teeth, he strolled down the hallway until he reached her side. Then cinching her waist with one arm, letting her head droop unsupported, he guided her toward her bedroom.

Her head hung so low she felt bitter bile lap at the back of her throat. She wanted to throw up. Instead, she swallowed convulsively. Last night she had succumbed, vomiting tea and stew. Maxey had lost his temper, screaming, "I told you not to do that!" and pinching her breasts until she had begged for mercy.

Now he dragged her inside the bedroom. "Your recuperative powers amaze me, Mary," he fumed, flinging her on top of the bed and reaching for the decanter.

"No," she said, rubbing her cheeks.

"A small dose, my pet. It's nap time. But tonight I want you awake, aware."

"Go to hell, you bastard!"

"Disobey, and you'll suffer the consequences. I promised not to lie with you, Mary, but I can take you standing up."

"Python," she whispered.

"Quit rubbing your cheeks. If you continue, we shall have to bind your hands. Now drink your brandy-wine, my angel."

"Please, Max... Mr. Stanhope. I shall stay in bed, I promise."

"I'll pour." One hand held the glass while his other hand hovered above her breasts. He snapped his fingers, and it sounded like a gunshot. "That way I can dictate the dosage," he said, snapping his fingers again.

Defeated, she opened her mouth like a baby bird.

"Later," said Maxey, "assuming you behave, I'll give you whiskey diluted with water."

Water, blessed water. Behind her closed eyelids, Calliope saw a lake. Brian stood on the shore, arms extended. As she walked toward him, he stepped backwards. She increased her pace, but no matter how fast she moved, he moved faster.

"Brian," she cried. "Brian, wait for me."

Brian laughed.

No. Maxey laughed.

❧

"Once I was happy, but now I'm forlorn, like an old coat that is tattered and torn."

"Stop it!" Maxey scowled. He had given the wench one full tumbler of whiskey to which he'd carefully added two drops of nightshade. Now she was chirping like a caged songbird.

"Left in this wide world to fret and to mourn, betrayed by a man—"

"Shut up!"

"Yes, Mr. Stanhope." Peering at the window, Calliope thought she saw raindrops pelt the pane. Her gaze touched upon Maxey. What demon twisted the soul that hid behind his black reptilian eyes?

Her vision was blurry, but she could see him pace from the window to the bureau, from the potbellied stove to the wardrobe, from the vanity table to the window again. She saw his reflection in the bureau's mirror, and then it was gone.

Halting abruptly, he drew a pocket watch from his gray waistcoat. "How do you feel, Mary?"

"Fine. I'm wondrous fine."

"Good. It's time to get dressed."

Calliope watched him open her wardrobe door, fumble among the contents, then remove her new emerald silk gown. Eve had done a truly remarkable job. The gown was cut low, its skirt draped over a small bustle. On the bustle, a cluster of pink roses— Eve's signature.

"Wear this," said Maxey, tossing the gown toward her pillow. "You must look your very best."

"Why?"

"We're going out."

Her heart was silent because fear… no, *terror* had momentarily stilled its loud pounding. "I won't go," she said, scrubbing her cheeks with her knuckles.

Maxey yanked her from the bed and circled her waist with one hand. Weaving the fingers of his other hand through her hair, he pulled until her head fell back against his shoulder. "When will you learn I mean business?"

Her heart resumed its thunderous thump. When would she learn that defiance incited Maxey's anger? Gesturing frantically toward the green gown, she tried to nod her head.

∽⤫∾

Johnson's office walls were covered with red damask, the windows draped with red velvet. Johnson's desk was a dark, polished mahogany. Maxey glanced at a framed painting of a circus parade and wondered if a wall safe was hidden behind it.

"This is the woman I told you about, Mr. Johnson," he said. "This is Angel."

"You told the truth, Stanhope. She's beautiful."

Maxey glared at Calliope. Why didn't the chit say thank you? Her eyes were enormous, the pupils dilated, and she stood there as if hypnotized.

Shifting his gaze, Maxey watched Johnson rise from the chair behind his desk. Lamplight turned his blond hair silver. He was clothed in a plain white shirt and brown trousers.

"Won't you sit down, Miss Angel?" Johnson nodded toward a red velvet settee. "What's wrong with her, Stanhope? Why doesn't she respond?"

"Angel's French," Maxey replied quickly. "She doesn't speak English." Staring at Calliope's bodice, he snapped his fingers, a gesture more effective than words.

"*Comment vous portez-vous, Monsieur Johnson*," she said softly. "*Son ses un long espace de temps*."

"How do *you* do, Miss Angel?"

"You understand French?" Maxey's voice betrayed his surprise—and his apprehension. He tried to snap his fingers again, but they were slick with moisture.

"I understand many languages, Stanhope."

"In your line of work I suppose you have to. I mean, your hostesses come from everywhere. Your establishment is famous for its variety."

"Let's get down to business. What do you want?"

"A line of credit. Shall we say a thousand dollars?"

"You already owe me more than that."

"I've repaid a large portion of my debt. When I win tonight—"

"What if you lose?"

"I won't lose. I feel lucky. If I'm still in debt, we'll make new arrangements."

"How does Miss Angel feel about that?"

"She will do as I say."

"*Non, monsieur. On ne peut so fier a lui.*" Calliope pulled the words from memory, from Angelique's frequent lapses into French.

Maxey scowled. "What did she say?"

"She said not to trust you." Johnson's gaze lingered on her red-patched cheeks. "I accept your proposition, Stanhope. You'll have your line of credit, but I want the woman for one full week."

"That's impossible!"

Calliope understood Maxey's dilemma. Ann and Raymond would return Friday. Saturday was Aaron Fox's party.

"No woman is worth a thousand dollars for one night, Stanhope, and that's final."

"I'll let you have her until Thursday. Shall we say

midnight? What's a thousand dollars to a man like you? They say you have millions."

"Wait here," Johnson said. Leaving the office, he slammed the door behind him.

"You'll fulfill his every desire, my angel," said Maxey, "or you'll be punished. Do you understand?"

Before Calliope could respond, Johnson entered. "This is Clarissa," he said, indicating the exquisite blonde woman who stood by his side. "Clarissa will escort you through the gaming rooms and serve refreshments. You drink corn whiskey, don't you?"

"Yes." Maxey's black eyes gleamed. "Will Clarissa service all my needs? Some of your whores refuse—"

"My *hostesses* make their own arrangements." Johnson quirked one eyebrow. "You've spent the night here without gambling, but after you wager you rarely quit."

"Seventy-two hours is a long time."

"You plan to remain here?"

"Of course. I must protect my investment."

"You consider Miss Angel an investment?"

"I always have." Turning toward Clarissa, Maxey crooked his arm. "Are you ready, sweetheart? If we don't begin soon, the dice'll cool."

Calliope watched Maxey exit. When the door had closed behind him, she stretched, trying to ease the sore muscles in her taut neck and shoulders.

"Won't you please sit down, Miss Angel?"

"No, thank you. That's a wonderful painting, full of detail, but the elephant's howdah is empty, the cats are uncaged, and the clown looks ever so sad. Did you paint it?"

"Yes. Would you care for a drink?" He nodded toward a well-stocked shelf in the corner. "Wine? Brandy?"

She shuddered. "Water, please." Accepting a glass, she took several sips. "I thought Clarissa was dead."

"It's not her real name. She calls herself Clarissa to please me."

"Your name is real, Bret Johnson. No more Jocko, no more clown. Aren't you afraid of discovery?"

"Clarissa's judge passed away ten months ago. The reward was dispersed among his eager relatives. For the love of God, Calliope, why does Stanhope control you like Brian O'Connor controlled his cats? No, damn it! A cat will snarl and show her claws. Your behavior is more like Dublin, blindly circling the ring. Are you playing some sort of mercurial game?"

Her reply stuck in her throat, so she merely shook her head.

"I've watched you struggle across a slick trestle," he continued. "I've seen you brandish your whip at a cage full of wild lions and tigers. I've heard you give orders to guy-out the tents when a windstorm threatened. What's the matter with you?"

"It's a long story, Jocko." Calliope drained the water from her glass and burst into tears.

He stepped forward and pressed her face against his chest. "Hush, darling. I'm sorry I shouted. You don't have to explain right away. We have time. Don't cry, little girl, I'll protect you."

Calliope felt her belly knot. Jocko had destroyed her circus. Maxey was satanic, but Jocko's sins were greater by far. He had murdered countless numbers of gillys, her animals, Brian. And Jocko's reward was a successful gambling house. How dare he offer protection!

"You look flushed." Scooping her up into his arms, he carried her to the settee. "Rest here. I'll make all the arrangements. A private room and dinner. There's no Cook Top at my establishment, but my chef is an expert." He lightly kissed her quivering lips then left the office.

How many rooms were inside his establishment? After alighting from the carriage, all Calliope could see was a brick building, three stories high, blending into the background with others along the lamp-lit side-walk. Trees shed leafy teardrops over a cobblestone path. Maxey had ushered her through the front door then guided her up a staircase, but she had seen the men and women laughing, whispering, watching her with curious eyes.

Lay-deez and gen-tul-men, the Congress of Freaks presents Calliope Kelley, a live, wingless angel.

She recalled her futile plan to find and assassinate Jocko.

Now was the perfect opportunity.

She would kill the clown, then find Maxey and shoot him. She'd aim for his reptilian eyes and forked tongue, because he didn't have a heart.

Her heart was pounding again. Rising from the settee, Calliope rummaged through desk drawers, searching for a pistol. There was no weapon except a sharp letter opener, and she truly doubted she could stab a man to death. A gun was quick, neat, a tug on the trigger, and she was an expert. How many times had she shot at a target, releasing her pigeons?

Damn and blast! There was no pistol. The letter opener would have to do. She hid the thin piece of metal inside her bodice.

Though the water had temporarily soothed her parched throat, Maxey's drug was having an effect. He had tempered the dose, but her heart sounded like the clickety-clack of her railroad cars. Maybe the sight of Jocko had caused her fever to soar. Her skin felt hot and dry.

With a whimper, Calliope rubbed her cheeks.

Office walls compressed, expanded, compressed again. Red damask rotated—a bloody, spinning vortex. Birds pecked at her skull with their pointed beaks. Why were the pigeons attacking when they were supposed to land on her arms?

Trying to avoid their wings, Calliope waved her hands and lost her balance. She plunged toward the floor. Upon landing, she felt an excruciating pain in her left breast. Behind closed eyelids, she saw Dublin circling the ring.

She let her body adjust to his comfortable gait. 'Round and 'round Dublin cantered, until she heard somebody call her name. Jocko? Brian? Papa?

"Blow your whistle for the next act, Papa," she said. But she wasn't sure Sean heard her. Because her words were *whooshing* like a flotilla of wind-swept, galloping ghosts.

Then the ghosts disappeared, and she saw the bloodstained hand of her evil leprechaun.

Nineteen

DIFFUSED BY SHEER DRAPES, SUNBEAMS FRECKLED THE bedroom and gave a greenish cast to the pale blue blankets. As Calliope shifted on the mattress, she felt a throbbing pain in her left arm.

She sniffed. *Chicken broth!* Damn! Why did she always awaken after a disaster to the potent perfume of boiled domestic fowl?

Jocko said, "Were you trying to kill yourself?"

He looked exhausted, even though he reclined in an armchair with his legs stretched out, ankles crossed and resting on an upholstered ottoman.

She blinked. "What happened?"

"As far as I can determine, you fainted and stabbed yourself on the blade of my letter opener. What was my letter opener doing inside your bodice?"

"I hid it there," she replied without thinking.

"Why?"

Last night came back in an almost overwhelming flood of memories, and her mind raced as she attempted to invent a plausible explanation. "Jocko, you run an establishment devoted to devious pleasures.

Gambling. Prostitution, even if you do call your women hostesses."

"Do you honestly believe I'd turn you over to one of my guests? Unlike your friend Maxey Stanhope, I don't consider you an investment."

"I was muzzy-minded."

"True. Why did you take belladonna?"

"Belladonna?"

"Don't play innocent with me, darling. Belladonna, sleeping nightshade, naked lady lily. I've covered your beautiful face with wet towels, poured glass after glass of water down your beautiful throat, and—damn it, Calliope! Belladonna is toxic. A larger dose and you could have slipped into a coma."

"How did you know? The belladonna, I mean."

"Some of my hostesses use the plant for cosmetic purposes. It dilates their pupils."

"That's where he got it," she murmured under her breath.

"What? I couldn't hear you."

"Rabbits," she said louder. "The Stanhopes breed rabbits and... and the rabbits ate nightshade. I was hungry, so I cooked up a rabbit stew."

Jocko was regarding her with disbelief, and Calliope wondered why she bothered to fib. Because she wanted to hang on to her tattered pride, that's why. How could she admit she had believed the empty promises of a snake in the guise of a man? How could she admit Maxey had abused her breasts until she begged for mercy? How could she admit Maxey had drugged his fiancée while his evil mind conjured up a plan that would benefit him and, at the same time, effect her total degradation?

Perhaps it might be prudent to change the subject.

Sitting up, she propped pillows behind her back. "How did you escape from the fire, Jocko?"

"I was inside the tent, waiting to exchange my gun for your ostrich feathers. When I saw the flames, I jumped on top of Big John's horse and rode for help. Upon returning, I couldn't find you. Cuckoo swore you made it out under the sidewalls, but we couldn't find you, even though Brian and I searched—"

"Brian?" Her breath shot out in short gasps. Bolting upright, she felt pain course through her shoulder. "Brian's dead! He died in the fire!"

Swiftly rising from his chair, Jocko eased her back onto the pillows. "Stay still, Calliope. Don't move so abruptly, or you'll start the bleeding again."

"Brian's dead," she whispered.

"No, darling. Brian managed to shift a cage away from the top's entrance. That's why so many gillys busted loose."

"If he's alive, where is he?" Calliope felt as though she stood directly beneath a pelting shower of icy pins and needles. She had never been so cold in her life.

Seating himself on the edge of her blanket, Jocko shrugged. "We went our separate ways. Many performers were injured, and Brian said he knew how to raise money to pay for their care. I left Denver. Brian… well… he… disappeared. Didn't he abandon you once before when you needed him the most?"

Jocko was him-hamming, she thought, either stumbling around the truth or downright lying. But why? The answer was simple. If dead, Brian remained locked in her heart forever. If alive, he had abandoned her again, and she would grow to hate him. It was to Jocko's advantage she believe Brian alive.

"How did you end up here?" she asked.

"I flipped a coin."

"What?"

"A coin, Calliope. Even a clown has coins. I flipped a coin. Heads I'd travel North, tails South. I sold my pig for passage money. On the stage to Colorado Springs, I met a man who commissioned a painting. When the portrait was completed, I used my fee as the stake in a poker game."

"You won enough to build your establishment?"

"I won the establishment and renamed it Cirque de Delices."

"Circus of delights," she translated. "What time is it, please?"

"Seven. The sun is setting."

"I slept a whole day?"

"Two days. It's Thursday. A doctor treated your punctures with a poultice. I woke you several times to force water and broth down your throat, change your bandages, and help you pee. Don't blush, Calliope, everybody pees. Unless, of course, they consume vast quantities of belladonna."

She rubbed her cheeks with her hands. "Who usually occupies this room?"

"Clarissa."

"Where did she spend her nights? With Maxey?"

"No. With me. Does that disturb you?"

"Why should it disturb me?"

"Vanity. Pride."

"My vanity was destroyed by a circus fire."

"And your pride?"

"Where's Maxey?" she asked, unwilling to discuss what little remained of her tattered pride.

"Stanhope hasn't left the gaming rooms. He's won a sizable amount, darling, but in the end he has to lose. You see, he doesn't know when to quit."

"Thank you for taking care of me."

"Thank you for taking care of *me*."

"What do you mean?"

"You knew I was hiding from something or someone when I joined your circus. After the lawman's visit, you kept on protecting me."

And you repaid me by torching my circus, she screamed silently, squeezing her eyes shut so he couldn't see the hatred smoldering as brightly as the flames that had consumed her Big Top.

And yet a feeling of doubt nudged the very edge of her brain, like a mouse nibbling at a piece of trap-cheese. Jocko wasn't her evil leprechaun. He had joined the circus after Mum's fall. He couldn't have tossed the nosegay; Brian would have seen him do it. Unless Brian's attention was wholly focused on Susan. Jocko could have lured Papa to the pie car and pushed Napoleon's buggy up against the cat cage, but what would be his motive? Why would he want Sean dead? Why would he want *her* dead?

The fire was a different story. She had provoked him with her confession. He had called her Jane. He had made threats.

Calliope pictured the fleeing shadow she had glimpsed while waiting for her act to begin. At the time she had thought it might be the clown, or

Panama, or her absent ringmaster. Could Jocko have really waited inside the tent? She had been so angry at Brian's announcement, she hadn't noticed. But if Jocko didn't lie about his actions during the fire, it meant he spoke the truth about Brian, and that wasn't possible.

If Brian was alive, he'd move mountains to find her. He'd investigate all rumors. Good Lord, he'd shout her name from every nook and cranny. Granted, she had hidden her true identity, but Brian would realize Mary Angelique O'Connor was Calliope Kelley. Wouldn't he read the newspapers? Immediately after the Spring Ball, the Denver paper had carried the announcement of her betrothal, and he would have seen the name Mary Angelique O'Connor. He would have put two and two together and… had Brian left Colorado? He wouldn't do that if there was the slightest chance she was alive.

Jocko lied. Brian was dead. If he wasn't, he didn't love her, had never loved her, and that couldn't be true.

"Calliope?"

"I'm fine. Wondrous fine." She opened her eyes. "Do you really have a million dollars?"

"What?"

"Maxey said you had millions."

"Not nearly that much, darling. But an establishment devoted to devious pleasures is very profitable. I've invested my earnings in real estate and the stock market, which, as you know, is merely another form of gambling."

"I attended a fancy ball and met rich gillys. Are you a rich gilly now, Jocko?"

"Perhaps. But I'm not a gilly-galloo. I remember

how you always wanted to be a lady. You hated what you called Marys, yet desperately wanted to be one. I think I made my fortune with that paradox in mind, just in case I found you again. What would you do with a million dollars, darling?"

"Buy a circus," she answered promptly.

"Of course." He grinned. "You may borrow one of Clarissa's gowns."

For the first time, Calliope realized she wore a negligee. If Dottie believed Mary Angelique's ball costume provocative, she'd faint at the sight of this wispy piece of cream-colored material. Calliope reached for the blanket but halted her motion.

Are you daft, girl? Who changed the bandages on your breast? Who held the chamber pot?

"Is my own gown beyond repair?" she asked.

"I'm afraid so. The letter opener was very sharp, and you bled a lot."

"The bloody hand. It was yours." Instinctively, she pressed her hand against her wound. "Why do you want me to clothe myself? Didn't you buy me for your pleasure?"

"No." He grinned, and Calliope could almost swear she saw the outline of a painted frown edging downward toward his chin. "Maybe. At first. With your injury, it's out of the question. Instead, you must accompany me through the gaming rooms. I shall be the envy of every man, while your beauty shall be the target of every woman's jealousy. Despite what you said before, my darling, I have the feeling your vanity is still intact."

"You allow women to gamble?"

He chuckled. "You'd be surprised at how many ladies contribute to the upkeep of my Cirque. Naturally, it's not their original intent. Yet they seem to lose more cheerfully than men. Women are more... shall we say, matter-of-fact?"

"I wouldn't lose cheerfully. I have no money, Jocko. I'm not a rich lady."

"Is that why you hooked up with Stanhope?"

"No."

"Then why, darling?"

"Maxey Stanhope is my fiancé."

"What?"

"It's true. I removed my engagement ring because it kept slipping off my finger." She laughed bitterly. "Due to a recent illness, I've lost weight."

"Why would Stanhope barter his fiancée for gambling money, Calliope?"

"Maxey would sell his soul for gambling money. In truth, he already has. I thought his soul was hidden behind his eyes, but now I understand he has no soul."

"What are you babbling about? You're not making any sense."

"Nothing makes sense. I'm a ward of Ann and Raymond Stanhope, engaged to their son. I said it was a long story, but it's not so long after all."

"Why don't you leave him?"

"*That's* a long story."

"If you have no place else to go, live here at the Cirque, with me."

"As one of your hostesses?"

"No. As my wife."

"If Brian's alive, I'm already wed."

There! I've paid him back in his own coin! It was to his advantage to have Brian alive, but it put a rather large snag in his proposition.

"You're not legally wed, Calliope."

"Brian and I said our vows before God."

"In that case, my darling hypocrite, you can't marry Stanhope."

"Maxey's parents are away on a visit. They return tomorrow. I'll invent some excuse and leave Colorado." She took a deep breath. "Will you lend me some money, Jocko? Please?"

"Not a chance," he said, rising from the bed. "Why would I help you vanish from my sight when I've finally found you again?"

"I own a very valuable mare. She was given to me as a gift and—"

"I said no, Calliope."

"Wait! Let me finish. I'll pledge the mare for a line of credit. You can name the amount."

"You plan to gamble?"

"Why not? If I win, I shall have enough to travel, perhaps even join a circus. If I lose, I'll forfeit my mare."

"I don't want your damned mare." Jocko stared at her body, clearly outlined by the flimsy negligee. "All right. I'll stake you to five hundred dollars."

"You gave Maxey a thousand!"

"And in return I received damaged merchandise. I'm not completely altruistic, Calliope."

"Why do I always forget how nasty you can be, Jocko?"

"The name is Bret, darling. Bret Johnson. Don't you want to hear *my* proposition?"

She blinked with surprise. "My mare... I thought... you said—"

"I said I didn't want your mare. If you lose, I'll expect you to become a member of my establishment."

Mulling it over in her mind, she gazed upon a waist-high vase of dried pampas grass. "All right, Jocko, I mean Bret. It's a bargain. If I lose—"

"I win."

As she nodded, Calliope discovered she wasn't the least bit muzzy. Her mouth didn't feel dry as toast. She could hear her heart, but its pounding was due to anticipation, not Maxey's drug. She flexed her shoulder. It felt stiff and sore.

Luckily, her left breast was injured. Because she needed her right arm to throw the dice.

∝

Calliope saw herself reflected in the gambling room's mirrored walls. Her borrowed gown was gold taffeta. Bret walked by her side, resplendent in a black shirt, gold brocade vest, and black trousers.

"The player who takes the box and dice must throw a chance for the company," he said. "It must be greater than four but not more than nine, otherwise he must keep throwing until he can produce five, six, seven, eight, or nine. Do you understand?"

"I've always been good at numbers," she replied. "Don't talk to me as if I were a child."

"This done, you must throw your own chance, which may be above three but not exceed ten. You don't look like a child, Calliope. You look beautiful, like a lady. Or should I say a Mary?"

"No. Please. Mary doesn't exist anymore. No matter what happens tonight, I shall be Calliope Kelley again."

So many people, she thought, glancing around the room. Where did they all come from? The air reeked of tobacco. Cigar smoke floated up toward the ceiling, which resembled a cloudy summer sky before a pending storm. Ceiling blades whipped through the smoke, adding to the illusion.

Excitement was palpable. Calliope felt as if she could reach out and capture lightning bolts on the palms of her hands. Voices shouted, loud as thunder. Trying to ignore the clamor, she brought her attention back to Bret.

"If you throw two aces or trois ace, commonly known as crabbing or crabs, you lose your stake," he said. "If you throw seven, and seven or eleven is thrown immediately after, it's called a nick, and you win. If eight is the number, and you throw eight or twelve, it's another nick."

"That sounds easy. No wonder hazard is Maxey's favorite game."

Bret quirked an eyebrow. "Stanhope owes the Cirque more than a thousand dollars, and tonight he plays poker inside a private room. Wouldn't you prefer a game of cards, darling?"

"No, thank you." Calliope's gaze touched upon Bret's employees. While she had clothed herself, he had bragged about his establishment. The man who dealt cards was called an Operator, and two Crowpees gathered money for the Bank. A man at the back of the room, near the roulette wheel, was called a Puff. He decoyed others to play the game. Dunners recovered money lost at play. Hostesses served refreshments and snuffed out candles, replacing them with fresh tapers.

Would she soon become a hostess? Only if she lost.

"I understand the rules," she said, raising her chin. "I throw a chance for myself and the other players. I keep throwing until I win with a nick or lose to the others. Even if I don't toss the dice myself, I can bet with the thrower by placing my money on the table, inside a circle. Hurry, Bret, please. I'm anxious to begin."

He grinned and nodded toward a Puff, who immediately relinquished his space to Calliope.

After an hour, maybe longer, she had lost most of her stake. Hazard was a slow game, and the big winner belonged to a group placing side bets. The man next to her smelled like Dottie "on holiday." He was short, rotund, and wore a light brown shirt. Calliope thought the wet patches beneath his armpits bore a remarkable resemblance to wet tent canvas.

Stepping closer to the table, she shook the box and tossed her dice. Ivory squares stared back at her. Two unblinking eyes. Maxey Stanhope's eyes.

"Snake eyes," she said as the Dunner collected her chips.

"That's a good one, little lady," said the short, fat man. "Snake eyes. Never heard *that* before."

The room was hot, stuffy. Perspiration trickled down Calliope's bodice, soaking her bandages and making her wounds itch and sting. Since it was unusual—practically unheard of—for a woman to cast the dice, men crowded around the table and watched. Several whispered in her ear, naming high amounts if she would retire to a room upstairs. "My hostesses make their own arrangements," Bret had told Maxey. But she wasn't a hostess, and she had no intention of ever becoming one. After tonight she would never let a man touch her again.

Unless you lose, whispered a voice inside her head. If she kept throwing those damn snake eyes, she would end up as Bret Johnson's personal property.

"Do you want to quit, darling?" he said. "Shall we rest? Perhaps drink a glass of wine?"

"No. My luck will change. It has to change." She placed chips inside the circle, betting with the fat man, and groaned when his throw came up trois ace.

"I did suggest cards, Calliope, or you might try the wheel."

"Explain the rules," she said, glancing at the back of the room toward the roulette wheel.

"You keep wrinkling your lovely nose as if you smelled a rat. Let's take a breath of fresh air." Offering his arm, he led her toward a door in the mirrored wall.

Dizzy from the heat, the smoke, and the hum of conversation, she clutched Bret tightly and leaned against him.

"Are you ill?" he asked, sounding concerned.

"I'm fine. Wondrous fine. But the noise is deafening. Can't it be heard in the street? I thought gambling was illegal."

"I've added shutters, closely fitted to window frames, which are padded and covered with green baize. There's an inner door placed along the passage, with an aperture. My employees can see all who enter, a precaution that prevents a surprise visit from any officer of justice. You'll learn all this, and more, when you become a member of my Cirque."

"Only if I forfeit my stake. I still have a hundred and fifty dollars left."

Guiding her onto a small balcony, Bret kissed her lips. At the same time, he very lightly caressed her shoulders.

She staggered backwards, and her hands rubbed her cheeks as if he had slapped her face. "Don't do that!"

"What's wrong?"

"You agreed to wait."

"Calliope, it was just one kiss."

"I know. I'm sorry but I can't..." She couldn't tolerate a man's touch.

Bret stared at her, a frown denting the area between his tawny eyebrows. "Okay," he said. "I get the idea. You want to play out this ridiculous game of chance. You've always been a stubborn gazoony."

"Please explain roulette." Calliope inhaled fresh air, hoping to calm her shaking body. Truthfully, she had overreacted, but Maxey's actions inside the stable had ruined any pleasure she might receive from a man's embrace.

"It's really quite simple, darling. The wheel has thirty-one numbers, one through twenty-eight, a single zero, a double zero, and a picture of an American eagle, which is the equivalent of a triple zero. You can place a bet on any number. When the ball drops into zero, zero-zero, or Eagle, the bank wins all chips except those on the winning symbol. You can bet on red or black, which pays even money."

"How much can I win on the zeroes or eagle?"

"Single number bets are paid off at odds of twenty-seven to one."

"So if I wager on a single number, I could win"—she swiftly added numbers in her head—"four thousand and fifty dollars."

"Not really. The Operator collects your original bet."

"All right. After paying the Bank and returning your five-hundred dollar stake, I would still have over three thousand. Correct?"

"Yes. However, there are table limits."

"Are you saying I can't bet all my money at one time?"

"Not unless I give permission."

"It's only a paltry hundred and fifty dollars!"

"I run this circus, not you."

"Will you let me wager my entire stake?"

"It's highly unlikely the ball would drop into your single number, Calliope. That's why the odds are so high. You'd be wiser to bet on red or black."

"Will you raise the limit, Bret? Please?"

"If you insist."

After they had reentered the gaming room, Calliope headed straight for the roulette wheel. Walking closer, she noticed the numbers were not in sequence. Five was followed by twenty-four, followed by seven, twenty-two, nine, then the American Eagle, representing three zeroes. *Three!* It was time to give the number three another chance.

Before she could change her mind, she placed all her chips on Eagle.

Bret joined the Operator. Both men glanced her way. Was Bret telling him to raise the limit? Or was

Bret telling him to cheat? If that was the case, she was doomed from the start. Bret had always wanted her, had burned down her circus in a jealous rage. The blasted paladin had even suggested roulette, yet made it seem her own choice. Could he rig the wheel? Of course he could. Cards too—the reason she'd decided to toss the dice. But the dice could easily be weighted. If Bret was a cheat, she really had no control over her destiny.

Roulette was certainly faster than hazard. One turn of the wheel, and if the Operator was honest, she might be free. Or she might be enslaved by Bret Johnson. One quick turn of the wheel, and if she couldn't control her destiny, at least she'd know her fate.

Bret stood by her side. Ignoring him, she watched the numbers spin, becoming almost a blur, until the ball slowed and stopped.

"Congratulations, darling." Bret grinned.

"Don't take my chips off Eagle, let it ride," she said, remembering words shouted at the dice table.

"Are you stark raving mad? Don't you realize how impossible—"

"Tell the Operator to raise the limit, please. No, don't leave my side. You bring me luck."

Bret hesitated then nodded toward the Operator.

Immediately, Calliope regretted her impulsive action. Why hadn't she collected her winnings and walked away?

Too late! The Operator had called "No more bets."

She would stab herself with a dozen letter openers before allowing a man to use her body. No, she amended sadly. If there was the slightest possibility

Brian was truly alive, she must find him. Maybe he had lost his memory… like Gwendolyn.

What would be the odds against both Brian and Gwendolyn losing their memories? More than twenty-seven to one.

Don't mull over Brian. Don't think about anything except the wheel.

The wheel wasn't a cage full of wild cats, and yet Calliope knew if she lost eye contact she'd forfeit her stake.

For the first time, there was total silence as everybody in the room stopped playing and watched the wheel spin.

It spun 'round and 'round. Calliope felt as if she performed inside center ring, galloping in a circle. Once she had stared toward a hoop of fire. Now she stared at the wheel with the same intensity.

Eagle!

Numbers whirled, blurred.

Eagle! Land on Eagle!

The ball slowed, bounced twice, once, and dropped on Eagle.

The crowd gasped. It sounded like a collective breeze.

"Do you want to continue wagering, darling?" Bret shielded her from the excited press of people. "I believe you've earned over a hundred thousand dollars. If you win again," he teased, "you'll own my establishment."

What a fine revenge, she thought, better than stabbing or shooting. Bret had destroyed her circus, and now she had a chance to ruin his. She was sorely tempted to let her bet ride.

The word "ride" echoed inside her head. She had enough money to buy a small circus, hire performers and a few roustabouts. She'd teach Brandywine new tricks, resurrect her act.

But she felt so lucky. Should she wager one more time?

What had Bret said about Maxey? *In the end, he has to lose. You see, he doesn't know when to quit.*

"I quit," she stated, her voice firm.

"Good girl," said Bret.

Men and women reached out to touch her, hoping her luck would rub off on them. For a moment, she tensed, wanting to escape their hands. Then she relaxed. They weren't threatening. They loved winners. They loved *her*. She wasn't a Kid Show freak. She was the star performer.

"When may I have my winnings?" she asked.

"Tomorrow." Bret escorted her through the room. "I'll have my bank draw up a draft. Or would you prefer cash?"

"Cash, please. It will make it easier to escape. I mean, leave."

Once again, that small frown appeared between his eyes. "Stanhope collects you at midnight. Please stay here, darling. You'll be safe, I promise."

"No. I must return to Ravenspur, Maxey's estate."

"Why must you?"

"I must say good-bye to Mr. and Mrs. Stanhope, pack my belongings, and make arrangements for my mare. *And attend Aaron Fox's barbecue!*

Eve might be there. Calliope planned to gently prod Eve's memory. Perhaps Bret told the truth. Perhaps the ringmaster had not been trampled, had not burned. Furthermore, Calliope might see other performers. Surely all of them wouldn't have left Colorado. It was a very slim chance, but a chance nonetheless.

Why not play Mary a few more days? With Ann and Raymond present, Maxey would leave her alone. She wouldn't drink anything except the water she poured with her own two hands, and the servants would serve meals.

As if he had read her mind, Bret said, "Won't you join me for a late repast?"

"Yes, oh yes. I'm hungry, starving. I could eat a horse!"

"We don't serve *equus caballus*, my darling."

"What?"

"Horse is not the Cirque's most popular fare. Crow. Sometimes foot. I've heard guests say they'd like to eat their words. What fine dishes may I instruct my chef to prepare, Miss Kelley?"

"Quail and caviar," she answered promptly.

"I'll bet a thousand dollars you've never tasted either."

He sounded younger, more like the clown she had once adored. "You win," she said. "Isn't gambling fun?"

"Only if you know when to quit. You haven't told me everything about Stanhope, Calliope, and I have a feeling… Please remain here as my guest."

"I'm not scared, Bret, not anymore."

"The cats didn't frighten you, and look what happened. A lion nearly bit your head off."

"I'm not scared," she repeated.

Picturing that long-ago evening outside the performers' entrance, she heard the echo of Brian's words: *You should be scared.*

Twenty

CALLIOPE STRETCHED, PLEASED HER SHOULDER HAD LOST its painful throb. Her cuts itched, but the irritating tickle meant her wounds were on the mend.

Rising from her bed, ignoring her slippers, she donned a blue velvet robe. Then she strolled past the dressing table and potbellied stove until she reached the window. An overcast midmorning sky reminded her of Jocko's smoke-filled ceiling, and she uttered a brief invocation. "Please, God, let the weather clear by tomorrow."

During their ride to the Cirque de Delices, Maxey had said Aaron Fox's party was to be held outdoors, with food spitted over pits. Maxey had said Fox had hired musicians. So it would be a circus again; a dance-to-the-music circus; a beef-cooked-on-spits-over-pits circus. Pre-senting Aaron Fox's Spit Circus.

Calliope stifled the urge to spit. Maxey had remained at the gambling house, unwilling to halt his winning streak. It was Jocko who had made the arrangements for her carriage ride back to Ravenspur.

Bret, not Jocko. She must remember he was now

Bret, even though, after he delivered her winnings, she had no intention of ever setting eyes on him again. She would try to forget her revenge scheme. After all, she had stripped his Bank of funds, and he had acted very nicely—like a gentleman.

But Bret would win that money back, and more. Last night, walking from the room, she had watched people crowd around the roulette table, placing their chips on Eagle. Her unexpected windfall had lured them to the wheel.

Calliope's mouth turned up in a wry grin. "I played a Puff," she said then whirled about when she heard footsteps.

"Aunt Mary, Aunt Mary, I'm home." Pollyann skipped into the room. "And you have a present."

"I do?"

"A big brown giant brought 'round a new traveling case. It has straps, and it's smaller than the grips we took to Kansas, but very nice. Are you going away, Aunt Mary?"

"Yes, darling."

"Damn!"

"Hush." Calliope hugged the child. "Your mother would not approve of that word, especially before breakfast."

"I already ate my eggs, and Uncle Maxey says that word all the time."

Calliope's heart skipped a beat. "Is Uncle Maxey home?"

"Where else would he be?" Pollyann's eyes sparkled with mischief. "He's asleep in his bed. I tried to wake him, but he shouted damn and lots of other bad words."

"When did your grandparents get home?"

"Last night. Very late. Mummy wouldn't let us see you. Mummy said you took medicine to make you sleep. She said you were sick and Uncle Maxey was scared out of his whips."

"Wits, Pollyann."

"Your hair's mussed, and your face is pink, Aunt Mary, but you don't look sick."

"That's because I'm all better now. Won't you join me for breakfast? I know you've had yours, but you can talk while I nibble my toast."

"No, Aunt Mary. I've been gone so long I have to say hello to my pony and my dead dollies."

"Dead dollies?"

"Yes. Poor dead things. They're buried in the vegetable garden. I must dig them up and kiss their poor dead faces and say a prayer for their poor dead souls. My new dolly almost died, the one Uncle Maxey gave me. It scared me out of my *whips*."

"Pollyann! I told you not to bother Mrs. O'Connor." Dottie walked into the room, followed by Ann. "Are you feeling better, Mary Angelique? We were all so concerned over the length of your illness, especially Maxey."

Maxey was at Bret Johnson's, you liar! This performance is for Ann's benefit, and you mention Maxey's name as a threat, in order to make certain I dovetail your trumped-up story.

"Aunt Mary doesn't look sick, Mummy. She looks pretty and smells like flowers."

Dottie's pale blue eyes narrowed, but her lips stretched into a thin smile when Ann rushed forward and hugged Calliope.

"I'm so glad you're feeling better, my dear," Ann gushed. "Goodness gracious, is that a bandage? What happened?"

Calliope caught Dottie's penetrating glare. She probably thought Maxey's nails were responsible for the breast-gash. Calliope didn't give a hang about Maxey anymore, but why disturb Ann's peace of mind?

"I tumbled from my mare and landed on a cluster of brambles. Two thorns left nasty scratches, but my injury is on the mend. Please don't fret, Ann."

"I won't, not if you say you're all right. I feel quite ruffled, my dear. First Dottie told us about your illness. Then she said Mr. Fox was holding a barbecue in your honor, to celebrate your engagement. Isn't that romantic? Goodness gracious, I nearly forgot. A rather large black man delivered a traveling case. He wanted to hand it over to you, Mary, but I told him you were indisposed. Then he refused to leave until I promised not to let the case out of my sight and brought it to you personally, unopened."

"Where is it?"

"Directly outside your bedroom door. Dottie wanted to peek, but I wouldn't let her. I gave the colored man my word."

"He was only a Negro, Mother Ann."

"A promise is a promise, Dottie."

"Thank you," Calliope said. "I purchased the grip for my trousseau. Then I foolishly left it at Eve's apparel shop. She must have packed my new gown inside and sent it here."

"Your gown for Mr. Fox's party, dear?"

"Yes," Calliope fibbed, knowing her dark gray

silk hung inside the wardrobe; she had discovered it last night. "I would remove my gown from the grip and show it to you, but I want my appearance to be a surprise."

Calliope darted a glance toward Dottie. Had the frowzy crone been present when Gwendolyn delivered the gown? If so, would she insist Mary Angelique open the case and show its contents?

But Dottie's plucked eyebrows merely drew together above the bridge of her nose as she stared down at Calliope's bare feet. "You're not planning to costume yourself in a gown that shows your petticoats and leaves your limbs bare, are you Mary Angelique?"

Calliope breathed a sigh of relief. Apparently, a maid had taken the gown from Eve and hung it inside the wardrobe. Didn't the maid wonder why Maxey's fiancée was missing? Yet even during her illness, when Dottie had cooked up her damned rabbit stews, the servants had pretended nothing was out of the ordinary. No one had visited her room to dust or even empty what the upstairs maid called the "slop jar." Dottie must have bribed them. Or perhaps Maxey had threatened them with instant dismissal.

"Of course she isn't planning to expose her limbs," said Ann. "*Are* you, Mary dear?"

"My gown is quite proper, its design brilliant. Eve sewed thin whalebone stays through the waist and bodice so I don't have to wear a corset."

"No corset? That's indecent!" Dottie's eyes widened with shock.

"No corset? How wonderful," Ann said at the same time.

"Mother Ann!"

"I hate the damn things." She blushed and looked around for Pollyann, but the child had already slipped through the open doorway and disappeared. "I'm going to pay Eve a visit first thing next week. Come, Dottie, let's allow Mary to get dressed in private while we help Cook prepare hot tea and toast."

"Please don't bother, Ann. I shall prepare it myself." Calliope held Dottie's gaze until the pawky Jane paled and looked away.

After both women had left her bedroom, Calliope swiftly retrieved the case, placed it on her bed, fumbled at the straps, and lifted the lid.

So much money! Bret had sent stacks of bills wrapped in bands of paper.

Staring into the case, Calliope saw a huge tent filled with happy gillys. She smelled popped corn and sawdust. She heard applause as Brandywine galloped 'round center ring. She didn't see money. She saw freedom.

Maxey would see freedom too. His, not hers. If he found the case, he'd steal it and use its contents to gamble.

She was sorely tempted to pack her clothes and ride toward Denver this very afternoon. Forget Aaron Fox's party. But she wanted to play the lady one more time and prove to Maxey her pride was intact, unimpaired. It was the only revenge scheme she could summon. She didn't care to charm the snake, but she wouldn't mind if he ate humble pie. And if she could somehow manage to put a lethal dose of nightshade in his pie, she would do so without a moment's hesitation. Since that was impossible, her lady-performance would have to suffice.

Meanwhile, she must hide her money. Where? In her bedroom? The stables? If Maxey had learned about her luck at the gaming tables, he'd search both places. Then she remembered Pollyann's dead dollies.

Braiding her untidy hair, donning her slippers, Calliope hefted the grip, carried it down a back staircase, and tiptoed past the servants' quarters.

The gardens were deserted, and the earth looked newly dug. Pollyann must have visited her cemetery and greeted her "corpses."

Calliope glanced toward the carriage house. Pollyann's pony would be tethered on the other side, near the stable. But the child could appear any moment, and that meant certain discovery. Pollyann would want to know why Aunt Mary was hiding the case and would tell Dottie, or even worse, Maxey.

Without further hesitation, Calliope plunged both hands into the dirt. She wished she had thought to bring a shovel, but the ground was soft from three days of intermittent thunderstorms. She dug at a furious pace, uncovering a floppy-eared stuffed dog and a Julia Grant doll. Unlike the president's wife, the doll's porcelain features were passive, even though its painted eyes were filled with dirt, and a plump worm crawled out from its matted wig.

Calliope shuddered. She had the distinct impression someone was watching her. She glanced about, puzzled. The gardens were deserted. Billowing clouds promised more rain, so nobody dared hang clothes on the line. Cook was preparing a welcome feast for

Ann and Raymond, while other servants polished the floors and dusted the furniture. Pollyann was nowhere in sight.

Slowly, Calliope's gaze shifted upwards until her gaze touched upon Maxey's bedroom. There he stood, half hidden by the window's plum-colored drapes. She couldn't distinguish his features, but she knew he was staring down at her.

Damn and blast! She'd have to find a new hiding place.

         *

Calliope hid the money then stuck like a cocklebur to Raymond or Ann, confessing she had missed them so much she couldn't let them out of her sight. She even suggested that Pollyann spend the night in her bedroom.

"I'll listen to Pollyann's prayers and read Mr. Aesop's story about the fox and the grapes," Calliope said. She sat at the dinner table but accepted her food only after the rest of the family had taken their portions. "Is that all right, Dottie?"

"Of course, Mary Angelique."

Thom had returned for the barbecue, and Dottie was no longer "on vacation." Bathed and perfumed, she looked subdued, guilty. Thom had spent the afternoon consoling Pollyann. "Mummy and Mary ate my bunnies," the child kept sobbing.

Not Mummy, just Mary.

She could tell by Maxey's dour expression and the barely suppressed coil of his body that he had lost everything at the Cirque, including his thousand-dollar stake. Bret was right. Maxey didn't know when to quit.

Calliope spent the next day prowling around Ravenspur, silently saying her farewells, stifling the urge to hug Ann and Raymond every few minutes. She'd miss them so much, but she had been born and bred to play the circus performer.

The circus was forever, even if love was not.

❧

Calliope was admiring her new gray gown, planning to slide it carefully over her curls, when Maxey entered without knocking.

"Get out," she said. "We leave soon for Mr. Fox's party, and I must get dressed."

"Where is it?"

"Where is what?"

"The money."

She didn't pretend to misunderstand. "Bret said he would deliver a bank draft tomorrow."

"Tomorrow's Sunday. The banks are closed."

"You've searched my bedroom, Maxey." She glanced toward Clarissa's gold gown flung carelessly across a small chair. It didn't matter that everything was out of place, since she planned to pack and ride for Denver at the crack of dawn.

"Why were you in the vegetable garden, Mary? Why were you digging a hole for your grip?"

"I wanted to surprise Pollyann, use the case as a coffin and hide one of her dolls inside. But I changed my mind. The idea suddenly seemed morbid, and my case would be ruined."

"Did you think I wouldn't hear about the lovely Miss Angel who played roulette and broke the bank?"

Striking a match on his boot heel, Maxey lit a cheroot. "Johnson's grip was delivered yesterday morning with your money inside."

"My grip came from Eve, with my new dress inside. Ask Ann or Dottie. Don't be such a horse's ass, Mr. Stanhope. If I had the money, I'd be long gone from Ravenspur."

"That's true." For a moment, his eyes clouded with uncertainty. Then they cleared. "Johnson must already have your bank draft. Tomorrow, early, I'll escort you to Johnson's office and help you collect your winnings. I'll protect your interests, sweetheart."

"Just like you protected my health?"

"Exactly." He scowled. "Did you purr, my beautiful circus cat? Or did you scratch?"

"What are you talking about?"

"Johnson."

"Bret was a gentleman. We spent many hours together but not in bed."

"Do you expect me to believe that?"

"I care not what you believe." She watched him clench his fists. "If you hit me or pinch my breasts, I shall scream until Ann and Raymond come running. You cannot cover my mouth throughout the day and night, Maxey, and I've been purged of the belladonna."

"Who purged you? Johnson?"

"Yes."

"Did you tell him how you got the drug?"

"No."

"Why not?"

"I don't know. I think he guessed, so you'd better be very careful. If I die—"

"Circus whore! You managed to cast a spell on Johnson the same way you bewitched me."

"Don't be ridiculous, Maxey. I said from the start we shouldn't wed. Bewitched? Hah! You are nothing more than a banana-backboned bully." She knew she was inciting his temper, but she didn't care. "It was a bully who dragged me to the stables then kept me prisoner with his deadly nightshade. And it was *you*, Maxey Stanhope, who sold me to Bret Johnson!"

Maxey's onyx eyes glittered. He grabbed Clarissa's gown, crushing it against his chest. "The men who witnessed your amazing win described you perfectly. A golden angel, they said. Gold in her hair and on her dress. Gold at her fingertips."

Furious, he stuffed Clarissa's gown inside the potbellied stove. Nights had been temperate, so the stove just squatted there, unused—a large, creepy, sleepy black widow spider, rust spots on its underbelly.

Calliope raced toward Maxey but stumbled over a footstool.

Ripping pages from her Aesop book, he lit them with the end of his cheroot.

"Don't!" she screamed, rising to her feet.

Shoving the flaming pages into the stove's square opening, he stepped back, his lips stretched wide in what some people might call a grin. Calliope knew better.

"No, dear God, no," she moaned, sinking to her knees. She heard the crackle of flames and could already smell ashes. Her eyes, nose, and throat were filled with ashes. She couldn't see, breathe, or swallow.

Maxey was enjoying her anguish. "I've destroyed your pretty gown, sweetheart. Your pretty golden gown." He stared at Calliope then the stove. "No! You didn't! Tell me you didn't..." He paused, his mouth open in horrified disbelief.

"Gone," she whispered. "All gone."

Dry-eyed, Calliope watched her freedom go up in smoke.

∽

A carriage bore Calliope down the road toward Aaron Fox's ranch. She ignored Ann's tangible excitement and Dottie's inane chatter. Instead, she kept thinking: *What will I do now? Dear God, what will I do now?*

Would Bret replace some of the burnt money? Of course not. He had behaved like a gentleman, but there were limits to a gentleman's generosity. And Bret could be nasty.

As they neared an intersecting road that led up into the thickly wooded mountains, Maxey nudged his roan closer to the open carriage. "You look as though you're going to a funeral," he told Calliope, his black snake eyes promising she'd pay dearly for her lies.

She didn't respond, merely gazed straight ahead at Raymond, who, with Thom, was perched on the driver's seat.

"Are you ill again?" Ann asked.

"No. Just a wee bit cold. I forgot my gloves."

"Cold? But it's hot, Mary Angelique. Do you feel a breeze? I don't." Ineffectively, Dottie fanned her face with her white-gloved fingers. "Lucky we've had so much rain recently. There's not one puff of trail dust to smirch our gowns."

Maybe I could join Bret's Cirque as a Puff. He might

let her do that. She would lure others to the tables. It wasn't dishonest, since the gamblers had a chance to win as well as lose.

She didn't hear the rest of Dottie's exchange. It was as if the setting sun had ducked behind a mountain peak, leaving the world shaded by shadows. Foliage sagged, weeping with defeat, and the aspen leaves were a sickly yellow rather than their usual shimmering gold.

Gold! Calliope dug her fingers into the seat's upholstery. She had believed Clarissa's gold dress lucky, but it was an illusion. Her evil leprechaun had won after all.

Or had he? Suppose she really did return to Bret's Cirque as a Puff or even a hostess? If she couldn't buy her own circus, she'd join his. She would be a different kind of lady; a lady of the evening; a painted lady; a lady of pleasure.

She would be a different kind of cat. A bawdy cat.

The carriage crossed a shallow creek and scaled a hill. Even before Fox's ranch came into view, Calliope could smell the savory aroma of beef and mutton.

As the carriage topped the rise, she saw a house with a wide verandah. Its blackened brick chimneys rose from slate gray roofs. Ivy climbed the white boards until verdant clusters reached the second story and curled over windowsills, nodding at the glass panes.

An audience of green gilly-sprouts, Calliope mused. How many clandestine events had the ivy plants witnessed throughout the years?

Fox's circular drive was filled with saddle horses and carriages. Guests alighted, shouting greetings. The front door was wide open, its vestibule swarming with people. Calliope thought it looked like a hive about to burst from too many bees.

The Stanhope carriage finally reached the verandah steps and halted. Calliope's eyes searched the crowd for Gwendolyn then lingered on a tall gentleman, powerfully built, leaning against the porch's front column. His hair was the color of coal dust except where silver wings crested at the temples. His dark beard and mustache, carefully trimmed, surrounded a mouth that quirked with cynical humor. Even from a distance, Calliope could see that his eyes were a deep, piercing blue.

"Who is that tall man?" Dottie's voice was very loud. "He looks like a horse thief."

"Don't you recognize him, my dear?" Thom patted his wife's plump shoulder. "Perhaps he looks different because the last time we met him he wore a white wig and black mask."

Thom turned his face toward Calliope. "That's our host, Mary. That's Aaron Fox."

Twenty-One

CALLIOPE'S HEART PLUNGED TO THE VERY TOES OF her cream-colored, gray-gaitered shoes. Although undeniably handsome, Aaron Fox was old—at least fifty. The Master Artist had kindly allowed Fox's mustache and beard to remain untouched by Father Time's paintbrush, but a profusion of webbed lines crisscrossed the weathered skin above and below his blue eyes. Fox's body was sturdy, his arms and legs muscular, the form of a much younger man. No wonder she had responded to his masculine strength during the Spring Ball.

She rubbed her hot cheeks with her fingertips, then dismayed, clasped her hands tightly together. This was one habit she intended to break. If Fox mentioned their dance together, she'd simply say, "Did we dance, sir? Forgive me, but I met so many people. Were you the Napoleon who trod on my toes?"

Raymond escorted his family up the porch steps onto the verandah. "I believe you've met my son, Thomas, and my daughter-in-law, Dorothy," he said to Fox. "I am Raymond Stanhope. This is my wife,

Ann, and my ward, Mary Angelique O'Connor. Her fiancé, my son Maximilian, is already on his way to the pits." Raymond smiled paternally. "I'm afraid Maxey has a voracious appetite."

Calliope shuddered at Raymond's prophetic words.

Aaron Fox greeted the Stanhope women with polite kisses on their gloved knuckles. Ann blushed, and Dottie simpered. Then Fox reached out for Calliope's hand, brought it to his lips, and kissed her palm.

She felt nothing. No tremble. No urge to melt against the broad expanse of his chest. "Good evening, sir," she said with a small curtsy.

"Good evening, Mary. May I call you Mary? I've heard you're from the South, but here in Colorado we tend to drop unnecessary formalities." Fox's dark brows drew close together, making his eyes appear very blue. "During my misspent youth, I played the charlatan. Upon aging, I find I cannot tolerate hypocrisy."

Dottie gasped at Fox's lack of decorum, but Calliope nodded then withdrew her hand. Aaron Fox couldn't tolerate hypocrisy, she thought, yet he was pretending they'd met for the very first time.

What an attractive, crocodilian rogue!

She smelled an unusual essence—flowery perfume and corn tortillas. Sniffing with delight, Calliope shifted her gaze toward the vestibule.

A lady wearing a crimson gown sidled through the crowded doorway, patted her blonde chignon in an ageless gesture of femininity, and walked straight toward the Stanhope entourage. Ignoring the women, she smiled at Raymond and Thom. Then she looked up at Fox. "Why do you allow cowboys inside the house, Aaron?" she said, her brown eyes wide and guileless. "Their boots are covered with horse shit."

Calliope almost echoed Dottie's second gasp. Not at the unladylike mention of animal dung, but because she recognized Marie Antoinette. It was Marie Antoinette from the Spring Ball, the very same woman who had rubbed her perfectly formed breasts against Fox's doublet.

"May I present Louisa Sandoval, my guest from Denver," Fox said. "She's a distant relative, and for some strange reason she's called Daisy."

The reason wasn't strange at all, thought Calliope. Miss Sandoval's hair was the color of a daisy. Brian had once told Calliope the word meant "day's eye," appropriate because the plant folded its petals at night then opened them in the morning with the sun. However, Calliope had a feeling this particular Daisy reversed the procedure.

After introductions had been completed, the Stanhopes moved away, down the long verandah. Calliope just stood there at a loss for words.

"You must be Aaron's little friend," Daisy said. "I understand this affair is in your honor, even though Aaron hired special musicians to please me. My parents are *gachupines*, of pure Spanish descent. I'm aware your mother was a French countess, so that makes us equals."

"Equals?"

"Social counterparts."

If Calliope had been a tiger, her fur would have bristled. "In America," she said, "everybody is equal. Even the cowboys who stomp shit through the house."

Aaron Fox chuckled while Daisy's brown eyes

glittered. "Your gown is very pretty, Mrs. O'Connor, however the severity of your coiffure ruins the effect." She patted the elaborate loops and swirls above her chignon. "Center parts are so infantile. Oh dear, that was thoughtless."

"On you," Calliope said sweetly, "a center part might appear too youthful. Your gown is beautiful, Miss Sandoval, and wherever did you find that perfume? It combines the essence of corn and orchids."

"Orchids have no scent."

"Did I say orchids? I meant cowslips. The cowslip is a *common* primrose, very fragrant, also called a marsh marigold."

"You know a great deal about horticulture, Mrs. O'Connor," said Daisy, placing an emphasis on the first syllable of the word horticulture.

"Please call me Mary, and with your permission I shall call you Jane."

"Jane?"

"Sorry. A slip of the tongue. You see, I recently finished the novel *Jane Eyre* and—can you read, Miss Sandoval?"

"Of course!"

"Then we must have tea together one afternoon and discuss *The Study of Sociology* by the British philosopher Herbert Spencer." Calliope had the impression Aaron Fox hid another chuckle within his discreet cough. "How are you related to Mr. Fox, Miss Sandoval?"

"We are cousins, very *distant* cousins. There are no blood ties between us."

Calliope understood Daisy's meaning clearly. The daft flower had staked her claim on Aaron Fox.

"Please excuse me, I must see to the Mexicans," said Daisy with a sniff of her perfectly formed nose. "I can speak their language, and Rosita adds chili powder to everything, including coffee and salad greens." She looked up at Fox again. "Your ranchero needs a well-bred woman's supervision, *querida*. Your servants sing too much, which means they are lazy."

With an enigmatic expression on his handsome face, Fox watched Daisy's red bustle wriggle through the open doorway. Calliope could almost swear he didn't approve of his cousin's last remark. Perhaps Daisy's well-bred bosom fuddled a man's intellect, and Fox assumed a different attitude when those obvious assets disappeared from view.

Hellfire! Calliope lowered her lashes, dismayed by her catty-clawed reaction to the blooming Daisy. Did Miss Sandoval's condescending attitude hide her vulnerability, just as Gwendolyn's long hair had once hidden her friendly intelligence? Jocko's clown makeup had shielded him from the law and obscured the depth of his shrewdness, while Maxey's teasing frankness had disguised his demonic wickedness. What about Brian? Had Brian's loving tenderness concealed his desire for control?

"Mary dear, I thought you were standing beside me." Ann wore a blue satin gown and a diamond pendent that captured the rays from the setting sun. "Goodness gracious, I began introducing Maxey's fiancée to my dearest friend, Mrs. Browne, and then I discovered you had vanished like a puff of smoke."

Calliope swallowed a half sob, half laugh at Ann's congruous description. Following tonight's performance, she *would* become Bret Johnson's Puff. The idea she had pondered during her carriage ride suddenly became a firm resolve.

Because, to be perfectly honest, after Bret's insistence that Brian was alive, Calliope had harbored the daft hope that Brian and Aaron Fox were one and the same. At the Spring Ball she had thought Fox's voice sounded familiar, and she couldn't forget her damfool reaction inside Eve's apparel shop.

'Tis barely out of nappies ye be, daughter.

Sean's words were as apt today as they had been in Iowa during that long-ago circus parade. Only a child would be so naïve, so crackbrained. Why on earth would Brian O'Connor change his name to Aaron Fox? Where did the ranch come from? Thin air?

And why, when confronted by Calliope, had he not immediately confessed his new identity?

"Mary?"

"Sorry, Ann, woolgathering."

"I was saying Dottie prefers to wait inside the house until darkness. She hates the heat. I shall accompany you to the barbecue pits." Ann turned toward Fox, who had been discussing something with someone who looked and smelled like a hired hand. "Will you join us, Mr. Fox?"

"Please call me Aaron. We're neighbors, you know. I would enjoy nothing more than escorting two beautiful women, but I must remain here as host."

Ann linked her arm through Calliope's. "Raymond was impatient to taste the mutton and is already on his way to the pits. I must admit the aroma is making my mouth water. Are you hungry, Mary?"

"No. Not really."

"I suppose a young girl would rather dance than eat," Ann said fondly. "Don't you agree, Mr. Fox... I mean, Aaron?"

Calliope studied Fox's face. Had he forgotten their waltz together?

Impossible. He had practically seduced her. She had practically swooned in his arms.

Fox smiled. "The musicians are tuning their instruments. That means the dancing will begin soon. Please save a waltz for me, Mary."

He did remember.

Anchored to Ann's side by her arm, Calliope saw Fox's trestle tables had benches on both sides and were surrounded by shade trees. Chairs were scattered about for those who didn't fancy benches. Smoke rose from the pits, and barbecue sauce simmered inside huge iron pots. Several dark-haired, dark-eyed Mexican girls sauntered back and forth, the bangles on their wrists jangling as they hefted gourds filled with wine.

Maxey watched the serving girls appreciatively. Then he turned his gaze on Mary. She was behaving strangely, and he didn't like it. She should be cowering in a corner, anticipating his revenge for the burnt money. Instead, she walked among the guests as if she were some damn princess. What an accomplishment! She read books and newspapers, which explained her cultivated vocabulary, but it didn't explain her graceful, almost regal air. You couldn't learn that from books.

Perhaps he should ignore her background and

marry her anyway. But then his children would be tainted with circus blood. No. He couldn't allow that.

The circus twit had bewitched him. She had used her circus, her *Gypsy* background to cast a spell on him. He desired her day and night. He wanted to possess her, but he had given his word he would wait until they were wed. And despite his many sins, Maxey Stanhope never broke a vow.

Tonight after the party, he'd wait until the household slept then carry her to the loft. He had purchased some more belladonna from that little whore at the Cirque, and he would pour brandywine down Calliope's throat. When she was drugged beyond control, he'd make her lay with *him*. Damn! Why hadn't he conceived that plan before?

Meanwhile, one of the serving girls stared at him, her dark eyes signaling. Why waste the evening? People would accuse him of deserting his fiancée, but when had Maxey Stanhope ever exhibited conventional behavior?

Calliope watched Maxey head toward what looked like a servant's cottage. Good. Now she could relax and enjoy herself.

As the sky darkened, lights from paper lanterns blazed like giant fireflies. Remembering her dream, Calliope stood stock still, her heart pounding. Then she shook her head. *Are you daft, girl?* She stood outside, not on some ballroom floor. Lanterns glowed, not candles. She was fully clothed, not naked as a jaybird. Furthermore, there had been no music in her dream.

Aaron Fox's hired musicians sat behind a large

stage, and already couples moved to their euphonious melodies. Footsteps on the wooden deck thudded, joining the guitars, mandolins, violins, and steel drums. Calliope's feet twitched.

"May I have the pleasure of this dance, Mary?" Aaron Fox winked. "I believe you promised me a waltz."

"Of course." Calliope held out her arms and let Fox guide her through the now-familiar one-two-three.

"The Spring Ball in Denver," she murmured. "Following our dance..." She paused as she felt her cheeks bake. "Following our dance together, I told you I was engaged to be married. Is that why you arranged this lovely party?"

"I didn't attend the ball, Mary. Spring is roundup time."

His voice was tinged with amusement. Was he making fun of her? "You were there," she insisted. "Your cousin, Daisy Sandoval, was there too."

"I have no doubt Cousin Daisy attended. She loves any event where she is the center of attention."

"Unfortunately, I was the center of attention."

"You were?"

"Yes. Don't you remember? I wore petticoat breeches." Calliope took a deep breath. "You were arrogant, presumptuous, and blamed your actions on the brevity of my costume. I thought you couldn't tolerate hypocrisy, Mr. Fox."

"Please call me Aaron. Petticoat breeches? My, my, that's a sight these old eyes would love to see."

Fuming, Calliope kept her silence, wondering why he disputed their previous encounter. What did he have to lose? His reputation? Surely it was too late for that.

A finger tapped her shoulder. Fox whirled her around then stopped, and she found herself looking up into icy blue eyes.

"Excuse me, Father," said the owner of the eyes, "but I claim the privilege of this dance. I've been searching all over for you, Mrs. O'Connor. I must confess I asked the musicians to play this waltz. Does it sound familiar?" Deftly, before she could comment, he swept her into his arms.

Her feet moved—*one, two, three*—but she stared at him fixedly. She was certain every stitch of color had drained from her face.

"Are you planning to faint?" he said, his voice low. "Don't faint, Calliope. The house is already chock full of swooning women."

"Swooning women," she repeated, dazed.

"Yes. A vaquero handed Dorothy Stanhope a plate filled with bull testicles. It's a delicacy, but the lady didn't appreciate his generosity. Neither did quite a few of the other women present. My vestibule is carpeted with bodies. What a shame there aren't any clowns handy. They could wave smelling salts. I have no salts, so don't you dare faint. I said no, Calliope. Damn it! Hold on, puss, I've got you."

"You're alive," she whispered, sagging against his hard body. "You're truly alive."

"Why did you believe me dead?"

"Gwendolyn saw… she swore… oh, God." Still woozy, Calliope swayed backwards. "After the fire, I prayed I might die too. If I had not been so weak, I would have killed myself. But then I thought there might be a wee lad or lass because… because of our night together inside the silver wagon and... Oh, God, you're alive!"

Hands outstretched, holding onto nothing except her pride, she savored his appearance. His dark hair was shorter than she remembered. It only emphasized his lean, reckless face with those cold blue eyes. "Why do you look at me like that, Brian? As if you didn't care?"

"Dance, Calliope."

"But I don't want—"

"One, two, three. One, two, three. We shall waltz to the edge of the platform and slip away. You haven't seen my father's gazebo, have you?"

"Your father?"

"Aaron Fox."

"I never realized—"

"That I had a father? Everybody has a father, puss, even bastards like me."

"And a fine bastard you have become, Brian O'Connor, you damn gilly-galloo! Why did you not tell me you were alive?"

"Dance, Calliope."

"Answer me!"

"Dance!"

Anger had caused her shock to fade, but she couldn't pull away from his unrelenting grasp on her waist or the fingers he had twined through hers, so she let him twirl her around, navigating their passage through the dancers until they reached the very edge of the platform. Then, still holding her hand, he ran, pulling her after him.

"Slow down!" she cried.

"You are Maxey Stanhope's fiancée. He has no reputation to protect, but for some daft reason, I'm trying to save yours. If people saw you strolling in the moonlight with Aaron Fox, they'd think the worst."

"Aaron Fox? Your father? I don't understand."

Calliope felt adrift in the darkness, twice as dark once they had left the lanterns behind. Filtered through leafy tree branches, the moon's glow bemused rather than consoled her. She and Brian plunged into dense, shoulder-high shrubbery. She felt prickly briars scratch at her arms. More briars caught in her hair, which soon tumbled down and curtained her face.

"Ouch! We can't be seen anymore. Brian, please!"

He responded to her cry of pain by slowing their pace a little. "Walk, Calliope. One foot in front of the other, just like the pie car. Remember?"

She stumbled forward, trapped by his grip, trapped by the weight of her heavy heart. "Brambles… my hair… brambles have snagged my hair. If you don't stop, I'll soon be bald."

They emerged from the shrubs into a small clearing. Her gaze didn't linger long on the gazebo. Instead, her eyes were drawn to a merry-go-round, where a master craftsman had carved leaping horses and swan boats in full, realistic detail.

Brian finally released her hand. She climbed four steps until she stood on top of the merry-go-round's platform. "Does it move?" she asked breathlessly.

"Yes. There's a rotating frame. Do you want me to explain the mechanism?"

"No. Don't spoil the magic." She reached out and touched the smooth wood of a graceful swan. "How

beautiful. I've never seen anything so beautiful."
Then, like a child, she lifted her skirts high above her
knees and danced 'round the horses. "That one there
looks like Dublin, and the chestnut looks a wee bit
like Susan. Or Brandywine. There, over there, Blackie
and Big John's gray Arabian. Oh, you beautiful things!
Where on earth did you come from?"

"My father carved them." Ignoring steps, Brian
bounded up onto the platform.

"Your father?"

"When he learned my mother was expecting a baby,
he tried to find her and was told she had died. It was
a mistake. Another equestrian had been fatally injured.
Father was penitent, conscience-stricken, so he built
this merry-go-round to honor Maureen O'Connor.
Perhaps he wanted his sons and daughters to use it, but
the woman he married was barren. She passed away
years ago. On the other hand, it was my good fortune
his wife couldn't conceive a child. I'm his only heir."
Brian lifted Calliope up onto the gray Arabian's saddle.

She clutched the rod that extended through its body.
He grabbed the leather reins attached to its throatlatch.
He jumped to the ground, and started running, the
reins held tightly in his hands. Her wooden horse
swung out past the platform, flying through the air as
if it had wings, and she heard the sound of cog and
pinion wheels. When the merry-go-round was in full
swing, Brian released the reins.

Calliope felt a rush of air cool her flushed cheeks
as her painted horse galloped through the night.
Trees blurred. She gazed up at the sky pierced with
stars and thought they looked like the glittering pins

on a bolt of Eve's black fabric. The moon was a pincushion without any pins. Aaron Fox's merry-go-round continued rotating, and suddenly all the puzzle pieces fell into place.

Brian had escaped from the fire. Jocko hadn't lied when he said Brian could raise money for the injured performers. He need only confront his father with the fact of his existence. Brian had been acknowledged as Fox's heir. Brian had paid all medical expenses to restore Gwendolyn's health, and he'd invested in her shop. Brian was building a restaurant with a stage larger than most opera houses. Brian was—

"Aaron Fox!" Calliope's head whirled faster than her merry-go-round horse. "You're Aaron Fox!"

Brian waited till she swung 'round again. "When I became his heir, Father insisted I take his name. I'm the third Aaron."

Still clutching the rod with one hand, Calliope pressed her other hand against her heart. How could she have been so blind? The Spring Ball. Their dance together. Blue eyes. Brian's eyes. He had disguised himself with a mask and wig, but she should have known from her reaction to his embrace. His voice. Why had she not recognized his voice? Because he had sounded like an educated gilly, not the Irish lad she loved. And she had thought him dead. In her heart of hearts she had thought him dead. Her heart, not her body, had betrayed her.

As the merry-go-round slowed then halted, she wanted to ask why he had kept his identity a secret from her, but she simply said, "You shaved your beard and mustache."

"Yes." He grasped the rod and steadied the swaying horse. "For tonight's party. For you."

One puzzle piece was still missing. Digging her nails into the horse's sculpted mane, Calliope said, "Gwendolyn swore you burned to death, Brian. She saw it happen."

"She saw it happen to someone else."

"No. That's impossible. The ringmaster... You can't mistake a ringmaster for someone else. He wears different clothes. Top hat and cane and... Why are you chortling like a hyena?"

"It's all so ironic, Calliope."

"What's ironic?"

"Your fat ringmaster returned before the show and begged for his old job back."

"Why did he not confront me?"

"Because you're a lass. To my credit and his misfortune, I suggested he stay and discuss it with you after your performance."

"So Gwendolyn did see a ringmaster burn." The wooden horse grinned. Calliope wondered what colors a craftsman would mix to paint anguish. "Why didn't you tell me during our waltz together at the Spring Ball? Why play that daft game of cat and mouse?"

"You dare accuse *me* of playing games, Mary Angelique O'Connor? You, the daughter of a French countess? Were you not raised on a Southern plantation?"

"I told the Stanhopes what they wanted to hear."

"No, Calliope, you told them what you wanted to believe." His voice simmered with barely suppressed fury. "You've always wanted to play the rich lady, and that's a fact. When you saw your chance, you grabbed it like a child grabs the ring on a merry-go-round."

"That's not true."

"No? Why didn't you return to the scene of the fire? And please don't tell me you did. I hired men from the ranch to keep watch. They even had circus posters with your likeness."

She opened her mouth then closed it again. He wouldn't believe her. Why hadn't she returned? Because even after her long convalescence, she couldn't deal with her vivid memories. Or her guilt. Look what had happened when Maxey brought her there. She had become violently ill and fainted.

And yet Brian spoke true. She should have returned and provided a grave, a headstone. She should have done that. She had made a big mistake and paid dearly for it.

"I was going to expose my new identity," Brian continued, "but then you bragged about your engagement to Maxey Stanhope."

"Not Maxey. It was another man, and I hadn't truly accepted him. I said he was my fiancé because you hurt my feelings. If you had only..." Her horse wobbled. She closed her eyes and clutched its rod.

If you had only told me during the Spring Ball, how much suffering would have been avoided.

"Calliope?"

She opened her eyes and raised her chin. "Since you are alive, Brian, I must call off my engagement. Before God, I am already wed."

"I won't hold you to your vows."

"What if I want you to honor yours?"

"Are you suggesting I announce our 'silver wagon marriage' to my guests? Should I explain in detail how the equestrian and the cat tamer consummated their vows inside that same circus wagon? Are you daft, lass? Your reputation would be destroyed. No decent woman would ever speak to you again."

Her reputation? Brian didn't know everything, even if he thought he did. He didn't know about Miss Angel and the Cirque de Delices. Eventually, that episode would surface, and decent women would avoid her like the plague.

"I don't care what people think, Brian."

"No, I suppose you don't. What does a small scandal matter? As my wife, you'd be wealthy beyond your wildest dreams. The Stanhope fortune is a dung hill compared to Aaron Fox's mountain of assets."

"Is that what you honestly believe?"

"It doesn't matter what I believe, Calliope." He laughed, but there was no joy in the sound. "You can't change the past. You can't change the direction of a merry-go-round. No matter how hard you try, it keeps turning in circles."

Tired. I'm so tired. She wanted nothing more than to enter the gazebo, sink down, and bury her head in her arms. But she couldn't even move her legs and slide from the horse's saddle.

"You've achieved your goal," said Brian. "You're a lady. And despite what you might believe, I'm a gentleman. If I recall correctly, we had something else in common."

His grin mocked as he scooped her from the horse and carried her toward the gazebo. For one brief moment, craving his protection, she nestled against his strong chest. Then she felt an almost unbearable panic, a dread beyond belief.

"Let me go, Brian!"

"Don't play the coy virgin with me, Calliope."

She struggled wildly and heard him swear under his breath, but he didn't release her. Tempted to blurt out the reason for her fear, she swallowed her words, confused by his new attitude. This wasn't Brian; it was Aaron Fox. She had loved Brian not Aaron. She had loved a cat tamer not a rich rancher's son and heir.

Inside the gazebo was an old blanket. It smelled frowzy, and its horsehairs prickled as Brian placed her on top, unfastened her gown, and pulled its bodice to her waist.

She couldn't move. Her head whirled as if she still rode the merry-go-round. Behind closed eyelids she saw dozens of snakes coiling and uncoiling their long, tapered bodies. Sounds of their hissing filled her ears.

She had accused Brian of playing cat and mouse. Now she recalled how Papa's circus reptiles had been fed mice. The tiny mice just stood there, unable to flee, mesmerized by the snakes until they'd been gobbled up alive.

Brian's lips fed on her closed eyes, her nose, her chin, the pulse at the base of her throat, and then moved toward her breasts.

"You have a nasty wound," he said, rolling away from her. "It's barely healed. What happened?"

She couldn't answer. If she opened her mouth, a snake would slither inside. She fluttered her fingers in a feeble attempt to wave away the snakes.

"Look at me, Calliope." Brian's hands captured hers, halting her useless motion. "Please look at me."

She obeyed. And saw his worried eyes, bluer than a cloudless summer day, bluer than the bunting on an American flag. The snakes vanished along with her fear.

Repeating her earlier gesture at the merry-go-round, she tentatively reached out to stroke his face. She had always loved his face.

He knelt above her, his legs straddling her hips, but he remained motionless, letting her touch his face, rediscover his features. Then he shifted his weight so he could remove their clothing.

"I dreamed," she began, her voice trailing off into a sigh as she felt the warmth of his hand against her belly, moving deliberately lower.

"I had forgotten how soft your hair is," he whispered, "even here." His hand traveled upwards, and he began to tease her nipple with his thumb and first finger. "Why do you flinch, lass? We've played this scene before."

"I'm scared."

"Of me?"

"No. Not you. Maxey."

"Stanhope will never find out, I promise."

"You don't understand."

Brian removed his hand. "Did Stanhope cause those wounds on your breast?"

"No. I swear. It was an accident."

This whole evening was an accident, thought Brian. He had planned to impress Calliope with his wealth, show that he didn't give a damn for her Stanhope connections. He had planned to laugh and walk away.

But he had forgotten the seductive curve of her body, the slant of her cat eyes, the swan-arch of her throat, her full young breasts.

His beautiful, beautiful circus cat. Her hesitation was driving him insane. And despite every instinct that screamed he was making a mistake, he wanted her.

Without warning, she reached out, wove her fingers through his hair, and pressed his face against her breasts. She murmured incoherently, something about the tug on her braids hurting but not hurting. He couldn't understand all her words. He thought she whispered, "I don't care if it hurts good."

The mounds of her breasts smelled like lemons, and Brian imagined the spinning moon might smell like that, taste like that. He had always enjoyed the tart taste of lemons, the tart taste of Calliope. Savoring her breasts, sucking each nipple in turn, he stroked every inch of her body until she spread her legs and shouted the familiar command.

"Now, Brian!"

Her body arched fiercely against his, and her supple movements blotted out everything except his insatiable need.

Calliope felt as though she'd been released from a cage. Brian's tongue cauterized her wounds, and she knew she would die a thousand deaths before allowing Maxey to enslave her soul again.

Craving Brian's touch, she guided his hands toward her face and felt him trace her lips with his thumb. Opening her mouth, she sucked his thumb like an infant. He responded in kind, sucking her fingers until she was nearly crazed with desire.

A purr trembled inside her throat. Brian had already penetrated, but now he timed his thrusts and placed his thumb, the thumb she had sucked, between their bellies. He slid his thumb lower, then lower still, until she gave voice to her pleasure. He then moved his hands to her buttocks and pressed their bodies tightly together, until his voice merged with hers.

After their passion had been spent, she covered her face with her hands and began to sob.

"What's wrong?" Brian asked, alarmed. "Are you all right?" He expected her to say fine, wondrous fine, but she merely lowered her hands, and in the moonlight shining through the open roof of the gazebo, he could see that her tears were tears of joy.

"I forgot," she whispered. "You made me remember. Maxey made me forget."

What the hell was she talking about? Brian felt a raging pang of jealousy at the thought of Maxey Stanhope. He made her forget? Forget what? The passion that had always existed between the circus equestrian and the cat tamer? Brian wanted to begin again, bring Calliope slowly to the brink of ecstasy, make her forget Stanhope. He reached out and—

"I care not what you say, Brian. Before God we are wed, and I love you."

I love you too, he wanted to shout. Then he thought about her actions after the fire. She had abandoned the circus, abandoned her performers, abandoned him.

"You love the wealthy Aaron Fox," he said.

"No. It's the opposite. I love Brian O'Connor. Why won't you believe me?"

"Too much has happened, Calliope. You can't change the direction of a merry-go-round."

"True, but you can get off." Rising, she walked away from the gazebo and stood, staring up at the sky. "Do you not want me, lad?"

Tangled hair tumbled to her waist and framed the smooth curve of her buttocks. Brian almost groaned out loud. "I'll always want you," he said, rising and walking toward her. He didn't care to wound her pride, but he really had no choice. "Have you met Louisa Sandoval?"

"Daisy? Yes."

"Tonight I will announce our engagement. Tomorrow, in church, the banns will be read."

Before his eyes, Calliope's appearance changed. She walked slowly to the gazebo and reached for her gown, her movements unsure, her grace gone.

"Daisy's father, Louis Sandoval, gave my father the money to start his ranching empire," Brian continued. "Permission for my marriage has already been granted. Even if I wanted to, I cannot disgrace Daisy and, in turn, her father."

"Does your father know who I am?" Calliope walked away from the gazebo.

Brian followed. "Yes. Father promised to keep his silence. If your circus background was revealed, the scandal would spread faster than wildfire."

"What about your circus background?"

"I'm a man. People would call it a youthful escapade."

"That's not fair."

"Who said life is fair, puss?"

"Does your father know you once loved me?"

"I still love you."

"You have a strange way of showing it."

"Damn it, Calliope, it was you who became engaged to Maxey Stanhope. This party tonight is in your honor."

"I thought you were dead."

"There. You see? We've traveled full circle, just like a merry-go-round."

She straightened, holding her gown against her body, hiding her beautiful nakedness. "Would you do me one favor?"

"Of course."

Her uncertainty was gone. "I'd like to borrow a horse, please."

"You already have your own, here at the ranch."

"The carriage horses belong to the Stanhopes..." She paused. "Dublin!"

"After the fire, I took him with me."

"That makes it easier," she murmured, fastening her gown. "Please escort me to Dublin's stall and inform your stable hands that I do not pirate your stallion."

"Are you daft, lass?"

"Dublin is no merry-go-round horse. I can choose my own direction, and though blind, he will obey."

"Forget this foolishness, Calliope. You must wed up with Stanhope and make the best of it."

"I cannot marry Maxey, Brian. A diddy predicted my loveless fate, but Maxey..." She shuddered. "Do not concern yourself with my wee hornet's nest."

"Why not? If we can't be man and wife, we can still be brother and sister."

She nodded toward the gazebo. "Do you honestly

believe that what just happened was the act of a brother and sister?"

"No. You're right. What are you planning to do?"

Once again, Calliope glanced up at the stars. Then she focused on Brian. Suppose she told him about Maxey? Brian would beat the man to a bloody pulp. Then he'd marry Daisy Sandoval. And in the process, Calliope's pride would be destroyed completely, beyond repair.

Moonlight silhouetted Brian's naked body. She had thought Maxey's form powerful, but Brian's rigid strength was clearly etched against the sky. She admired his furred chest, lean hips, taut belly. She especially loved his hands, now hiding what she assumed was the beginning of a second erection. She wanted to lose herself in his arms, press herself close to his heart until their two heartbeats became one. And yet, despite his obvious desire, he would never believe she hadn't betrayed him and left him for a more opportune future.

Dreams are merely rainbows. Rainbows were beautiful, but you couldn't capture one and fling it across your shoulders like a colorful cloak.

Tonight Brian had opened the door to her cage. She would always be grateful for that.

Walking forward, he tilted her chin and stared into her eyes. "What are you planning to do, lass?"

"Fly away."

Twenty-Two

"BLOW ON THE DICE FOR LUCK, IRISH."

"Of course, me brawny lad. 'Tis your plan to break Mr. Johnson's Bank, I'm thinkin'." Bending forward, Calliope pursed her lips and blew a half whistle, half sigh just above the young man's hairy knuckles.

"My name's Kyle," he said. "If I win this toss, will you come upstairs with me?"

The men placing bets stopped short. One gasped. Nobody invited Irish Angel upstairs. She belonged to Bret Johnson.

"If you win your toss, lad, 'tis another toss of the dice you'll be takin'." Calliope pasted a smile on her face. Kyle couldn't be more than twenty, her age, yet he flung his money around with careless abandon and didn't seem to mind if he won or lost.

Staring at her bodice, he drew a wad of bank notes from his pocket. "I'll make it worth your while."

"'Tis honored I am at your askin', sir." Calliope beckoned toward a small, dark-haired girl. "Emily shall bring you refreshments and all else you might be needin'."

"Don't want her, Irish, want you." Dice forgotten, Kyle lurched forward, his mouth creased in a petulant scowl. "Defy me and suffer the consequences."

Momentarily, Calliope's vision blurred, and she began to press one hand against her cheek. Then, halting the gesture, she said, "Defy *me*, lad, and ye shall learn what the word consequence means."

As if by magic, a huge man—over seven feet tall—appeared by the Irish Angel's side. Candlelight shone on his handsome ebony face and bald pate. Although properly attired in evening clothes, the players could imagine the hard muscles that rippled beneath his shirt and jacket.

"'Scuse me, Miss Angel," he said. "Mr. Johnson wants you inside the salon."

"Begging your pardon, gentlemen, but I must take my leave." She nodded toward the dice table. "If hazard proves unlucky, join my game of cards. I oft lose and never cheat."

Placing her hand atop the black man's extended arm, she walked away. "You arrived just in time, Jack," she said. "We nearly had a bit of a clem. Did you note the greenish cast to that young gilly's face? Soon he shall toss his whiskey along with the toss of our dice. Please remove him gently or by the seat of his pants, I care not. Let him grovel on the curb like a mangy dog—" She took a deep breath. "Sorry. Does Bret really want to see me?"

"Yes, Miss Calliope," Jack replied, the three words floating down from his great height.

She grinned up at him. Black Jack was yet another man from her past. He had appeared in her Kid Show as "Jack the Giant, Tallest Man in the World." He and Bret were the only two at the Cirque de Delices who knew her true identity. She had played Irish Angel for six months and had never been challenged.

"Would you ask Bret to come to my room, boy-o? I must make myself presentable for the game."

Black Jack nodded. Grinning at Calliope's boy-o, his teeth shone very white. Nobody had ever called him that, not even when he was a boy, growing so tall so fast he had entertained his whey-faced mistress on the eve of his thirteenth birthday. She had borne his daughter. As a consequence, Black Jack had been sold to another plantation. Then came the war, freedom, Sean's circus, Bret's Cirque.

"Thank you again for the timely rescue, my friend." Lifting her skirts, Calliope ascended a winding staircase until she reached the second floor. She turned left, entered the first bedroom, and sat in front of her dressing table. Above the table, her mirror was fitted with candles.

She opened a jewelry box. Sifting among its contents, she tried on several pairs of earrings. No pair seemed to coincide with her mood, so she discarded them all.

Her elaborate gown was stiff black satin. By contrast, her arms and shoulders looked as white as the January snow that swirled outside her windowpanes. Removing the pins from her topknot of curls, she shook her head, and her hair tumbled free to her waist. She reached for her hairbrush.

"Let me do that."

Meeting Bret's eyes in the mirror, she handed him the brush.

"Black Jack says a young pup made crude advances."

"True. But he shall soon forfeit his courage along with his whiskey. I heard the tremor in his voice, as if a wee cub had swallowed a huge fur ball."

"Did his paws touch your body, Calliope?"

"No, Bret, honest."

"Black Jack says you invited several guests to join your poker game."

"Yes." She leaned back, enjoying his deft strokes. "I doubt they'll leave their dice, but what does it matter? There's more than enough cards to go 'round."

"Not tonight, Calliope. Tonight you deal a private game for high stakes."

"How high?"

"No limit."

Her eyes widened. "What's our cut?"

"The usual five percent. You'll deal while Clarissa sits in for the house."

"That's not fair, Bret. Let her deal. I'm the better player. Clarissa uses her obvious assets to distract, but an earnest player won't be bamboozled."

Bret bent his head over one bare shoulder and lightly kissed the mounds that rose above her low-cut bodice. "You would never use your obvious assets to distract, would you darling?"

"Not in a serious game for high stakes. Why can't I play for the house?"

"Because the host asked that you deal."

"Who's the host?"

"Aaron Fox."

"The son or the father?" she asked, daring to hope.

"The son."

"No! I won't do it!"

"You will," Bret said as he returned to the business of brushing her hair.

"Don't make me play. Tell them something, anything. Tell Aaron Fox I'm sick."

"You're not sick, Calliope, and you'll deal the cards." Lifting her thick strands, Bret nuzzled her nape. "Or would you prefer to play a Puff again?"

"Why do I always forget how nasty you can be?"

He straightened and placed her brush on top of the dressing table. "A Puff doesn't share in the profits, darling. As a Puff, you'll never save enough money for your passage to France."

"If I accepted the offers to retire upstairs, I'd be in Paris lickety-split."

"If you dare accept one offer, you shall find yourself on the sidewalk, penniless, rubbing the hurt from your French-Irish ass."

"Yes, I do believe you'd boot me out, Bret Johnson. Jealousy has always been your weakness."

"And my strength. Look what I've achieved from cupidity."

"Cupidity is a desire for material gain. I'm not a possession. I can't be bought."

"I know, my love. That's why you won't retire upstairs with an ardent guest no matter how much he offers."

Her anger faded at the truth of his words. She braided her hair, twining scarlet ribbons through its shiny abundance. "You would think that after six months I'd have enough money for my ticket," she murmured. "But my gowns cost dear, even though Eve charges me half what she should."

"Marry me, Calliope, and you won't have to worry about the cost of a gown."

"If I marry you, I can't book passage to Paris."

"We can go to Paris for our honeymoon."

"As your wife, I wouldn't be able to join the Nouveau Cirque. That's my dream, Bret."

We've had this discussion a hundred times, and just like a merry-go-round, we always come full circle. Brian was right about that.

"Must I deal tonight?" she asked, keeping her voice modulated. Bret was still brainsick with jealousy. He wouldn't set fire to his Cirque, but he might destroy her horse-charm necklace. He had told her to remove it, and she had refused, incautiously suggesting he might as well tell her to remove her heart.

Now her heart pounded wildly at the thought of facing Brian again.

Naturally, she had learned all about his activities, carefully questioning Eve during their many dress fittings. She knew his marriage to Daisy Sandoval was planned for June, and the construction of his hotel and restaurant neared completion, though often delayed by nasty weather. She hadn't set eyes on Brian since she'd ridden away from his ranch. Atop Dublin, she had galloped through the night, finally knocking on Bret's door, incoherently pleading for sanctuary, protection, for her job as a Puff.

Then fearfully, she had waited for the summons to Bret's bedroom. But it never came.

"I want your love, Calliope, not your body," he had told her one evening over a game of rummy. Staring pointedly at her necklace, he had added, "I'll wait until you can no longer resist my charms."

But she had resisted. Resisted her desire to be held and petted. Resisted Bret's teasing touch and knowledgeable hands.

Now she gazed at his reflection in the mirror. Ash-blond hair the color of a tiger's underbelly. Eyes two shades lighter than a tiger's stripes. In appearance, Bret and Brian were as different as day and night. Yet it was the nights when she wanted nothing more than to slip under Bret's blanket and press her body close to his.

Lately she had been weakening. Brian had released the snake-demons, and her passionate nature demanded physical fulfillment. Only the thought of Bret's role in the circus fire kept her from offering her love.

Bret had known all along that Brian O'Connor and Aaron Fox were one and the same, and she couldn't forgive him for that. If Bret had told her, she might have visited Brian before the barbecue, accepted his rejection, returned to Bret, collected her winnings, and left Colorado. Instead, Dame Fortune's roulette wheel had dictated her new destiny—first Puff, then Operator.

"I don't understand why Brian requested me," she said, rising from the dressing-table chair. "He hates me. He believes... Oh, it doesn't matter what he believes."

"I told you O'Connor would betray you. Do you hate him, Calliope?"

"Yes. More than any man alive, with the exception of Maxey Stanhope."

Bret tilted her chin with one finger. "Do you hate me?"

"No."

"Do you love me?"

"No."

"You will. Someday you will."

"Now you sound like Jocko."

"A bit of the clown and a bit of the fool, eh darling?"

"If you bide your time, waiting for my love, why do you tempt the fates by forcing me to deal Brian's game?"

"Is that what I'm doing? Tempting the fates?" Circling her waist, drawing her close, he kissed her. Unlike his usual kisses, this one contained a savage passion.

"Stop it, Brian," she cried. "My dearest love, there is no time to—"

Bret released her so abruptly she staggered against the dressing table. Perfume bottles toppled, two shattered, and she smelled roses and apple blossoms. Bret stood there, hands fisted at his sides, his eyes slits of anger.

Her temper flared. "Why do you look at me like that? Is it because I cannot say I love you and kiss you back? I'm sorry if you feel you must possess my soul as well as my body, but I belong to no man."

His expression altered. "You don't even know what you said. _I'm_ sorry, Calliope. Did I hurt you?"

"Hurt me?" She realized she still clutched the table, one hand resting on slivers of broken glass. "My scent tonight shall be overwhelming, but I'm fine. Wondrous fine."

"You don't have to deal." Bret lifted her drenched hand and kissed her fingertips. "I'll make your excuses."

"No. I've changed my mind. Why shouldn't I come face-to-face with Brian O'Connor? He means nothing to me. My only request is that, after a while, I change places with Clarissa. I want to play. I want to win."

"I'd like to win too."

"Don't fret. I shall play well and make sure the Cirque wins," said Calliope, wondering why Bret sounded so unhappy.

Twenty-Three

Shortly after Calliope had graduated from Puff to Dealer, she had swiftly added numbers in her head. "Dash it all! I never realized."

"Realized what, darling?" Adjusting the lamp's flame, Bret had sat back in his chair and shuffled a deck of cards with one hand.

"Five percent for the house doesn't sound like much," she had said, pacing up and down the small salon, "until you add the figures. Let's assume each player starts with... oh, say a hundred dollars for simplicity's sake. The usual game has eight players, so the total amount at the start is eight hundred dollars. Let's also assume each player receives the number of good, bad, and indifferent hands probability says he can expect in the long run. That means the dealer collects three hundred and sixty dollars, leaving only four hundred and forty in the game. Each player has paid forty-five dollars out of his original hundred, and our small five percent has grown to forty-five percent."

"Very good, Calliope. I'm impressed."

"Wait. It gets better. Suppose the game lasts several

hours? If, by that time, six players have gone broke, leaving two, they will have two hundred dollars between them. The dealer has taken a charge of six hundred out of the original eight, or seventy-five percent of the total amount the players brought into the game. No wonder you're a rich man."

"Players can indulge in private games without a dealer, but they're afraid of being honey fuggled."

"Have *you* ever cheated?"

"Choose a card, Calliope." He fanned his deck, and she drew one out. "Ten of hearts," he said.

"How did you know? Tell me."

"The cards are marked."

"But that's impossible. It was a new deck. I saw you break the seal."

Reaching into a box, Bret pulled out six decks, all sealed. "One of these is marked, darling. Let's see if you can find it."

Calliope sat across from him. She examined the backs of the cards, an arduous task. After thirty minutes, she couldn't spot the marked deck. "All right, Bret, I give up."

"I'll confess. I lied when I told you one deck is marked."

"You pawky galloo! What a dirty trick!"

"As a matter of fact, all six decks are marked."

"I don't believe it!"

With a wicked grin, Bret read each card from the back. When he had finished, she said, "I've never cheated in *my* games."

"And never will. That's why we charge the five percent." He grinned again. "Would you like to learn these cards?"

"Yes, please."

"Good. I shall also teach you how to detect a cheat. Come, darling, move your chair next to mine, and we'll have some fun."

❧

As Calliope thought about the evening, her mouth quirked at the corners.

"You look happy. Are you?"

Startled, she gazed into Brian's dark blue eyes. He hunkered down, very close to her chair. She said, "Why did you not join the others at the refreshment table, Mr. Fox? You need fortitude if you want to continue your winning streak."

"Why aren't you eating? Nervous?"

"Why should I be nervous?"

"This is a high-stakes game."

"I've played for higher stakes, Mr. Fox. Sometimes I win; sometimes I lose. That is the nature of the game. On the other hand, you always seem to win. You once said I was a cat who landed on my paws, but I think it's the other way 'round."

"You smell like roses and apples."

"You smell like Brian O'Connor," she said and heard the wistfulness in her voice.

"Would you like a glass of wine, puss?"

She winced at the word "puss" then shook her head. She wasn't hungry or thirsty. Ever since the poker game's beginning, she had erased everything from her mind except the job at hand. Fuming, she had watched Clarissa lose big pots. Her bluffs were useless, and she stayed in the game when she should have folded. In truth, Clarissa was a much better player, but she spent too much time flirting with the man Brian had introduced as Senior Louis Sandoval—Daisy's father.

"Are you happy?" Brian asked again.

"I'm content. I've been trying to save enough money for my passage to Paris. I want to join the Nouveau Cirque."

"As an equestrian?"

"No, an equilibrist." She took a deep breath. "Why did you request me? I mean to deal your game?"

"I wanted to see if you were all right. You left in such haste the night of—"

"Damn your soul!" Glancing around the room, she lowered her voice. "Did you expect me to remain and listen to the gossipy tittle-tattle over your betrothal to Daisy Sandoval?"

"Be fair, Calliope. The barbecue was in honor of your engagement to Maxey Stanhope."

"But I told you I'd call it off. Never mind, Brian, you're starting up the blasted merry-go-round again."

"Does Stanhope know you reside here?"

"I assume he does. I've never made an appearance while he gambles, which isn't very often. His source of funds has apparently dried up," she said and heard the sarcasm in her voice.

Brian didn't acknowledge her sarcasm, or else he chose to ignore it. "If you were my fiancée," he said, "I'd sling you over my shoulder and shoot anyone who tried to stop me. Why doesn't Stanhope knock down your bedroom door and rescue you from this life of degradation?"

"Degradation? Oh, if you only knew."

"Knew what?"

"Remember Black Jack, the giant in our Kid Show?"

"Of course."

"You sound flummoxed, Brain."

"I'm confused by your abrupt change of subject, Calliope."

"The subject is Maxey Stanhope. Our old friend Jack is now a member of Bret's establishment. If Maxey took one step toward my bedroom, Black Jack would boot him out and none too gently."

"So it's over between the two of you?"

"Yes. How... how do Mr. and Mrs. Stanhope fare?"

"They were devastated by your disappearance. That wasn't very smart, Calliope. You could have married. You've never been religious, and we're not legally wed."

She burst out laughing, the sound tinged with bitterness. Her laugh drew stares from Clarissa and Señor Sandoval, who stood nearby, sharing the contents from a glass of champagne.

"I don't consider us wed," she whispered, "not anymore. Did you believe I left Maxey because of our vows? Is that what you really thought, you swell-headed, bumptious bastard?"

"Don't call me names, you vainglorious circus brat," he whispered back.

"Self-serving, self-worshipping spalpeen." She had never in her life made such an effort to keep her voice subdued yet audible.

"Over-proud, overweening gazoony." His blue eyes blazed. "Self-serving? You dare call me self-serving? It was you who deserted me, abandoned your circus. And look at you now. A whore in a brothel."

"A high-class brothel, Brian. I'm a lady. A fancy lady but a lady nevertheless. Don't you know how much the hostesses earn here?"

"No, and I'll never find out. I won't bid for your services, Calliope."

"Why should you? I gave myself to you freely. Now I can't be bought for love or money."

"What did you say? I couldn't hear you."

"Do you want me to shout my words to the whole casino? Never mind. They already know. You're the only galloo who's too thickheaded—damn and blast! Why can't you leave me alone?"

Before Brian could respond, the door opened and a beautiful woman entered. Her gaze swept the room then came to rest on Calliope. There was instant recognition.

Rising, Brian walked forward. "How nice of you to join us, Daisy, even though I did suggest you might find other amusements."

"I played the roulette wheel, darling, and lost all the money you gave me," she said, staring at Calliope.

"Let me introduce our hostess." Brian grinned recklessly. "Her name was Mary, but she enjoys changing it every so often, and I believe she is now called Irish Angel. Is that correct, Miss Angel?"

Still fuming, Calliope nodded.

"This is my fiancée, Louisa Sandoval," Brian continued, completing the introduction. "She's called Daisy."

"Miss Angel reminds me of another woman I once met," Daisy said, "but of course that's impossible. The other woman was a lady of impeccable breeding."

"Miss Sandoval reminds me of another woman too," Calliope said sweetly. "But of course that's impossible. The other woman was named for a light-weight hat of natural straw, hand-plaited from the young leaves of the jipijapa. The other woman's name is Panama. She straddled the back of an elephant. Have you ever mounted an elephant, Miss Sandoval?"

Brian shot Calliope a murderous glare. Then he unclenched Daisy's fisted fingers and folded them around a thick wad of bank notes. "Why don't you give the wheel another chance, sweetheart? If you bet small amounts on red or black, it will keep you occupied, and you'll have a chance to double your money. Or would you prefer to return to my ranch with your friends?"

"I prefer to play cards with Miss Angel." Daisy tossed the bank notes on top of the table.

"This is a gentleman's game for high stakes." Shaking off Clarissa, Señor Sandoval stepped forward.

"Oh do hush, Papa. I have no intention of disrupting your silly game." Daisy kissed Sandoval's bristling mustache then dimpled at the others. "Do you mind if I play a few hands while you eat and drink? Please?"

Brian scowled. "Daisy, return to the casino right now."

"Let her play, Fox," said a man who wore a check-ered vest. "Do you know poker rules, my dear?"

"I think so. I've watched the vaqueros on Papa's ranch."

"If you gentlemen agree, I'll let the ladies play for half an hour."

Calliope rose to her feet, surprised by the sound of Bret's voice. He had apparently seen Daisy enter and followed her inside.

"There will be no house percentage, since they share the deal," Bret continued. "I'll stake Miss Angel to any amount she requires."

"Good. Shall we begin?" Daisy smiled prettily at Bret and sat in the chair Brian had occupied.

"We can cut for first deal," said Calliope, also sitting.

She stared at Daisy from across the table. Like Calliope, Daisy was clothed in a black gown that left her neck and shoulders bare... except for jewelry. Daisy wore a magnificent spray of rubies; Calliope her horse-charm necklace.

Bret strolled up behind Calliope. Brian took a seat at the end of the table.

Each player made her cut, with Daisy winning the first deal.

It took about ninety seconds to play out a hand, and after ten minutes it became obvious Daisy had done more than just watch her papa's vaqueros.

"Does this win?" she'd ask, smugly showing her three of a kind to Calliope's two pair.

She was experiencing a run of extraordinary luck, thought Calliope, unless the ranch hands had taught Daisy more than the fact that a full house beats a flush.

Calliope felt her cheeks bake as she realized Daisy Sandoval was cheating. No doubt about it. She was palming the cards. Palming could be learned by almost anyone, but doing it well required talent and assiduous practice. Daisy was doing it well, palming cards and placing her hand on her arm in a natural curved position, or resting her hand, fingers together, flat on the table.

Before Calliope could expose her, Daisy lost a small pot and tossed the cards toward her opponent.

Calliope played the odds, winning the next three hands. Finally, she lost.

This time Daisy seemed to be dealing honestly, and Calliope couldn't detect her cheating method. Bret would probably tell her later. Why didn't *Bret* expose the bamboozling Jane? Was he afraid of offending his high-class company?

"This is too easy, and I'm bored," Daisy said. "Let's finish the game with one hand." Smiling complacently, she pushed all her money toward the middle of the table.

Bret counted and reciprocated, then added a thousand dollars.

"But I don't have any more money," Daisy said.

"If you can't match my thousand, you forfeit," Calliope said. At the same time, she wondered why Bret had raised the stakes. Hadn't he detected Daisy's cheating?

"Aaron, please give me more money."

"No." Brian stood, stretched, and walked over to Daisy's chair. "I didn't approve of this to begin with, and I'm sure the gentlemen wish to resume their game. Call it quits, Daisy. The house has bested you with the oldest trick in the book."

"But I'm sure I can win. I'm the better player. Papa, will you lend me the money? Please?"

"I agree with Aaron, daughter. You've risked your entire stake, and you must assume the consequences."

"That's not fair!" Daisy pouted, pondered, and removed her engagement ring, a huge emerald surrounded by tiny diamonds set in gold filigree. "This is worth more than a thousand dollars, Mr. Johnson."

"Are you crazy?" Sandoval's mustache bristled. "That ring has been in Aaron's family for generations."

"Hush, Papa, I have no intention of losing. Luck is on my side. Skill, as well. Mount an elephant, indeed! This baseborn hostess is a slut, a sham, and needs to be taken down a peg or two."

"Louisa! That's enough!"

Brian's sharp words effectively stopped Daisy's angry tirade. "I can't lose," she said, staring up at Brian, her eyes wide and tear-stung. "You don't mind if I bet the emerald, do you, darling?"

He shrugged.

"Will you accept my wager?" Daisy, dry-eyed, shifted her gaze to Calliope.

"I really don't think—"

"We accept," Bret said.

Was *he* crazy? Calliope deliberately lifted her eyebrows, attempting to hide her dismay.

I've got to do something, she thought desperately. But she couldn't figure out how the reechy weed was cheating. The shuffle. It had to be in the shuffle.

Calliope pictured Daisy rifling the cards. All at once it became clear. Of course. How simple. Daisy simply put the cards she wanted on the bottom of the deck. Then during the shuffle, she pulled one from the bottom and one from the top.

But it's too late to expose her. She's already shuffled, and I've made the cut. If I insist she show the cards, she'll claim it's coincidental.

"I believe a wager of this magnitude calls for new cards," said Bret, retrieving a sealed deck from a box.

"But I want to use these." Daisy gestured toward the cards she had just shuffled. "They've been lucky."

"Our rules state that a losing player can request a new deck at any time." Bret turned toward Calliope. "Would you like new cards, Miss Angel?"

"Yes, please."

Breaking the seal, Bret removed the cards and shuffled with precision.

"I don't care what the rules say!" Daisy screamed, and Calliope thought she sounded like Pollyann Stanhope.

"Let's get this over with." Brian reached out, accepted the new deck from Bret, and handed the cards to Daisy.

Immediately, Calliope recognized the markings on the back. It was one of the six decks Bret had teased her with the night he'd taught her how to detect a cheat.

By the time Daisy finished dealing, Calliope saw the fuming woman held two pair—aces and fives—while Calliope's hand included two sevens and two deuces.

Hesitating, trying to look indecisive, Calliope finally pulled one card from her hand and placed it face down on the table, hoping Daisy would believe she drew to complete an inside straight. Upon receiving the new card, Calliope made a quick *moue* of disgust.

Daisy discarded a Queen.

Calliope watched Daisy clutch the next card and knew from its markings that it was another Queen.

"Are you ready to resume the betting?" Calliope asked sweetly.

"But we've finished. I've more than matched your stake."

"You said you were bored. You said I was a slut and a sham. You swore you were the better player."

"I am! I can beat a painted *puta*. Besides, you're bluffing."

"Am I?"

"Yes!"

"In that case, call my bluff." Calliope unclasped her chain and placed her horse charm on the table. "I'll wager my necklace against yours."

"Are you mad? These rubies are worth—"

"My charm was a birthday gift from a dear lad, and I've always treasured it. However, you're right. It doesn't match your rubies. So I shall add a diamond solitaire ring that rests in my jewelry box upstairs. It was a gift from Maxey Stanhope."

"She's bluffing," said Daisy, almost spitting the words. "I saw her try and draw to an inside straight, and although she hid her disappointment, not very well I might add, she didn't get the right card. She's bluffing."

"Call my bluff."

"All right, I will. I remember your diamond ring. It should make a pretty brooch." Daisy tossed her ruby necklace onto the table and fanned out her cards. "Two pair, ace high," she called triumphantly. "Now show me your straight."

"I don't have a straight."

"I knew it!"

"But I do have a full house, sevens and deuces."

"What? You cheated. You must have. I saw the look on your face when you drew the last card."

"That, Miss Sandoval, is called a bluff." Calliope stood up and stretched. "Thank you for your patience, gentlemen. Clarissa may deal now. Perhaps in a short while I shall join you as a player." She turned her face toward Brian. "Is that satisfactory, Mr. Fox?"

"Of course. But I'm afraid I must withdraw from the game. My fiancée is rather distraught. Won't you sell her ring back to me? I'll give you twice its value."

"No, Mr. Fox. You may buy the rubies and my golden-horse necklace, but I prefer to keep the emerald. Its color matches my eyes."

Brian said, "How much is your horse charm worth, Irish?"

Turning toward Daisy, Calliope scooped her necklace from the table. "Here, Miss Sandoval, I'll let you have my charm for nothing, just to prove I'm a good loser."

"But you won," Daisy said.

This time Brian didn't say anything, yet his fierce, almost riveting glare said it all.

I didn't abandon you or my circus, Calliope screamed silently. *I'm not a whore, and I don't cheat.*

Her whole body felt naked, vulnerable. She had never taken the necklace off. Now she felt Bret lightly caress her shoulders and throat. He reached the precise spot where the horse charm had rested and stroked with his thumb.

Watching Brian escort Daisy through the open doorway, Calliope wanted to weep. But she knew she wouldn't. Because her heart was missing.

It had left the room with her necklace.

Twenty-Four

MERRY-GO-ROUND, MERRY-GO-ROUND, MERRY-GO-ROUND. Calliope didn't feel very merry as she paced in an irregular circle from her bed to her window, clothespress, chiffonier, dressing table, bed again. In one hand she clutched an unwrapped parcel. Within its layers of thin tissue paper were six red roses and her horse-charm necklace. The card was signed "Aaron." There was no salutation, no message.

After besting Daisy Sandoval, Calliope had thought she'd heard the last of Aaron Fox. Now, three days later, he had stirred her emotions anew, like a stone skimmed across a placid pool of water.

Why send back the necklace? Why include the roses? It should have been a paper bouquet of flowers drawn from a magician's sleeve. Hadn't their love for each other proved to be nothing more than a fantasia?

Since it was the first day of February, the roses must have come from a hothouse.

Hothouse—another name for a brothel! Was that Brian's hidden message?

She sank down onto her counterpane. Perhaps he

had sent back the necklace hoping she would reciprocate and return his emerald ring. Well, she wouldn't.

Caressing one rose, she felt a sharp thorn prick her thumb. Then almost immediately, she felt a small pinprick of guilt. She tried to shrug the sensation away. Daisy had cheated. She had not. True, she had known the woman's last hand in advance by reading the markings on the back of the cards. But that made no difference. Daisy had controlled the shuffle.

Had she shuffled? Calliope probed her memory. Daisy had reached out and accepted the deck from Brian. Then she'd dealt the cards. Which meant—what?

Could Bret have fixed the cards in advance?

During their lesson on cheating, Bret had showed her a false shuffle. He had demonstrated a method called the pull through, a dazzling and completely crooked shuffle that didn't alter a single card.

But how could he know Daisy wouldn't reshuffle?

Because Bret was an excellent student of human nature; that's how. He would have anticipated Daisy's reaction to the appearance of a new deck, her anger and disappointment.

Daisy had not shuffled.

Calliope flung her horse charm and roses toward her pillow. Rising, she walked over to the dressing table, gazed into the mirror, and saw that her eyes were very bright, very green—as green as an emerald. She glanced down at her open jewelry box where the Fox emerald lay amidst her earrings, along with Daisy's ruby necklace.

The ring is mine, and I won't give it back!

And yet she had no right to keep it. She knew, without a single doubt, Bret had pre-arranged the deck.

She couldn't return the bank notes, the original stake, since that belonged to Bret. He had let her keep the jewels. She had a feeling Bret was challenging her. If the valuable gems were pawned or sold, she'd have enough money for her ticket to Paris.

The diamond solitaire engagement ring had been a bluff. Winding thread around its band until it fit, she had worn it to the barbecue and then foolishly sent it back to Maxey as soon as she arrived at the Cirque de Delices.

She had also sent a letter to Ann and Raymond, the ink blotchy from her tears. What could she say so they'd understand? Your son abused my body and drugged me? Aaron Fox, once known as Brian O'Connor, is very much alive? My husband who is not my husband wants no part of me, so I dwell inside an opulent, high-class hothouse? In the end, she had merely thanked the elderly Stanhopes for their care and kindness and suggested that Brandywine, now well schooled, be trained as a mount for Pollyann.

A few days later she received an envelope with Brian's wedding band and a note from Ann. The paper smelled of lavender and read: "Raymond and I love you, Mary. You are always welcome in our home."

Calliope owed the Stanhopes so much, but she should have sold the diamond. Maxey owed her that and more. Much more. What had Brian called her? Over-proud, overweening gazoony. Yes, she had acted like a stubborn child by returning the engagement ring, by allowing her pride to dominate reason.

Calliope shrugged. It was done, finished, and couldn't be changed.

Now she had a second chance. The rubies and emerald would be more than enough to provide the funds for her journey, and Dublin's, as well. She'd audition for the Nouveau Cirque as an equestrian rather than an equilibrist.

But she hadn't won the pot fair and square, because Bret had used a false shuffle.

Daisy cheated first.

Dottie would say two wrongs don't make a right.

Paris, thought Calliope. She could leave Colorado, leave Maxey and Bret. And Brian.

According to Señor Sandoval, the ring had been in Aaron Fox's family for generations. So if she kept the emerald, she was, in effect, cheating Brian.

I'm not a whore, and I don't cheat.

Twenty-Five

STROLLING ALONG THE TREE-LINED STREET, CALLIOPE ignored the ethereal landscape. Everything was white, even the sky whose curtain of clouds promised more snow. She walked to the site of Brian's hotel for two reasons. First, the snow was at least a foot deep, with higher drifts piling up at every street corner, making it virtually impossible for a horse or carriage to plow through accumulated mounds. Second, she didn't want Bret to know about her decision. Let him believe she'd deliberately chosen to remain at the Cirque, even though the emeralds and rubies would have bought her freedom.

She couldn't send the parcel by messenger for the same reason. She had no desire to visit Brian's ranch, the scene of her humiliation and broken pride, and if Black Jack delivered the jewels, he'd surely tell Bret. She must never forget Bret could be nasty as well as nice, especially where Brian was concerned. Hadn't "Jocko" set the circus fire in a jealous rage?

But Jocko wasn't her evil leprechaun. Perhaps her leprechaun had died in the fire. If so, Sean and Angelique would have been avenged, and she would never learn the leprechaun's identity. So what? The circus wasn't forever. The Cirque was. Thus the leprechaun, not Bret, had ultimately dealt Calliope her dismal cards.

And he, or she, didn't even have to shuffle.

Scrambling over a huge drift, clutching the paper-wrapped parcel in her furry muff, Calliope resisted the urge to slide down the other side on her rump.

It was so cold her breath created smoky puffs as she shouted, "Damn your soul, Brian O'Connor! I'll prove I'm not a cheat. You can have your blasted ring, and I'll not charge you a penny. Then you can go straight to the devil!"

She hadn't donned her corset and bustle, but over her boots and beneath her long woolen skirt, she wore one of Eve's creations: a pair of trousers made from soft beaver pelts. Her hair was captured under a fur bonnet whose green ribbons were tied at the side of her chin. Her coat was also lined with fur, but only once before had she ever felt as cold as she did this very moment— the night Bret had told her Brian was alive.

"It would have been better if you had truly died in the fire, Brian O'Connor!" she shouted and swallowed a blast of icy air. Superstitiously, she crossed herself. "I didn't mean it," she cried, her voice sounding strange in the eerie silence of the empty street.

She pictured Brian, not as he had appeared at the poker game but the way he had looked while standing outside the gazebo. And wasn't his nakedness a sight to behold? Broad shoulders, lean hips, long muscular legs, and that glorious part of his body that brought her such pleasure.

She shivered, but this time it wasn't from the cold. She felt a pleasant throb between her thighs as she remembered their lovemaking on the gazebo floor— the passion that had erupted, destroying demon-snakes, subduing everything except her insatiable need to be kissed, touched, fulfilled.

By the time she reached the hotel site, she was warmed by her memories and her need to see Brian again, having almost forgotten the true purpose of her mission.

It had never occurred to her the recent blizzard would halt construction or Brian wouldn't be at the site supervising his workmen. Her mind, like her old railroad cars, had been following one track until she reached her destination.

Hellfire! The place was deserted. And it was snowing again, snowing so hard she couldn't see the tips of her boots as she placed one foot in front of the other. The storm was a huge monster with a voice that was low and rumbling, occasionally interrupted by a high-pitched whine. The storm was a Kid Show freak of nature, dominating a circus of snow-shrouded horses and elephants. The storm played center ring, but there were no gillys or tent walls, only uprooted trees and mammoth snow banks.

Before the snow had obliterated her vision, she had glimpsed the outline of a wagon and even managed to make out a few crudely painted letters on the wood: F XF RE MA R.

Where was the damfool wagon? Snow stuck to her long lashes as she plunged recklessly forward. The whole world was pure white. She released one hand from her muff and reached out blindly, hoping to encounter wheels, steps, anything that offered a solid hold for her fingers.

Nothing. Only a wall of swirling flakes that pelted her mercilessly. Only the monster's voice, now a constant wail. If someone had slashed a pillow and stuffed the feathers inside her mouth and up her nose, she couldn't have been more frightened. Or miserable.

Falling to her knees, still clutching the parcel, she crawled forward, not even knowing if she headed in the right direction. "Brian, help me!" she shouted, aware that her words seemed to melt the moment she uttered them.

He wasn't daft enough to venture outside. He was probably at his ranch, sitting in front of a roaring fire, consoling his grief-stricken weed of a fiancée, mending her broken pride.

"Brian, for the love of God, help me!"

"Calliope?"

"Brian?" Was she asleep? Dreaming? Dead?

"Calliope!"

"Brian, where are you? I can't see you?"

"I can't see you, either. Keep talking, and I'll follow the sound of your voice."

"Wind… loud."

"Talk, Calliope. I'll know the difference between the wind and your voice."

"All right. I had to come."

"Louder!"

"I had to come, Brian. I had to tell you. I'm not Bret's hostess. I'm not a whore. Oh, God, I can't breathe."

"I'm here, Calliope. I've found you. Can you stand up?"

"Tired."

"I know, puss. Put your arms around my neck, and I'll lift you. Calliope, let go of that blasted muff and put your arms around my neck."

"Can't… muff… emerald."

Shit! What the hell was she talking about? What the hell was she *wearing*? Whatever it was, Brian thought, the sodden garments made her weight tenfold.

He managed to place one arm under her knees and one under her shoulders. Then with a mighty effort, he lifted her up into his arms—and smelled wet fur.

"Calliope, drop that damn muff! I'd rather suffocate from snow than a wee animal's dead pelt."

"You sound very Irish," she murmured. Flinging her muff toward a snow bank, she wove her fingers through the hair at his nape.

"Ow! You're pulling my mane out by its roots," he said. "Now I know how Dublin feels. Can you not hold still for two minutes?"

"Damn your soul, Brian O'Connor! Drop me and be done with it!"

He staggered up four steps, kicked open the wagon's door, and lowered her onto the cushion of a large stuffed armchair.

She removed her bonnet, and Brian watched rich golden-brown strands cascade to her waist. Then shivering, she drew her legs up to her chest and hugged her knees. Snow melted on her lashes and glistened like shiny teardrops caught in cobwebs. Her eyes stared accusingly.

"What," she said, "are you doing here?"

"It's my wagon, you daft colleen."

"I only meant you should be at your ranch, sitting in front of a roaring fire, consoling your weed—"

"What the hell are you babbling about?"

"Daisy Sandoval."

"Daisy's in Denver, where she belongs."

"Does she wear another ring on her left stem?"

"As a matter of fact, she does."

"Then my venture was for naught," Calliope said, hugging her knees tighter.

As Brian shook the snow from his hair, everything fell into place. Muff. Emerald. The daft lass had plodded through the snow to return his ring.

Briefly, he felt an acute sense of disappointment. She had not braved the elements—challenged death as it turned out—to see him again.

"Your venture was the act of a gazoony," he said with exasperation. "I should spank your lovely backside."

"If you spank me, you shall get a handful of wet fur."

"Wet fur? That's a new way to put it. I have a mind to wash out your mouth with soap."

"What? Oh." A series of musical giggles spawned more shivers. "Such a boozlebrain you have become, Brian O'Connor."

"Why do you chortle like a hyena?"

"When I said you'd get a handful of... I only meant that under my skirt I wear soft, thick breeches." Again, she burst into peals of laughter. "I must tell Eve. No, I cannot tell Eve. Yes, I shall tell her. She, for one, will appreciate..." Abruptly, Calliope's giggles subsided. "Wash out my mouth with soap? How dare you suggest... Why, you depraved, pinch-beck, gilly-galloo!"

A chameleon! I once compared her to a chameleon, and she hasn't changed one whit.

"Calm down," he said.

"Don't tell me what to do, you flummery buffoon! Why do you always misunderstand everything I say?" Rising, Calliope clutched her soaked garments closer to her body. Eve's breeches, the wet fur between her legs, was now a hindrance rather than an asset. Every inch of her skin erupted into goose bumps. "There's a parcel buried in the snow, Brian. It's valuable, so I suggest you retrieve it. I must return home. Good-bye."

"Have you completely lost your mind, Calliope? How far do you think you'd get in this blizzard?"

"I d–don't w-want to be alone with you," she said, her teeth chattering like castanets.

"I don't want to be alone with you, either, but I can't see what choice we have." He thrust several chunks of wood into a potbellied stove. "Take off your clothes."

"No! Not for love or money, you pawky bastard!"

"Damn it, Calliope, take off your wet dress, or you'll catch your death from pneumonia. Here." He tossed her a man's dressing gown: purple with a tasseled sash.

She stamped her small, booted foot. "I'll take my clothes off if you leave yours on."

"And wouldn't you love to step over my frozen corpse tomorrow, lass?" He removed his boots, trousers, and shirt. "Do you honestly think I'm brainsick enough to stay in wet duds just to appease your sudden sense of modesty? Or do you fear I shall do more than spank your lovely backside?"

She stared, mesmerized, at the sight of his tall body clad in long johns. The top was unbuttoned, allowing his dark chest hair to escape from its opening. The bottoms, especially between his legs, left very little to the imagination.

Slowly, she dropped his dressing gown, along with her coat, boots, and sodden fur breeches.

"I'm sure you've seen many naked men at Bret Johnson's establishment," he said.

"Oh! You bastard!" Calliope stiffened her cold fingers into claws and rushed forward to rake Brian's face. "I hate you!" she screamed. "I'll kill you dead! You'll never say another hurtful word to me again!"

Brian deftly sidestepped.

Calliope's forward motion sent her sprawling. She landed on her belly and lay there, trying to regain her lost breath.

Brian knelt and carefully turned her over, startled by the expression he saw in her beautiful eyes. There was anger, and yet there was also a soulful sorrow that tugged at his heart. "You cannot kill the truth, puss," he said.

She didn't answer. Instead, tears gathered, overflowed.

"Aw, don't cry," he murmured, feeling like a small lad who had suddenly been handed a broken toy. Calliope Kelley never cried. She had bawled, briefly, inside the menagerie tent. She had faced the cats with bravado then wept, mourning Sean's death. She had cried during that long-ago night inside the silver wagon. Her eyes had brimmed over at the Spring Ball, and she had sobbed with joy inside the gazebo. Not a hell of a lot of crying, considering that most of the women Brian knew, Daisy included, often gushed waterfalls.

He cradled her face and gently wiped away her tears with the fingertips of his right hand. His other hand accidentally brushed her bosom.

She gave an almost eerie screech. Then she bit his thumb, her sharp teeth drawing blood.

"Why, you little tiger." He would have said more, but his words died unborn at her look of pure terror. "Calliope?"

Her eyes were unfocused, far away. "Calliope, look at me," he said, recalling how he had encountered the same reaction inside the gazebo. But this time she didn't respond.

Now his trepidation matched hers. He sat cross-legged and pulled her into his arms so her legs straddled each side of his waist. In this position, with her damp skirts and petticoats up about her hips, her naked thighs were enticing, and yet he could almost smell her fear.

"Calico Cat, what is it? What's wrong?" He stroked her back beneath her silken hair.

She cringed, drew away, and with a drugged motion finished unbuttoning her gown. Then she thrust her breasts forward above her chemise, trembling so fiercely Brian though she might shatter in his arms like a piece of fragile glass. Her charade wasn't the teasing gesture of a woman in the throes of dawning passion. Hell, no! She bared her breasts as if they were a couple of sacrificial offerings.

Despite her obvious terror, her motions were provocative, and Brian felt his erection burst through the slits in his johns, meeting the soft whorls between her thighs. With the greatest control he had ever exerted, he kept from spilling his seed. Instead he sat motionless, whispering his pet name for her over and over.

"Calico Cat, Calico Cat, Calico Cat."

"Brian?"

"Yes?"

"Is it you? Is it truly you?"

He watched her stare at his face. Her eyes were finally focused and had lost that muddy grayness. Then a different expression clouded their brilliance, and he realized desire had replaced fear. It was safe to remove her bodice and chemise, lower his mouth, and lick the graceful arch of her throat until he reached her rosy nipples.

With a gasp, she leaned forward, inviting him... no, *urging* him to feed on the creamy perfection of her breasts. He obeyed.

She spread her legs, and he had no choice but to insert his full-fledged erection into her moist opening. When his entire length was buried deep, he cupped her face with his hands and thrust his tongue inside her mouth. She met his tongue with hers and began to spasm, but he held back until he felt her grind her nipples against his chest, suck his tongue toward her throat, then release it altogether as her head fell back and she issued the familiar "Now!"

Calliope listened to Brian's low hum of pleasure. She felt his steady stream of desire. She bit at the edge of his open undershirt, scissoring with her teeth. As the shredded garment fell apart, she nuzzled his coarse chest hair until she found his nipples. She licked the hard nubs, faster and faster. With satisfaction, she heard his renewed moans.

He shifted until they lay on the floor with her body on top, still united in a oneness of bonded flesh. When he withdrew, she sighed, disappointed. "Why did you leave me?" she cried, dimly aware she meant more than the sudden loss of his hard heat.

"Hush, puss. Let's get rid of these damn clothes. There should be nothing between us."

Nothing between us, she thought, *except the fire, Maxey Stanhope, Bret Johnson, Daisy Sandoval*.

Brian's fingers brushed tantalizingly at her belly button then her brown-gold whorls, still wet from his ministrations. "Soft," he murmured. "I always forget how soft... My beautiful, beautiful Calico Cat."

"Encore!" she screamed, her spasms building anew. "I want you inside me! Now!"

"Of course, puss."

Instead, his first finger continued exploring. Pressing her palms against the floorboards, she raised herself up the length of her arms, giving him easier access to the pulsating throb he had created. He inserted his finger and felt her contractions. She was more than ready, and so was he. Removing his finger, he penetrated, plunging deeper as her flesh enfolded him.

Calliope had never realized a man could plunge upwards. It was against the laws of gravity, like a ropewalker plummeting toward the tent top rather than the net. Wasn't it?

Apparently not, because Brian defied gravity very nicely.

Her arms lost their temporary strength, and she

collapsed against his chest, her long hair fanning out like the strands of an unwoven blanket.

Recapturing her face, Brian licked her lips. His tongue tasted her rippling crescendo of whimpers. Her breath was sugar-sweet as she whispered, "I love you, lad, evermore."

Afterwards, he wrapped her in a downy patchwork quilt and placed her on top of an army cot. Long lashes fanned her flushed cheeks. She looked so vulnerable, so different from the stately, black-gowned hostess who had presided over Bret Johnson's poker game, so different from the woman who had pledged her horse-charm necklace then offered it to Daisy to prove she was a "good loser."

Daisy didn't understand, but Brian did. The circus cat had severed all ties to the cat tamer.

He had sworn up and down he would never see her again. Then impulsively, he had sent her the horse charm and roses. He should have sent a clown's paper bouquet of flowers. Wasn't their love an illusion?

Yes. But not their passion. That burned as brightly as the green fire in Calliope's beautiful cat eyes.

He knew there would be no encore to this performance. The show was over. He had obligations. To his father. To Daisy. He had been fully prepared to visit his father, threaten a scandal, collect money for the injured circus performers, and leave straightaway. But to Brian's surprise, Aaron Fox said he'd desperately tried to find Maureen O'Connor and was devastated by her death. A bond had formed between father and son—a bond that had nothing to do with money or property.

In truth, Brian thought, he should be at the ranch

right now. Rounding up the stock. Fighting the blizzard. Fighting his love for Calliope. It was Calliope who had caused him to visit the construction site. Alone, he wanted to mull over his feelings. Well, he'd mulled. Then with her almost ghostly appearance, all his firm resolutions had melted away, just like the snow on her dark lashes.

After stoking the fire, Brian donned the dressing gown she had discarded, blew out the lantern, and lay beside Calliope on the narrow cot, unmoving, staring into the darkness of the wagon. Mulling.

❧

"The rope! I'm going to fall!"

Brian stirred and opened his eyes. He had finally dozed, but his whole body was cramped from remaining in one position.

He felt his legs protest as, rising, he stared down at Calliope.

"The rope's burning," she cried.

He knelt by the cot. "Wake up, puss," he said, keeping his voice low, hoping he wouldn't startle her. "You're having a bad dream."

"Brian, why did you leave me? Where are you? Oh, I'm going to fall off."

"Hush, puss." He smoothed the tousled hair away from her forehead. Shit! She was burning up. He listened to her cough, a rattling sound that seemed to come from deep within the recesses of her chest. Then he recalled the words he had so carelessly flung at her: *Take off your wet dress, or you'll catch your death from pneumonia.*

"Brian," she whimpered.

"Calliope, I'm here. Lie still."

"Hurts. Hurts bad, not good."

"I know. Don't move." Brian glanced toward the small window. He couldn't determine the time, because thick snowflakes surged against the dark panes, but he thought it might be close to dawn. "I'll light the lantern and…" His voice faltered as he watched Calliope, still coughing, lean over the cot's side.

Swiftly, Brian caught her heaving shoulders with one arm and pressed his other hand against her hot forehead as she retched, spewing forth a thin stream of phlegm and bile.

When she finally sagged back onto the stretched fabric, he reached for a nearby canteen, unscrewed the cap, and pressed the opening against her lips.

"Drink, lass."

With a great effort, she managed to swallow. Then she gave a pathetic moan and once again moved her head toward the edge of the cot.

Brian circled her shoulders, felt her tense then lose all control as water gushed from her open mouth.

"Die," she gasped.

"No!" Gritting his teeth, he forced more water down her throat and watched helplessly as she vomited for the third time. Clutching her belly, she rocked back and forth. The cords in her neck strained as she tried, unsuccessfully, to vomit away her pain.

"You will not die!" he shouted.

He stroked her forehead, wondering if he spoke the truth, dimly aware she must retain liquid if she were to survive. With one last whimper, she lapsed into unconsciousness.

She needed a doctor! Brian raced toward the door and grasped its knob. Stuck! The damn door was stuck! With a strength born of desperation, he pushed, every muscle straining. The wood yielded a few inches, and he found himself facing a solid wall of pure white snow.

They were trapped. If Brian was Hercules, Atlas, and Samson, all in one body, he'd never move that accumulated mountain of snow.

His calm belied his anguish as he shrugged off his dressing gown and pulled on his shirt and trousers.

The damn snow was good for something, he thought, gathering enough to fill a dented tin basin. Carefully, he tore Calliope's petticoats into wide strips, dipped the strips into the basin, and began to bathe her fevered body.

Twenty-Six

THE HAND THAT CARESSED HER BROW WAS COLD. Calliope struggled to lift her heavy lashes. Finally succeeding, she saw Sean Kelley. And realized his corpse-cold hand had been stroking the tangled hair away from her forehead.

"I'm sick, Papa," she whimpered. "Terrible sick."

"Suck the peppermints," he said. "'Tis good for the digestion."

"I'll eat the mints if you don't go near the pie car."

"Do not be tellin' me what to do, daughter. 'Tis barely out of nappies ye be."

"Papa, I'm seventeen."

Her vision blurred then focused, and once again she saw Sean. Younger, he stood in center ring. His green eyes twinkled, his black hair was parted in the middle, and his clear voice reached every seat.

"Our French Angel, at great danger to her lovely person, will tiptoe across the rope. Lay-deez and gen-tul-men, she will dance through the air, straight up to heaven."

"Your arms, Mum!"

"Do not be forgettin' to wrap your arms about your chest," Sean pleaded, "or they'll catch between your legs."

"I can't wrap my arms about my chest, Papa. Don't you understand? Somebody's holding me down and dousing me with frozen water."

"Wash down the elephant," Brian sang, sloshing more water in her direction.

"I'm not an elephant. Aren't you the confused boy-o?"

"It's time for Calliope's Saturday bath."

"Stop it, Brian! I'm cold!"

In truth, she was possessed by a shivery sensation that shook her whole body. A quilt was tucked around her, and somebody had added blankets, her coat, even her fur-lined breeches.

"Ain't you shamed for the fibbing, lass? 'Tis hotter than the devil's front parlor."

"She's burning up again, Aaron. Fetch more snow."

"I believed you a man, Brian O'Connor. But now I see you are merely a spalpeen in manly form."

The musicians executed a drumroll.

"Now!" screamed Calliope, and Susan B. Anthony leaped gracefully through the hoop. But someone tossed a flowered nosegay. Jocko? Panama? Susan kicked out with her hind legs, and Calliope felt herself falling.

The heat! Brian had not caught her after all. She must have landed inside the ring of fire. The tent was filled with fire, and flames singed her hair.

The heat was unbearable. She thrashed about to escape it, kicking away at the quilt and the blankets and the coat and the breeches. Opening her eyes, she thought she caught a glimpse of Gwendolyn.

"Have you seen Brian? The cat tamer. Tonight he also played ringmaster."

"Oh, the ringmaster. He's dead."

"Are you sure?"

"Yes, I swear. It was the ringmaster."

The room smelled of chicken soup. The man wore a top hat and a batwing collar and his necktie's knot sported a stickpin with a diamond as big as an acorn.

"Brian?"

"I'm here, puss."

"Brian?" It hurt Calliope's face to whisper.

"She must mean her husband," said Ann Stanhope.

"Then he's truly dead?"

"Do you remember your name, dear?"

"Mary Angelique O'Connor."

"Pollyann wants to thank you. She even finger painted a picture just for you, a picture of her favorite cat."

"Calico Cat. Poor wee Calico Cat."

"You must get some sleep, Aaron."

"No. You sleep. If I sleep, she might die."

Possessive lips kissed her hot forehead.

"Try that once more, and I shall slap your face."

"You'll like my kisses, Angel, and that's a promise."

"I'm not certain I like you, Mr. Stanhope. In any case, you've made a mistake. I'm not an heiress. I couldn't even make a wish at the cherub's pool."

Maxey mounted his horse. "I don't usually make mistakes."

She had the whim-whams. Maxey gave her the whim-whams.

"You can't marry me, Mr. Stanhope. I told you last night. I'm not an heiress."

"You didn't say anything about becoming my father's ward. Don't you understand what that means?"

"Yes! Your parents will take care of me for the rest of my life. Why do I need you?"

"But I need you."

"Please, puss, I need you. Please don't die."

The animals stared accusingly, fire reflected in their eyes. A long line of performers and gillys passed each other buckets of water to douse the fire, and someone stroked her body with a cool cloth. But it didn't help. She writhed about in suffocating heat. Her breasts ached. Her whole body ached. Her throat was dry as toast, and she heard the loud pounding of her heart. One, two, three. One, two, three.

"When we're alone, you must call me Mr. Stanhope. Open your mouth, Mary. Eat the pretty bunny and drink the deadly nightshade."

"Open your mouth, puss. Try to drink."

"Go to the devil, you bastard!"

"If you do what I say, I won't hurt you again."

"I'm sorry, puss. I know it hurts to swallow, but you must try."

"I never thought the name Mary suited you, but I do now. Drink the belladonna, Mary."

Once she had watched a sparrow hawk and wondered how it felt to fly with no net beneath. Once she had stared at a snake—

"This is Angel, Mr. Johnson."

"You told the truth, Stanhope. She's beautiful."

"Your name is real, Bret Johnson."

"For the love of God, Calliope, why does Maxey Stanhope control you like Brian O'Connor once controlled his lions and tigers?"

"If Brian's alive, where is he now?"

"We went our separate ways. Brian disappeared. Didn't he abandon you once before, Calliope, when you needed him the most?"

"You're Aaron Fox!"

"When I became his heir, Father insisted I take his name. I'm the third Aaron."

"She feels cooler, Aaron. Perhaps the fever will break soon."

"This is my fault. I should have taken off her wet clothes. Instead, I played the lustful—"

"Hush! Don't go to pieces on me now. She needs both of us. Heat some more broth."

"She won't swallow."

"She must. Hold her still."

"Brian, put me down."

"Don't play the coy virgin with me, lass."

The wooden horses grinned.

"Why didn't you return to the scene of the fire?"

She opened her mouth to reply then closed it again. He wouldn't believe her. He thought she had abandoned him, abandoned her circus. If she told him about Maxey, he'd beat the man to a bloody pulp and marry Daisy Sandoval.

"How much is your necklace worth, Irish?"

Calliope tossed her heart toward Daisy. "I'll let you have this just to prove I'm a good loser."

"But you won."

"No. The leprechaun won. And he didn't even have to shuffle the cards."

"Calliope! Oh God, Eve, we're losing her."

"Brian, where are you? I can't see. I can't breathe."

"I'm here."

"Tired," she whimpered. "Hurts bad, not good."

"I know, puss. I'm so sorry."

Brian grasped the reins with one hand and started running. The stars looked like glittery pins stuck through a bolt of black fabric. The pins pierced her legs, belly, and heart. Then she heard Eve croon, "There, there, Aaron, don't cry. I think her fever has finally broken."

Calliope felt Eve remove the pins, and darkness cloaked her in soft silk. She was covered in silk from head to toe, her new Spring Ball costume. The mask had no eye-slits but that didn't matter, because Aaron Fox was whirling her around the dance floor, crushing her against his broad chest. One, two, three. One, two, three.

"Brian, you're alive!"

◈

Calliope opened her eyes. It was so quiet she could hear the drip-drip of melting snow and ice.

She must have fallen from the cot, because she felt bruised, as if every part of her body had been beaten with the end of Brian's whiplash. Turning her head, she winced at the slight movement. Then her puzzled gaze swept the wagon's interior.

A washbasin had been placed near the cot, and strips of white material hung across a rope above a potbellied stove. The dripping sound came from a small window where icicles glistened in the bright

sunshine. She wore Brian's purple dressing gown. Eve
was asleep.

Calliope raised herself up on one elbow, groaning
at the painful effort.

Eve's eyes opened. Rising from the stuffed armchair,
she raced toward Calliope then slowed and smiled.
"How do you feel, Mary?"

"What happened? I feel as if a horse trampled me
beneath his hooves. Did I fall from the cot?"

"You've been ill for six days. For a long while we
thought you weren't going to make it." Sinking to the
floor beside the cot, Eve settled her skirt and petticoats
above her crossed ankles.

"We?"

"Aaron and I."

"Did I say anything? I mean, did I talk out loud?"

"You were very sick," Eve replied, sidestepping
the question.

"Where is he?"

"Aaron? He returned to his ranch. I imagine everything's a mess out there too."

"A mess?"

"The snow."

"He left me again," Calliope said. "That's always
been his answer to any problem."

"No, no, he didn't leave, not until your fever
broke. He hardly slept the whole time, Mary, and he
promised he'd come back soon."

"How did you get here?"

"I almost didn't. You see, snow blocked the
wagon's door, but Aaron hauled himself out through
the window. He planned to fetch the doctor."

Calliope glanced toward the window. She tried to picture Brian's broad shoulders fitting. He must have wriggled and—

"The doctor was in the mountains, delivering a baby," Eve continued, "trapped by the storm. So Aaron came to my place. I live above my shop, and there's an outside staircase. It was so cold the snow was packed hard, solid. We walked on water, Mary."

"Thank you for taking care of me."

"You're welcome, but I didn't do much. If it wasn't for Aaron, you'd have been a goner. He even blamed himself for your illness, insisting he should have removed your wet clothes."

Now I understand. Brian blamed himself when I got sick. He tended me from a sense of guilt. Nothing has changed.

Eve said, "Are you hungry?"

"No, not really." Carefully, Calliope moved her legs over the edge of the cot, dismayed by her lack of strength. In this new position she could see the wall at the end of the wagon. During the blizzard, in the dim light from Brian's lantern, she hadn't noticed a circus poster depicting an elephant's head. How could she have missed it? Bright and colorful, it drew one's gaze. Above gleaming white tusks and a long gray trunk, red letters spelled out:

FOXFIRE MANOR PRESENTS CIRCUS ACTS
TRANSPORTED TO COLORADO SPRINGS BY AARON FOX

Foxfire Manor. The letters on the wagon had spelled out Foxfire Manor. No wonder Brian was building a stage "larger than most opera houses." He planned to present circus acts for his hotel's grand opening. What a brilliant scheme.

Calliope heard a loud knock. Reluctantly removing her gaze from the poster, she turned her head toward the door.

"Aaron," said Eve with a smile. But before she could get to her feet, the door swung open, and Bret Johnson entered.

Above the brown fur collar of a long coat, his face was paler than the bleached petticoat strips that hung above the stove. Strands of ash-blond hair were darkened by melted snow. His gaze lingered briefly on Eve then encompassed Calliope, and his expression swiftly changed from anxiety to relief.

"They said there was a dead woman inside Fox's wagon," he stated without preamble. "They said she was trapped by the storm and had frozen to death."

"Who is they?" asked Calliope.

"Fox's workers, gambling away their wages at my dice tables."

"How did you know they were talking about me?"

"Who else would visit Brian O'Connor during a raging blizzard?"

Eve stood and advanced toward Bret like a lioness protecting her cub. "Leave Mary alone. She's been ill."

"Stay out of this."

"I won't, you weasely bastard. Mary... Calliope didn't visit Mr. O'Connor... Mr. Fox. Oh dear, I'm fuddled by all the names."

"*My* name is Bret Johnson, and I own the Cirque de Delices." He turned toward Calliope. "I told you I don't like to play the fool, darling. I made it very clear you'd be out on the sidewalk, penniless, rubbing the hurt from your—"

"Are you blind, Mr. Johnson?" Eve's slender hands splayed across her hips. "Can you not see she's sick? Mary doesn't need your blasted accusations when she's just sat up for the very first time."

Bret backed away from the bonfire of fury in the small woman's sherry brown eyes. *Yes, I'm blind when it comes to Calliope. She's right about that.*

He recalled his abject disappointment at Calliope's disappearance. At first he assumed she planned to trade her jewels for a ticket to France, since the emerald ring and the ruby necklace were missing from her jewelry box. Then when she didn't return, he and Black Jack tried to battle the storm, but it was impossible. They couldn't plod more than a hundred feet through the swirling flakes and icy needles. The Cirque de Delices, just like the rest of Colorado Springs, was trapped by Mother Nature's whimsical sense of humor.

When the snow finally stopped, he and Black Jack renewed their search. But Calliope had vanished into thin air. Bret seriously considered hiring a man with bloodhounds. Then he heard the workers talking about the frozen woman who lay inside Aaron Fox's wagon.

It couldn't be Calliope, Bret told himself. Or if it was, she couldn't be dead. He'd know. Deep down in his heart, he'd know. After the circus fire, he had built his gambling empire with the certainty he'd find her again. This was no different.

Now he reached into his pocket, removed a handkerchief, and wiped away the water that streamed from his wet hair. In his haste to reach the construction site, he hadn't bothered to retrieve his hat, snatched from his head by a frivolous gust of wind. Staring at Eve, he said, "What do you mean she wasn't visiting O'Connor's wagon?"

It's as if I'm not here, thought Calliope, sinking back onto her cot in sudden exhaustion. They were talking around her. Maybe she had truly died, and this was a new kind of purgatory. No, not purgatory, hell, because she'd briefly believed Brian really loved her. But he had treated her from a sense of guilt, a sense of honor, like he'd treat a tiger he had wounded in the taming.

"Answer me, woman!" Bret shouted. "Or I'll throttle the truth out of you."

"Don't you dare threaten me, Mr. Johnson. I'm not afraid of any man nor beast."

A small smile twitched at the corners of Bret's mouth. "I apologize, Miss Eve. That's your name, isn't it? I promise I'll not threaten or throttle if you will kindly tell me exactly whom Calliope planned to visit."

"Me."

"You?"

"We had an appointment for a fitting." Instinctively, Eve knew she must protect her friend from this attractive man who, even in his bedraggled state, radiated a distinct aura of power. "Mary became lost in the snowstorm. She caught pneumonia. Mr. Fox and I nursed her. Mary's fever broke this morning at daybreak, and Mr. Fox returned to his ranch."

Uncertainty clouded Bret's hazel eyes, which roved around the wagon's interior until they lit on an unwrapped parcel atop a small wooden table. "Do you take me for a fool, Miss Eve? Why would Calliope bring her emeralds and rubies to a fitting?"

"A fool indeed, Mr. Johnson. Men are such dunder-heads. Of course she brought her jewels. We planned to choose fabrics that would match their colors."

Calliope blinked at the fib. Why was Eve lying? What difference did it make if Bret knew the truth? Her whole world had turned to ashes with Eve's carelessly uttered words: *He even blamed himself for your illness.*

Why hadn't God allowed her to remain in that wondrous cloak of darkness? Why cure her? Why bring her back to fight demons over and over when she could never claim a victory?

The wagon walls began spinning. Pressing both hands against her forehead, trying to crush her anguished memories into particles of dust, Calliope moaned.

Eve turned and raced toward the cot.

Bret reached the cot first. "Calliope, look at me," he said. "Can you hear the horses? Black Jack has arrived with a closed carriage warmed inside with a brazier."

"Brazier," she repeated.

"Yes. We hoped to find you alive. I came first." Kneeling, he tenderly stroked the tangled curls away from her forehead. "You don't feel fevered, darling. I believe it would be safe to take you home. I'll bet you a thousand dollars Jack is tying my horse's reins to the back of the carriage. In another moment he'll knock at the door."

"You win," said Calliope at the sound of fists rapping wood.

Walking forward to answer the summons, Eve prayed Aaron stood on the other side. She didn't want her charge removed from the wagon, but she knew she was powerless to stop Bret Johnson.

Opening the door, she gazed up at a tall man. He looked so familiar. Where had she met him before? She had the feeling they'd worked together. But where? When?

Momentarily, the huge dark-skinned man looked startled. Then he grinned and said, "Hello, Miss Gwendolyn. I'm Black Jack. Remember?"

Eve's mind whirled with images. People pressing forward, laughing, reaching out to touch her long hair. Men shouting crude remarks about winding her hair between their legs. Women squealing at the men's insinuations, while at the same time, their eyes gleamed with lustful appreciation.

Eve shook her head, hoping to erase the images. "I believe you've made a mistake, sir. We've never met. You work for Mr. Johnson, don't you? I've never set foot inside his estab..." She paused, terrified by a sudden realization.

Bret Johnson looked familiar too! In her former life, had she been one of Bret's employees? She had heard the rumors that Johnson was a whoremonger from Georgia. Had she been one of his hostesses? Had his hostesses attended the circus and become trapped by the fire? Had Johnson kept silent, not wanting to ruin her new life with old memories?

Bending his bald pate, Black Jack entered. Immediately, his puzzled eyes sought Bret's.

Calliope had confided in Bret, relating Gwendolyn's story. Meeting Black Jack's gaze, Bret shook his head—a gesture that promised he'd explain later.

"I'm sorry, ma'am," said Jack, turning his head toward Eve. "I didn't mean to distress you."

"I'm distressed by Mr. Johnson's lack of judgment," Eve said, regaining her composure. She sensed a gentleness and compassion in the handsome giant. "You see, sir, Mr. Johnson is planning to remove a very sick lady from her warm resting place and expose her to the cold winds outside." Eve widened her eyes until they filled with tears. "He shall kill her, and this after I've labored so long to bring her back from the grave."

As if to belie her words, there was a series of sharp cracks at the window. Icicles shattered, scissored by the increasingly brilliant sunshine.

Ignoring Eve, Bret wrapped Calliope tightly in the quilt. "Let me have your coat, Jack. It's twice again as large as mine." He buttoned Black Jack's oversized garment around the quilt.

This time Eve's tears were for real. "Won't you let her eat something first, Mr. Johnson? Just one cup of broth? Please?"

There was a muffled sound from within the quilt.

"What did you say, dear?" Eve watched the colored giant hoist his bundle. Only Mary's eyes, nose, and mouth were visible through the cocoon of quilt and coat that rested easily in Black Jack's muscled arms.

"Don't stop him," Calliope said more clearly.

"But Aaron will be back any minute."

"No."

"Yes, dear. He's checking out his ranch then fetching the doctor."

"No!" Calliope knew her eyes were as hard as gray granite, as unrelenting as the Fox emerald. Brian had tended her from a sense of duty. He didn't love her. Like Maxey, he merely desired her body.

Only one man loved her enough to arrange, in advance, for the roulette wheel to land on Eagle. Only one man loved her enough to let her keep the valuable jewels from her poker game, understanding full well he could lose her by that magnanimous gesture.

Brian's lips caused her to soar with passion. But only one man loved her enough to let her fly free.

"I don't want Aaron," she said. "I want Bret."

Eve saw the joyous intensity that lit up Bret Johnson's face. She saw that beneath his ash-blond hair and pale brow, his eyes burned with a sudden radiance, and she pictured yellowish flames blazing upwards toward a sky filled with white velvet clouds.

Velvet! Eve plied her needle through the soft, dense material. But didn't the word velvet also mean the winnings of a player in a gambling game?

Or, she thought uncomfortably, a profit beyond ordinary expectations.

Twenty-Seven

BRIAN O'CONNOR STOOD OUTSIDE THE CIRQUE DE Delices.

For the first time in its history, the gambling house was closed even though lights dotted every window. ENTRY BY INVITATION ONLY read the printed sign on the door. Brian didn't have an invitation.

The assemblage included wealthy businessmen, accompanied by their mistresses. Many of the guests were familiar to Brian—ex-circus performers who had settled in Denver or Colorado Springs. He saw roustabouts, hired to construct his new hotel and restaurant. He saw Cuckoo, the lovely Bird Girl, who was now wed to a cattle rancher. He saw Junior, who had once tended the circus cats and who now assisted an animal doctor. Desperately clinging to Junior's arm was a heavy woman who wore a mourning veil. From the back, she looked like an upholstered wing chair.

"Let me inside for five minutes." Brian's eyes were blue steel, yet his voice revealed an uncharacteristic pleading tone. "I'll leave directly after."

"Wish I could," Black Jack said. "But Bret don't want you here."

"Please? I've got no hidden weapons."

Black Jack stared at the area between Brian's trousers. "You got one mighty fine weapon, boy. Recall how it used to puncture Panama Duncan."

"I recall how your weapon did the same." Brian grinned then scowled. "C'mon, Jack, we've been friends a long time. I even taught you how to tame my lions and tigers."

"Yep. And almost made me lose *my* weapon in the bargain, not to mention the rest of my body. Seems them cats preferred dark meat for dinner."

Brian glanced toward the Cirque. Not one sound escaped its red brick walls, and yet he could practically hear the house hum with excitement. He had seen the minister enter. If Black Jack couldn't be persuaded soon, it would be too late.

In a fair fight, Brian thought he might have a better than even chance to subdue the ebony giant. Black Jack was bigger, but Brian was quicker. However, even if he managed to get past Jack, there were still the dogs. Two dogs from the same litter, named—if he remembered rightly—Nietzsche and Blake. Their mother was a German shepherd bitch who had mated up with a wolf, and the dogs were trained to kill on command.

Perhaps he should just tell the truth, thought Brian. Appeal to the compassion that lurked beneath the giant's fearsome exterior. "Let me explain how it is, Jack. Will you listen?"

"I'll listen, but you ain't getting inside. Bret don't want you." Black Jack hunkered down and scratched one of the killer dogs behind an ear that flopped like a maple leaf. The other ear looked like a miniature mountain peak.

The lop-eared dog was in ecstasy, thought Brian, its tongue lolling between razor-sharp teeth.

"Calliope was very sick, but you already know that," Brian said. "Didn't you rescue her from my wagon?" He scowled again, thinking how he had returned a scant ten minutes after Bret and Jack had driven away from the construction site. "Well, you see, Calliope was delirious, and she talked… She didn't realize what she was saying, but in her delirium she…"

Shit! This was the hardest speech Brian had ever made in his life. Meanwhile, Jack's ebony face remained impassive.

"Damn it, Jack, she was drugged! Poisoned!" With satisfaction, Brian watched the giant's eyes register surprise, concern, anger. "Maxey Stanhope was the lickfinger no-account who fed Calliope deadly night-shade." Brian took a deep breath. "Stanhope's gone, the yellow-bellied bastard! If he returns, he's dead meat. I thought Calliope abandoned her circus for the life of a rich lady, but I was wrong. She truly believed me dead. I was such a fool. She has to understand how much I love her. Please let me inside."

"Bret don't want you here."

"Calliope doesn't love your damn clown. She loves me!"

"Mebbe. But she's marrying him."

"That's why I have to see her."

"Bret don't—"

"Want me here. Yes, I know." Brian heard the

dogs growl at the fury in his voice. Trying to tone down his anger, he said, "If I can't see Calliope, will you at least let me talk to Eve?"

"Eve?"

"Gwendolyn! Surely you remember Gwendolyn. You appeared with her in Calliope's Kid Show."

A gentle smile softened the giant's features, revealed by the porch lamp's glow. "Miss Gwen's playing bridesmaid. She can't be disturbed for nothing."

"This isn't nothing, damn it. It's very import…" Brian paused, startled by Jack's canoodled expression. "Does Gwendolyn recall her past?"

"Yep. Inside your wagon, Bret and me jogged her memory, and the pieces came together after that."

"I'm glad. Will you do me one favor?"

"Mebbe. Depends what the favor is."

"A few days ago, when I learned about the wedding, I delivered a gift. For Calliope. I wasn't thinking straight. Irish temper. It's a plain box from Eve's Apparel. No card. Would you fetch it for me?"

"You must think I'm crazy, boy. Soon's I'm gone, you'll find a way to get inside."

"I'll wait right here. You have my word on it."

"Mebbe so, mebbe not, but I can't take that chance."

"I lied."

"Lied?"

"When I said I had no weapon." Brian drew a knife from his boot and pressed its tip against Black Jack's throat.

Slowly, the giant stood up. "Neechee, Blake, stay outa' this," he said, snapping his fingers.

"Escort me inside," Brian ordered. "One wrong move, and I'll slit your throat."

"Won't do you no good, boy. There's a locked door with a window. Keeps out the law."

"Johnson will tell them to open the door when he sees me with a knife at your collar."

"Don't count on it."

"Quit stalling."

"Whatever you say."

Black Jack took a few steps backwards. Then quicker than Brian could have believed possible, Jack ducked away from the blade, captured Brian's hand, and pressed hard against his pulse until he released the knife.

"Sorry." Black Jack shook his massive head. "But you couldn't get in yesterday or the day before, and you ain't gonna make no surprise appearance tonight."

Somebody flung open three windows, then the patio door, and Brian heard music—"El Caballero." He almost grinned, thinking how in character it was for Calliope to choose that bold music rather than the standard wedding march.

Wedding march! The ceremony had begun.

He played his last card. "Is your clown afraid to let me see Calliope? Is he scared I'll change her mind?"

"Mebbe," said the imperturbable giant.

"Let me talk to her for five minutes, and if she still wants to marry Johnson, I'll deed over five hundred acres of the richest land west of the Rockies. Go tell your boss. It's a fair gamble. One hundred acres a minute."

"I'll tell him tomorrow."

"Tomorrow will be too late!" Totally frustrated, Brian drew back his fist, aimed it toward Jack's belly, and felt the pain from a split knuckle.

Black Jack merely grunted then snapped his fingers at the dogs. "Stay put, Neechee, Blake!" Turning to Brian, he said, "Don't make me have to fight you, boy. Don't hanker to knock loose what little brains you've got left."

Okay, thought Brian, he had underestimated Jack's muscular strength. But every man was vulnerable in one spot, and Brian planned to make sure this particular colossus wouldn't be able to produce little giants for a month of Sundays.

He circled Jack. A flicker of intent must have gleamed briefly in his eyes, because when he lashed out with his foot, Jack deftly caught his boot, twisted his leg, and Brian found himself on the ground, his arms and legs extended like a four-tentacled octopus.

With a roar of rage, he leaped up and flailed his fists.

"Shit," swore the giant.

Brian felt a slab of iron connect with his chin. His legs turned to water. Before he could count the stars that clouded his vision, the earth became a vortex of black sky, black house, and Black Jack.

Jack caught Brian's sagging body and carried it away from the Cirque de Delices.

"Mebbe it's better this way, boy," he muttered. "Mebbe it's better you're out cold and don't hear nothing." He glanced toward an open window where the minister's voice floated through the night.

"If there be any reason why Bret Johnson and Calliope Kelley should not be man and wife, speak now or forever hold—"

"There's a reason," another voice interrupted eagerly. "And you won't perform this piss-proud service when you hear what I've got to say."

Twenty-Eight

"SHE LIED THROUGH HER TEETH," CALLIOPE WAILED. "What little teeth she's got left."

"You didn't say your vows before God?" Gwendolyn unfastened the tiny buttons on the back of Calliope's peach silk wedding gown. Then she untied the bow of a green velvet sash.

"Of course I did. But there was no preacher present. For the love of heaven, my so-called wedding ceremony took place in the middle of the night during a wind storm."

Gwendolyn halted her motion of removing pins from Calliope's complicated hairstyle. "What has a wind storm got to do with the price of beans?"

"Nothing. Everything. Don't you understand? Panama witnessed my sworn pledge, but she made up the rest. There was no preacher, no 'marriage paper.'"

"Panama said your license burned in the fire."

"There was no license, I swear. Why did she lie? It was Brian she desired, not Jocko."

"It was you she hated."

"I know." Calliope sighed. She pictured Panama

Duncan, now a widow. Panama's additional girth was still inadequately constrained by a tight corset, and her crinkled hair was dyed a brassy yellow, yet somehow she'd managed to latch onto Junior, attending the wedding as his consort.

Bret had ordered the minister to continue, but the devout gentleman refused. Not until the confusion was settled, he had insisted, because although Miss Kelley… Mrs. O'Connor… had portrayed herself as a young widow, apparently her husband was very much alive.

Successfully hiding the murderous intent that clouded his expression, Bret had invited the guests to enjoy the sumptuous wedding feast. "We shall settle this confusion in due time," he had said with a smile, "so we must all celebrate in advance."

Clasping Calliope's gloved fingers in his, ignoring Junior's red-faced apology, nodding toward a brawny bouncer, then Panama, Bret had sauntered through the room.

"I can't stay here," Calliope had whispered, stumbling by his side. "Please make my excuses while I retire upstairs."

"You shall remain, darling. That's an order. Do you want to give credence to that harridan's claim?" Halting, he had stared directly into her eyes. "How do you feel?"

"Miserable."

"How do you feel, Calliope?"

"Fine. I'm wondrous fine," she had said, lifting her small, dimpled chin.

Now she corralled her recollections and walked toward the clothespress.

"Bret wanted me to wear white," she said, carefully

hanging her peach gown inside. "But I couldn't. It's not that I have any objection to appearing virginal, but it would remind me too much of Dottie Stanhope. Drat it all, Gwen. I'm married but not married. I wonder if that means I'm destined to singe in purgatory rather than burn in hell."

"Hush! What a thing to say."

"Dottie said it first." Calliope thrust out her bottom lip.

"Why did you agree to hold the ceremony so quickly?" Gwendolyn asked, thinking how Calliope had the body of a woman and the face of a rebellious child. "It's only a week since your recovery from a serious illness. Why couldn't you have waited?"

"Bret didn't want to wait."

"Why?"

"You know the answer to that as well as I do. Brian O'Connor. You keep insisting Brian loves me. You're wrong. He never loved me. He loved Angelique's daughter."

"Oh, Calliope." Gwendolyn shook her head. "Brian loves you, not your mother's memory."

"If true, why didn't Brian pay a visit to the Cirque? I'll tell you why. Once I'm Mrs. Bret Johnson, Brian is relieved of any further responsibility. There's passion between us, but that's all it is. Even when we were inside his wagon, before my illness, he admitted he didn't want to be alone with me. He doesn't love me, Gwen. If he did, he would have come here to stop my wedding." Calliope dabbed at sudden tears with the hem of her petticoat.

"So that's it. Damn your stubborn pride! You were testing Brian, weren't you?"

"Yes! And he failed my test, didn't he?"

"No, dear. Brian tried to see you a dozen times and was always turned away by Black Jack. I've had a dozen clems with Jack over that very issue."

But their fights didn't last very long, Gwendolyn thought. Jack was too sweet, too patient. "Mebbe," he'd say, never giving an inch.

After their confrontation at the wagon, she had begun remembering incidents from her past, starting with her name. Jack had visited every day, taking her for rides into the mountains. They couldn't travel very far because of the snow, but they would dismount and she would unlock a new memory and Jack would hold her close as she wept her pain, her humiliation, her relief.

Too bad they'd never be more than friends. A colored man couldn't consummate his relationship with a white woman. If Jack had been white and she had been black, they might have taken their chances. But he wasn't and she wasn't and that was that.

Gwendolyn watched Calliope's face light up like sunshine after a thunder squall.

"Are you telling me the truth, Gwen?"

"I swear."

The joyous expression dimmed. "But that night at the barbecue, Brian said we couldn't stop the merry-go-round. He's engaged to Daisy Sandoval."

"Brian can't marry Daisy. Panama—"

"Lied through her teeth."

"I believe you, Calliope, honest I do. And yet you must admit Panama's untimely claim puts the proof of the pudding on Brian. And gives you a chance to think."

"Perhaps you're right." Calliope seated herself in front of the dressing table and reached for her hairbrush.

"It isn't fair," Gwendolyn said. "Three of Bret's hostesses are brown-skinned, and nobody believes it's wrong if they sleep with white men. Rich colored men have white whores, and nobody says boo."

Calliope instantly grasped the subject of Gwen's musings. "Do you love him?" she asked.

"Yes. I finally remembered my past, but now I have no future. Any relationship with Jack would be a big mistake."

And you're making a big mistake too, Calliope Kelley! Because of your wounded pride, you're engaged to a man you don't love.

Gwendolyn stared fondly at the woman she had come to regard as her dearest friend. Calliope was so young, and she had been through so much. She was still half kitten, half cat.

But she was Bret's pampered pet, not Brian's.

With a shudder, Gwendolyn imagined the confrontation between Bret and Calliope. Gwendolyn wouldn't trade places with Calliope tonight, not for all the tea in China.

Not for all the gold in Colorado.

⚬⚬⚬

Three candles glowed, but their reflection in the mirror made them look like six burning tapers. As Calliope stared at Bret, she couldn't decipher his expression.

"Did you enjoy the party, darling?" Sitting on the edge of her bed, he clasped her hand in his.

"I never realized before how many rich gillys... I

mean, well, some of your guests came from the best families…" She paused, thinking how two of the wealthiest families had been absent: Fox and Stanhope.

"Respectable wives stayed at home," Bret said, "fretting over their lost opportunity to view the inside of an honest-to-goodness brothel. Does that bother you, Calliope?"

"No. Yes. A little. I would have liked the Stanhopes to witness my happiness."

She shrugged her slender shoulders. Ann and Raymond would never enter Bret's establishment. Neither would Thom and Dottie. Maxey had disappeared from Colorado Springs, thank God.

The senior Aaron Fox had been invited and declined, most likely because Calliope had humiliated the daughter of his old friend, Louis Sandoval. Shame on Aaron! The card game was such a wee hullabaloo. Brian had gotten his emerald back and would soon marry his cheating Daisy and become a pompous gillygalloo and raise a parcel of dande-lions and fox-gloves.

Or would he? Gwen had sworn Brian tried to visit the Cirque. Why? To stop the wedding? Perhaps Brian simply meant to tell her about Panama Duncan. But how could Brian know Panama had witnessed their vows inside the silver wagon? Hellfire! It was all so confusing.

"You're thinking about him, aren't you?"

"Who?"

"It doesn't matter, Calliope. You're mine now."

"Not until the 'confusion' is settled."

"I've already taken care of it."

"Really? How?"

"Panama shall never interrupt our wedding ceremony again. In fact, she shall never play your 'evil leprechaun' again."

"What? Panama? She's my leprechaun?"

"Yes. While you visited the water closet, I stepped outside to question her. Threatened with bodily harm, she was compliant. She was also spitting mad, a sight to behold considering half her teeth are missing. Bobby Duncan guyed-out your mother's rope, Calliope. He wanted Panama, and she promised to satisfy his every whim. He didn't consider the consequences. Panama said the sag would stop Angelique's act and make her mad. After that, Duncan was trapped. Panama threatened to tell on him, and Duncan was too dull witted to realize if Panama tattled, she would incriminate herself."

"When I crossed the trestle, Bobby pulled me up the embankment. His grip on my wrist... I thought he might drop me. Panama must have told him... Oh, well, it doesn't matter now. What about the pie car?"

"Panama lured Sean to the car by pretending to be Angelique. It wasn't difficult. He was very drunk. Then she saw you and—"

"Changed her mind. The cats?"

"Dressed as a clown, she pushed Napoleon's buggy next to the cage. I could kill her for that."

"The law will kill her, won't they?"

"No, darling. Duncan murdered Angelique. Unfortunately, we can't prove Panama threw the nosegay or lured Sean to the pie car or pushed the buggy—"

"Why did she do it?"

"She loved Sean. It's that simple. When your mother fell from the rope and your papa didn't respond to her advances, she married Duncan. But her hate for Angelique's daughter festered, so she became your evil leprechaun, responsible for Susan's skittishness, Sean's death, and the agitation of the cats."

"That's all?"

"That's not enough?" Bret arched an eyebrow. "She effectively stopped our wedding."

"Where is she now?"

"In jail. Tomorrow she'll be hauled before a magistrate."

"For what?"

"Prostitution. It's illegal, you know."

Calliope caught the spark of amusement in Bret's eyes. "And afterwards?"

The brief glint abruptly vanished. "Panama played a losing hand, Calliope. After she's released, she will be taken to a seaport and placed aboard a ship."

"A ship?"

"You don't want to know the details, darling. Let's just say she won't last a week, and if she does, she'll wish she hadn't."

Calliope felt somewhat sorry for Panama. Then the feeling faded, replaced by the knowledge that Bret hadn't mentioned the fire.

And why would he, you daft lass? After all, Panama didn't set the fire. The fire had nothing to do with wanting Papa, and Panama couldn't know for sure I'd die in the blaze. What's more, if the circus burned down to the ground, she'd be out on her fat backside, jobless and penniless.

Aloud, Calliope said, "You always win, don't you?"

"Always, especially when it comes to you."

"What does that mean?"

"My darling Irish Angel, the wheel was rigged, the dice were loaded, the cards were marked." Unclasping her hand, he ran his first finger across her palm. "I've always said Brian O'Connor would betray you."

"I don't want to talk about Brian."

"All right, darling, let's talk about us. In a few days, after this—what's your word? Oh, yes, hullabaloo. After this hullabaloo has settled down, we'll travel to Denver and say our vows. Meanwhile, I see no reason why we shouldn't consummate our marriage tonight."

"That would make me an adulteress."

"Nonsense, Calliope. You're not married. The consummation of our engagement would make you promiscuous, not illicit."

Lord, she was tempted. She could never override Bret's logic, and she wanted to be held, petted, comforted. Although her immediate reaction had been dry-eyed numbness, she knew that eventually she would be devastated over Panama's confession, especially the part about Papa.

On the other hand, what if Gwen spoke true? What if Brian planned to break off his engagement to Daisy?

Mistaking her silence for acquiescence, Bret rose from the bed and walked toward the dressing table. Barefoot, bare-chested, he was clothed in a pair of trousers. Calliope admired the smooth muscles in his shoulders and back. He might not be a dark, dangerous panther, but he had the grace of a stalking animal.

Opening the first drawer of her chiffonier, Bret

removed a box. "This is for you," he said, returning to her side.

"What is it?"

"A wedding gift. It arrived three days ago. No card, no message. I must admit I peeked at the contents."

Puzzled, she began to open the box. Then she stopped, overcome by a sudden realization. "I don't want this, Bret."

"You haven't even looked inside."

"I don't care. I don't want it."

Aaron Fox's negligee! She recalled his words: *The gown must be transparent in all the right places.*

"It would please me if you wore your gift tonight, darling," Bret said.

His voice was polite, but his smile was ugly. It twisted his features into a hard mask of demonlike jealousy. How did he know Brian had ordered the negligee? Bret had the instincts of a wild animal, but he wasn't a mind-reading magician. Then she saw the neat lettering on the box: EVE'S APPAREL.

It didn't take a magician to put one and one together and get three.

One, Gwendolyn, two, Brian, three, Calliope.

She sat up and plumped the pillows behind her back. "Do you have a deck of unmarked cards?"

Bret reached into his trouser pocket. "I always carry cards, the same way you used to tote peppermints. Remember how you fed mints to your monkeys?"

"Let's not talk about the circus."

"Of course, darling. We must not discuss the circus or Brian O'Connor. Anything else?"

"Don't be nasty. May I have the cards, please?"

Bret handed her the deck. Kneeling by the side of the bed, he watched her shuffle.

"Stop staring at my hands," she said. "You know I never cheat. We shall make one cut each. Highest card wins. If you win, I'll open the box and wear its contents."

"And if your card is higher?"

She nodded toward the fireplace, where flames consumed a structured pile of thick logs. "If I win, you shall throw the box, unopened, into the fire. Are you ready? Damn, it's hot in here."

"Don't cuss, darling."

"I'll cuss if I want to." She let loose with a series of oaths, all strung together, ending with what sounded like elephant sheets. "So there," she added, kicking off the blanket.

Bret was staring at her body, at her pink velvet dressing gown. "Put down the cards," he said, his voice raspy.

"Make your cut."

"No. I've changed my mind. You don't have to open the box."

"I'll go first." She held up the king of spades.

Bret shrugged and cut, exposing the ace of hearts.

"Damn, damn, damn," she swore. "Let me have Brian's gift, please."

"How do you know the gift is from Brian?"

"I'm a diddy with a crystal ball," she said sarcastically. "Hand over the box, Bret."

"I said you didn't have to open it."

"I keep my word. Or did you cheat?"

"I don't cheat, Calliope, not unless I have to."

Maneuvering her legs toward the edge of the mattress, she stood up. Bret opened the box and tossed her the garment. With a decisive gesture, she took off her dressing gown and put the negligee on.

It was red satin—sleek, glossy, buttery to the touch. But it wasn't transparent in all the right places. It was *missing* all the right places. The shiny red material encompassed her rib cage then stopped, and a small draft from the window cooled her breasts. Shoulder ribbons kept the negligee securely fastened. Calliope felt like the most brazen of whores. Was this what Brian truly thought of her?

All of a sudden, she had an awful revelation. Brian O'Connor didn't want her for his wife. Aaron Fox wanted her for his mistress. That was why he had argued with Black Jack. That was why he had tried to invade the Cirque. Aaron Fox wanted to marry Daisy and set Calliope up as his paramour, just like the rich gillys who had attended tonight's aborted ceremony.

Passion is for paramours.

One fat tear rolled down her cheek.

"I'm sorry," Bret said.

He didn't sound sorry. He sounded nasty.

"God, you're so beautiful." Scooping her up into his arms, he placed her on top of the bed again.

"Wait until I take off my neg—"

"Leave it on!"

The lust in his voice was abrasive. Where was the man who claimed he wanted her love, not her body?

"Bret?" She wriggled underneath the blanket until her breasts were concealed. "Please listen. I have an important request. There's no earthly reason why you should agree, but if you do, I swear on my life I shall belong to you forever."

"I agree."

"But you haven't heard my request." She took a deep breath. "I want another wedding, a big one. I want you to invite every family, perhaps even cancel their gambling debts if the men attend *with their wives.* I want our ceremony to coincide with the opening of Aaron Fox's hotel. Do you understand? The very same night!"

Bret pursed his lips in a soundless whistle. "'Vengeance is mine; I will repay, sayeth the Lord.'"

"Exactly." Her eyes glittered. "I told you once before that I hate Brian more than any man alive, except Maxey Stanhope. I haven't changed my mind."

"I assume we shall not consummate our engagement until I fulfill your request."

"You assume correctly."

"Don't you trust me, Calliope?"

"I trust no man."

"All right, darling. Do you mind if I spend the night? You have my promise I won't ravage your lovely body."

"I don't mind if you move your belongings inside my room. I can be magnanimous too, and you have your reputation to consider."

"What about your reputation?"

"When did I ever worry about that? I wore petticoat breeches to my first society ball."

He blew out the candles, slid beneath the blanket, and buried his face within the mounds of her breasts.

Stroking his finespun hair, she turned her flushed face sideways, searching for a cooler piece of pillow. She saw the fireplace. Flames licked at the logs, and the resulting sparks sounded like snapping fingers.

Fire. She squeezed her eyes shut, but it didn't help. She smelled the acrid odor of smoke and heard the screams of animals and gillys.

How could she have agreed—twice—to marry the man who had set fire to her circus?

Allowing her the freedom to fly had been a calculated gamble. Bret had clipped her wings from the very start, and she had merely traded one cage for another. Bret was an excellent student of human nature. His winning trump had been her gratitude after he salved her broken heart and bandaged her wounded pride.

Brian O'Connor was her strength, but he was also her weakness. It was a fact she would have to accept, just as she would have to accept the fact that she was engaged to the man who had torched her circus.

Following the legal ceremony, Bret could possess her body whenever he pleased. But she would never give him her heart, her soul, or the pure love he craved.

Opening her eyes, Calliope glanced down at Bret's head, still nestled between her breasts.

And saw the red satin of her negligee...

...rippling...

...glossy red...

...flames.

Twenty-Nine

No matter how hard she tried, Calliope couldn't forget Bret had torched her circus. The monkeys seemed to haunt her draperies.

Bret honored their verbal bargain, and yet while he slept, she would curl up on her side of the mattress, picture red-hot flames, and suppress her sobs with her pillow.

"Why do you always weep into your pillow?" Bret's angry voice pierced the room's darkness. "You're thinking about him, aren't you?"

"No."

"Yes, you are. I've given you a home, beautiful gowns, and soon you shall wear my name. What more do you require?"

"Nothing. I swear."

"Don't swear, Calliope. Since our betrothal, you've taken to cussing the way a duck takes to water. Would you like to forget our agreement and get married right away?"

"All right."

"What do you mean, all right?"

"I won't cuss."

She felt Bret's weight shift until he lay on his side, his body turned away from her. There were only a few inches between them, but it might as well have been a chasm. The next day Bret collected his clothing and moved back into his own bedroom.

A week later Calliope decided to settle the rift— explain her misgivings and discuss the fire. Perhaps with the words spoken aloud, she could finally banish the demons who plagued her memories and orchestrated her dreams.

She brushed her hair until it cascaded down her back like a golden-brown cloak. Bret loved her hair. He said he loved the silky strands fanning out across his chest as she lay spoonlike, within the curve of his body. He often kissed her hair, her nape, and she would be on the verge of capitulation. Then the heat of his hands would conjure up the image of her burning Big Top.

But not tonight. Tonight she would discuss her fears calmly, rationally. She would let Bret tell her how he saw the flaming canvas and rode for help. This time she would believe him.

Naked, she opened the door a crack and peered down the hall. Hellfire! The beautiful blonde hostess, Clarissa, stood just outside Bret's bedroom.

Calliope donned a robe. Furtively, she tiptoed along the hallway. Then pressing her ear against Bret's door, she heard Clarissa's lust-filled laughter.

Early the next morning, Calliope joined Bret for breakfast served outside on the patio. He smiled politely, held her chair, even buttered the toast she couldn't swallow.

"That's a lovely gown, darling," he said. "You should always wear gold. It brings out the color in your eyes."

"My eyes aren't gold."

"Did I say eyes? I meant hair."

"Where's Clarissa?" she asked, dispirited by his nastiness.

"Asleep. Clarissa's exhausted, and not from weeping into her pillow."

"Why do you humiliate me?"

"I thought you lost your vanity during the circus fire."

"I still have my pride," she said between clenched teeth. "Perhaps you might be more discreet."

"I once had a hostess who betrayed me." Bending sideways, Bret petted Nietzsche, who lay by the side of his chair. "Her left leg was chewed into strips of jerky, and she still walks with a limp. Here, have some fresh tea."

"Are you saying you'd set the dogs on me?"

"And mar those lovely limbs?" Bret looked like Jocko, his face miming horrific disbelief.

She buried her gaze in her bowl of strawberries. "We have to talk about our engagement, Bret."

"If it pleases you. Of course we can't mention a certain cat tamer, can we? If I recall correctly, you and what's his name weren't exactly discreet."

Maxey exposed his cruelty with deeds, while Bret's whiplash is his tongue.

"That's not fair," she said, "and you know it."

"Good morning." Clarissa's turquoise dressing gown swept the patio's tiled squares. "What a beautiful day."

"Beautiful," said Bret. He kissed her on the lips, held her chair until she sat, then buttered her toast.

"Eve hasn't finished my new gown," she complained,

pouting prettily. "Irish once borrowed a gown from me. May I borrow one from her?"

"That's up to Irish."

"Take two or three," Calliope said. "Hell, take them all."

"Thank you." Clarissa gazed up at Bret through her thick blonde lashes. "I don't want to gamble tonight," she said. "Can Irish deal the cards?"

"Of course."

Calliope stifled a gasp. She hadn't played Operator since her engagement. Bret's response was a slap in the face.

Tilting her chin, she said, "The Cirque's profits have diminished while I assume the role of pampered fiancée. It shall be refreshing to experience action again."

Was that a flicker of admiration she saw in Bret's eyes? No. She must be mistaken. His expression merely registered indifference.

Why did he continue this damn charade? Why make plans for their wedding ceremony? Was his grudge against Brian so profuse he'd use her as the pawn in a human chess game?

She fed her breakfast to Nietzsche, who rewarded her with a grovel and a growl.

❧

Divested of her clothes, Calliope slipped her tired body into the hot mineral pool. She was alone—except for a family of curious, chattering squirrels.

Watching the water spill over moss-shrouded rocks, she felt the steamy heat unravel knots in her back and shoulders.

"Hot springs, God bless 'em, are full of life-giving minerals from holy mother earth," Raymond Stanhope had once said. "Minerals are absorbed into the human body through the skin and lungs, Mary. People suffering from anxiety find a soothing soak to be the best of sedatives. Ponce de Leon and Cleopatra even claimed that mineral springs turned back the age clock."

I wish I could turn the clock back three months before I swore I would belong to Bret.

If gamblers wondered why Johnson's fiancée had returned to her role as Operator, they never mentioned it out loud. If hostesses were aware Clarissa had moved her belongings into Bret's bedroom, they remained silent in Calliope's presence. And yet every night her pride suffered.

She could marry Bret right away. If she did, Calliope understood that his liaison with Clarissa would be over. "I don't cheat," he had said, "not unless I have to."

Or she could leave Colorado. The honorable Brian had sent her a wad of bank notes for the emerald and Daisy's ruby necklace. With that stake, she could travel east and find a circus, perhaps even set sail for France. But what about her bargain with Bret?

He had commissioned a new wedding gown from Gwen. He had ordered invitations engraved with real gold lettering. He had made arrangements for exotic flowers and food.

Her thoughts were rudely interrupted by the nervous gibber-jabber of the squirrels. Calliope looked up through the steamy mist.

"What are you doing here?" she asked with dismay, sinking deeper into the water.

"This is my property," said Brian. "It belongs to Foxfire Manor."

"I'm sorry. I didn't know. Raymond Stanhope showed the pool to me. If you turn around, I'll get dressed and… Why do you chortle like a hyena?"

"I'm tickled by your sudden sense of modesty, Calliope. Do you display bashful prudishness in front of your clown?"

"No. But I don't indulge in promiscuity, either. I learn from my mistakes. Bret and I shall never come together as man and wife until our vows are legal."

"Do you expect me to believe that?"

"I don't give a damn what you believe." She heaved a deep sigh. "Will you answer one question, Brian?"

"If I can."

"Why did you try and see me after I returned to the Cirque de Delices?"

"Does it matter?"

"Yes."

"I wanted to say I'd keep you safe, warm, happy. *Are* you happy, puss?"

"You've asked me that before," she said despite the sudden lump in her throat. She had been correct. Brian wanted her for his mistress; 'else he would have mentioned love.

"Answer me honestly, Calliope."

"I'm safe." Eyes downcast, she studied the steamy water. "And warm."

"I've heard you plan to hold a new ceremony that will coincide with my hotel's grand opening."

His voice had changed from tender concern to brittle contempt. Lifting her lashes, she said, "You've heard rightly, Brian."

"Johnson's scheme?"

"No. Mine."

"Why try and thwart the success of my venture, Calliope?"

She swallowed. "It seemed a good idea at the time."

"And what time was that?"

After I received your wedding gift and garbed myself in a wee, blood-red whore's nightie. "I don't remember," she fibbed, her words a mere mumble.

"Your scheme is for naught, lass. There are more than enough people to attend my opening and your wedding. In truth, I've already taken steps to thwart your venture."

"What do you mean?"

A new thought occurred. Perhaps Brian had discovered Panama and convinced her to halt the original ceremony. *Are you daft, girl?* If Panama's foolish claim had been allowed to stand, it would have ended Brian's engagement. And while he might possibly secure a mistress by that action, he'd lose a wife.

Unless he wanted to marry *her*. She shook her damp mane of hair as she imagined Brian introducing Calliope Kelley to his swank friends.

Lay-deez and gen-tul-men, pre-senting Dream Dancer, Mrs. Aaron Fox, circus equestrian and gambling-house Operator. She will bemuse you with her bookish vociferation, dazzle you with her décolletage.

"What do you mean?" she asked again. "Do you plan to stop my wedding?"

"Of course not. I only meant that Aaron Fox and Bret Johnson are well matched. But Brian O'Connor, born and bred under the Big Top, has an advantage over Jocko the Clown."

"I don't understand."

"You will. Soon."

"What are you do… doing?" she stammered, watching him unbutton his shirt.

"I told you. This is my property."

Indignantly, Calliope advanced through the pool. And felt her toes slip on a patch of muddy foundation. With a muffled oath, she submerged.

By the time she regained her footing, Brian had shed his shirt, boots, trousers, and underwear. She watched him step into the water. Shamefaced, she opened her arms wide. The wealthy Aaron Fox might not love her, but he desired her. And despite all her denials, she desperately wanted a lad named Brian O'Connor, even if he merely desired her too.

Brian stared at Calliope's face. What expression lurked in the depths of those gray-green eyes? Hate? She must hate him, or else why schedule her new wedding to take place on the night of his grand opening?

Yet her slender arms beckoned, and her wet lips, slightly parted, invited kisses. What daft game was she playing now? He was tempted to tell her about his clem with Black Jack but didn't want to admit he'd been felled by one punch. She'd laugh her damfool head off.

"I never thanked you for my wedding gift," Calliope murmured. "Though but a wee wisp, it must have cost dear, and as you know, I always repay my debts."

"What the hell are you gabbing about?"

"During the poker game you said you wouldn't bid for my services, but you obviously changed your mind."

"Do you mean the negligee? I sent it because I thought you had betrayed me again."

"Bret fights betrayal with a dog that is half wolf, while a man that is half Fox sends a wee nightie." She took a deep breath. "Are you still engaged to Daisy Sandoval?"

"Yes. I gave my word."

"So did I." Wanting to wound him, pay him back in his own coin, she lifted her chin and said, "Since you do not consider the negligee a fee for my services, you might commission a gown from Gwendolyn. One of the Cirque's hostesses pirated my clothespress and—"

"Calliope, shut up!"

Brian tried to control his temper. How dare she offer herself to him for the price of a gown? He wanted to spank her lovely rump. Instead, he took a few steps forward and stroked the wet, tangled hair away from her forehead. Then circling her waist with his hands, he lifted her high above him and buried his face against her belly, licking the few drops of water trapped inside her navel.

Calliope shivered at the surge of cold air and the loss of bubbling heat. But Brian's tongue traveled lower, drinking thirstily, and she was soon consumed by a new warmth. Losing all control, she leaned backwards until the misty fingers of steam wove through her long hair and covered her eyes like a gauzy veil. Brian's tongue worked slowly, and she felt her body spasm, each quivering explosion bringing her closer to the brink of forgetful ecstasy.

He slid her body down the length of his. Realizing his intent, she straddled his hips and clasped him tightly with her legs, providing easy access. He needed no further incentive as he buried his erection in the recesses of her moist cave, wet from the pool, wetter still from his tongue's ministrations. He captured her mouth, breathing her whimpers of pleasure toward the back of his throat.

My dream, she thought, *the good part, not the bad*.

Instead of a ballroom, Brian circled the mineral springs as she rode him like a merry-go-round horse. Steam rose above their waists, adding to the illusion. She felt the earth tilt and the sun shimmer, and she rocked back and forth.

"Now, Brian, now! I want to forget. I want to fly."

As he brought them both beyond the brink, she wasn't Maxey's Mary or Bret's Irish Angel, only Brian's Calico Cat, following the music of his invisible pipes.

Inevitably, he withdrew and helped her regain her balance.

"What a wondrous dream," she whispered, pressing her face against his wet chest. "Please let me never awaken. Let me dream evermore."

Her prayer was absorbed by the misty waters as Brian said, "That was our final performance, Calliope. I never want to see you again."

Thirty

"DAMN ALL MEN!" CALLIOPE'S ANGRY STRIDES WERE AT odds with her demure gown and bonnet. "May they be welcomed by the devil's embrace and rot in hell."

One week had passed since Brian's appearance at the mineral springs, and she had almost convinced herself the whole experience had been a dream. Almost. Because the gown she wore was from Brian. It had not been stitched by Gwendolyn. In truth, it was ready-made, the plain white calico printed with repetitive *daisies*.

She hadn't really meant to barter her body for a gown. Boozlebrained boy-o! Yet the dress, like the negligee, told her what Brian truly thought of her. The negligee shouted she was brazen while the calico gown indicated a definite lack of originality, and she kept hearing his words over and over like some muddlepated mantra: "I never want to see you again; I never want to see you again; I never want—"

By all that was holy, he would damn well see her again! He'd have no choice. Because she planned to audition for Brian's stage manager, and she damn well intended to be hired!

Brian's colorful posters adorned walls, from the saloon to the courthouse. Circus acts would be transported from all over the country. Colorado Springs was abuzz with excitement. Aaron Fox had even announced he would hold try-outs for local denizens, and every woman at the Cirque de Delices preened before her mirror, hoping she might be selected to join the opening spectacle.

That, of course, was Brian's scheme to thwart Calliope's venture. When it came to the circus or a wedding, the circus would win every time.

Furious, she had asked Bret to schedule their ceremony for midnight. He had agreed without hesitation. "Do you want to attend the grand opening?" he had asked. "I can get front-row seats."

"No, thank you."

She would not attend as a member of the audience. She wasn't a Mary. She wasn't a gilly. Furthermore, unlike her friends at the Cirque de Delices, she didn't care one whit about the opening spec. She planned to resurrect her old equestrian act. She knew that famous circus owners—including the great P.T. Barnum himself—had been sent invitations. Perhaps a representative from the Nouveau Cirque would attend, and she would be offered employment.

Then she could leave Colorado, start over again. What about Bret? After the aborted wedding, would he truly set Nietzsche and Blake on her? Not a chance! He would remember she had once shielded him from the law. He would soothe his wounded pride with Clarissa. Or any other hostess he might choose.

Her wounded pride had healed completely.

Last week, after Brian had walked away from the hot springs, Calliope had decided to sink down into its watery depths. The beautiful pool would be her grave, a mossy rock her headstone. She would submerge until the bubbling stream brought peaceful oblivion. But she soon discovered it was easier to think about drowning than actually perform the deed, especially since the pool was merely bosom deep. With her first loss of breath, she struggled to the surface, gasping for air. Awkwardly climbing over slippery rocks and donning her chemise, she had stretched out on the flat surface of a sun-baked boulder.

Are you daft, girl? Why give up now?

A part of her had died when her circus burned and she had believed Brian gone forever. She could have killed herself during Maxey's physical abuse and mental torment. She had almost expired with pneumonia. Why turn up her toes just because a stony-hearted cat tamer had dared to scratch her tattered pride?

She felt a small whisk broom tickle her nose. Lifting her head, she saw a squirrel sitting on her chest, above her bodice. He was chattering away to beat the band.

"I am Calliope Kelley," she said, "daughter of Sean and Angelique."

Surprised by the sound of her voice, the squirrel scampered toward another boulder, his tail again sweeping her nose.

"I was put on this earth to perform, Mr. Gilly-Rodent. My life isn't over. It's just beginning."

Calliope brought her attention back to the present. She heard Dublin nicker and realized that, lost in thought, she had been zigzagging down the street, leading her blind horse first left then right. She led rather than rode her stallion because she didn't want to tire him.

"Sorry, lad," she murmured, clutching Dublin's reins tighter. "In any case, I believe we've finally arrived."

Foxfire Manor was a gingerbread Victorian-style hostelry with a grab bag of balconies, turrets, and cupolas. It had a broad verandah from which guests could sit in rocking chairs and watch the world go by. Calliope had heard that workmen were completing a basement tunnel that would lead to the baths and mineral pool.

Today the hotel was surrounded by a cloud of purple haze, giving it a somewhat eerie dignity. The sound of hammers echoed in the street, shattering the mystical illusion, and she saw wagons transporting red sandstone bricks.

"What are the bricks being used for?" Calliope gazed up at one of the drivers.

"Fox's restaurant," he replied, wiping his brow with a blue-patterned neckerchief and staring with obvious delight at Calliope's trim figure. "Was you wantin' to try out for that circus flummadiddle?"

"Yes, sir. Is Mr. Fox about the grounds?"

"Mr. Fox is at Canyon Diablo, loadin' bricks. I take my hat off to a rich man who don't mind gettin' hisself sweated up with the rest of us."

Calliope pictured Brian's muscular chest and arms "sweated up" and remembered how many times he had joined the guying-out crew, tightening tent ropes. Oh, what a glorious sight!

"You don't want to see Mr. Fox nohow, miss," the

driver continued. "Fox don't do the hiring. You want Mike Levine."

"And where is Mr. Levine?"

"Inside the restaurant with them gals, like he was yesterday. All of 'em beggin' to be picked." The driver winked. "You ain't got nothin' to fret over, miss. You sure got 'em beat. Mike's crazy if he don't hire you."

"Oh, dear."

"What's the matter?"

"Well, you see, Mister… Mister…"

"Al. My real name's Al-oh-wish-us, but my friends call me Al."

"Well, Mr. Al, my papa forbade me to audition. You know how it is, I mean, a circus, well, it's not like trying out for the church choir, is it? I want to be in Mr. Fox's show, but I can't join those other girls. One of them might recognize me and tell my papa. Oh, dear."

"Hitch your horse to the back of my wagon, Miss…"

"O'Connor. Mary O'Connor."

"Mike owes me a favor, Miss O'Connor, so I'll ask him to talk to you alone."

"Would you really do that for me?" Calliope attached Dublin's reins to a small iron ring on the back of the wagon. Then she climbed the spokes and sat next to Al. "You're a wonderful person, Mr. Al."

"After Mike hires you, I'll buy us a beer at the saloon."

"A beer at the saloon," she echoed.

"Would you let me buy you a beer, Mary?"

"I'll do better than that. If Mr. Levine hires me, I'll purchase a couple of front-row tickets, one for you and one for your wife. You are married, Mr. Al, aren't you?"

"Ummm."

"How many children do you have, sir?"

"Seven," muttered Al-oh-wish-us.

⚬⚭⚬

Brian had moved his wagon from the hotel site to a grassy area near the restaurant. Glancing around the wagon's interior, Calliope recognized the cot, tables and chairs, potbellied stove, elephant poster, even the dented washbasin. Only Brian's purple dressing gown and her petticoat strips were missing.

Mike Levine was a small, balding man who didn't really need the suspenders that held up his brown trousers. The buttons on his plaid shirt were stretched to the limit. His light blue eyes possessed a feral gleam.

Al had followed Calliope inside. "This is her, Mike," he said.

"How do you do, miss?"

"I do very well, thank you." Turning to Al, Calliope said, "Would you hitch my horse to a tree, please? Be very careful; he's blind."

"Your daddy lets you ride a blind horse?"

"Yes." Placing her hand over her heart, Calliope sighed. "Usually my papa is very protective and would shoot anybody who tried to harm me. But Dublin is well trained. I trained him myself. Thank you again, Mr. Al. Give my best to your wife and seven children. Seven is a lucky number in the game of hazard. It's called a nick, and you win."

Al's weathered cheeks reddened. "Good luck to you, Miss Mary," he said, backing out through the entrance and closing the door.

Calliope heard him stumble down the steps. Then, all business, she looked at Mike Levine. "I want you to hire me for your circus," she said without preamble.

"Lift your skirts and show me your legs," Mike said with a grin.

Why had Brian employed this nasty little man? "That won't be necessary. I don't plan to flaunt my legs during your opening spec. I'm a professional equestrian."

"Sit down, Miss Kelley. Calliope Kelley, isn't it?"

"You've heard of me?"

"Indeed I have."

"Then you know I've been performing since I was a wee lass."

"Yep."

Calliope stared at Mike, wondering why he still wore that foolish grin. She felt like a cat trapped by a mouse. "Am I hired, Mr. Levine? Or would you prefer to see my act first? I brought my horse."

"Sit down, Miss Kelley."

"No, damn it! I won't sit. Am I hired?"

"I've already engaged an equestrian act."

"I'm better. I'm the best. I can adjust my act to fit theirs. And," she added, playing her last card, "I won't charge a fee."

"I don't care if you perform stark naked and spread your legs—"

"How dare you!"

"I've been given my orders. You ain't allowed in my show, and that's final."

"It's not your show, you dirty little man. It's Aaron Fox's show. Oh! Now I understand. Fox was the one who gave the order, wasn't he?"

"Don't reckon how he knew you'd try out, but he did. So you see, Miss Kelley, I can't hire you."

"But I can hire you."

"What?" Mike's grin finally vanished.

"How would you like to be my manager? After Fox's grand opening, of course."

"Are you mad? I don't care how good you are. There's dozens of good equestrian acts."

"Yes, I know. But how many ropewalkers can perform a forward somersault?"

"None. It can't be done."

"Do you remember my mother, Angelique Kelley?"

"Angelique… the French Angel. You're her daughter?"

"I am. Before Mum died, she taught me the forward."

"Then how come you ain't performed it? Barnum himself would pay a fortune. In fact, I heard he once offered your mum a fortune."

"The Nouveau Cirque would pay an even bigger fortune. As my manager, you'd collect ten percent."

The feral gleam had returned to Mike's eyes. "Twenty."

"Fifteen. And I'll pay all travel expenses."

"Show me the forward today, right now."

"Certainly." Calliope's heart momentarily stopped then started beating again. "Do you have a rope strung? Is it guyed-out?"

"No, damn it! Fox didn't count on ropewalkers. We've got ourselves a cat tamer, clowns, equestrians, but we couldn't find a suitable trapeze artist, so there's no rigging."

"A wee dilemma, easily solved."

"And no net."

"I perform without a net."

"You *are* mad." The predatory look in his eyes had been replaced by a glint of respect.

"Then it's a bargain?"

"Nope."

"Why not?"

"Fox will watch rehearsals."

"I won't rehearse. All I need from the musicians is a drumroll. Just make sure the rope is strung tight, for if I fall, it's your loss."

"Nope," said Mike. "I can't chance it."

"Why, damn it?"

"Fox'll find you backstage. And don't tell me you'll hide from him. Even if you do, he'll draw the curtain the minute your foot hits the rope. Nobody will see your act, and I'll be dead meat. Fox is one strong son of a bitch, and I have a feeling that, when crossed, he can be mighty mean."

"You have a point. All right. I'll perform blindfolded. Bri... Fox... the strong son of a bitch won't recognize me until it's too late."

Mike's eyes narrowed. "You're lying through your pretty teeth, Miss Kelley. Nobody can perform a forward somersault blindfolded. It's impossible."

"I won't try the forward with a blindfold, you daft man. I'll wear a mask at the beginning of the act, walk to the middle of the rope, execute a series of back flips—" She shut her eyes, picturing her performance. "Drumroll. I remove my mask. Then, before Fox realizes what's happening, I'll be finished with the forward, and the gillys will be on their feet, cheering."

"Nope."

"What do you mean, nope?" Opening her eyes, Calliope watched her lovely fantasy dissolve.

"It's too risky. If you fall, I'll be out my percentage, Fox will beat me to a bloody pulp, and I'll lose my job."

"Damn your soul! All right! Suppose I pay you a thousand dollars before the show starts? Then if I fall, you shall have a stake until you find employment."

Brian's bank notes for the rubies and emerald!

"If I'm successful," she added, "you can use that money for our passage and—"

"Make it two thousand."

"No! I've had enough, you pawky bastard! I'll talk to Barnum, arrange my own audition."

"Hold your horses!" He offered his hand. "It's a bargain. I sure do admire a lady who can use rough language, Miss Kelley. Shows grit."

"Call me Calliope," she said, giving his hand a firm handshake. Mike seemed lewd and lazy, but he wasn't. No wonder Brian had retained him. He'd make a fine manager.

Now all she had to do was learn the forward somersault.

Thirty-One

TIS THE COCKSHUT OF THE EVENING, THOUGHT CALLIOPE, remembering Sean Kelley's favorite description for twilight.

She wondered if the rooster would be hoot-a-doodling for her tomorrow morning.

Glancing toward the mountains, she was almost blinded by the brilliance of the setting sun. A golden haze obliterated jagged peaks. Perhaps the pot of gold at the rainbow's foot was the sun's gilded incandescence, not the glow of coins as she had once believed.

"Why am I going through with this daft plan?" She held her wet palms in front of her face, as if by that action her small whiff of whispered breath might dry the nervous moisture.

Then she recalled Sean's long-ago warning: *Cease, me precious darlin'. There's no net beneath. Do not be attemptin' a foolish stunt for these hulligans.*

Gazing into the distance, she said, "Forget the hulligans, Papa. They don't matter. There will be circus owners watching. Even the Nouveau Cirque has sent a representative. My stunt shall be attempted for them, Papa, and soon I shall play center ring, just like Mum."

Just like Mum.

Calliope shook her head, trying to erase memories. She must forget the past and concentrate on the future.

If she had a future.

Because she hadn't rehearsed, much less perfected, the forward somersault.

There was no place to do it. The Cirque had a clothesline. So did Gwen's small backyard. Calliope had diligently practiced her splits, but the ropes were too loose for a somersault. She needed a guying-out crew, and that didn't exist, except, she hoped, at Brian's theatre.

She had once heard Angelique performed her first forward on top of a cowboy's lasso strung out between two trees, somewhere near Missouri. But Mum was an equilibrist.

Last night, after drifting into a fitful slumber, Calliope had dreamed about the ballroom and her dance across the burning rope. Would her demons never go away? Perhaps her performance tonight would banish them outright.

I will succeed, she thought, as she had all through the long morning and endless afternoon. The forward was difficult but not impossible. She had watched her mum complete it dozens of times, and Angelique's last performance was indelibly printed on her brain.

Calliope pictured how her own act would proceed. Splits, spirals, somersaults, then the forward. A high leap and a wrap of arms about her chest, letting gravitational pull work for her, not against her.

That was Mum's mistake. Mum forgot about her arms and landed slantwise. Perhaps she'd realized too late the rope possessed a sag. Perhaps she had harbored the daft notion that if she plummeted she could grab the rope with her fingers.

"I won't make the same mistake," Calliope said. "If I fall, I fall like a bird shot in midflight. I won't grab the rope. I won't scream. If I fall, I shall fly with dignity."

Even the sun wasn't daft enough to attempt a forward somersault. It preferred the more conventional back flip, at long last vanishing behind the mountains. Darkness descended, a tent top lit by stars, and the full moon shone down upon the cobblestones that led to Brian's newly constructed restaurant and theatre.

Calliope shifted her gaze toward the empty carriages, buckboards, and riderless horses secured to trees and hitching posts. A few late arrivals scurried inside. Drivers peeked through windowpanes, their boots crushing Foxfire Manor's newly planted herb patch.

A dirt path catercornered the building and led to a backstage entrance. Calliope resolutely stepped onto the trail, clutching her small case. Inside the case was her costume. Gwendolyn had altered the red negligee, hemming it knee-length and adding a bodice strung with layers of brightly colored spangles. While she stitched, she muttered, "I didn't know it was you, Calliope, but I should have. I'll never forgive Brian. I won't even talk to that bushy-tailed fox until after his grand opening, because I'm sure to lose my wits and tell him what for."

Knotting the thread, biting its end, she had added, "There won't be any corset or bustle to restrict your leaps astride. The spangles will catch the light's glare, and the red satin will be seen clearly from every seat, no matter how fast Dublin gallops."

Gwendolyn believed her friend was performing as an equestrian. Nobody, except Mike, knew about the ropewalking. Mike had improvised an elaborate story about a man who juggled objects atop a rope. Thus, the stage was strung with rigging.

Yesterday, very briefly, Calliope had met Mike outside Eve's Apparel. Everything was arranged, he told her, even though the expression in his eyes revealed an anticipatory anxiety rather than a feral gleam. She had given Mike the thousand-dollar stake just before she'd retrieved her altered negligee from Gwendolyn.

Now Calliope heaved a deep sigh. Under her daisy-print gown and petticoats, she had already donned her white tights, but she needed a concealed area where she could safely change into the rest of her costume.

Perhaps the donicker, she thought. Donicker—one of the circus terms that had given her away.

As she conjured up an image of Dottie and the scene beneath Ravenspur's balcony, she could almost swear she smelled the smoke from Maxey's cheroot, an expensive, pungent, vinegarish aroma.

"Well, well, what have we here? Planning to join Aaron Fox's circus, Angel?"

Calliope skidded to a stop and made an about-face.

"I figured I'd find you at Foxfire Manor when Clarissa said you weren't at the Cirque." Maxey puffed furiously on his slim cigar. "Are you performing, sweetheart? Or do you solicit new clients? Is spreading your legs for Johnson's gambling friends not enough for you?"

"I spread nothing but my arms, Maxey. I deal the cards; that's all. I'm engaged to Bret. Our wedding ceremony is tonight at midnight. I sent a personal announcement to your family, so I'm sure you've heard all about—"

"Johnson made a wise investment. I sold you for a paltry thousand. He must collect at least that much every week."

"Damn your soul, Maxey Stanhope! I'm not a whore. I never was."

He snapped his fingers. "You'll obey me, Angel, or suffer the consequences."

"Leave me alone," she cried, backing away.

"God, I forgot how beautiful you are… your face… your eyes."

"You cannot see my eyes in the dark," she spat, her terror turning to anger, her Irish temper flaring. "If you could read the expression in my eyes, you'd see hatred, perhaps even a wee bit of sorrow. Yes, I feel sorry for you, *Mister* Stanhope. You have everything. Money. A caring family. And yet you must make threats in order to subdue a slip of a girl who once would have given her love gladly, unconditionally."

"What do you, a thieving circus whore, know about love? I fell in love with a girl named Mary when I believed her a virtuous widow from Georgia."

"You did not! You said I was an investment. You said you desired my body—"

"And still do."

"Hah! You bastard of a gilly-galloo! Galloo is the

Dutch word for eunuch. Did you hear me, Maxey? Eunuch! I have lain with a man, a real man, a man who possesses a tree, not your pawky stub of a twiggy branch."

"What did you say?"

"My man is no galloo. His instrument provides pleasure. Thank God I have no intimate knowledge of your lovemaking, but I've heard all about your aberrations. My man knows how to satisfy a woman. My man doesn't need to pinch a breast or—"

Calliope swallowed the rest of her words, aware she'd gone too far. Maxey had once said his pride was intact, only his judgment impaired. Now her scathing words had wounded his vanity as effectively as if she had pierced his heart with a rapier's blade. Too late, she remembered his response after she had turned down his marriage proposal: "Am I so ugly?"

A vain, prideful question. At the time, she had even thought it a woman's question.

A woman scorned was chancy. Her evil leprechaun, Panama Duncan, was a prime example. What about a scorned gilly-galloo?

Dropping her case, Calliope turned to run.

Maxey reached out, caught her arm, and twisted it cruelly behind her back until she was crushed against his shirt. His hot breath scorched her cheek as, laughing at her helplessness, he bent his head forward, over her right shoulder. She struggled to wrench herself free when he dropped his cheroot and caressed her collarbone, his fingers hovering just above her breasts, just above her nipples.

No! Please, not again!

Bitter bile lapped at the back of her throat, and she swallowed convulsively. Now was no time to be sick. Now was no time to faint, even though she was nearly driven out of her mind from the pain of her twisted elbow. She couldn't see Maxey's face, but she knew he would break her arm without a single qualm.

If he breaks my arm, I cannot perform. I cannot wrap my arms about my chest.

She felt him fumble through the pocket of his open jacket. Then she felt the familiar lip of his flask pressed against her mouth. Oh, God! Belladonna!

Abruptly halting her struggles, she gritted her teeth and hung her head. He couldn't release his tight hold on her arm, raise her head, and feed her the drugged wine all at the same time. And he couldn't pinch her breasts when both his hands were occupied.

"Damn you!" Dropping the flask, he forced her to her knees. "I promised I wouldn't lay with you until we were wed, but you will lay with me."

"Go to hell and rot there evermore, Maxey. I prefer death."

"Do you really?"

"Yes!"

She heard him click his tongue against the roof of his mouth. Then without warning, he released her arm, pushed her onto her back, straddled her hips, and reached for his discarded cheroot. He puffed then held the glowing tip an inch away from her face. The smoke made her eyes water.

"The carriage drivers," she gasped. "Leave me alone, or I'll scream my head off."

"If you scream or disobey, I'll use this. First I'll

scorch your chin and cheeks, then your breasts. By the time the drivers get here, you'll be scarred for life. Do you understand?"

"Yes. I won't scream."

"Good. Keep your eyes open and your mouth shut. I can't reach my flask, sweetheart, but I can reach the buttons on my trousers. Soon I shall fill you to bursting with my stub of a twiggy branch. Open your mouth. I want to see you panting, anxious to fulfill my every desire. Well, what are you waiting for?"

"I can't shut my mouth and open it at the same time."

He whistled through his teeth. "I've always admired your courage, my angel."

"She's not your angel," said a familiar voice. "She's mine."

Startled, Maxey whipped his face and hands around. His fingers released their tight grip on the cheroot. Fortunately, it landed near Calliope, not on top of her.

"I admire courage too," Bret continued, yanking Maxey upright, "and there's nothing I despise more than a bully. Why don't you pick on someone your own size?"

"You're my size, Johnson," Maxey said with a sneer, shrugging his shoulders free from his jacket.

That's not true, thought Calliope. The men were equal in height, but Maxey outweighed Bret by at least thirty pounds. She looked around for Nietzsche or Blake or Black Jack. No dogs. No giant. Just empty shadows.

Rising to her knees, spying the cheroot, she picked it up off the ground and puffed the unlit end, disgusted by its harsh taste. Then she thrust and had the satisfaction of hearing Maxey's enraged howl as the glowing ashes struck him smack-dab in the seat of his trousers. She watched his hand search out the hole.

All of a sudden, she realized he wasn't reaching for his singed backside.

"Look out, Bret!" she shouted. "Maxey has a knife!"

"Good. It will make the contest fair." With a grin, Bret unfastened the gun belt that circled his lean hips. A gun would be too quick, too easy. Bret wanted blood to stain his knuckles. And he wanted to erase that arrogant smirk from Stanhope's face.

Arrogance was a familiar garment. Outwardly, he maintained his arrogant demeanor, but he had been in an irritable mood ever since packing up and leaving Calliope's bedroom. The liaison with Clarissa had been a mistake, a clown's pratfall. He didn't want Clarissa or any other woman. Calliope had been his solitary love from the moment he had seen her standing in front of the Big Top, a child on the brink of full womanhood. He had watched her body blossom and grow while her fine mind stretched beyond the restrictions of a limited education. He had always admired her intelligence and courage as well as her beauty.

He understood how shamefully he had behaved. Handing over the red satin negligee. Insisting she return to the casino as an Operator. Flaunting his affair with Clarissa. He had wounded Calliope's pride, possibly beyond repair, and all this after he had chanced so much to possess her.

Then this evening he had knocked on her bedroom door, entered, and found her gone. Without a single doubt he knew her destination. Foxfire Manor. The grand opening. He was equally certain she planned to perform.

Leaving Black Jack in charge, Bret had ridden like hell toward the Manor, arriving in the nick of time. Nick: a win in hazard. He would win this contest too, and his prize would be Calliope's gratitude. If he couldn't secure her love, he'd settle for her sense of obligation.

He itched to watch Stanhope's blood flow, but he advanced slowly, staring at his adversary's eyes rather than the wicked blade that flashed in the moonlight.

Calliope managed to rise. Cradling her sore arm, she leaned against the pink-tinged bricks. Although frightened for Bret's safety, she delighted in the predatory expression on his face. He looked savage, ferocious, wolfish.

Maxey lashed out with the knife, but Bret adroitly stepped aside. At the same time, he struck a glancing blow on Maxey's chin.

Surprised, Maxey circled more warily, feigning left and right, until Bret whirled and kicked out with his foot.

Bret's boot tip connected with Maxey's wrist, and the knife spun to the dirt.

Once again Maxey looked surprised. Obviously, he'd anticipated an easy victory. Taking advantage of the heavier man's confusion, Bret sunk his fists, one after the other, into Maxey's belly, then let loose with an uppercut that sent Maxey staggering into the wall. Dazed, Maxey clutched his stomach. Conceit gone, he looked as if he might cry at any moment.

Bret picked up the knife, tested its sharpness on

his thumb, and grinned as a drop of blood bubbled to the surface.

"We had a performer in our Congress of Freaks," he said. "I remember painting him on our banner line. 'Gargoyle, the Ugliest Man in the World.' Poor Gar. His face was so misshapen..." Bret shook his head. "You wouldn't believe it, Stanhope, unless you saw for yourself. One of Gar's eyes was set an inch above the other. His ears were flaps, and his nose... Come to think of it, he didn't have a nose, just a deep hole where his nose should have been."

"What the hell are you talking about?"

"Are you not following my drift, Stanhope? I could describe Gar's appearance more fully, but why waste time?" Bret gestured toward Maxey's face with the knife. "Would you prefer the cigar? No, I think not. What should I brand across your face? Despoiler of defenseless women? Too many letters. You wouldn't have any face left. Perhaps rapist will do."

"I didn't rape her."

"Poison is one form of rape, especially if you drug your victim slowly. You robbed Calliope of her will and then had the gall to sell her body. That's rape, Stanhope."

Maxey cringed and pressed his back against the wall. "Please, Johnson, I swear I'll never bother her again. Tell him, Angel. Tell him I swore never to lay with you and kept my word. Tell him Maxey Stanhope never breaks a vow."

"*On ne peut so fier a lui.*" Calliope felt a primitive joy at the thought of Maxey's face slashed to ribbons.

"What did she say?"

"Don't you remember, Stanhope? I believe Miss Angel used the very same phrase the night you sold her to me. She said not to trust you."

"You can credit my word, Johnson. I'll ride back to Denver. I'll never see her again. I'll join my family and…"

Calliope suddenly realized that while Maxey was slavishly pleading, he had inched closer to her. Before she could move away from the wall, she felt him reach out and grab her body, using it as a shield. One arm circled her waist. His other arm squeezed hard across the strained arch of her throat.

"Get rid of the knife, Johnson," he said. "If I wrench my arm, her neck's broken."

No! Don't trust him! Calliope wanted to scream the words, but her throat was held too tightly by Maxey's relentless grip. With despair, she watched Bret fling the knife toward the tall weeds that grew by the side of the path.

"You dare threaten me?" Maxey's disposition was fueled rather than tempered by relief. "First you steal my fiancée and then you threaten to scar my face. She's mine now, do you understand? My angel! All mine!"

"Yes," said Bret. "Loosen your arm."

Choking, Calliope struggled.

Maxey laughed, but there was no joy in the guttural sound. His hand released her waist and traveled boldly down along her hips. His fingers slid across her belly. "If I had a third hand, I'd lift your skirts and mount you the way a stallion mounts a mare," he said into her ear, guiding her forward until they stood above Bret's discarded holster.

Once before, Calliope had pretended to faint, hoping to secure freedom from Maxey's abuse. It hadn't worked that night in the stable, but it might work now. Desperate, she shut her eyes, issued a pathetic moan, and sagged backwards, against Maxey's body.

With his attention focused on Bret, Calliope's limp weight, slight though it was, threw Maxey off balance. Trying to compensate, he released her, and she sank to the ground. Maxey teetered as Bret rushed forward. Falling to his knees, Maxey grabbed Bret's pistol.

Calliope heard a click. Was the gun unloaded, or had Bret not chambered the first bullet? Swearing a blue streak, Maxey squeezed the trigger again.

She hoped to hear another click, but this time the gunshot blended with the sound of loud music, and she was dimly aware Brian's opening spectacle had begun. Eyes wide with horror, she watched the force of the bullet drive Bret against the wall. His head struck with a sickening thud. Dark stains smeared the sandstone bricks as he slid down to the dirt. Blood flowed and matted his ash-blond hair. Another stain soaked his shirt and spread across his upper chest.

Maxey tossed the gun aside, reached out, and grabbed Calliope's long hair. Ignoring the pain, she crawled toward Bret, but Maxey's grip was stronger, and her head was forced backwards until she thought her legs would snap at the knees.

His face loomed above her. "Spread your legs, circus whore," he sneered. "Let's celebrate my victory."

"What victory?" she managed, though her throat felt sore and bruised. "You shot an unarmed man. Coward! How I loathe and despise you."

Passive, her eyes open, she tried to control her shudders when Maxey ripped open her bodice. She wouldn't give in to her pain or fear, for his lust fed on both. Suddenly, above his shoulders, she saw icy blue eyes.

Brian pulled Maxey away by his shirt collar, flung him toward the side of the trail, and leaned over Calliope. "I heard a gunshot, lass. Are you all right?"

Before she could respond, Maxey stood up. In his hand, he clutched the discarded knife.

"Look out, Brian! Knife!"

Although her words were a mere whisper, Brian swiftly turned toward Maxey. At the same time, he reached for his own knife sheathed inside his boot.

Weak with fear, Calliope cast a frantic glance toward Bret. Then she focused on Brian. He must have been backstage, readying the cats. She saw his bare chest glistening with perspiration and blood. The blood oozed from a deep scratch that could have been caused only by a lion's or tiger's needle-sharp claws.

"Have you tasted the sweet nectar between her thighs, Fox?" Maxey taunted, lunging.

His knife came within a hair's breadth of slicing Brian's belly. On the next swing, Brian captured Maxey's wrist in a hard grip, but Maxey reached out with his left hand and caught Brian's arm. Both men toppled, fell, and rolled over and over in the dirt. When they finally stopped, Brian was on the bottom, looking up at the sharp blade aimed toward his throat. His arm muscles quivered as he strained to hold Maxey away, but Calliope could see Brian was tiring rapidly. Loss of blood had debilitated him.

Heart slamming against her chest, she pressed her hands over her mouth to stifle her screams. She must not interrupt Brian's concentration.

With an almost herculean effort, he shifted his body so he and Maxey rolled over again, and this time he straddled Maxey.

The music inside the restaurant reached a crescendo.

Raising his own knife, Brian hesitated at the abject terror that constricted Maxey's face.

"Castrate that useless piece of meat that hangs between his legs!" Calliope shouted. "That trifling twig will never give pleasure! Cut it! Cut it! Cut it off!"

The fear in Maxey's eyes diminished. Enraged by her words, he lifted his head toward Calliope's taunts, his lips drawn back in a primal snarl. His movement was so abrupt, Brian had no chance to react. Maxey sank to the dirt, the hilt of Brian's knife protruding from his neck. Blood spurted like a fountain.

Like cherubim spitting! "Make a wish, Mr. Stanhope," she said, "for it shall be your last one on this earth."

"I wish," he began, but before he could finish his wish, he lay motionless.

Calliope crawled toward Bret and cradled his head against her breasts.

Brian hunkered down by her side, his blue eyes darkening as comprehension dawned. "The shot I heard," he said. "Johnson."

"Calliope." Bret's voice was very weak.

Dear God, he's alive! "Don't move, my darling," she said, her eyes ablaze with joy at this miracle. "We'll find a doctor and—"

"Too late." He cocked his head, wincing at the

pain. The band had begun playing "El Caballero." Bret smiled at the sound. Then he grimaced. "Stanhope?"

"He impaled himself on Brian's knife. A fitting end for a yellow-bellied bastard. You were so brave, Bret. Neither clown nor fool. Just a man, a very brave man."

"I love you."

"I forgive you," she said as she watched his life slowly ebb with the tide of unstoppable blood. "I truly understand why you set the fire, dearest. You lost your wits when I told you about the silver wagon."

"Bret had nothing to do with the fire," Brian said. "It was Bobby Duncan who torched the menagerie tent."

"Bobby Duncan?"

"Panama was inside the menagerie tent, waiting for the show to end, waiting for me. Duncan found her there. She taunted him until he lost his temper."

Calliope remembered the large shape she had seen fleeing around her Big Top's corner. She had thought the form Jocko or Panama or her absent ringmaster. She had never once considered it might be her dull-witted strong man.

"Bobby guyed-out Mum's rope the night she fell," Calliope said, "and left a wee sag. If I had only discovered the identity of my evil leprechaun sooner, how much anguish would have been avoided."

"The fire spread from the menagerie tent to the Big Top," Brian continued. "When Duncan saw the result of his deed, he crept through the sidewalls. He must have carried a dozen people to safety before the flames consumed him. He lived long enough to confess to Big John, Bret, and me. How could you not know this, Calliope? It was in all the newspapers."

"I was ill, barely conscious for ten days. Once I recovered, the Stanhopes thought it best to avoid any mention of the fire because... because of your death. Oh, God," she wailed, "I didn't know. I swear!"

"Don't swear, Calliope." Bret coughed, and red spittle appeared between his lips. "A lady never swears, and you've always been a lady. Please... a favor."

"Anything."

"Were you planning to perform tonight?"

"Yes."

"Perform well... for your clown."

"Yes, I swear. I mean, I promise." Tears streamed down her face and mingled with the blood that soaked her torn bodice.

"Bury me in the mountains. High. I want to watch over my Cirque. Remember the roulette wheel, darling? When you see an eagle, think of me." Bret smiled, took one last breath, and stared up at the starry sky.

Brian carefully placed Bret's head on the ground. Lifting Calliope to her feet, he settled her face against his shoulder and felt her hot tears sting his bruised skin. "I love you, puss," he said. "So many misunderstandings. How I wish we could start all over again."

"I wonder if starting all over again was Maxey's last wish. Maybe, facing death, he found his conscience." Reluctantly, she pulled away from Brian's soothing touch. "Will you send somebody to fetch Black Jack? Please? He'll take care of Bret. I have to get ready."

"Ready for what?"

"My performance." Noting the angry expression that clouded Brian's face, she said, "Don't blame

Mike. I pestered, cajoled, even bribed him until he gave in. It's my fault."

Brian glanced around. "Where's Dublin?"

"In his stall. You might as well know everything. I plan to do a forward somersault."

"No! I won't allow it!"

"You cannot stop me."

"Yes, I can. This time it's *my* circus, Calliope, not yours."

"If you keep me from your stage, I'll string a lasso between two trees, just like Mum did, and execute my act for the gillys when they leave."

"Are you daft? String a lasso?"

"A rope, then. Any rope."

"And who will guy-out the line, you stubborn gazoony?"

"I will. With Black Jack. He'll do it when I tell him it was Bret's dying request."

"Bret thought you planned to ride Dublin, not walk the rope."

"What's the difference, Brian? Don't you see? I've made so many mistakes, been wrong about so many things." Her breath shot out in short bursts. "It was my fault, Bret's dying. We could have found happiness if we had only talked about the fire, talked about Duncan. Oh, God!"

All at once she was in Brian's arms again. His hands caressed her tense shoulders, and his lips brushed the top of her tangled hair. "There, there, puss," he crooned. "You're in shock, not thinking straight. We shall discuss this tomorrow, after you've had time to rest, sleep, think clearly."

"I don't want to rest, sleep, or think. Let me go!"

"I've told you before that I won't take orders from a wee lass," Brian said, his voice tender.

She stepped back, away from the comfort of his arms, and stared up into his dark blue eyes. "I'm not a wee lass," she said, her voice calm, her brief hysteria gone. "I'm not a lady, either. And I'm not a child. Please don't treat me like one."

"You talk like a child, Calliope. Have you forgotten there are two men dead?"

"No. But you've forgotten your background, Brian, and mine. The circus never came to a halt after an accident. Remember the night Mum fell? They carried her broken body away from the ring while Papa whistled for the next act to begin."

"This is different."

"You're wrong. It's not." Refusing to lower her gaze, Calliope had the feeling that if she won this contest she'd lose Brian's love forever.

But it didn't matter. Nothing mattered except her desire to honor Bret's dying wish. She owed him that much. Bret had sheltered her, loved her, while she had responded with silent accusations. They had never really discussed the fire, because she had tiptoed hither and yon, like a ropewalker surreptitiously crisscrossing a spider's thready web.

So she would perform well. For Jocko. For Gwendolyn. For Gargoyle, Cuckoo, Junior, and Black Jack. She would perform well for all the circus performers she had abandoned.

Mary O'Connor and Irish Angel were gone. They had died with Maxey and Bret. She was Calliope

Kelley, daughter of Sean and Angelique, and the circus was in her blood.

Even if she spilled it.

Thirty-Two

HAVE YOU FORGOTTEN THAT THERE ARE TWO MEN DEAD?

No, thought Calliope. She had not forgotten. She'd never forget. Tomorrow she'd grieve. Tomorrow she'd allow memories to overwhelm her. Tomorrow she'd wail like a banshee. But tonight she'd perform.

Or die trying.

She stood on a tiny wooden platform. Looking down, she could see a blur of faces. The gillys were seated at tables. Entertainers crowded the side of the stage, pressing against each other to get a better view.

It's the lack of a net that intrigues the other performers!

Shifting her gaze, she searched for Brian. Was he watching from the side of the stage? Or had he joined Daisy Sandoval and her parents at a ringside table?

Calliope's heart beat fast, and she was seven years old again, following the strains of the Piper's flute—

Brian, wait for me.

Then she remembered there would be no more music.

"Perform if you must," Brian had said, standing beneath the moon and staring into her eyes. "Your stubborn pride is more important to you than our love. It always has been."

"That's not true!"

"Yes, it is." As if memorizing the contours of her face, he cradled it between his palms. "I cannot order you to leave Colorado, Calliope. However, if we should meet again, it will be as strangers." Then turning away, he had walked swiftly toward the back-stage entrance.

"Wait! Brian, wait! Where are you going? The sheriff—"

"Tell him Aaron Fox will give a statement after the show. Most people respect my position, obey my demands."

"Most people," she had cried, "are not me!"

She had remained with Bret's body until Black Jack arrived, thinking how she had won the hand but lost the game. Her single-minded determination had led to a victory, yet it was a hollow triumph and possibly for naught.

Brian had left her alone on purpose, knowing she wouldn't leave Bret's body, hoping to defer her performance.

It almost worked, but fate intervened. The cats were obstinate, and Calliope wondered if their trainer had sent a lioness or tigress into the cage during her season to excite the other cats and make them more ferocious. That would account for Brian's nasty scratch. There was a long delay while the tamer labored to control his wild beasts, and the band played "El Caballero" over and over until Calliope thought she'd scream.

However, that gave her the extra time she needed to console Black Jack, explain the events that had caused Maxey's fatal knife wound, and change into her costume.

Mike played Brian's ringmaster. After she admitted Aaron Fox knew all about her ropewalking, Mike announced her act with expertise and enthusiasm.

"Lay-deez and gen-tul-men, presenting Calliope Kelley, also known as Dream Dancer, the first female equilibrist to perform a forward somersault."

Calliope heard a surprised murmur and suspected it came from the astonished circus owners and their agents.

"Picture tossing an egg into the air," Mike continued, "a plain, ordinary hen's egg. Imagine, if you will, stretching a piece of sewing thread out in front of you and trying to catch the rotating egg. What happens if you miss?"

The murmurs became a collective gasp as the gillys visualized Mike's concept.

Clothed in a ringmaster's garb, he waved his gold-tipped cane. "I know what you're thinking. You're thinking Dream Dancer has eyes to see where she'll land, while an egg doesn't. Not true, ladies and gentlemen. Dream Dancer's legs will come between her eyes and the rope, permitting no optical help with her landing."

Another gasp.

"The forward somersault requires the utmost in bodily coordination, muscular precision, and fault-less technique, and to my knowledge has never been successfully completed by a woman, at least not during a circus performance. Furthermore, Dream Dancer will perform…" He paused dramatically. "Without a net! That means, if she falls… Well, picture the egg."

My cocky manager plans to earn his percentage, Calliope thought, as whistles and cheers erupted from every corner of the room.

Mike held up his hands, palms facing outward. "Thank you," he said. "We value your appreciation. But now I must ask for silence. Not one cry, not one cough or sneeze, we beg of you. Even though Dream Dancer performs splits and flips before her somersault, she does this too, with no net beneath. Pre-senting our daring young lass… Calliope Kelley."

Since Brian already knew about her act, Calliope had rejected a blindfold. Smiling until she thought her face would crack like the shell of Mike's damfool egg, she danced a bolero then executed a split and a series of somersaults. Now, decisively, she stood on the platform and prepared—mentally—to begin her forward somersault.

Three oversized wagon wheels, fitted with candles and suspended from the ceiling, shone down upon her crimson gown with its glittering spangles. She was so lofty she could smell the melting tallow and smoking wicks. Perhaps the scent in her dream had been burnt wick rather than hemp. Perhaps, in her dreams, she had stood poised above an empty stage.

Empty, she reminded herself, as if she needed reminding. The boards were bare except for sawdust.

"Do not be looking down," she whispered, "for it will make you dizzy."

What else had Brian said during her daring climb across the slick trestle?

Look up or straight ahead.

Pretend you're a monkey.

Are you all right? Calliope, answer me!

"I'm fine. Wondrous fine," she whispered then danced nimbly to the center of the rope and took a deep breath. "This is for you, Bret. This is for you, Papa. This is for you, Mum."

She leapt toward the candles. At the same time, she threw her head down. Wrapping her arms about her chest, she felt her body rotate. All she could see were her knees.

Chairs toppled as every member of the audience jumped to their feet.

"*Merde*," said the representative from the Nouveau Cirque, his expletive full of admiration rather than derision.

Gwendolyn's breath caught in her throat, and her heart slammed against her chest. What courage! If Calliope could perform on the rope, perhaps she, Gwen, could find the courage to love without fear, without reservation, mindless of hurtful gossip and condemnation. *Mebbe.*

"Goodness gracious, it's Mary," said Ann Stanhope. "Look, Raymond dear, it's our precious Mary."

Raymond squeezed his wife's hand. After receiving young Fox's invitation, Ann had begged to attend the hotel's grand opening. She thought it sounded "romantic." She had also insisted—with a kittenish purr and an iron will—that they attend Mary's wedding. Mary had brought romance back into their lives. She had been like a breath of fresh air sweeping through an old attic. No matter what she had become, Raymond would always be grateful for that.

"Be not forgetful to welcome strangers, for thereby

some have entertained an angel unaware," Dottie whispered. She had a feeling she might have misquoted the psalm, yet its meaning was crystal clear.

Thom glanced toward the empty seat at their table. Maxey had failed to attend, as usual. He was probably diddling some performer backstage. How did his brother get away with it? Lucky Maxey!

Louis Sandoval stroked his mustache. After this *circo*, he would attend Bret Johnson's wedding. Then he would spend the night with that lovely *mujer rubia*, Clarissa. Sandoval's pulse quickened, and his groin throbbed.

Daisy Sandoval scowled as she twisted her engagement ring. She didn't understand Aaron's obsession with his damn carnival. And she couldn't comprehend the announcement from that fat little rodent with the cane. Why toss an egg into the air? If it fell and shattered, it made such a bloody mess.

Brian shut his eyes, but he was unable to block out the sight of Angelique soaring through the air, landing in a heap, her body crushed, her neck broken. Shit! He should have scooped Calliope into his arms, placed her across his saddle, galloped toward the gazebo, and soothed her through the night until she came to her senses.

Her pride! Her damfool pride! Just like Angelique!

Would Angelique's daughter suffer the same fate?

Opening his eyes, Brian forced himself to look upwards, as if by that action he could keep his tenacious circus cat safe. Warm. Happy. Alive.

Calliope's golden-brown hair escaped from her braid and whipped around her throat as she landed slantwise then teetered on the rope's edge.

Thirty-Three

LORD, HOW SHE HATED WASHING CLOTHES. HER PARTIC-
ular bête noire was an evening gown slashed with red,
white, and blue stripes.

Scrubbing the occasional smear of mud had been
much easier in America. There she sometimes had
a whole riverbank on which to perform her task,
beating out both the dirt and her resentment upon
the rocks. In Paris she had no nearby river, just an old
wooden tub.

She roomed inside a small hotel on the Place
Pigalle in Montparnasse and indulged herself by
creating her own bonnets. One was of natural straw
with black velvet ribbons and colorful plumes.
Another was bergère white straw with red ribbons
and pink roses. Her most daring creation was a fawn
beaver tricorne.

Paris inspired her. She wanted to display her
couturier's artistry outside, perhaps take a leisurely
stroll through the park, but she rarely found the

opportunity. During the week she had very little spare time. By Sunday, exhaustion had set in.

She glanced toward her window, where a small piece of sky was visible. The sun shone so brightly it reminded her of a needle threaded with silver darting through the seams of a burnished gold and blue gown.

⤳

There was no such thing as a buzzing butterfly, thought Brian O'Connor. If there was, it would talk French.

Brian had met circus performers from all over the world, and he'd picked up a few words and phrases in almost every language. German was guttural, Russian incomprehensible, but French was music to the ears.

What a beautiful day. Kites floated through the clouds, and small lads chased hoops down the park's twisted path. Beneath leafy trees, artists had set up their easels and were sketching bustled women shaded by colorful parasols.

Only one thing was missing. Calliope. Brian wanted to share the sight of kites, hoops, bustles, and parasols. He wanted to share the smell of candied apples and the sound of buzzing butterflies. God, how he missed her.

Over there in the clearing was a merry-go-round—the French called it a carousel. He could almost swear he saw Calliope sitting sidesaddle atop a sculpted white stallion. But the lass he glimpsed wore a shapeless black gown, unadorned, and she hid her hair beneath an awful fur hat shaped like a triangle.

Ruefully, Brian shook his head. He tended to see Calliope in every woman. Sometimes it was long golden-brown hair, sometimes gray-green cat eyes, sometimes simply a saucy rump. If he could fit the pieces of each individual woman together, like a picture puzzle, he'd reconstruct his lost love. He'd add a wee bit of Irish temper. Pride. Stubbornness. A giving, passionate nature. He'd create a human chameleon and then gaze adoringly at every fickle change of color and mood.

One thing for certain. Calliope had never been tedious, not like Daisy Sandoval. With tact worthy of a circus opener, he had broken off his engagement to Daisy, no longer able to endure her conceit, her selfishness, her downright stupidity. She had passively accepted his rejection, her vanity unimpaired, then focused her attention on a wealthy young widower named Charles Doone.

The Fox ranch thrived, Foxfire Manor was eminently successful, and Brian had never been so miserable in his life.

Remembering Calliope's dream to join the Nouveau Cirque, he had impulsively embarked upon the long ocean voyage, arriving in Paris late last night.

Now he wandered through this beautiful park, thinking he saw Calliope everywhere. He stopped to study a circus poster nailed to a fence post. Several acts were featured, but his gaze was drawn to an illustration of a woman riding a horse. The letters above the artist's rendering spelled out PETIT ANGE. Then there were a few more French words, ending with AUX AILES D'ANGE.

Brian tapped a gendarme on the shoulder. "Do you speak English, sir?"

"*Oui*, monsieur. Lee-tle."

"What does it say on that poster, above the girl who rides the horse?"

"Her *nom*... She is called Lee-tle Angel. She rides the *cheval*, monsieur, and she is *aux ailes d'ange*, a wing-ed angel. *Danseu d'corde*... How you say? Necktie? Clothes-hang? No. Rope. *Oui*. Lee-tle Angel dances through the air—"

"Thank you, Monsieur Gendarme. *Merci*. Could you please give me directions to your cirque?"

The Nouveau Cirque was housed in an octagonal building, with seats facing three sides of a single ring. Along the ringbank were plush red boxes. Behind the boxes were arena seats, then a gallery that extended to the roof. There was no menagerie or Congress of Freaks, but the audience could descend to the basement and inspect the horses. A forty-piece string-and-woodwind orchestra occupied a platform above the performers' entrance.

Open from April to February, the circus changed its bill monthly, holding over the most popular acts. For the first two months, Calliope had performed as both an equestrian and a ropewalker. Sometimes she didn't complete her forward somersault, but the circus owners insisted on a net, so she emerged from each fall unhurt.

Then Mike Levine wouldn't let her continue.

"You've gained weight," he said. "The Cirque will keep you on as a rider."

"But Mike, the posters say I dance the rope."

"Use a skipping rope as part of your equestrian act. I don't want anything to happen to you."

"Because you'd lose your percentage?"

"That's right."

"Liar."

"Marry me, Calliope."

"Thank you, Mike, but I won't ever wed. You see, a diddy predicted my lonely fate."

Tonight I do feel off balance, she thought, braiding her hair with red, white, and blue ribbons. Her star-studded evening gown looked like an American flag. She'd worn the same costume since July Fourth, celebrating America's centennial.

With a muffled moan, she pressed her hands against her belly. Perhaps it hadn't been such a good idea after all, meandering through the park. And she really shouldn't have ridden that whirling carousel. Or eaten that candied apple, even if it did taste wondrous fine.

Should she tell Mike to cancel tonight's performance? She felt queasy and quaggy.

But I've never missed a show! She sucked a peppermint, trying to settle her rebellious stomach.

She had even performed the night of Brian's grand opening, despite her horror over Bret's death, despite her broken heart. Teetering on the rope, she'd heard a voice from above, Bret's voice. "I'll bet a thousand dollars you can blow out those candles with one breath, Calliope."

Still wobbling, about to fall, she'd somehow managed to look up. A shadow of spread wings dominated the ceiling. Angel or eagle? Life or death?

Regaining her balance, she had whispered, "Daft clown, you lose. The candles are a wee bit too high."

"So are you, my love. Finish your dance across the rope and then climb down."

"Bret!"

But it was no use. The eagle's shadow had vanished.

So had Brian O'Connor.

Calliope corralled her wandering attention and focused on the ringmaster.

"*Messieurs et mesdames et enfants...*"

She automatically translated his recital: "Men and women and children of all ages. Wearing a full-length evening gown, Petit Ange will jump from the ground to the top of a galloping horse. Then she and her horse will leap through, not one, not two, but three hoops of fire, the only woman in the world to accomplish this difficult feat."

Swiftly leading Dublin into the ring, Calliope hoped action would settle her tummy. If she concentrated on her performance, perhaps her queasiness would go away.

The ringmaster looked surprised at her early entrance, but he merely waved his cane at the orchestra. The music's tempo increased. Dublin quickened his pace from a controlled canter to a stylish gallop. Calliope watched him intently. Then she ran across the ring, swung into space, and landed astraddle.

Rising, she untied the rope fastened about Dublin's neck and began skipping across his wide, dappled back.

A loud, piercing whistle sounded from one of the seats.

Dublin broke stride, prancing toward the whistle.

Calliope desperately tried to maintain her balance, but it was no use. She toppled over the ringbank, smack-dab into a red box, and landed in front of a pair of boot-clad feet.

"You damn gilly-galloo!" she shouted, pushing away the tangled hair and ribbons that had tumbled down her face. Then in perfect French, she added, "How dare you make a noise during my performance!"

Too late, she remembered she had interrupted the ringmaster before he requested complete silence.

"Why do you not you answer me, monsieur? Cat got your tongue?"

The man had covered his face with his hands, trying to stifle his laughter. Between his fingers, he said, "A wee cat has oft captured my tongue. I recall a silver wagon and a hot springs and—"

"Brian!"

"Are you all right, my brave, foolish Calico Cat?" Settling her on his lap, he stared at her with those scintillating blue eyes.

For a moment she was transported across an ocean, back in time, to the inside of a menagerie tent. She heard the sound of rain thudding against the canvas like a drum roll. She heard the *whooshing* whisper of tigers rubbing their tawny, striped hides against the bars of their cages. She heard the trumpet of an elephant, the roar of a lion, and thunder.

"Brian, what are you doing here?"

"I came to see the angel who can fly through the air with the greatest of ease. Her figure is handsome, all men she can please—"

"Hush! You ruined my performance, ruined it

good," she said, aware that clowns had entered the ring and were bent on capturing Dublin. Her blind stallion, recognizing, first Brian's whistle, then his scent, was now dancing a one-horse fandango.

Brian waved at Mike, who nodded and waved back.

"Damn and blast," Calliope swore. "Mike knew you were here, didn't he? You and Mike hatched the whole plan."

"Not your flip-flop into my box, lass."

"Why didn't you simply walk downstairs to the basement? You must have known I'd be readying Dublin."

"I wasn't sure how you'd greet me," he replied, his voice deadly serious. "You left Colorado without a word, not even a proper good-bye. When I begged Black Jack to tell me where you'd gone, all he'd say was 'Calliope don't want to see you.'"

"You said you never wanted to see *me* again."

"I've said the same before. Why did you believe me this time?"

"How is Black Jack?" she asked, sidestepping his question. "And Gwendolyn?"

"Jack works for me now. He manages the restaurant at Foxfire Manor. Gwen opened a second apparel shop inside the hotel. She has more business than she can handle, so she hired a young seamstress, Lizbet, transported all the way from Denver. Jack and Gwen plan to wed next Christmas. At first Jack said no, but Gwen showed a muleheaded stubbornness, not unlike a certain equestrian named Dream Dancer."

"That's wonderful news." Her eyes widened. "Oh! Oh, he doesn't like this slumpy position. He's kicking like Susan B. Anthony used to kick. Please, Brian, sit me up straighter or hold me tighter."

"He? He, who?" Brian's gaze traveled from her face to the belly-bulge beneath her gown. "How many months, puss?"

"Six." Tears overflowed and coursed down her cheeks. "It's the reason I left Colorado."

"Did you truly believe I'd wed Daisy if I had known?"

"Are you wed, Brian?"

"No. Why didn't you tell me about the baby?"

"You thought me Bret's *fille de joie*. If true, the child could be his son."

"What makes you so sure it's a boy? It might be another daft colleen, another Calliope." The expression in his eyes shifted from tenderness to anger. "And why were you galloping around the ring, you foolish gazoony?"

"Who are you to be giving me orders, you swell-headed, bumptious spalpeen?"

"The father of your child."

"You don't know that for certain. My son, or daughter, could have been conceived in a misty-fingered hot springs or beneath the roof of an opulent casino."

"What difference does it make? The little lad or lass might have dark hair like mine and Sean's, or light hair like Bret and Angelique. It doesn't matter one whit. He or she will be mine if I say so."

"You would claim the child as yours?"

"The child *is* mine, just as you are mine and always have been. Don't you know that yet?"

"I thought you… well, desired me."

"I do." He grinned. "If you can ride Dublin, you can ride the proof of my desire."

She lowered her lashes to hide her tears. She wept more often nowadays, but her tears didn't hurt, not even a little bit. Maybe it was easier to cry in French.

"I love you, Calliope," Brian said, "with all my heart."

"I love you too, and I swear on the souls of Sean and Angelique that I never made love to Bret, not once. So you see, Brian, only you could be his or her papa."

"Happy birthday, puss." Slowly, his fingers reached out and caressed the golden horse charm that lay within the mounds of her breasts.

"Golly Jehossafrat, I forgot it was my birthday!"

He grinned at her old childhood expression before he said, "Make a wish."

"I wish to be your wife."

"And so you shall. Tonight or tomorrow, as soon as I can arrange it."

"May I have a second wish?"

"Of course," he said, settling back in his seat and stroking her belly.

"May we name our baby Bret?"

"What if it's a girl?"

"We'll call her Bret."

"It's different. She won't like it, Calliope. Remember how you hated your name?"

"Well then, if it's a girl, we shall call her Bret Mary. Please, Brian?"

"I have no objection, but it will cause talk. People in Colorado will remember Bret's Cirque. What about your reputation?"

"What about yours?"

"I'm a man."

"And I'm a lady. Besides, when did I ever worry about my reputation?"

"When you lived with the Stanhopes and played the role of a conventional lass."

"Fiddlesticks! I wore petticoat breeches to my very first society ball. You've become quite the gilly, Brian O'Connor."

"But not a gilly-*galloo*." He laughed. "When you fall from your horse, you must mount him again. Let's leave, puss. I wish to be alone with you."

"Are we not alone?" She blinked with surprise as her gaze swept the filled arena.

A flying act was in progress, trapeze artists twirling end over end, grabbing each other's wrists at the last possible moment.

She and Brian would be like those trapeze artists. With or without a net, they would soar through the air, full of buoyant passion.

Calliope opened her mouth to tell Brian. But he kissed her, plunging his tongue through her parted lips, and she felt as though she'd begun a forward somersault that would endure until the last syllable of recorded time.

The circus was forever, and so was love.

Acknowledgments

First and foremost, I'd like to thank the research librarians at the Penrose Library in Colorado Springs. They not only found a book on merry-go-rounds (called "carousels" in France), but they discovered a slim volume with authentic "circus lingo."

A huge, heartfelt thanks to Deb Werksman and Susie Benton at Sourcebooks and my copy editor Gail Foreman. "They make my books better" is an understatement.

Finally, I'd like to acknowledge my two best friends: Gordon Aalborg and Lynn Whitacre. (If I didn't mention Lynn, she'd stop taking me to the best shops for discount shoes and consignment clothes.)

Read on for an excerpt from

THE Landlord's BLACK-EYED Daughter

6 April 1766

Seated beside the open coffin, the watchers waited. They waited to see whether Barbara Wyndham's body moved. They watched intently while mourners trailed past. Blind belief said that if Barbara's body began to bleed, 'twould identify her murderer.

There was some question as to whether Barbara had suffered a seizure of the heart and fallen and hit her head on a rock. Or had she been struck by some unknown hand?

Seven-year-old Elizabeth Wyndham watched with the watchers, but her mother remained motionless.

"Mama," Elizabeth whispered, "are ye sleeping?"

"Your mother sleeps evermore, my Bess," said Lawrence Wyndham, lifting his daughter up into his arms.

Elizabeth pressed her tear-streaked face against his shoulder. At the same time, she wondered with a twinge of fear how it would feel to sleep evermore.

One

30 March 1787

"I wonder why Fleet Street calls us Knights of the Road," John Randolph Remington said to his partner. "I'll wager no knight ever spent his days hiding in a copse."

Zak Turnbull swatted his hat at a circling fly. "They call us knights, Rand, 'cause 'tis a snappy title and no one can deny we be a fine pair o' prancers."

Rand gazed north, where the straight highway took an abrupt turn. For the past three hours nothing had passed their way except for a handful of dilapidated coaches and shabbily-dressed travelers. While Zak wasn't particular about whom he robbed, Rand agreed with Robin Hood: proper criminals should take from the rich.

"How much bloody longer is it gonna be?" Zak pulled at his wig. "I'm sweatin' like a bloody barrister 'neath this poll, and I've got so many fleas tormentin' me, ye'd think I was a heap o' dung."

"Patience," said Rand, shifting in his saddle and

trying to ease the stiffness in his right leg. "The reason you've spent the last twenty years breaking out of every prison in England is because you grow careless. And then you're caught."

"'Tis a fine observation, comin' from someone who's been in the business a mere two years. Ye know as well as I that a gagger, though he be rich as King George himself, will dress poor just t' trick us." Zak wiped his sweat-streaked face with his vizard. "And I'm warnin' ye. If a proper gagger don't come along soon, I'll be millin' meself a flat."

Rand mentally translated Zak's cant into something resembling the King's English. Basically, Zak meant you could seldom tell a man's wealth from his attire and he planned to rob the next traveler, no matter what the size of his purse.

"And as far as ever bein' habbled again, it ain't gonna happen," Zak continued. "Ye've brought me good luck, cousin."

"London's poor law enforcement has provided all the luck we need," Rand said with a droll grin.

In truth, London's press had proven to be a far more formidable opponent than the city's decrepit watchmen and underpaid constables. After every robbery, editors of the *Gazeteer* and the *Monitor* and the other daily papers howled for the apprehension of the "Gentleman Giant and his Quiet Companion." But the resultant publicity hadn't brought Zak and Rand any closer to capture. On the contrary, it had turned them into local heroes.

"If I'm gonna have t' wait, I'm gonna spend me time in a more enjoyable fashion." Zak dismounted and stretched his six-foot-five frame upon the grass. He covered his face with his wide-brimmed hat, then clasped his hands across his prodigious belly. "Rouse me if ye see a ratter what meets yer specifications."

Almost immediately Zak's rhythmic snores blended with the buzzing flies and the distant bleats of sheep. Rand tried to ignore his now throbbing leg and his own wig, which was bloody uncomfortable. Generally he wore his thick black hair long and natural, for that was the way the ladies liked it. But disguise was a necessary part of his profession. Today he was dressed as a gentleman. Doeskin riding breeches hugged his thighs and his feet were clad in knee-high, glossy brown boots. His loose-fitting shirt couldn't completely hide his rugged chest, which tapered to a narrow waist, lean hips and a flat belly. In an age where gentlemen prided themselves on their girth, Rand figured his slenderness was the only part of his disguise some observant magistrate might question.

So why did he feel so apprehensive?

He had experienced the same uneasiness before the Battle of Guilford Court House. The night preceding that colonial battle, he had dreamed of war. But the war in his dream belonged to another age, an age of broadsword and chain mail and mace, of armored men clashing on the summit of an emerald green hill. This dream, which had troubled him since childhood, always ended the same way, with the delicate mournful face of a flaxen-haired woman. Over the years he had sought possible interpretations. Eventually, he had stopped probing. It was better to accept the fact that the dream forecast change. Violent change.

The thud of hooves and the squeak of coach springs interrupted Rand's thoughts. He straightened in his saddle. While he couldn't see anything above the distant hedges, a prospective wayfarer was obviously headed their way.

"Zak," he whispered.

A gleaming black carriage, pulled by four high-stepping greys, came into view.

Zak's snoring continued, undisturbed. Rand maneuvered Prancer, his black stallion, closer. "Cousin, wake up! This is it. Time to earn your keep."

"I'm ready, I'm ready." Rising, Zak secured his hat atop his wig, stumbled toward his horse, and swung up into the saddle. "Who've ye decided we're t' be this time?" he asked, concealing the lower half of his face with his vizard.

"Irishmen," Rand replied. It was necessary to disguise one's voice along with one's appearance.

"And here's me shillelagh, boy-o," Zak quipped, raising his pistol.

Rand lifted his own vizard into place. As the coach rumbled toward them, his muscles tensed. This was the best part of his profession: the anticipation of the chase, never knowing what danger would come within the next few minutes or what surprises waited behind the curtained windows. He scrutinized every inch of the approaching carriage, from the gilded coat of arms on the door to the red plumes topping the heads of the greys, and the brightly polished gold buttons on the liveries of the coachman and footman.

"Now," he breathed.

Bolting from behind the stand of trees, he rushed

forward, grabbed the bridle of the nearest grey, brought the carriage to a halt, then trained his pistol on the coachman's chest.

"Stand and deliver!" Zak barked, yanking open the door.

A nervous young whip hastily exited. "My auntie's still inside," he said, his voice cracking. "May I pull down the steps? She suffers from an inflammation of the joints and—"

"Ye need not be deliverin' a sermon, ye chicken-hammed chatterbox. Do it and be quick about it."

The whip scrambled to obey. When his aunt climbed down, she turned out to be a formidable-looking dowager with a jutting jaw and a ramrod straight posture. Smoothing her satin skirt, she eyed Zak. "I'm Lady Avery," she said, "and I was robbed by a footpad only last month. Perhaps you've heard and will think to spare me."

"Prancers, I mean highwaymen, don't rub shoulders with footpads, m'lady, especially *Irish* prancers like we be." Ever mindful of his reputation with the press, Zak kept his voice respectful. "Now, if ye'd be so good as to give me yer bit… uh, yer purse… and yer rings. And ye, sir…" He gestured with his pistol at the whip's feet. "I'll have yer watch, and them be a handsome pair o' shoe buckles."

Lady Avery tapped her first finger against the bridge of her nose. "I know who you are. You're the Gentleman Giant."

Zak dipped from the waist in a half bow. "Aye, 'tis the gospel truth, m'lady."

"I don't recall the *Morning Chronicle* mentioning

that you were Irish." Her watery brown eyes turned toward Rand, who still had his pistol trained on the coachman and footman. "Well, no matter what your nationality, you're both impressive specimens." She swiveled her head toward her nephew. "Are they not, Roger?"

"We're being robbed, Aunt Maude." Roger fumbled with the watch and gold fob-seal in his waistcoat pocket. "I'll reserve my opinion for a more propitious time."

Zak pointed to a circle of diamonds nestled in a crevice of Lady Avery's towering coiffure. "I'll have that, m'lady."

"I should never have removed my bonnet, nor my gloves," she murmured, unclasping the circle. But her wedding ring proved a more difficult matter. "It's this damnable arthritis," she said. "I cannot get anything over my joints." In a tone that brooked no argument, she added, "Never grow old, young man. Though in your profession that can't be much of a worry."

"Forget the ring, m'lady, for I'm sure it holds sentimental value. I'll settle for yer earbobs."

"Thank you, Giant. Truthfully, my husband was a poor father and a poorer spouse, and I seldom mourn his passing."

"Aunt Maude!"

"I'm sorry to hear that, m'lady," Zak commiserated, dropping her jewelry into his coin purse. "I'll take that there cameo, if ye please."

"I don't please, but I suppose I have no choice."

"Hurry," Rand urged. Zak was a great one for talking when he should be tending to business. Rand fancied he heard hoofbeats. While Zak assured Lady Avery that she would soon find a more compatible husband, Rand guided Prancer to the carriage door and began retrieving everything within easy reach. The gold and enamel snuffbox would fetch a few coins, and the handsome walking stick was worth at least ten guineas from a good fence. He hesitated when he spied a novel. Entitled *Castles of Doom,* it rested on the velvet seat. The novel had little monetary value, but one of his ladies might enjoy it.

Two riders rounded the ragged hedge. They were moving slowly and looked like harmless merchants or respectable tradesmen. On the other hand, one never could be too careful, Rand reminded himself. "Time to go, boy-o," he said to Zak.

"Been a pleasure, m'lady." Zak leaned over and kissed the elderly woman's hand. She flushed beneath her rice powder.

"Help, highwaymen!" Roger shouted.

"Don't be such a nincompoop, nephew," said Lady Avery.

The oncoming riders were now only yards away. "Keep yer distance, ye bloody coves!" Zak shouted, and fired into the air.

Glancing over his shoulder, Rand saw both riders scramble for the ditches. The road stretched ahead, deserted save for a peddler who trudged along beneath a huge back pack. Spurring his stallion, Rand chucked the startled man a guinea. Then, shadowed by Zak, he raced toward London's turnpike.

"Hurrah for the Gentleman Giant and his Quiet Companion!" Zak bellowed to the grazing sheep, the freshly plowed fields, and the bright spring sky. "We're a fine pair, ain't we, cousin?"

True to his epithet, Rand merely grinned.

❧

"Are ye certain ye'll not be joinin' us?" Zak's arms encircled the waists of two pretty bunters.

Tonight Rand wasn't interested. "My leg's bothering me, cousin. I think I'll take a walk, ease the stiffness."

"Ye're not sufferin' one o' yer black moods again, are ye?"

"No. I just need to walk."

But once he was alone, Rand couldn't bring himself to leave their lodgings. While the rooms were clean and graced with quality furnishings, he need only draw aside the lace curtain at the window to look down upon a scene of unimaginable squalor.

Rand and Zak lived in London's Rookery, christened for the thievish disposition of rook birds. Even night watchmen avoided the area, calling it a den of ruffians, cock bawds, and beggars, although he and Zak had never been harassed. In fact, the primarily Irish coal-heavers, laborers, porters, and gaunt-faced children who were the recipients of Rand's largesse considered him something of a folk hero. Yet, as he pictured the filthy houses which sold beds for two pence a night and rotgut gin for a penny a quart, he felt the crushing weight of despair. The tiny, windowless, dirt-floored hovels housed up to fifty people each. If Rand robbed every lord from here to Scotland, the Rookery's poverty would not be alleviated one whit.

"I must leave London," he whispered, "for my soul is dying here."

He longed for the gentle hills and stone cottages of his native Gloucestershire, or the vast unpopulated landscapes of America. But he had made his decision following the War with the Colonies and there was no turning back.

Once, Rand had admired the rich. As a boy, he had dreamed of emulating the lords driving past in their gilded carriages. Lords attended by liveried footmen who wore scented wigs and supercilious expressions. Lords surrounded by black slaves who wore silver collars round their necks and the marks of the branding iron upon their arms. Someday, Rand thought, he would own a mansion on a hill. Someday he would be wealthy beyond measure.

As an adult, he had nearly achieved his dream. But the War with the Colonies had shattered his fantasies along with his leg. The war had been senseless and stupid, the lives lost on both sides wasted. When he returned to Gloucestershire, he sold his successful cabinetmaking business and did virtually nothing for two years—just walked and brooded. During that time he often asked himself whether England had changed, or was he viewing it through different eyes?

Increasingly, the world reminded Rand of something out of an opium dream, hazy and elusive, a place where reality could change in an instant. Because reality depended on the whims of the rich and powerful, never on truth itself.

"Platitudes," he whispered. During the war he had heard so many platitudes. The rebels declared their independence by founding a nation based on the concept of liberty and justice for all. Which meant, of course, liberty and justice for a few landed white men, not their slaves, nor their women, nor their poor. The war was fought over power and property, rather than principles, no matter how many noble phrases the rebels wrapped themselves in.

But England is far worse, thought Rand. *Here only the lives of the wealthy possess value.*

Now when he looked at the gilded coaches, he saw carriage-makers toiling for starvation wages. He saw servants working for cast-off clothes and straw mattresses to sleep upon. Parliament prattled on and on about passing laws against the enslavement of the Negro. Paying no heed, ladies treated their blacka-moors like trained pets. And the mansion on the hill that Rand had once longed for had been built by men who exploited their workers. "The rich are more deserving," the wealthy justified. "If we weren't, God wouldn't have blessed us with wealth in the first place."

For the upper classes, laws, like women, existed only for men's pleasure. Rand had seen a young fop slit a wigmaker's throat over the price of a wig, while a second ran his sword through a total stranger during a game of cards. Both had received pardons, whereas Rand's fourteen-year-old niece had been hanged for hiding, *on instructions from her employer,* some counter-feit shillings.

Rand had been gone, fighting for England, when the hanging of his niece occurred. Fighting for a country where orphans were sold into servitude to ship captains bound for America or India, and no one raised an objection. Fighting for a country where churchgoers nodded approvingly over sermons advocating that abandoned children should be allowed only enough education to obtain the meanest job. And those same children should learn to read a little so they could decipher the appropriate biblical passages that reinforced their lowly status.

Outside London coffeehouses, ten-year-old whores sold themselves for the price of a loaf of bread. Bucks drank champagne from the slippers of their mistresses while the bastards they spawned off their servant girls were left to die in the streets. Rand never ceased to be amazed, as well as enraged, by the sheer hypocrisy of it all.

With a sigh, he stretched out on the soft feather mattress and tried to sleep. Suddenly, he remembered the novel he had retrieved from Lady Avery. Although Rand was an avid reader, he had never opened a Gothic romance. According to conventional wisdom, such writings required the womanly virtues of imagination and sensibility, but not intellect, so they were a waste of time for serious—meaning male—readers. Not that Rand had ever paid much attention to conventional wisdom. Now, on impulse, he retrieved *Castles of Doom* from his saddlebag.

The novel had been manufactured in three slim volumes. Rand opened the first installment, and a folded piece of paper fell out. It was an invitation to meet the pride of Minerva Press, Miss B.B. Wyndham. Some biological facts followed concerning the lady, as well as the date of the party: 1 April 1787—three days hence.

Licking his thumb, Rand flipped to Chapter One.

The first sentence read: *That most malevolent of men, Baron Ralf Darkstarre, paced the length of his watchtower, which overlooked the churning waters of the North Sea, and impatiently awaited the arrival of his liege lord, Simon de Montfort.*

Rand felt as if all the heat from the stuffy room had rushed into his body. Simon de Montfort was a familiar name, a very familiar name. Rand had long believed that his recurring dream was connected with Simon de Montfort and his rebellion against King Henry, which had occurred more than five hundred years ago.

His breath uneven, Rand continued reading: *Despite his evil nature, Lord Darkstarre was a comely man of impressive height, and possessed of an arresting countenance. Lord Darkstarre's brow was wide and noble, and it was only after one gazed into his eyes that one could detect a flicker of the madness that would ultimately consume him.*

Swiftly Rand scanned the pages until he found the next mention of Simon de Montfort.

Three hours later, Zak stumbled inside, his waistcoat half-buttoned, his voice mangling the strains of a bawdy tavern song.

Rand was still reading.

"Ye bloody flat!" Zak shouted. "What kinda prancer be ye, spendin' yer nights with books 'stead o' bunters? Damn, lad, what's wrong? Ye look like ye've seen yer own death."

Reluctantly, Rand left the pages of the past and returned to his cousin. How could he possibly explain what was wrong? The whole thing seemed as mad as B.B. Wyndham's antagonist. "I'm going to attend a party," he finally managed. "I do believe I should meet the pride of Minerva Press."

"What the bloody hell are ye talkin' 'bout?" Zak tossed his beaver hat toward a wall peg. "Are ye daft?"

"Yes," said Rand. "Perhaps I am."

About the Author

Former singer/actress and perennial rule-breaker Mary Ellen Dennis is the author of several award-winning historical romance novels and culinary mysteries and is growing her audience for both. She is married to novelist Gordon Aalborg (aka Victoria Gordon), whom she met online through a writer's group; they live on Vancouver Island. Mary Ellen likes to hear from readers. Her email address is maryellendennis@shaw.ca.

THE *HEIR*

GRACE BURROWES

AN EARL WHO CAN'T BE BRIBED...

Gayle Windham, Earl of Westhaven, is the first legitimate
son and heir to the Duke of Moreland. To escape his father's
inexorable pressure to marry, he decides to spend the summer
at his townhouse in London, where he finds himself intrigued
by the secretive ways of his beautiful housekeeper...

A LADY WHO CAN'T BE PROTECTED...

Anna Seaton is a beautiful, talented, educated woman, which
is why it is so puzzling to Gayle Windham that she works as
his housekeeper.

As the two draw closer and begin to lose their hearts to each
other, Anna's secrets threaten to bring the earl's orderly life
crashing down—and he doesn't know how he's going to protect her from the fallout...

**A *PUBLISHERS WEEKLY* BEST
BOOK OF THE YEAR**

"A luminous and graceful erotic Regency...a captivating love
story that will have readers eagerly awaiting the planned sequels."

— *Publishers Weekly* (starred review)

978-1-4022-4434-6 • $6.99 U.S. / £4.99 UK